Sto

Swept

Jan -

Best wishes!

[signature]

Marvin Reem

Storm Swept

Marvin Reem

Copyright © 2014 Paris Mountain Press

ISBN: 1500804444
ISBN-13: 978-1500804442

Books by Marvin Reem

The Beryl Cathcart Series

Night Swept
Storm Swept

The Lane Johnson Series

Consequential Actions

Other Books

The Clear Path Ahead

Written as Ward Wagher

The Saga of Scott Baughman

Hannah Sorpat's Eye – A Novel of Alien Abduction
Without Beginning of Days
Witnesses in the Cloud

The Montora Series

The Mountains of Montora
The Margrave of Montora
The Snows of Montora
Christmas in Montora
The Diamonds of Montora

DEDICATION

To my wife Debbie, who gave up her extra time to help edit this book.

CONTENTS

MARVIN REEM

ACKNOWLEDGMENTS

To the pastors I have known, who have experienced many of the embarrassments, heartaches, hilarity and victories illustrated in this book.

MARVIN REEM

CHAPTER ONE

I was wondering what I had run into tonight. I had left my home and church in Appleton, Illinois after the Sunday evening services this Thanksgiving weekend in 1965 and begun my drive to Rockford. Classes at Mid-North College would resume Monday morning and I had already missed plenty during the semester. My classes didn't meet until Tuesday, but I needed to get back to the campus and jump into my pending homework.

The sky had been clear when I started my trip and the brilliant beacons of the late fall stars saged the coming Christmas season. Somewhere along the road north a ghosting overcast had drifted across the sky, and I didn't notice until snowflakes began spinning in the headlights of the Dodge. Within the space of about ten minutes the picturesque and relaxing flakes had been transformed into dense curtains of snow, driven by the sharply increasing wind.

The snow was rapidly accumulating on the highway and I was getting nervous. My still new '65 Monaco was a heavy car and would probably acquit itself well in the snow, except that in the rush of events over the previous several months, I had not found the time to get snow tires installed. In the pre-radial tire era, this could cause serious challenges on the road.

It was puzzling because the weather forecasters had predicted clear skies for the next several days. Their abilities were notoriously unreliable, but this was a bit much. I felt like I was caught between first and second base. I was about halfway between Appleton and Rockford and wasn't sure what to do.

My first couple of winters at Appleton Baptist Church I would drive the country roads and run the snow drifts just for the fun of it. I was always within easy walking distance of one farmstead or another, so I could get help if I really buried the car. By that time I knew most of the farmers in the area, so the consequences, at worst, would be my enduring a lot of teasing about my driving. My church members just *loved* finding things to tease me about.

This stretch of U.S. 51 did not have many houses close by and my nervousness changed to worry. The car was starting to slide just a bit as I plowed through some of the deeper drifts. *Okay, Lord, I'm not sure what's going on tonight, but I think I am going to need some help here really soon.*

One of the things the Lord had beaten out of me during the preceding months was my bad habit of waiting until the proverbial snow drifts were over my head before it occurred to me to talk to Him about the problem. I had jumped into a Masters Degree program and begun commuting to Rockford for classes as a way to help my friend Nigel Robart. Nigel was the president of Mid-North. I didn't bother to talk to God about it until after the arrangements were made.

An escalating set of trials had put me under incredible pressure and culminated in a series of terrifying events. I had been run off the road by a tow truck and later faced a couple of maniacs with guns. Along the way I had fallen in love with a blond goddess and then was forced to break off the relationship. The Lord had used this to finally drive me to my knees and beg him for help.

God is *so* gracious! I was none the worse after being banged around, and I witnessed the Lord doing some amazing things, both at Mid-North College and at Appleton Baptist Church. As things settled down we were hoping for a renaissance at the college. We were in the middle of a significant moving of God's Spirit at the church. People were getting saved and people were getting right with God. It was an exciting time and I was thrilled to be a part of it.

Of course, it might all end tonight with me stuffing the Dodge into a tree or freezing to death, or both. My normally relaxing, late evening drive had turned into a white-knuckled death-ride through a frozen ragnarok. I was hunched over the wheel trying to anticipate every untoward movement of the car and working hard to keep it on the road – which was now largely unseen. I was now traveling at about thirty MPH and struggling to maintain control.

During the summers between my years at McKisson University, my father had found me work on construction projects in New York City. Not only had I made very good money, but I was exposed to a side of American civilization I did not know existed. I heard an astonishing amount of colorful vocabulary. While I was always very careful to watch my language and maintain my testimony, there were a lot of words rattling around in my brain watching for an opportunity to escape.

So when the lights of an oncoming tractor-trailer filled my windshield the first word I uttered was *holy* and I clamped down on my tongue as I crowded the right side of the highway. There was six to eight inches of snow on the road at that point and more alongside. I couldn't tell where the ditches were. Apparently the other driver couldn't either.

A wave of snow from his tires swept across the windshield as he came by. I heard a loud *poinck* and then the right tires of the car dropped off the pavement. The truck was past and I turned the wheel to get the car back on the road. The car continued to plow ahead and I saw in front of me the reflectors of a bridge abutment. Now panicking, I quickly turned the steering wheel all the way to the left and the car kept going straight. The front wheels were caught off the edge of the pavement and were simply skating on the snow. I heard a whining sound coming from between my tightly clenched teeth. At that moment it was like I heard a voice that sounded like my dad saying *turn the wheel straight*.

In an instant I whipped the steering wheel back to center, then eased it to the left again. The front wheels jumped out of the rut and I was back on the highway. The back end of the car came around and I was now sliding sideways on the road. I got off the gas and spun the wheel the other direction as I slid across the bridge. There could not have been more than a foot of space between the ends of the car and the bridge railings. The car continued to spin, and slowly turned around where I was facing the direction I came from and slid to a halt. My whining turned into a long, drawn out *sheesh*!

In the snow fogged distance, I could see the brake lights of the truck, then the dancing beam of the driver's flashlight as he sprinted back to where I sat. I was shaking so badly I could hardly move. The truck driver came up to the car and tapped on the window.

"Mister, are you all right? Mister?"

I looked down at the red oil light glowing on the instrument panel – I had killed the engine during my frantic maneuvers. I managed to pull loose the buckle on my seatbelt and grab the door handle. I stepped out into the snow. The breathtaking cold quickly sobered me up, but it was several long moments before I could speak.

I shook my head. "Man!"

"Are you okay, Mister?"

I shook my head again. "I thought that was it. I started praying when the weather turned bad and I was sure the Lord decided it was time to call me home."

The truck driver turned his flash light toward the Dodge. The mirror on the driver's door had been sheered off when I passed the

4

truck, but it looked like the side of the car was not even scratched.

"I guess the Lord was looking after us tonight," I said. "I just cannot believe it. We couldn't have been any closer."

The truck driver was now shaking his head. "I'm not sure I would admit this to anyone, Mister. But I was sure we were going to hit and when you were right there... I don't know if it was a swirl in the snow or what, but I could swear I saw an angel standing in the road right where the center line should have been."

I was cold, but I felt an unearthly chill travel up and down my spine. At that moment I was convinced that his eyes were not lying and that God had indeed sent an angel to stand between us on the snow and night swept highway, and keep us from probable death.

I looked at the driver. "Are you a believer?"

"Yes, Sir. I trusted Jesus when I was five years old. I'm fifty-five years old now and I don't think I've ever seen anything like what just happened tonight."

I was not anywhere near his fifty-five, and I was sure I never wanted to see anything like that again in my life.

"Well, we both need to thank the Lord Jesus tonight for not only saving our souls, but for protecting our physical bodies," I said.

"Amen to that."

Looking back down the road just traveled, I saw another set of headlights. A snow plow slowed down to halt next to the truck. The driver got out and walked across the bridge to where we were standing.

"Is everything all right?"

"Everything is just fine," I replied. "We just had the closest of close calls, but I think..." and I took a deep shuddering breath. "...I think everything is okay."

I was able to pull the car around behind the snow plow and follow it north. The snow tapered off, and the snow plow pulled off as I drove through Rochelle, Illinois. When I arrived at my apartment in Rockford, the sky had cleared and there was nothing on the ground. I looked up at the clear pinpoints of light and pondered the chance meeting on the snowy road. To this day I wonder where that freak storm came from.

CHAPTER TWO

Nigel Robart, the president of Mid-North College and Divinity School was holding court in the living room of my parents' home in Rockford, Illinois. He was sitting in an easy chair in one corner of the living room. His cast-encased leg was resting on the ottoman in front of him. The end table next to him was covered with various bottles and tins of medicines. The floor on the other side was covered with paperwork from the college, newspapers and magazines. In his lap a copy of *Till We Have Faces* rested open and face down.

Nigel had always been a bit pudgy as long as I had known him. The past month had not been kind to him, however, and he was looking gaunt. A final confrontation between a thieving board chairman and an insane property developer had resulted in Nigel catching a bullet in his right leg. His femur had been shattered and he had nearly died from blood loss. He had endured three surgeries and today was his first day out of the hospital since the *incident*.

"When did you get back into town?" he asked me.

"About 1 AM this morning. It was quite the trip."

"That I can understand. I'm surprised the people at your church let you out after dark."

"There was no moon, so it was safe enough. At least they haven't felt the need to keep me locked up in a hospital for weeks at a time."

"Oh, that was cruel, Beryl! I can assure you my mental faculties are as good as they ever were."

"I'm surprised they let *you* out, then." I said.

"Right. And I'm still not good for much. I slept for two hours after they brought me home."

My mother brought in a bowl of soup on a tray. "Here you go, Nigel. Now, take your time with this."

"Thanks, Mrs. C. You are too kind."

"Anything for you, Beryl?" she asked.

"No thanks, Mom. I just had lunch."

She fluffed the pillow behind Nigel and checked the rest of the room before retreating to the kitchen.

"Very kind of your parents to invite me to stay here."

"Where else were you going to go?" I asked. You're not only weak as a kitten, but you have to drag that cast around. Besides, speaking from experience, it's nice having Mom fuss over you."

"I feel so guilty just lying around like this."

I chuckled. "You'd better get used to it, buddy. If you are seen on campus anytime before Commencement, I, for one, will be surprised."

"I feel guilty taking a salary when I'm not capable of working."

"Don't. You were injured in the line of duty. Besides, how do you know Dad is still paying you?"

After Nigel had talked me into helping him with his problems at Mid-North, I asked my dad to help as well. After a board meeting where the results of Dad's audit had culminated in the resignation of the board chairman, Dad had been placed on the board and elected chairman by the grateful members. Later, after Nigel had been critically wounded, the board had appointed Dad as the acting president.

"Aha!" he called out. "He *promised* me."

"He said nothing to me about that," I said.

"Remember," Nigel grinned, "he likes me better."

Nigel was not related to me, but we had become close friends while attending McKisson University in Elmira, New York. Dad treated him like a second son, and while I truly believed Dad loved me more, I think Nigel didn't rank far below my sisters in the esteem of my parents.

"We're not going into that," I sniffed.

"Wise. Very wise, Beryl. Now what was it you were trying to tell me about your trip last night before your feeble brain got sidetracked?"

"My brain didn't get sidetracked last night," I responded.

Nigel just grinned at me. I had just set him up to hit one out of the park and we both knew it. I decided to just ignore it for the moment. I told him about the sudden snow storm and the near miss with the tractor-trailer. His eyes widened when I told him about the angel.

"What do you think the driver actually saw, Beryl?"

"I'm not prepared to deny what he saw. The truck clipped my side mirror when it went by, but the car wasn't scratched."

He nodded. "I think we could call that *close*."

"I guess it confirms the Lord has something else for me to do before he calls me home."

"As long as it doesn't involve madmen waving guns about, I'll be happy to keep you in my kennel."

"Or maniacs driving tow trucks," I replied.

"Or Ellen driving the tow truck."

I groaned. I had suffered through an abortive romance with Nigel's secretary, Ellen Holgate. During the incident on U.S. 51 in Rochelle,

Illinois, I had briefly entertained the thought that it was Ellen driving the truck and trying to get her revenge after I broke up with her. Nigel thought that was hysterically funny and still brought it up.

"I don't know why I tell you these things," I said. "You just throw them back at me every chance you get."

He laughed again. "It's just that you're so easy, Beryl."

I was glad to see him in a good humor, although he was starting to look tired.

"How's the leg, by the way?" I asked him.

He grimaced. "It hurts a lot. And it never stops hurting."

"You know I've been praying for you. And the people at the church have too."

"I think the prayers of God's people are what have pulled me through so far," he said. "I don't think I've ever said this before, but I really appreciate your friendship – and your dad's too."

He had said it a lot, but he had other things on his mind, too.

I shrugged. "Hey, Nige, that's what we're here for."

"True, but I still appreciate it."

"Well, I suppose I should be on my way, Nigel. I have mountains of homework and I have no desire to be terrorized by Dr. Voysey tomorrow."

He chuckled. "We might make a wise man out of you yet."

"No chance of that. I guess I'll probably see you tomorrow." I waved as I walked into the kitchen to say goodbye to my mother.

"Won't you stay for supper, Dear?" she asked. "It'll just be me and Ruth with Nigel tonight. Your father has a dinner meeting."

Ruth was my youngest sister. My other two sisters were at Gordon College in Massachusetts. Ruth was in the ninth grade.

"Dad asked if I could eat with him tonight. He has some local real estate investors dining with us at the country club."

"Oh, I understand. Maybe tomorrow night, then?"

"I'll plan on that, Mom. You're still my favorite cook."

I walked out the back door and around the front of the house where my car was parked. Mom and Dad had bought the model home in the subdivision where my house was located. My house past tense. During the contretemps the previous month, someone had burned it to the ground. Everyone assumed the fire had been set by Roland Fordyce, the property developer who had tried to wrest ownership of the Mid-North campus away from us. He was in no position to argue the accusation since he had been killed by Charlie Bigelow, the former board chairman, who had subsequently stuck the gun barrel into *his* mouth. This was after he shot Nigel.

The charred remains of the house had been removed, but little else had been done on the replacement because of the winter weather. I was renting a two bedroom apartment a couple of miles away. An apartment was just as good as a house for my purposes; maybe better. I commuted to Rockford every week to take classes and needed a place to stay. Dad had talked me into buying the house as an investment. The investment had gone up in smoke.

I stopped by the apartment to change into a suit and tie. Dad wanted to make sure I made a good impression and had made a point to tell me that just a sport jacket would not do. Being in a pastoral ministry meant I was used to wearing suits, but it was easy to get careless on the Mid-North campus where the male students were much more casual.

After arriving in the lobby of the Rockford Country Club, I handed my overcoat to an attendant and then made my way to the private dining room. I made sure to be early because Dad would want to give me final instructions for the evening.

"Ah, Beryl, here you are," He said. He and I were of similar height and build, but where I had Mother's light brown hair and features, he had black hair and was almost swarthy.

"Now, tell me again, this is a *getting to know you* meeting, right?"

"That's right Beryl. You will sit at the opposite end of the table from me tonight."

I looked around the room. "And we have eight guests?"

"Yes. I have prospectuses printed. You may want to review it before our guests get here."

I picked up the heavy folder and looked at the neatly typed documents on the Cathcart Company letterhead. "Very nice, Dad. So you are not soliciting proposals for any particular project tonight, then."

"That's right. This is just to let them know we have an office and are open for business."

"Do you have time to actually develop anything in Rockford right now?"

He grimaced. "Honestly, no. I'm talking to Merrill Talbert about his moving out here from the city and managing the day to day business."

"Will he?" I asked.

"I think he will. When he heard we were moving out here, he got very interested."

"Just curious, but what are your plans for the operations back in the city?"

"I don't know at this point," he replied. "If my work at the school turns in to a long term thing, I should probably start unwinding things in the city. Commuting would get old."

"Setting up an office here will make things easier," I said.

"Yes, but sometimes I wonder whether the Lord wants me to get out of the real estate business altogether."

"Could you do that?"

"Oh, yes. There is nothing sacred about the family business. It's in the Lord's hands."

Out of the corner of my eye I saw our first guest walk in. Dad touched my arm and we walked over to meet him. Dad and I had a pretty easy-going relationship most of the time. But when we were dealing with clients and potential clients, he was all business. His track record showed he obviously did something right. He spent a career in the New York City real estate development market and had accumulated substantial wealth.

It was not a long dinner – these were busy people and Dad stayed on point. Most of the prospective clients were either elderly, or approaching retirement age. I had always liked older people and got along well with them. I understood now why Dad wanted me in the meeting. I kept the conversation going and was attentive to our guests.

I was out of there by 8 PM and got back to my apartment in time to bury myself in homework. I had gotten a lot accomplished during the afternoon, but it was still a long evening. In those days, college professors thought nothing of assigning homework to keep the students occupied over the holidays. Plus I had preached three times over the weekend and *that* had soaked up a lot of study time.

I hoped things would settle back into a routine now with Nigel out of the hospital. The past month had been a frantic time of shuttling between the hospital, campus and Appleton. Fortunately things at the church had settled down following the influx of disaffected Methodists, followed by their newly converted pastor. I struggled to maintain my schoolwork while spending every spare minute in the office helping Dad hold the school together. The evenings at the hospital were most frightening as Nigel's wounds were life threatening, and after three surgeries, I didn't think he was really out of the woods yet.

The lessons of the past few months were still very real to me, and after I closed my books at 2 AM, I spent a half-hour talking to my Heavenly Father. I knew I couldn't do all this on my own, and I was done trying. I once again placed my body and soul on the altar and put myself in God's hands.

One of the benefits of being excessively busy is that bedtime is welcome. I rarely had trouble sleeping, and during these days I was asleep within about ten seconds of my head hitting the pillow. I was only slightly surprised I had never run into Cain, considering my extensive travels in the land of Nod.

CHAPTER THREE

Dr. Voysey was working his way through the minor prophets. The short time between Thanksgiving and Christmas was the home stretch for the semester, and everyone was anxious to be done.

"And now, what is the great lesson we can draw from the book of Jonah?"

Voysey paced the front of the classroom as he lectured. The students were no longer as intimidated as they were earlier in the semester, and Voysey seemed to revel in the spirited discussions.

"Working backwards we could say it is a great illustration of Christ's command to pray for our enemies," Stephen Gardiner spoke up unbidden.

Voysey raised an eyebrow as he looked at the student. "Not bad, Garner. There may be hope for you, yet."

"That's Gardiner, Sir."

Voysey raised a hand dismissively. "Whatever. Now that Mr. Garner has launched himself out on a limb, who wants to administer the reward for his impetuous ways?"

I stuck my hand up.

"Speak, Cathcart!" he commanded.

"The book teaches God's sovereignty. He is willing to reach down and rescue a people, who would otherwise be condemned for their wickedness."

"That's *mercy*, Cathcart," another student commented.

Voysey looked down his nose at the other student. "Don't interrupt, Steuben. Now, Mr. Cathcart, I think we could make the argument that any of the minor prophets demonstrates God's sovereignty."

"But, that doesn't invalidate what I just said, Sir."

Voysey rocked his head back and forth, and then tried, once again, to stick his hands in the pockets of his tweed sport jacket. He had been attempting the same action repeatedly through class, without success. The tag hanging surreptitiously from one sleeve told me he had just bought the thing, and the pockets were still sewed closed.

I thought it was hugely amusing, but cracking a smile in that class was like blood in the water. And I had not desire to rupture my uneasy truce with the professor.

"What's so funny, Cathcart?"

Uh oh. He somehow recognized I was laughing at him. Since I was the son of the acting president of Mid-North College, I had received numerous warnings from my dad on how not to embarrass him. I had become very careful of my deportment around the campus, though this was out of character for me.

"I'm just enjoying the discussion, Sir."

Voysey snorted, and then looked around the room. "Is no one going to cut off that limb on which our Mr. Garner has so gloriously perched?"

"Will no one rid me of the turbulent priest?" someone said *sotto voce*.

Voysey managed a single bark of laughter. "Ha! Our Mr. Garner is far from being another Thomas Becket."

"It's Gardiner, Sir," Gardiner protested plaintively.

"Shut up, Garner. Now, I'm not planning on letting the rest of you off the hook. What's the problem with our limb-dweller's thought?"

The end class bell rang. Instead of galloping out of the classroom, Voysey stared at the hapless Gardiner. "I'm not letting you off your branch so easily, Garner. I expect to see you perched up there this Thursday morning where we can use you for target practice."

"It's Gardiner, Sir."

He nodded. "Uh huh. And, Mr. Cathcart, a word with you please."

He turned and walked back to the desk at the front of the classroom, and began arranging his notes. The assumption was that class was dismissed, and the other students shuffled out of the room. I gathered my things and walked over to the front of the desk, facing him. He jogged the stack of papers containing his lecture notes, and slid them into a binder. He then looked up and gave me his disconcerting stare.

"You are aware, Cathcart, of the incredible brouhaha this conference of yours is going to cause here on the campus?"

I wasn't expecting a direct assault, and I hadn't believed Voysey even was aware of my role in planning The Mid-North Symposium on the Reliability of Scripture. Nigel and I had hatched the plans for the conference as a way of smoking any heterodox faculty members into the open.

I did not know what Voysey's angle was, although I believed him to be the most conservative member of the faculty – and how would I even answer a question, such as the one he just posed. I mentally shrugged.

"Dr. Voysey, I believe the symposium will bring the faculty and the students together in a better appreciation of the Bible."

"Then you are either hopelessly naïve or you're a liar."

One of the oddly attractive things about Clarke Voysey was that there was never any doubt where you stood with him. I was not so sure I enjoyed the distinction at that moment. He had me on the spot. I had kept my wits about me throughout the semester, but at this moment, he had me rattled. And, I'm sure he knew it.

"Well, Sir, unfortunately I cannot confess that I have never lied, but I'm certainly telling you the truth, right now, as I know it," I babbled.

He seemed to stare right through me, and I wondered where he was going with this, until I saw that slight twinkle in his eye. Okay, there was a punch line coming, and Voysey was having fun tormenting me.

"Cathcart, Saint Paul teaches us that the Lord often uses the foolish things of this world to confound the wise. That being the case, I have some faint hope that the Lord will use you to rescue this place."

With that, he gathered up his things, and launched himself out of the classroom. I stared at the open door, and tried to decide whether to be insulted. My first thought was to trot over to the Administration Building and tell Dad about the incident, but Dad had his hands full being both chairman of the board of Mid-North College, as well as acting president. I could tell him next time I happened to see him.

Besides, by staying away from the Administration Building, I also stayed away from Ellen. While she was unfailingly polite when I stepped into her office, it hadn't been that long since our relationship had ended. I had no desire to rip the scab off my wound, and I didn't think Ellen would appreciate it either.

I supposed I could run over to Mom and Dad's house, and breathlessly relate Voysey's behavior to Nigel, but I did not want to add to Nigel's worries. He had enough on his plate just recovering from the surgery. Besides, I would be there for dinner, anyway.

Actually, I really could do none of those things at the moment. Voysey's class let out at 10:45 and the daily chapel service started at 11. I left the classroom building, and walked across the campus to the chapel in the teeth of a freshening winter breeze. It had grown noticeably colder since I had arrived on campus that morning. A thin skein of clouds had slipped past the sun. I did not take the Rockford paper, nor did I have a television in my apartment, so I was ignorant of the weather forecasts. Since I was remaining in Rockford until Friday, a winter storm presented nothing more than an inconvenience for me.

The chapel was nearly full when I arrived. I took that as a good sign.

Nigel's mandatory chapel attendance requirement had been met with some resistance by faculty and students. It looked like a majority were present. I slipped into the back row, and moved to the middle. Sancy Pearlman strode into the chapel, and moved down the row to sit next to me.

"Beastly cold outside, Beryl," she piped.

I smiled at the English professor, who was oddly likable despite her quirks. "And it's getting worse, Miss Pearlman. I suspect the students will be frolicking in the snow this evening."

She leaned back in the wooden theater seating. "I saw a few snowflakes spitting about out there. I fear my freshmen will spend the class hours staring out the windows."

"And with dire consequences for the week's assignments," I riposted.

She groaned. "I hadn't thought of that. You do bring up the worst thoughts, Pastor Cathcart."

I laughed. "It's just my naturally cheerful, and optimistic character, Ma'am."

"You will come to an evil end, yet, young man."

"People keep telling me that."

"You should listen to them. Now, who do you suppose will be speaking this morning?"

I leaned out to see past a group of students standing the row conversing. "Well, it looks like just Dad and the song leader on the platform so far."

"Nobody has entrusted Phil Brooks with anything beyond song leading for years, so we can safely assume Dr. Cathcart will be bringing the message."

I was still getting used to hearing my father addressed as *Doctor* Cathcart. Dad had received a law degree from the Harvard Law School, and therefore had his JD. But lawyers were rarely addressed as doctor, and Dad never made a big deal about his learning. Academia operated under different rules, though. Professors with earned doctorates were the highest caste of academic civilization, and they guarded their prerogatives jealously. And the academic culture insisted on addressing anyone with a terminal degree as *doctor*.

Sancy had confided to me that there was some discussion among the college faculty about the appropriateness of addressing Dad that way, because he was, after all, a lawyer. Graduating from the Harvard Law School was no mean feat, however, and a consensus was reached that Dad was entitled to the dignities of his degree. Many still looked at him askance because of his lack of experience in higher education. I decided they felt he hadn't paid his dues.

On the other hand, it was gradually seeping into the consciousness of the employees of Mid-North College that without the hundreds of thousands of dollars that my dad had invested in the school, they would all be on the streets at the end of the semester in a few short weeks. And to those inveterate score-keepers on campus, the ledger-books weighed heavily on Dad's side, and so they gave him due deference.

Whatever Sancy Pearlman's opinion of Phil Brooks, he was an enthusiastic song leader. The Thanksgiving weekend marked the beginning of the season where Christmas carols were appropriate in religious services. We all stood and sang "Hark the Herald Angels Sing." It seemed to me there was a good spirit among the students and they sang well, although not with the volume I experienced at my church in Appleton.

After the song, Brooks called to one of the students in the congregation to pray. Then following some perfunctory announcements, he turned the platform over to Dad. He stepped to the podium, and opened his Bible.

"Turn, please, to Second Timothy chapter three, and verse sixteen."

I was surprised. Dad and I had worked our way through a heated argument on the necessity of upholding the doctrine of the inerrancy of Scripture at the school. It was not that he and I disagreed over the doctrine, rather he was ambivalent about anything that would seem to run at cross purposes with his mission to save the school from financial ruin. Nigel and I had suggested holding a symposium on the reliability of Scripture, and he had embraced it as a way to avoid familial strife, I thought. Plus, he thought it would bring in visitors, who could be convinced to contribute to the school financially.

Dad launched into a serious discussion on the foundational nature of Scripture to our evangelical faith. He touched obliquely on inerrancy by quoting Lorraine Boettner, who had commented that God's purpose in inspiring the Bible was to ensure a reliable record. I glanced around the room to see if Dr. Carper was in attendance. After his statement in class requiring students to attend chapel as a condition of passing the course, I couldn't imagine him *not* attending.

Dad's Sunday School teaching experience showed in his careful application of the verses to the lives of believers. He was a good teacher, and I found myself getting caught up in the text, and his exposition, forgetting briefly the issue that was front and center for me and Nigel. It was again at the center of my attention as he concluded the message.

"I would like to take this opportunity to formally announce the Mid-North Symposium on the Reliability of Scripture, which will be held in March here at the college. This is a project President Robart was working on before his recent injuries incapacitated him. He has told me that he very much wishes this project to proceed."

"We have initiated this project for several reasons: first of all, we see this as a wonderful opportunity to gather as a group to focus on the Word of God, and meditate upon His greatness. Secondly, there are numerous strong Christian colleges in the upper Midwest, and as a small school, we kind of get lost in the herd. This will be a chance for us to promote our strong religion department, and vital student body."

"I recognize this is very short notice to plan something as complex as a conference, and we are going to look for support from all the faculty and students. There will be further announcements as we make plans. There will be weekly prayer meetings on campus to help us prepare. These will begin next week, and there will be an announcement on the time and place. Now, let us close in prayer."

After the prayer, the students jumped to their feet in their haste to either grab lunch, or head to their next class. Sancy Pearlman looked over at me with one eyebrow crooked. "It would appear our President Robart has grasped the nettle."

I hadn't heard that expression before, but her meaning was clear. It didn't matter what most of the students and some of the faculty thought, Dad had just fired the opening shot in the war that would be fought over the soul of Mid-North College in Rockford, Illinois. I wondered if he realized it.

Dr. Carper stopped me as I stepped out of the chapel. I moved to the side to keep from being run over by the crush of students as the headed to their next appointments.

"Can I buy you a cup of coffee, Cathcart?" he asked.

I shrugged. "Sure."

We walked towards The Gutter together. I shoved my hands into my coat pocket and shivered. He looked over at me and grinned.

"A bit cold today, for sure."

"Yes, Sir. I have never really learned to appreciate winter."

He chuckled as we walked. "Unfortunately there is little you can do about it. I grew up north of Minneapolis. Believe me, this is balmy."

"If you say so, Sir."

We continued in small talk as we crossed the campus. At least The Gutter was warm, even if it did have a stupid name. We gathered our coffees and retreated to a corner table. Carper took a sip of the brew and grimaced.

"I sometimes think drinking the stuff here constitutes cruel and unusual punishment."

"It's hot and has caffeine," I said. "That's about all I can say about it."

"Quite a little plan you and your father cooked up," he said without further preamble.

I tilted my head and raised my eyebrows. "We had some help from Nigel, but yes."

"What are you trying to achieve?"

I thought carefully as I took advantage of the opportunity to take another sip of coffee. I wondered if he was genuinely curious, or if he was looking for an attack vector.

"Several things, I guess, Sir. As Dad mentioned in his message, we think it is a way to put Mid-North on the map. Nigel particularly wants to set a standard for this school as to where we stand with our Bibliology. Those two things, mainly."

Carper nodded, and drank some more coffee. He appeared deep in thought.

"Are you trying to turn this school into a Fundamentalist outpost, then?"

"No. Dad is solidly Evangelical as is Nigel. They would not allow it."

"But, isn't this a back-door way of introducing Fundamentalist doctrine?"

"I believe Harold Okenga holds to an inerrant Bible." This was the first thing that came to mind, but there was a point I needed to make. "This is not just a Fundamentalist doctrine. Not all Evangelicals hold to it, but I think a majority of them do."

Harold John Okenga had coined the term New Evangelical and had credibility with this crowd. Even though he was a Fundamentalist bogieman, I had to admit his core doctrine was solid.

He waved his hand in a throwing away motion. "Okay, I'll grant your point. But we have never made a litmus test of inerrancy. That is a very Fundamentalist thing to do."

"Do you believe in the virgin birth?"

"Absolutely. That is cardinal doctrine."

"Do you believe that someone who does not hold to the virgin birth can really be saved?"

"I do not. And I see where you are going. The virgin birth of Christ is a historical position of the church. Inerrancy, as you hold it, is not."

"I believe it is, but we would probably server no purpose by sitting here saying *yes it is; not it's not.*"

He laughed then. "I will concede your point, Cathcart."

"Nigel feels strongly about this," I said.

"Strongly enough to quash diverse points of view?"

A tough question. "Dad has been pretty outspoken in his view that we should not tear the school apart over this."

"But what does Beryl Cathcart really think?"

I smiled. "Beryl Cathcart is trying very hard to follow his dad's instructions not to stir up trouble."

"I am forced to agree that you are not a typical Fundamentalist."

"You may be right," I replied. "I grew up in Evangelicalism."

He seemed to stare in the distance. "You know. I really love this place. It has been the great joy of my life to teach here. It is such a thrill to help bring the lives of my students into conformity to Christ. I would like very much to grow old here. I want to be like that tree planted by the rivers of water."

He slid his chair back and stood up. "Thanks for your time, Cathcart."

Before I could reply, he turned and walked quickly from the little coffee house.

CHAPTER FOUR

I was thoughtful as I fixed my bologna sandwich that noon in my apartment. I had actually made a grocery run that Monday, and was eating at home for a change. I could have gone to my parents' house. Mom would have been happy to fix me something, and I could have passed the time talking to Nigel. But, I wanted to get ahead of the curve in my homework. I had an easy A in Systematic Theology, and wasn't worried about finishing the semester that way. But, I was hovering between a B+ and an A- in Dr. Voysey's Old Testament Introduction, and I really wanted to come out on the top side. I think part of that was that I wanted to prove to Dr. Voysey I could indeed do the work.

As I ate, I paged through Berkhof's *Systematic Theology*, and reviewed the material Dr. Carper would be covering that afternoon. I was fully engaged in the class, not only because I was fascinated by theology, but also due to my need to isolate and document Dr. Carper's doctrinal declension. There was little I could pinpoint beyond his thoughts on inerrancy, but he loved studying Barth, Neibuhr and Tillich, and quoted them regularly. The Fundamentalists were deeply suspicious of the Neo-orthodox writers, and rightfully so. However they were widely studied at the Evangelical schools and were respected by even the most conservative of those scholars.

Dad had thrown the gauntlet down, and Carper was quick to react. From our conversation at the Gutter, I concluded that the professor viewed the conference as an existential threat to his career at the college. I *knew* it was. While Nigel and I differed on many points of doctrine and practice, he was firm in his conviction that even a mild form of doubt on the nature of inspiration was dangerous to have around the school.

Voysey was another case, altogether. He was so solid he reminded me of an immovable block of granite. He was unapologetic in his defense of Biblical truth. But, he was also unmerciful to any student who was less than fully prepared in class. His eclectic teaching style moved between strong Biblical preaching, and Socratic dialog. He had an uncanny instinct for spotting students whose attention was drifting, and those who were unprepared. The result was a group of students who had been trained to stay with the instructor, and interact in the classroom.

Once I had gotten over the quirks of Clarke Voysey, OTI provided a massive boost to my knowledge of the Old Testament, as well as honing my expositional skills. He succeeded in developing an eye-opening interaction and debate with the students. I felt like my coursework at Mid-North had contributed to my ministry in Appleton, particularly in the pulpit. Of course, the Lord had used the terrifying experiences of the preceding months to force me into His care, like nothing else had in my entire life. On net, I saw great gain from the experience. Not for me personally, but rather in the smelting that refined me as a tool in the hands of the Father.

As I munched on my sandwich, and reviewed my homework, the background noise changed. The wind, which had been rushing around the apartment building in repeated gusts dropped off. I glanced out the window to see the snow now falling vertically, and growing heavier. Snow is just magic. The drift and drive of the infinitude of flakes against the background of the winter-scarred trees was both mesmerizing and relaxing.

One of my life-long day-dreams was to be in a room with a blazing hearth, sitting next to the girl I loved, and watching the ethereal winter storm. Such events seemed to be rare in human existence, and non-existent for me. I sometimes wondered whether this represented a subliminal longing for the eternal rest that the Lord had promised his children. I did know it wasn't going to happen that day.

As I burrowed back into my homework, another sound intruded into the background. It was a rhythmic *squeak-clump* that seemed to me to be the sound of wood on wood. Once I became aware of it, I was driven to isolate the sound and identify it. I slide my chair back, and walked into the living room. The sound was definitely coming from the apartment above me. I went back to the kitchen table and tried to get into my studies again.

The funny thing about studying is that you have to get into the zone, as it were. Once that concentration is broken, it is a challenge to climb back into it. Now, the continued noise was now abrading my concentration. I finally looked at my watch in exasperation. I hurriedly finished my lunch, and grabbed my books. I drove over to the campus, and spent the rest of my spare time in the library until class started.

The snow tapered off, and the sun came out that afternoon. It appeared my predictions to Sancy Pearlman of a winter wonderland on campus were mistaken. By evening, the accumulated snow had melted, and the streets were dry, once again.

#

Dinner that evening was interesting. Arrayed around the table were my parents, my sister and I, along with Nigel. Ellen Holgate had also contrived an invitation to dinner. She was actively managing Nigel's life. I wasn't sure if she was acting in the role of his secretary, or driving towards something more serious. My parents were mainly bemused.

"Here, let me get that for you, Nigel."

Ellen reached for the bowl of potatoes, and then spooned some on to Nigel's plate.

"I don't need that much, Ellen."

"Yes, you do," she replied. "You look like a skeleton in that wheel chair. You need to put on some weight. The starch will help."

I was doing a poor job of concealing my smile, when he looked across the table at me.

"Shut up!" he said.

I shrugged. "I didn't say anything, Nige."

"Yeah, well, the look on your face said it all."

"I have no idea what you're talking about."

Dad jumped in, probably to forestall a sniping session around the table. "So, Beryl, were there any comments after chapel today?"

I grinned at him. "You might say that. Dr. Voysey remarked to me about it, but that was before chapel."

Dad nodded. "I explained the Symposium to the faculty last week before Thanksgiving."

"He seemed to think I was deeply involved, for some reason," I replied. I was reluctant to go into more detail, mostly because I didn't want to give Nigel more ammunition for our sparring wars.

"What about the students?" Dad persisted.

"Actually they're not saying much to me about it. They are pretty much aware I'm the son of the acting president, and are circumspect about it."

"That's interesting," he said.

"After you were introduced as the board chairman, everyone pretty much forgot about it, I think. But now when you are up on the chapel platform every day, more people started making the connection. There was more, though."

Dad waited as I gathered my thoughts.

"Dr. Carper intercepted me after chapel and dragged me to the Gutter for a cup of coffee."

Ruth giggled. "I thought you were going to say he dragged you to the gutter and beat you up."

"Actually, I worried about that briefly," I said. "No, he wanted to make the point that Evangelicals do not universally hold to inerrancy."

"They do at my school," Nigel said. "Or they should, anyway. That's why I feel I must put up with you, Buckwheat."

I cleared my throat loudly. "As I was saying before I was so rudely interrupted by the peanut gallery, Dr. Carper said that he really loves this place and wants to grow old teaching here."

"That poor man," Mom said. "This is really going to put him on the spot, isn't it?"

"Probably."

"Interesting," Dad said, but he didn't comment further.

I used my fork to mold a lake in the middle of my potatoes, and reached for the gravy boat. Most restaurants whipped their potatoes, but the result was rarely exceptional. Mom's potatoes were always light and fluffy, always tasty. I filled Crater Lake with the beef gravy, and poured some over the slices of roast on my plate.

"You should watch what you eat, Beryl," Ellen said. "The weight gain will sneak up on you."

I grinned at her. "So far I'm keeping my svelte figure. And besides, look at my parents. They're thin too. But, I think you're entirely correct in helping Nigel control his appetites."

"Thanks, Buddy," he said.

Ellen sniffed, as if further comment was unnecessary. Her attitude towards me had seemed to thaw a bit in recent weeks. I was still recovering from the effects of our breakup, which had occurred weeks previously, and I hoped she was too. It was much easier when we both pretended we were merely friends. My thoughts about her were somewhat more than that, but I thought I had finally succeeded in controlling it. And since she had assumed the role of mother hen for Nigel, and since Nigel and I hung around together a lot, Ellen and I were forced into one-another's company on a regular basis.

I remembered back to McKisson University, where I had taken my undergraduate education, and asking a classmate about his on-again, off-again romance. He replied that it was complex. I decided that was as good a description of our relationship as any.

I turned to my sister, Ruth. "And how are things at West High School?"

She made a face. "Still getting used to it. Being the new kid on the block really is tough sometimes."

"Sorry to drag you all the way out here, Cakee." When she was a toddler, she had developed a taste for dessert, and anything sweet was termed *cakee*. The nickname stuck.

"No need, Beryl. Plus, you didn't drag me out here. When Mommy and Daddy decided to move out here, I begged them to bring me along. I was going to have to live with Grandma and finish school in the city."

I looked the other direction at Dad. "I hadn't heard that. You were going to leave her in New York?"

"We were concerned about uprooting her," Mom said. "Making adjustments like that is hard on a child."

"I am not a child," Ruth proclaimed. "Besides, I didn't say I wasn't having fun. And the kids at the church are great."

Ruth had been attending a nearby Evangelical Free Church with my parents, and had immediately bonded with the young people in

30

that congregation. I had visited one Wednesday night, and had really liked the people of the church, too. Generally though, I attended the Baptist church in Love's Park when I was in Rockford.

My parents had initially visited their church because it was where Nigel was a member, plus they were not really comfortable in the Fundamentalist churches where I hung my hat. I was delighted to see them attending a good church. I had long since come to the conclusion I was not going to convince my dad to adopt by separatist convictions, so this seemed like a good solution.

"How are things going at the Cathcart offices?" I asked.

Dad now shrugged. "Merrill Talbert moves out here next week, but I really don't expect things to start moving until after the first of the year. He'll have a chance to get the offices sorted out. We need to get a secretary / receptionist hired. Darlene Swanson applied."

I grinned broadly at him. "And the Property Management Partners of Rockford would be delighted to send her our way?"

"Why would that be?" Ruth asked.

"Apparently she has a big mouth," I replied. "At least that was the word around town."

"Actually, she is highly valued by her current employer," Dad said. "I've had a couple of back-channel conversations with the owner. In spite of her difficulties with confidential information, she brings a lot of business to the firm."

"So, in other words, she's probably fine right where she is?" I asked.

"Correct, Bery," Dad said. "There's hope for you in this business yet."

"Ha!" Nigel said. "He hasn't learned how to help run a school yet."

"Of course I have," I riposted. "I learned from you, didn't I?"

"And he doesn't even know when he's failing the course."

Ruth joined in the merriment. "I remember Dad yelling at him a lot when he was growing up. I guess it's hard for him to learn."

I shook my finger at my younger sister. "You stay out of this, young lady. Your day is coming."

She stuck out her tongue at me.

"Children are such a joy, don't you think?" Now Mom was chiming in.

I looked down at my plate, and started stirring the gravy into the potatoes. Nigel just snorted. It seemed I wasn't going to get ahead in this group. On the other hand, I was used to it by now.

Anything planned for tomorrow, Beryl?" Dad asked.

"I need to see if I can find a replacement for the side mirror on the car. That and do homework. What do you need?"

"Ogden Routh recommended an events management company for us to use for the Symposium. There's a Clarence Rutherford coming by the office in the afternoon, and I'd like you to be there for the meeting."

Nigel was just taking a drink of his water, and nearly choked on it. We looked at him in amazement, except for Ruth, who laughed.

"What gives?" Dad asked.

"TV character, Dad."

Okay. It looked like Ruth and Nigel were the connoisseurs of TV trivia in the room. It certainly sailed over my head.

Then Ellen started giggling. "*Leave it to Beaver*, right?"

"I wonder if he will be as stuffy as the TV character," Nigel said.

"It's a good thing we're keeping you locked up here," Dad said. "If I had you and Beryl both in the same room tomorrow, we might just as well call off the whole conference."

"Ha!" I said. "You must be referring to Nigel's relative immaturity. No one would question my grave demeanor."

Dad rolled his eyes, then looked at Mom. "Will this dinner never end?"

She slapped him on the arm. "Oh, hush, Daryl. Eat your dinner."

After the dinner we helped Nigel to his favored chair in the living room. Ellen was in the kitchen helping Mom with the dishes. I didn't know where Dad was.

"Hey, Nigel?"

"Yeah?"

"Can you get Ruth down here for a few minutes?"

He looked at me carefully. "I think so. What do you have in mind?"

I pulled the rubber snake out of the pocket of my sport jacket and showed it to him.

"Oh, Beryl, that is wicked," he said. "I love it."

"Hey, Cakee!" I yelled.

"What do you want, Beryl?" she called down from her room.

"Nigel wants to talk to you."

"Just a minute."

She came bounding down the stairs as I headed up towards the bathroom. I made a short side trip and slipped the snake under the covers of her bed.

CHAPTER FIVE

"Ho, ho, ho, shopping for groceries again?" Sully asked.

On my first visit to the Chrysler-Plymouth dealer in Rockford, I had flipped a smart remark back at the salesman in response to his question about whether I was car shopping. He had thought I was enormously funny, and that he was my best friend. This was a case where I really regretted my awful mouth.

"How're you doing, Sully?" I asked, in reply.

"Not bad. Not bad at all."

"Business okay?"

"Not too bad for the winter. I do okay."

He probably had customers signing the papers to buy cars just so they could get away from the noxious aura of his body odor. The chicken-soup smell of body sweat was in abeyance in the winter cold, but he smelled as though he had been chain-smoking all morning. This was in addition to the clear evidence he had been having the odd nip.

"I need to talk to your parts man." I pointed to the driver's door of my Dodge. "I had the closest of close calls over the weekend, and need to replace the mirror."

"Well, come on in out of the cold, young Mr. Cathcart. Our body man doesn't have much going on today, so if Chester's got the part, we can probably fix you up, while you wait."

"That would be wonderful, Sully."

"Not a problem, not a problem." He opened the door and ushered me on to the showroom floor. "And how is your dad doing?"

"Doing fine. He recently moved here to Rockford from New York City."

"Is that so? I read in the paper where he's the acting president of that school you attend."

I nodded. "Yes, but just until Dr. Robart gets back on his feet."

"Such a horrible thing to happen. I tell you, I was shocked. I mean, we have some rough people here in Rockford, but shooting a college president. I don't know what the world is coming to."

Connie Seabright raised an eyebrow as we walked past the business office. She gave me a smile and a small wave. I hoped, maybe, I would have a chance to talk to her.

We stepped into the shop, and Sully waved to a dark-haired lanky man in the corner. "Hey Slatts, I got a job for you."

"Yeah, what is it, Sully?"

"Mr. Cathcart here got his driver-side mirror knocked off. If we have a replacement, can you put it to rights for him?"

Slatts looked around. "Kind of chilly out there, Sully."

"Well, bring the car inside, Slatts. I'm not making you work in the snow." Sully turned to me and winked.

I pulled the keys out of my pocket and handed them to the body man. "It's the black '65 Monaco."

"Right." He stepped over to the wall, and punched a button. The big door slid open and a wave of frigid air swept in. He stepped out into the parking lot.

"Geeze it's cold," Sully said. "Come on into the office. Slatts is mad because I found something for him to do."

"Who left the door open?" A portly middle-aged man stepped from the shop into the show-room. He accompanied his question with a fair measure of profanity.

"Slatts went out to bring a car in," Sully said. "I found him some work, Mr. Brinker."

"Good for you, Sully. Oh, excuse me." He turned to me. "Your car?"

"Yes, Sir. I needed to replace a mirror."

He stuck out his hand. "I'm Hans Brinker. I guess you could call me the proprietor."

"Beryl Cathcart," I replied, shaking his hand. I managed not to snort at his name. I really needed to be more considerate of people, especially since I had a funny name too.

"Is Sully helping you?"

"Yes, Sir. I bought a car from him a while back, and he's helped me a time or two since."

"Good, good. Sully, make sure Mr. Catfart goes away happy."

I managed not to drop my jaw, as he shook my hand again. Sully watched as Brinker marched back to his office.

He turned to me, with an apologetic look. "I'm sorry about that, Mr. Cathcart. Mr. Brinker doesn't hear too good, sometimes."

"Don't worry about it, Sully. I don't offend easily."

I wasn't going to tell him it was the funniest thing I had heard in months. My main problem at that moment was that I didn't know anyone I could repeat it to. Dad would tell me to grow up. Lane Johnson, the chairman of my deacon board, would be embarrassed. And Nigel would view it as an opportunity to bludgeon me with a new nickname.

I heard the sound of my Dodge as Slatts rolled it into the garage, and the door came rattling down. I wandered up to the front of the showroom, thinking I could escape the Sully fumes. Since I was his best friend, however, he followed me. Sitting on the showroom floor was a bright red 1966 Plymouth Belvidere two-door. The 66's were all new, and I admired the crisp, square-cut lines of the car.

"I think those are pretty," I said.

"Let me show you something." Sully walked past me to the front of the car. He reached under the bumper and pulled the hood release. He raised the hood, and said, "Take a look at this, Mr. Cathcart."

It took me a few moments to figure out what I was looking at. The distributor was at the front of the engine, just like my Dodge, but the spark plug wires disappeared into a series of four rubber plugs in the center of each water-trough sized valve cover. The engine seemed jammed into the compartment, and the lettering around the top of the air cleaner said, *426 Cubic Inches*.

"You heard about the new NASCAR racing engine?" Sully asked.

"I really don't follow racing closely. Are you telling me that this is what that is?"

Sully nodded. "Yep. Chrysler has started putting a few into street cars. I can't believe Mr. Brinker managed to snag one."

"This is his?"

"Oh, no. I meant, he usually doesn't like to stock vehicles like this."

I stepped around to the side, glancing at the dog dish hubcaps, and looked at the window sticker, then whistled. "They are proud of that engine, aren't they."

"They oughta be," he replied. "Richard Petty has been stomping Ford into the ground with this engine."

I peered into the interior. It looked like a typical low-rent Plymouth, other than the column mounted automatic shifter. "What kind of horsepower?"

"It's rated at 425."

I shrugged. "There's a couple versions of the 413, like in my car, that come close to this."

"Yer talkin' about the Max-Wedge, Mr. Cathcart?"

"Well, yeah."

"The thing t'remember, Mr. Cathcart, is that 425 is what they put on the spec sheet. I've heard a couple people claim it's putting out north of 500 horsepower."

"Naaah," I said.

"Yeah," he said nodding.

"That's a lot of engine."

"Wanna find out?"

Slatts stuck his head through the door from the shop. "This a warranty?"

"What?" I asked.

"Is this a warranty repair?" Sully explained.

"Oh. No. I'll just pay for it. I was in a minor accident over the weekend."

"Huh," Slatts commented. "There's not a scratch anywhere else. We got a mirror in stock. I gotta pull the door panel. Mebbe an hour or so."

"That's fine," I said. "I have all afternoon."

I turned back to Sully. "You were saying?"

"I was wondering if you were up to a test drive."

"In this?"

"Why not?"

I shrugged. "Sure."

"Let's get the doors open, so I can back it out on to the lot. Then we can take it for a spin."

Maybe it was the enclosed space. While the engine in my Dodge put out a solid rumble, when Sully fired up this Plymouth, it sounded like thunder. I had never heard anything quite like it. After he had eased the car out of the building, I pulled the double-doors closed. I then trotted around and climbed into the passenger seat.

Sully rolled up the window, and adjusted the heater. "Cold day for it," he grunted.

"I'm just glad the snow melted off," I said.

He eased the car down to the street and pulled out. It seemed like the automatic transmission shifted through its gears almost instantly. From my experience in my Dart, I knew that the Chrysler automatics liked to stay in high gear. Sully jazzed the throttle slight, and the car leaped ahead.

"I'll bet this thing could get to be a hand-full," he said.

I nodded, and watched the scenery go by. The car seemed to ride more stiffly than my Dodge as Sully negotiated the frost-heaved concrete streets of Rockford. I could feel the throb of the engine up through the floorboard and into my feet. It seemed like a monster was chained under the hood.

Sully pulled into a gas station, and put the car in park. "Why don't you take it, Mr. Cathcart."

"Don't mind if I do."

I was pretty careful, since it wasn't my car. Following Sully's instructions, I turned on to US 51. The car felt a little nose heavy, but, then again, there was a lot of engine under the hood. The car was definitely lighter than my Dodge, but seemed to ride and drive well. I eased it up to about 50 miles per hour. Sully leaned over.

"How's the temp?"

I looked at the temperature gauge. "Looks like we're in the operating range."

"If you're going to play around, you don't want to do it with a cold engine. Stomp on it, Mr. Cathcart."

I shoved the accelerator to the floor.

"Holy cow!" It was like being shot out of a cannon. The car just exploded. The thunder turned into *loud* thunder. I glanced down to see the speedometer sailing over 100. I got off the gas, and started braking. "I can't believe this," I shouted.

Sully was giggling. "Talk about strapping yourself to a rocket."

"And this is street legal?"

"Depends on how you drive it," he laughed.

I managed a couple more bursts of insane acceleration during the all too short test drive. As I pulled the Plymouth on to the dealer's lot the words going through my mind were, *I want this car!*

"Do you want to pull it back on to the showroom floor?" I asked Sully.

"Naah. I'll take care of that later. Why don't you come into my office, Mr. Cathcart?"

As I followed Sully to his office, I had this feeling of being led to the slaughter.

"How was the test drive?" I looked over as Connie called to me.

"Impressive."

She nodded knowingly. I wasn't sure what she thought of me. I already had one nearly new car, and a two year old car as a *beater* for the country roads. And here I was looking at 426 cubic inches of pure, unadulterated insanity. *But, I wanted this car!*

"Now, Mr. Brinker wants to get full list for this car. They are kind of rare, you know."

"I can understand that," I replied.

"What I can do, Mr. Cathcart, is to get you top dollar for your Dodge."

I leaned back in the chair across from his desk. "I don't know Sully. This is kind of quick."

"If it's a problem with financing, we could probably work something out with the bank."

I thought about the red Plymouth parked outside, and wanted it so badly I could taste it. I had never driven a car like that before.

"When did you get your Dodge?" he asked.

"Last July."

"Lemme go take a look at it."

He jumped out of his chair, and left the office with a quickness that belied his girth. I was rather surprised at how quickly things were moving. I had come to the dealership planning to get the mirror fixed, and then maybe catch a word with Connie. The red Plymouth had completely captivated me. I stepped out of Sully's smoky office for some fresh air, and saw through the window Sully along with Mr. Brinker walking around my Dodge. Connie was busy typing, and didn't look up as I stood in the breeze way between the showroom and the shop.

Sully and Brinker stepped close together briefly, then Brinker nodded. Sully spun around an marched back through the doorway from the shop.

"Come on back in here, Mr. Cathcart."

He dropped into his chair, and scribbled some numbers on a sales form. He spun the form around for me to study.

"Here's what we can do. Mr. Brinker really likes your car, and would like to trade."

I looked at the sales order. They were offering me $500 less for my Dodge than I had paid for it in July, which was not bad at all. And Sully had discounted the Plymouth $125.

"You can see we decided to drop the price on the Plymouth a bit. We would really like to trade with you."

I took a deep breath. Dad gave me an allowance, which he called missionary support, so that I wouldn't have to live in penury at my pastorate in Appleton. There was no way to spend all of it, living in a small town, so I could easily write a check to buy the car, even without the trade-in. I felt myself shivering on the edge of a decision.

"I'm getting ahead of myself, Sully. I'm not going to make a decision today."

"But this price is good today, only."

"Uh huh. I'll tell you what I'm going to do. I'll come back by tomorrow afternoon, or call you. It you have to change the price, or the car gets sold that'll be the end of it. I really need to pray about this."

"What would we have to do to make a deal today?"

I grinned at Sully. "I'm not going to insult you're intelligence. You've been very helpful to me before. I learned last fall the consequences of getting ahead of the Lord's will. The results were unpleasant, and I didn't want to do that again."

I saw the strange look on his face, and was reminded that I was once again thinking about Beryl, and not the people around me.

"Tell me, Sully, have you ever made a decision to accept Jesus as your Lord and Saviour?"

That stopped him. His mouth dropped open, and then closed again. He visibly tried to speak a couple of times before he managed a sentence.

"I go to church sometimes. I'm a good person. I believe in God."

"Those things are fine," I said. "But, Jesus said, 'unless you believe that I am He, ye shall die in your sins.' You have to have a personal relationship with Jesus."

Sully started to slide his chair backwards, but couldn't get very far because of the wall.

"Uh, I guess we could hold the car until tomorrow, Mr. Cathcart. I don't want to twist your arm, or anything."

"You're a great salesman, Sully, but I need to think about this."

"I understand. Slatts has finished the work on your car. Would you like to leave it here, and drive the Plymouth home tonight?"

I found myself wavering again. I really wanted to get behind the wheel of that red rocket, again. I stood up.

"No. Thanks, though. No, I just need to get on my knees and talk to God about it. He has always shown me the right thing to do."

"I wish I was that sure, Mr. Cathcart."

I looked at the middle-aged salesman, and for the first time saw him as a human being. He was a genuinely nice man, and a successful salesman. But, he was using tobacco and liquor as a way to quell the urgings of his heart. He needed the Lord.

"You can be sure. All you need to do is ask the Lord. John 3:15 says that 'whosoever believeth in him shall not perish, but have everlasting life.'"

"I gotta think about this, Mr. Cathcart. Nobody has ever talked to me about this before."

I felt guilty, then. "Listen, Sully, whatever I decide to do about the car, I'll come back by here tomorrow afternoon. We can sit down and look at these things in the Bible together."

He looked at me, and bit the corner of his lower lip. "You know, I think I'd like that."

"Thanks again for your help, Sully," I said. "Let me get the invoice paid, and I'll get out of your hair."

I left his office, and he remained in his chair, staring at his desk. I was once again amazed at the power of the Gospel. This was apparently the first time he had really heard it, and it had his attention. I knew I would spend some time in prayer that evening for his soul.

I retrieved the invoice from Slatts, and walked over to the counter to pay it.

"Are you going to buy that car, Beryl?" Connie Seabright asked.

I looked at the thin brunette with the olive skin and decided she was attractive. "I don't know. I need to pray about it."

"It's good to pray about those things."

"Yes, it is. And I have another thing to pray about."

"What's that?"

I nodded over to the sales office. "I had a chance to share the Gospel with Sully. I'm going to come back tomorrow afternoon with my Bible to talk to him again."

Her eyes glowed. "Oh, that is wonderful. We could pray for Sully at church tonight. You are coming to church, right?"

I had planned to attend the Baptist church in Love's Park that Wednesday night, and I was suddenly very excited about doing so. "Yes. Yes, I'll be there."

"Good. Maybe we could pray together for Sully."

"Maybe we could, at that."

I left the dealership on a cloud. I had belatedly remembered my responsibilities as a believer, but God had seemed to bless anyway. I was excited about the possibilities of purchasing a truly exciting automobile. And I looked forward to seeing Connie at church.

CHAPTER SIX

I stepped into Dad's office about 7:30 the next morning. He had already arrived, and was going through a stack of mail, which had arrived the previous afternoon.

"It's not like you to leave your desk like this at the end of the day."

He grinned at me. "Yeah. Look at this mess. Ellen diverts a lot of it, but it keeps piling up."

"How did Nigel do it?" I asked.

"I don't know. He must be gifted. Every time I visited him in his office, his desk was clear. I thought I was good at shoveling paper, but I guess I was just fooling myself."

"There are benefits to being a small-town pastor. A Bible and an offering plate just about completes my equipment."

"Uh huh. Listen, could you run this folder over to Nigel? I forgot to take it last night, and it's stuff he needs to see. If I send Ellen, she'll spend half the morning fussing over him, and I won't see her back before lunch."

"Is something going on there?"

Dad looked at me carefully. "Yes. I think so. Is that going to bother you?"

"No. Well, not personally. I worry about Nigel. He's not really in a position to defend himself, if she decides to take over his life. What?"

Dad was grinning at me. "You may not know your friend as well as you think. They've already had a couple of sharp exchanges. Nigel guards his turf."

"I should hope so. Dating her was a lot of fun, but the end game was rough."

"Have you gotten over it?" he asked.

"Yeah. I think so. There's a girl at church I'm thinking of asking out."

"Based upon recent events, I trust your judgment, son."

"Thanks, I think. Let me get this over to Nigel. If he and I get started talking, I'll be late for class, otherwise."

"Please don't."

"Right. See you later."

As I walked out to the car, I wondered whether Dad's faith in my judgment was misplaced. I had almost made a big impulsive purchase the day before. For the first fifteen minutes after I left the dealership I couldn't wipe the grin off my face. I had never driven anything like that Plymouth. At some point my mind engaged. There was no place I could drive that car the way I wanted – at least not without risking an enormous traffic ticket or killing myself. I would also be giving up the power windows and air-conditioning. The interior was not nearly as well trimmed as my Dodge. By the time I had arrived at my apartment the fever had completely left me, and I was left with that depression that was the result of getting too enamored with *things*.

Besides, other than the black color, which showed dust horribly, the '65 Dodge Monaco was the perfect car for my needs – a fast, comfortable, open-road machine that effortlessly chewed up the highway miles. I was a little embarrassed with my behavior the previous day – slobbering over that car. And I was going to have to go back over there this afternoon and tell Sully to forget it. I wondered how that would impact my attempt to witness to him. I was going to have to spend some time in prayer before I visited there again.

Nigel was once again enthroned in his chair in the living room of my parents' house. Along with the medicine bottles and tins, a stack of books was next to the chair. He devoured nearly as many books as I. On this day, though, he wasn't reading. His head was against the backrest, and his eyes were closed. He looked wan, and he was breathing shallowly. He opened his eyes when I slipped onto the sofa.

"Hey, Beryl, how's it going?"

"I should ask you, Nige."

"Rough morning," he replied. "My leg really hurts."

"Anything I can do?"

"Nope. The doc told me there was going to be pain. He wasn't kidding. I just gotta tough it out."

"Don't you have anything for the pain."

"Yes, but I don't like to take it. It makes me too dopey."

He looked over at the grin on my face. "Shut up, Beryl. That's no way to treat a sick man."

"Listen, I know you are hurting, so I won't stay long. I brought a folder over of stuff Dad said you needed to look at."

I handed it to him, and he laid it on the top of the stack of books.

"I'll look at it later. And please hang around for a little bit. When we talk, I don't think about my leg as much."

"Okay. I'll try not to think about it, either."

"Thanks, Buddy. So what's going on."

"Let's see, I didn't buy a car yesterday."

"What?"

I related to him the story of my test drive, and my mad desire to immediately purchase the red rocket. He seemed more alert and listened closely.

"You always have been a sucker for a pretty car. This one sounds cool."

"I'm glad I didn't buy it. I would never had heard the end of it from you and Dad."

"You may be growing up, yet, Beryl."

"Don't hold your breath. On the other hand, I did get a chance to witness to the salesman. I promised him I would go back over this afternoon with my Bible and show him some things."

Nigel nodded. "I can't do much else right now, but I'll pray for you."

"Thanks. But pray that he will get saved. He seemed very open."

"That's what I meant. I pray for *you* all the time."

I looked at him, and decided he meant it.

"Hey, listen, I spend a lot of time on my knees, talking to God about you, Nige. I want to see you on your feet, again."

"As I said, I can't do much else right now. So I pray for you, and your Dad. I pray for the school. I've been asking the Lord to show me what he wants me to learn from this trial."

I felt a lump in my throat. "I would give anything to have that bullet hit me instead of you," I replied. "But I think it's wonderful that God is using this to help you grow."

"I've learned to thank Him for it. That wasn't easy, let me tell you. But I can clearly see where God did this, not just for His glory, but to help me understand His glory. And I am thankful."

"Why don't we pray?" I suggested.

"I would like that."

We prayed for about an half hour. I looked at my watch.

"I gotta skedattle, Nigel. Voysey gets cranky when people are late to class."

He chuckled softly. "Voysey is always cranky."

"Next time I'm over here, I'll have to tell you what Voysey told me Tuesday after class."

"You could tell me, right now."

"No time, Nigel." I waved. "See you later."

"I am going to kill you one day," I heard him mutter as walked through to the kitchen.

Mom was standing at the sink peeling potatoes. I stepped up next to her, and gave her a quick hug.

"I think Nigel really needs to take his pain medicine."

She shook her head. "I already tried that, and he refused."

"When's he go to the doc, again?"

"Tomorrow," she replied.

"Maybe you can get the doctor to yell at him about that. He looks like he's about ready to pass out from the pain."

"Good idea, Beryl." She looked up at the clock on the wall. "And you'd better get going."

"Right, you are. See, ya, Mom."

# # #

Sully looked up as I walked into his office. "Did you bring a check?"

"No, Sully. I'm not going to buy it. I'm sorry to put you to so much trouble."

He made a throw-away motion. "Don't worry about it, Mr. Cathcart.

That's not the right car for you anyway."

"Really?"

"That Plymouth, there, is made for one thing only, and that's running the drag strip. No, you already got a much nicer car."

"I sort of reached that conclusion, myself. Once I slowed myself down, that is."

"You almost bought it, yesterday, didn't you?"

"I almost did. And you would have sold it to me."

He shrugged. "Of course. It's my job."

"Well, no offense, Sully, but I'm glad I talked myself out of it."

"None taken, Mr. Cathcart. I guess you came to talk to me about the Bible?"

"That's right, if you have time."

He opened the desk drawer, and slid a Bible on to the desk top. "You got me thinkin' yesterday. I went home and pulled this out. You had mentioned the book of John, so I started reading there."

I was surprised. It was rare to have anyone show such immediate interest in God's Word. I sensed that God had already prepared this man's heart.

"What did you think about it?" I asked.

"I'm kind of confused, to be honest. What is this *born-again* stuff? I hear preachers on the TV talk about it, but they don't really explain it. Then I read about this guy that visits Jesus, and he's confused too."

I settled into the chair across from his desk. "Can you open your Bible to that page?"

"Yeah, sure."

He fumbled with the Bible, but, I saw he had placed a slip of paper in the passage. "Here we go."

I felt like I was talking to a modern-day Nicodemus. Sully followed what I taught him, and asked perceptive questions. He didn't try to throw up road-blocks, and he didn't get defensive. I would explain a paragraph, and he would ask a piercing question. The last time I had encountered anyone so open to the Gospel was when I led Edgar and Eileen Forsen to the Lord, at my home in Appleton, weeks previously.

The look of childlike wonder on his face nearly brought me to tears. "You mean, all I have to do is ask Jesus to change me?"

"That's the new birth, Sully. It's a gift, freely offered. Jesus paid the price."

"Could I ask Him, right now, Mr. Cathcart."

"Yes, you certainly can," I nodded.

And, he bowed his head. "God, I never talked to You before. But like Jesus told this man about getting born again, well Mr. Cathcart here told me about it too. And I want that. I want to be born again like you promised, here in the Bible. And thank you for Jesus, because He paid for it. Thank-you. Thank-you."

He raised his head up, and I saw the tears streaming down his face. And I felt the tears running down my face.

"Mr. Cathcart. Thank you for telling me about Jesus."

"I was my.... Sully, I am honored to be the one to bring you to the Savior. This is a wonderful day.

"You know, Mr. Cathcart, I think this is the greatest day of my life. I feel like I was blind before. Everything seems different."

I was once again amazed at his perception. "Everything *is* different. You are now a child of God."

"What should I do, now?"

I stood up and wiped my eyes with my sleeve. "Come out here, with me."

I led him over to the office counter. "Connie, Sully has something to tell you."

With a look of wonder, he said, "I just got born again."

She jumped up and trotted around the counter, and threw her arms around him.

"Oh, Sully! That is wonderful news. I am so happy for you."

I had planned to drive back to Appleton that evening, but Sully had insisted on buying dinner for me. And he invited Connie along, too. We found ourselves at the diner of the Scrumptious Pork Chop – a nickname I had given to the place I had eaten on my first trip to Rockford.

We dawdled around the table for nearly two hours, as I showed him passage after passage in the Bible. He carefully took notes, and promised to study the passages on his own. He agreed to visit the Baptist Church in Love's Park on the upcoming Sunday, so he could tell everyone how God had changed him. I dropped Sully and Connie back at the dealership. Connie's mother was waiting in the family Ford. She had used the pay phone at the restaurant to call her mom as we left. In a way, I guess I considered this a first date with Connie, although the conversation was almost entirely with the converted car salesman.

On the way back to my apartment, on impulse, I swung into the entrance gates of the campus. Dad's car was still in his parking place in front of the administration building. The outer doors were locked, so I tapped on the glass with my key. He stuck his head into the hallway, and then walked down to let me in.

"What are you doing here?"

"I should ask the same," I said. "You're working late."

"Not much choice tonight. Come on back to my office."

I followed him down the hall and stepped into the office behind him. Sitting in a chair across from his desk was Dr. Carper. He stood up and stuck out his hand.

"Hello, Beryl. It seems we have *père et fils* tonight."

I had never learned French, but had a pretty good idea of what he meant. I looked over at Dad.

"If I am interrupting something, I can leave. I was just in the neighborhood."

Carper gave me a crooked smile. "I was walking to my car and saw the light on here, decided to just drop in myself."

Dad motioned me to the other chair, and walked back to his chair. Carper sat down again.

"We were discussing my concerns about this symposium," he said.

I looked at him, and then at Dad. "This is along the lines of our conversation, then?" I asked him.

"Indeed."

"I have to be very honest, Dr. Carper," Dad said, "I knew that this project would make some of the faculty members uncomfortable."

"Does that honesty compel you to announce you will fire anyone who disagrees with you?"

"Of course not," Dad said. "I intend to establish Mid-North as a center for conservative Biblical scholarship, but I also recognize there will be some diversity of opinion."

"And that is Nigel's position?"

Dad stared at Carper for a few moments. I wondered how he was going to handle this.

"I believe you could say there is some difference of opinion on that score. I have made it clear that there will be no witch hunts on this campus."

Carper looked over at me. "What would you do, Beryl?"

Now I was on the spot. But, I thought I had a ready answer.

"I am a Fundamentalist, Dr. Carper. My opinion doesn't really hold for Mid-North."

"What if this was your school, then?"

"Then I would ensure that the faculty were all inerrantists."

"So therefore you are influencing your father to drag this school into the Fundamentalist orbit," he said, pointing his finger at me.

"That would be dishonest," I said.

"So? When has that ever stopped a Fundamentalist?"

"Dr. Carper, you are making a value judgment," Dad snapped. "My son is not a liar, nor are any of the other Fundamentalists I have ever met."

Dad and Carper glared at each other for what seemed like a full minute. I held my breath, waiting to see which way things would break. Finally Carper looked over at me again.

"You're right, Dr. Cathcart. Beryl has behaved honorably in my class. Beryl, you have my apology."

Now I was on the spot. While attending Carper's Systematic Theology class, I had compiled a paper detailing the doctrinal aberrations of Dr. Alan Carper. That had left me feeling a little underhanded and dirty. I was holding his apology in my hand like a grenade minus the pin.

"I... don't know what to say."

Dad interrupted smoothly. "Please understand, Dr. Carper, that I have no intention of turning Mid-North into Fundamentalist school. Though my son is strongly of that persuasion, I am not."

Carper waved a hand. "Oh, very well. But that does not solve the basic problem, though."

"And what is that?" Dad asked.

"How can I teach my students to be faithful to the Word when my school is promoting an extra-Biblical cant. You are putting me in an impossible position."

Dad was now leaning back in his chair, rubbing his chin as he thought. "While I understand that this is an area where Evangelicals have historically disagreed, there always seemed to be an unstated agreement to simply disagree. What I do not understand is the level of invective you have thrown into the argument."

"Once again, I apologize," Carper said. "I bring a lot of passion to my arguments. I love having the freedom to argue these points in the classroom. It just saddens me to see this campus being undermined by a silly little conference."

It seemed to me that Carper couldn't avoid his invective. I noticed Dad's eyebrows raise.

"Nobody is forcing you to curtail your approach," Dad said. "It seems to me you are manufacturing a crisis where none exists."

Carper jumped to his feet. "I can assure you, Dr. Cathcart, that there *is* a crisis. I believe it will tear this school apart."

Dad raised his hands, palms upward. "I have tried to reassure you any way I could, Dr. Carper. What more can I do?"

"You can leave this place and leave us to serve Christ the way He desires us to serve Him!" And he turned and stalked out.

Dad waited until he heard the outer door to the administration building close, and then turned to me.

"That did not go quite as I expected."

"It was like talking to the wall, Dad."

He snorted. "That is as good a way to say it as any, I think."

He stood up.

"I really need to get home. Your mother just called a little while ago and asked if she should just throw out dinner. I was getting ready to leave when

Carper walked in."

"Ouch," I said. "Anyway, I had something I needed to tell you about."

"This doesn't sound good."

"You remember the salesman we bought the Dart from?"

He looked up at the ceiling, then snapped his fingers. "Sully, right?"

"Right. I got to lead him to the Lord this afternoon."

"Praise the Lord. You know I need to leave right now, but let's stop and thank God first. This is wonderful news. I really wasn't having a good evening, until you showed up."

Dad and I got on our knees. Dad was not a shoutin' Fundamentalist, but there was a lot of joy in his prayer that evening.

CHAPTER SEVEN

I had returned to my apartment before nine on Thursday night, and was so tired I had immediately gone to bed. It had been a busy week, and I had run flat out. I slept through the night, and awakened at 3:30 Friday morning. I lay staring at the ceiling for about ten minutes, and decided I was not going back to sleep, so I got up and got on the road. I would arrive in Appleton early enough to put in a full day with my ministry there. I was near my turn off from US 51 when the winter sun finally dragged itself into the eastern sky and illuminated the crisp winter day.

I walked through the door into my kitchen, and noticed something new. Mrs. Marsden, my housekeeper, usually left a stack of notes on the kitchen counter. She functioned as the church secretary, and her notes informed me of who was in the hospital, or requested a visit, or any of the dozen other things a pastor needed to know. And the breeze from the door swinging open would often sweep the notes onto the floor.

On the counter was a block of wood, with a six-inch nail driven through it. The notes were now carefully arranged on the spindle, with the nail driven through them. I raised an eyebrow at that. It was a clever solution, and I immediately wondered why I had not thought of it. I walked through the house and dumped my books on my desk, then headed for the bathroom. I had not stopped on the trip home to Appleton, and I was about at the limit of my capacity. As I was drying my hands, I heard the back door open, and the foot-fall of Mrs. Marsden. She was a big woman and it seemed the whole house shivered when she walked through.

When I got back to the kitchen, she already had a skillet out, and was pulling things out of the refrigerator.

"What time did you leave, this morning, Preacher?"

"About four o'clock," I replied. "I woke up feeling rested, and decided to get on the road. I figured I could get a full day's work in that way."

"Well, you're not leaving here until you've sat down to breakfast."

When Mrs. Marsden made a decision for you, you could either immediately acquiesce, or you could fight it, but the end result was the same.

"In that case, let me go get cleaned up, then I can eat."

"Don't take too long, Preacher."

I was never entirely sure how I acquired a housekeeper in Appleton. Mrs. Marsden and her husband Harvey were spry septuginarians who kept the church and parsonage clean. She also cooked my meals for me when I was in town. Harvey managed a real estate brokerage, apparently in his spare time.

I sat down to two eggs, sunny-side up, four strips of bacon, and whole-wheat toast.

"This is wonderful, Mrs. Marsden."

"Hmmph. You don't eat well enough, Preacher. I have to take care of you when I can."

I had no reply to that. When I was home, Mrs. Marsden set the rules.

"Looks like a big stack of notes," I said. "Anything I need to pay attention to in particular?"

"Dennis James' mother is in the hospital again. He asked if you could go see her."

I nodded. "She's had a rough time of it lately."

"Yes, she has. Poor lady. And the new Methodist minister in Oneida called and would like to have lunch with you. His name is Roland Klegg."

I raised an eyebrow. "That's interesting. What did you tell him?"

"You're to meet him at noon at the *Mister Steak* in Galesburg. If you can't make it, I will call him."

"I should probably see him," I said. "It might be interesting, though."

"Seemed pleasant enough."

I worked my way through the breakfast as she continued. Mrs. Marsden always seemed to find the tastiest bacon – it was very good.

"Lane wants to have a deacons meeting tonight. They will come here at eight o'clock."

I nodded again. During the winter we kept the heat at the church only at a level to avoid frozen pipes, then kicked the temperature up on Sundays and Wednesdays. The old building cost a fortune to heat, otherwise, so a lot of the other meetings were always held at somebody's house. This time it would be my turn.

"Fine. Is the big coffee-maker here?"

"Yes, Preacher. I brought it over last night."

"Mrs. Marsden, you're just too efficient."

"Somebody has to be."

I took that as a slam against my disorganized nature. I wasn't naturally disorganized; it was just that the light demands of a small church brought out the laziness in me. In terms of keeping me busy, my adventures at Mid-North were probably a good thing.

"And the Forsens would like to come see you tonight, after he gets off work."

"Okay, I have the deacons coming at eight. What did you tell them?"

"They are coming at six. I will have dinner ready for you at five."

And that pretty much lined out my day. I backed the Dodge Dart out of the garage, and pulled the Monaco in. I would be driving all over Knox County on this Friday, and wanted to keep the good car off the lousy roads. I had bought the Dart from Sully when the Monaco was in the shop, and after I had lost an encounter with a tow truck. That incident had turned a pristine '53 Ford sedan into a crumpled ball of metal and glass.

I took US 150 to Knoxville, and then hopped on I-74 to Galesburg. The four-lane interstate highways would be wonderful if they ever got them finished. I stopped at my tire dealer and had a set of snow tires put on the Dart. I had been fortunately so far, but I fully expected to need the extra traction before too long. I then made the rounds of the local hospitals, and arrived at the steakhouse on Henderson Street just before noon.

Roland Klegg (call me Rollo) was a tall, beefy man. When they passed out joviality, I think he must have gone through the line twice.

"You're not what I expected," I blurted out.

He laughed, and he had a big laugh. "Believe it, or not, there is not standard size for Methodist ministers. Although if we could generalize, I would be on the large side."

That was the truth. And, I guessed we all had our crosses to bear. "I've been told I look on the young side to be a preacher."

He laughed again. "Mr. James told me I should watch for somebody just out of grade school."

"He didn't."

Klegg just smiled. "Let's get inside, Reverend Cathcart. I want to beat the lunch rush."

"Sounds good to me."

The restaurant was a little short on ambiance, but the food was good. They had a creative menu, and I selected something that was a glorified hamburger, but with bacon and cheese in the center. It was very good. I was mainly interested in what the Methodist minister had to say. After all, two thirds of his members were *former* members, and now attended Appleton Baptist Church.

"I did a little asking around, after I arrived in Oneida," he said. "When your bishop pulls you out of a perfectly good situation in a tearing great hurry, it tends to raise a lot of questions."

I nodded, wondering where this was going.

"From what I heard, the bishop displayed unusual common sense when he suggested that Edgar Forsen was not well suited to a pastoral occupation."

"I don't think I could argue about that," I replied.

"As I understand things, it seems you were handling a lot of his job, by default."

"Not intentionally, on my part. I met Mr. James, I guess, by accident. When he couldn't seem to get his minister to call upon his mother, when she was in the hospital, he called me."

"I heard about that accident, Reverend Cathcart. You saved his life."

"I just happened to be in the right place at the right time."

He looked up as the waitress delivered the food. "Why don't you let me ask the Lord's blessing upon our lunch."

I nodded, and bowed my head.

"We thank you for this lunch, our wise and loving heavenly Father, and for the opportunity to meet our brother in the Lord. Bless the food and the conversation. We pray in the name of our Savior, whose blood was shed for our sins, Amen."

I looked up in surprise, and he grinned. "No, I am not your run of the mill Methodist minister, Reverend Cathcart."

"Please, call me Beryl."

"Okay, Beryl. I had my encounter with the Lord when I was seventeen years old. I immediately knew that I wanted to spend my life bringing the same message to others. I somehow managed to maintain my faith, in spite of attending a theological seminary you would probably call a mausoleum."

"And you believe the Bible?" I asked.

"Oh absolutely. It's God's inspired and inerrant Word."

I looked at him carefully. This was something outside of my experience. "Please pardon me, and I don't mean to offend, but what are you doing in the Methodist Church?"

He laughed loudly, and the other patrons in the restaurant looked over at us. "I grew up in the Methodist Church. There are a lot of good people in my church. You should know; most of the ones from Oneida are now attending your church."

I held up my hands. "I just want you to know, I wasn't actively engaged in sheep-stealing..."

"Oh, I know that," he interrupted. "Edgar Forsen did a magnificent job of running them off. No, the bishop wanted me to see if I could pick up the pieces. You see, they don't quite know what to do with me. I go into dying churches, and get people excited about God's Word. Attendance and offerings pick up. They like that. They don't like what they call my *Fundamentalism*, no offense."

"No offense taken," I replied. "But... why do you stay in that church. I mean, if I stopped to think about it, I would realize there are probably a lot of redeemed people in the pew. But the denominational structure is largely," I thought about the word, "apostate."

He looked at me for a few moments. "Apostasy is such an ugly word, Beryl."

We were on my ground, now, and I was pretty sure I knew what I was talking about. "You're right. It is an ugly word. But can you deny the truth of that?"

He shook his head slowly. "No. You're absolutely right. And that is why I am such a thorn in their sides. I grow their churches, and send them money. And I make sure the people in the churches know that their leadership is not serving the same god." He laughed again. "It makes the bishops uncomfortable."

"So why do you stay that church? It's hopelessly compromised."

He smiled sadly. "Let me give you another ugly word: schism. Separation is the job of the church hierarchy. They make the decisions, and try to protect the church as a whole."

"But they're not even saved."

"You're right. But our Lord instructed us not to try to pull up the tares. He said He would do that at the end of the age. Moses had to deal with the mixed multitude. It would be the height of arrogance for me to compare myself to Moses, but I have a similar problem. Besides, I enjoy tweaking the prelates."

I looked down and busied myself with my lunch. I looked up again. "You know, there are probably a lot of things we won't agree on. But, I am glad to see a brother in the Lord working with those people in Oneida."

"Thank you for that, Beryl. For the record, I am not going to try to bring those people back to my church, even though my bishop directly ordered me to try."

"Hey, if they felt the need to return, I wouldn't stand in their way." I grinned. "I would, however, instruct them in the perils of belonging to an apostate denomination."

"Touché," he murmured. "Dennis James did tell me, by the way, that he was planning to stay in your church."

"I really like Mr. James," I said. "He's a salt of the earth kind of guy."

"And what about Edgar Forsen?" he asked. "I understand he followed the people to your church. What was their reaction to that?"

"This is where it got interesting, Rollo. After the bishop fired him, he and his wife showed up on my doorstep. They had no money, and no place to live. I was able to lead them to the Lord."

"You don't say. So something good did come out of this," he said.

"He made his confession in front of the church, then apologized to everyone."

"I would suggest the Lord really did get hold of him."

"There was not much question about that."

Klegg leaned back in his chair. "Okay, now that we have that settled, your Mrs. Marsden told me you were commuting to Rockford to go to school. Tell me about that."

I spent the rest of the meal recounting my adventures in Rockford. Roland Klegg was a rapt audience.

CHAPTER EIGHT

I came to the conclusion that soul-winning was a gift. I had been present on numerous occasions when God reached down, through his Spirit, and rescued poor lost sinners. I was more convinced than anything that I had done nothing other than be obedient to the Lord's command to spread the seed. God commands each of us to preach the Gospel, but it seemed that it fell to some to be harvesters. I worried about pride, but each time I led a soul to Christ I felt very small.

Edgar and Eileen Forsen had changed since that night I had opened the Bible to them, and they had seen the power of the Gospel. Oh, they were both still cadaverous middle-aged people, although it looked like they both might be putting on some weight. But now they radiated joy.

"I've read through the New Testament three times," Eileen said. "I decided to start going through the Old Testament. I am in Leviticus, and it's heavy going."

She had a whisky voice, I guess from years of drinking and smoking, but rather than the harsh cawing she exhibited the first time I met her, she sounded mellow and relaxed.

"I have a tough time in Leviticus, too," I replied. "The apostle Paul talks about the milk and the meat of the Word, and this area is definitely meaty."

"But how do I get to where I can understand it?" she asked.

"That's a good question." I looked over at Edgar, who was listening carefully. "Maybe, just skim through it the first time. Try to get the gist of what Moses was saying. If something jumps out at you that really drives your curiosity, just ask the Lord to help you to understand it, and move on."

She tilted her head as she considered what I said. "I don't know, Pastor Cathcart, that seems like a kind of a lazy approach."

Edgar snorted and shook his head.

"Oh, I'm sorry, Pastor," she said. "That didn't quite come out the way I meant."

I held up my hand. "No, that's all right. Most people don't realize that Bible study is hard work. It's sort of like... well, you've seen the construction crews working on the interstate highways. When they need to cut down a hill, they do it a layer at a time. That's way to approach this. Just try to ease through what you understand, and leave the rest for the next trip."

"You're pretty good at this, Pastor," Edgar said. "Where did you learn it?"

"Some of it was on-the-job training, Edgar. But, mainly I was blessed with some tremendously gifted teachers when I was at McKisson."

"I wish I knew the Bible as well as you do. I feel like I spent three years in seminary and did not learn a thing."

"It takes being born again to truly understand the Bible," I replied. "You're just starting out. The good news is that with some consistent study and growth, you can catch up to me."

"Do you suppose it would help if I spent some time at a Bible school somewhere? I mean I'm a run-down retread Methodist, would they even look at me?"

I chuckled. "They sure would. But don't get in a hurry. Keep on doing what you're doing, and see what the Lord has for you."

"And we really need to get back on our feet financially," Eileen said. "I mean, God has been so good to us, but we have a ways to go."

Edgar now worked at one of the factories in Galesburg, and Eileen worked as a receptionist for a surveyor's office. They had roughly the same schedules and were able to commute together from the small house they rented in Dahinda. He had commented to me that they were living on his wages, and putting Eileen's paycheck directly in the bank.

"I can't believe we let ourselves get into such a condition," he said. "It was just like we didn't care."

I smiled. "It says a lot about the effects of sin. Like Paul says in Romans One."

"There are some pretty horrible things described in Romans One," Eileen said. "I would never think of doing anything like that."

"True. Most people are not as sinful as they could be. But, Paul illustrates the human heart. Man is basically not good; he is inherently sinful and in rebellion against God. I believe it's the influence of God's people that keeps the world from being as bad as it could be."

"It's kind of sobering," she said.

"Yes, it is. It is also what makes Christ's work so powerful, and so necessary. There is no way we could save ourselves."

"I guess I have a lot to learn."

"We all do." I paused. I slid a couple of booklets across the table. "I signed you up to receive mailings from the Radio Bible Class. Every month they send out booklets on a particular topic in the Bible. I thought you could study these, along with the Bible, then we can get together and talk about it."

"Thanks, Pastor," Eileen said. "What does this cost?"

"It's free. Oh, they are supported by gifts from God's people, so if you feel led to send them some money every once in a while, they would appreciate it."

I had to wrap things up, because of the pending deacons meeting. From experience, I knew the Forsens would happily spend the evening with me, talking about the things of God. They absorbed the Word like water poured in sand. They just soaked it up, and came back for more. I enjoyed most aspects of the ministry, but times like this were the most rewarding, I thought.

My good mood persisted after the Forsens left, and later as the deacons started arriving at the house. Mrs. Marsden had the big coffee maker primed and ready to go. I plugged it in about twenty minutes before eight. The deacons drank a lot of coffee. Mrs. Marsden had also baked a coffee cake, and left it on the counter.

The four deacons fit comfortably around my kitchen table. The chairman, Lane Johnson, sat at the opposite end of the table from me. Over the five years of my ministry at Appleton Baptist Church Lane had become not just a father figure, but a friend as well. We had shared the victories and the trials that are the normal part of life in a country church. Most recently I had conducted the funeral for Lane's father, Fred Johnson, who had passed away suddenly early in the fall.

Larry Smith sat to my left, along with Lister Coons. Larry was the song leader at the church, and owned a farm south of Appleton along US 150. Lister Coons worked a farm further to the west, about halfway towards East Galesburg. Sigmar Carlson lived in Oneida and worked at a farm implement dealer. Lane owned and managed nearly a thousand acres of farmland along the Fremont Road, north of Appleton.

Lane opened in prayer, and we proceeded through a half dozen routine items. The most controversial was the furnace replacement. The oil-fired antique in the basement of the church had been long overdue for replacement, but everyone quailed at the expense.

"What do you think, Preacher?" Lane asked.

That was my cue. "Sooner or later we're going to have a really cold Sunday, when the furnace quits. We have the money. Let's get it done."

"I don't know," Lister said. "That's a lot of money. I wonder if we can get through another winter with it."

Sigmar Carlson shook his head back and forth slowly. "Lister, I'm the one that has to fight with the thing every time it acts up. It's not going to last the winter. Besides, I think it's getting dangerous."

"Maybe we should get a real furnace repairman out here," the other deacon said. "We always seem to have the most problems when we try to do something ourselves."

Carlson leaned back and turned his hands palms up.

"Come on, Lister," Larry said, "Sigmar knows these machines as well as anybody. He's repaired the things part time for years."

"Yeah, well I just wonder what we've been missing, here."

"How old are you, Lister?" Lane asked suddenly.

"Hey, I know I'm only thirty-five, Deacon Johnson, but I'm not stupid."

"I'm not saying that. What I meant was that when we put that furnace in, your ma was still carrying you to church."

"Surely not."

Lane looked over at Sigmar. "It was, what Sigmar, late 1928?"

The white-haired mechanic nodded. "That's about right, I think. It was before the crash of twenty-nine. Nobody had any money after that."

"And you've been taking care of it ever since."

Carlson chuckled. "I put the thing in."

Lane stroked his chin and smiled. "That's right. I had forgotten that. I remember Pa yelling at me when Billy and I were running around in the church basement. He and you were fightin' with it, trying to put it together."

"Yep. Whoever had welded the frame had the thing a quarter inch out of true. Didn't think Fred and I would ever get it together."

"Be that as it may," Lister jumped back in, "we shouldn't be a wastin' the Lord's money on things like that."

I sat back and listened to the debate. Every once in a while, Lister Coons got the bit in his teeth, and the discussion would get spirited. Sometimes he would get mad and walk out of the meeting. While we didn't really have factions in the congregation, each of the deacons had a group of families who took their cues from the leadership. Lane and I were careful to keep the arguments from getting out of hand.

"And if the burner blows out, we could burn down the whole building," Sigmar said.

"Oh, surely not."

"Is that right?" Larry asked.

Sigmar shrugged. "Well, probably not. But it could happen."

"A lightning strike could do it too," Lister said. "Sometimes you just have to trust the Lord."

"That's why we have lightning rods on the building," Larry said. "The Lord expects us to use our brains."

"What are you suggesting, Larry?"

"That you're not thinking, Lister."

Lister put his hands on the table and pushed himself to his feet. "That's it. I'm out of here."

Okay, I could see a church split happening in front of my eyes. I really hated it when people got this way. And I really didn't know what to do. I glanced over at Lane. I think he saw the desperation in my eyes. He stood up and put his hand on Lister's arm.

"Lister, let's take a walk into the other room for a minute."

Lister Coons looked into Lane Johnson's eyes and visibly wilted. Lane was somebody else who did the intimidation thing well, too. Lane propelled him out of the kitchen, and a few moments later I heard the door to my study close. The three of us remaining looked at each other uncomfortably. I cleared my throat and two pairs of eyes snapped over at me.

"Perhaps we were pushing him a bit hard," I said.

Larry snorted. "You mean I was pushing him too hard, Preacher." He shook his head. "I guess I will need to apologize to him when he comes out."

"Lister wears his feelings on his sleeve," Sigmar said. "I always have to remember that. He gets upset easily." He looked over at me. "Does that make him the weaker believer, Preacher?"

"In that one area, I guess. He does have a point about trusting the Lord, though. It's too easy to assume money solves everything."

Carlson raised a finger to concede the point. "In this case I think the Lord has given us the money to solve this problem."

"It's just that Lister hates to spend it," Larry said. "You've seen that wreck he drives."

I tilted my head. "Lane told me Lister gets more mileage out his farming equipment than anybody he knows."

"True," Sigmar said. "I don't know how he keeps it running. He's better at it than I am."

I had an idea. "Maybe you ought to ask him to help you with the furnace, Sigmar."

Now Carlson laughed. "I did once. You should have seen the pieces of scrap he brought in to repair the thing. Scared me to death."

"Forget I said anything."

Sigmar looked up as Lister and Lane walked back in the door to the kitchen.

"Listen, I'm sorry I blew my stack like that," Lister said. "You all know I'm tight with my coin. I sort of get in the habit of looking around for ways to keep from spending it."

Larry stood up. "Hey, I'm sorry, Lister. I said some things that were out of line."

The two men shook hands. Lister gave us a crooked grin. "Let's vote on this thing before I change my mind again."

"That much money, it's going to have to go before the congregation," Larry said.

I nodded. "Yup. If we have a consensus to do this, you guys need to button-hole the men in the church. We can call a brief meeting after a Sunday night service, and vote on it."

One of the lessons I had learned from one of my professors at McKisson was that whenever a large expenditure, or a difficult decision came before the congregation, it was wise for the deacons to talk to the men of the church individually. That way no one was surprised when it came up in the meeting, and everyone had talked through the issues. Alternatively, the leadership would discover entrenched opposition before the embarrassment of having the thing fail in a vote. Or worse yet, having a close vote.

Sometimes you had to face controversy head-on in the church. Taking a stand on principle, or clear Biblical teaching was always mandatory. But low-keyed communication was a wonderful way to avoid fights within a congregation, or worse yet, splits.

The deacons around the table nodded. They would start talking to the other men in the church. The business meeting would be a formality. I wasn't terribly concerned about this decision – everybody knew we had to do something soon, with the possible exception of Lister Coons.

"Any thoughts about when we can hold a formal vote?" I asked.

"Week from tomorrow?" Larry asked.

Once again everyone nodded. I would have liked to get the thing done this coming Sunday. The old furnace worried me. However, it was still more modern than the oil stove that heated my house. At least the discussion was fairly short. That should have worried me, but I was just relieved I wouldn't be sitting there with the deacons until 11 PM as we meandered through the agenda.

"Okay," I said. "Anything else?" I was anxious to get back to sermon prep.

"One other thing we've kind of been talking about, Preacher," Lane said.

One of the problems with being out of town all week in Rockford was that the church members would discuss an issue during the week, and then spring it on me when I got home. I think they truly enjoyed ambushing me. This was along with the general teasing I endured.

"And what is this *one other thing* we need to discuss, Deacon Johnson?"

The other deacons grinned in anticipation. I started to get concerned.

"Why don't we get some more coffee before we start on this item?" Lane asked.

With a scraping of chairs, the other men stood up and clustered around the coffee maker. The glint in Lane's eye led me to believe he was setting me up. The deacons were all in on it, and they were having a great time. Everyone was back in their chairs and Lane looked at me.

"Aren't you going to refill your coffee, Preacher?"

"No, because while I'm doing that you'll think of some other reason to delay."

"Me?"

"You don't do *innocent* very well," I replied.

He chuckled softly. "It's really not anything that you should worry about, Preacher. It's just so much fun to pick at you."

"And you do it *so* well."

The other men laughed then.

"What we were thinking about, Preacher, was that with all the extra people we've had attending church recently, that it's got to be tough keeping up with things."

I didn't think they were getting ready to fire me, but I wondered what they were up to.

"So, what we had in mind was to pay Avis Brody to go full time as our assistant pastor. I think he spends all his spare time out here, anyway."

After spending time in the hospital, following my altercation with a tow truck one night, we had asked Avis Brody to fill the pulpit, while I was stranded in Rockford. Brody was a recent McKisson graduate, and a very solid young man. He now covered most of the Wednesday services, and taught a Sunday School class, as well. His wife Christine also taught a childrens' Sunday School class, and accompanied her husband when he handled some of the visitation chores for me.

"Have you talked to Avis about this?" I asked. I felt distinctly behind the curve.

"Yes, Preacher. As you know, he stocks groceries at the A&P in Galesburg"

"Yes, I know that."

"And grocery stores don't pay that well. We would be able to at least cover what he makes now."

"But what about his commute out here?" I asked. "He's got to buy gas and he has the wear and tear on his car. It's not a new car, either."

That stopped him. I wasn't necessarily against what the deacons were proposing, but I wondered if they had thought things through.

Lane scratched his head, and managed a sheepish grin. "To tell the truth, I hadn't thought about that, Preacher."

"I wonder if it wouldn't be cheaper just to rent a parsonage for him around here somewhere? He wouldn't have to pay taxes on that."

Lister Coons spoke up. "The Gibbons place is empty. The coal company owns the property. They would probably be happy to have someone looking after it."

"Could you look into that, Lister?" I asked.

"Sure thing, Preacher. I can call them first thing Monday morning."

I looked around the kitchen at the men sitting at my table. "You've thought this thing through, haven't you?"

"Yes, Preacher," came the chorus.

"And... I suppose you've kind of talked it around the congregation?"

There were more sheepish looks. "Yes, Preacher."

"We really weren't trying to go behind your back, Preacher," Sigmar Carlson said. "We just got started talking about it, and it seemed like a good idea."

"I'm not saying it's a bad idea," I replied. "Avis has done a good job here, and the people like him. I guess, what I'm asking, is would it be better if I just quit school at the end of this semester and stayed home?"

"No, Preacher," came the chorus again.

"We think it's important for you to get additional education," Larry said. "In fact, with the growth we are seeing, I think we would be looking at getting some additional staff here, anyway."

I was thinking hard, as the conversation rolled around the table. At first blush, it seemed to me to be a good idea, too. But after my experiences during the past summer and fall, I was wary of running ahead of the Lord.

"Okay, let's do this," I said. "This makes sense to me. But it's come at me cold. Give me a week to pray about it. If the Lord doesn't put up a red flag, or block the path, I think we should do this."

It was like the whole table heaved a sigh of relief. I don't think they realized they were on thin ice until Lane made the proposal during the meeting. I was a little surprised – Lane usually thought ahead better than that. I guess anybody could have an off day. I was certainly capable of it.

CHAPTER NINE

Sunday was anticlimactic. My mind was in turmoil because of what the deacons had sprung on me Friday night. I had somehow managed to get the sermons prepared, and homework done on Saturday. I still didn't know what to make of the proposal to hire Avis Brody as the assistant pastor. I didn't think the people of the church were trying to ease me out. Lane Johnson would have a very direct conversation with me, if that were the case. Or so I thought.

I assumed, therefore, that congregation was trying to help me. Did that mean I was not doing the job, and they were keeping me around out of kindness? Or, were they truly supporting of my ministry, and were doing whatever they could to help, Avis Brody being the solution. I wanted to believe this was the case. But, it was a new experience for me, and I worried.

I invited Avis and Christine over after the Sunday night services. As usual, I forewarned Mrs. Marsden of my plans, and she had prepared another coffee cake, along with sandwiches and coffee. I was comfortable around them. They were fellow graduates of McKisson and had become my friends. The young couple was understandably nervous about their new status, and was aware that this had come together without my knowledge.

The Brodys were both tall, thin and blond. Christine had grown up in Galesburg. Since a ministry had not immediately developed after their graduation and marriage, it was natural for them to locate near her parents.

I had sat on the ordination council for him at one of the fundamental churches in Galesburg, and he was a natural choice for substitute preacher when I was overcome by events in Rockford.

"I feel a little funny about this, Preacher," Avis said. "I think if they had surprised me with this, I would be upset."

"So this wasn't a surprise to you?" I shouldn't have said that, but the straight line was just too good to pass up.

"Oh no, Sir, that was not what I meant at all."

"He's pulling your chain, Avis," Christine said. Very little got past her. "I'll get you for that, Beryl."

Since the Brodys had begun attending Appleton Baptist Church, Christine and I had struck up an unusual friendship. We tormented each other unmercifully. The congregation was a willing participant in that game and constantly watched our sniping. Avis was usually bewildered by the back-and-forth. He was a long way from naive. He generally took any conversation seriously at first, and then later thought about whether someone was funning with him. Early on, I had learned not to poke at him. Christine subjected him to gentle teasing, which he took with good grace.

"Okay, Preacher, you got me. What I meant was that I didn't see this coming either. I'm embarrassed they didn't talk to you first, before they spoke with me."

I took a sip of my coffee and collected my thoughts. "Let me say first of all, that I don't have a problem with this proposal at all. You've done a great job for us, and I would be honored to have you a part of the team here."

He visibly sighed in relief. Christine merely patted his hand. I would have been tempted to roll my eyes, but he was so serious.

"The deacons meeting *was* interesting, however," I continued. "I think they probably let their enthusiasm get ahead of their good judgment."

"I sort of wondered if that was the case," Christine said. "They really like

Avis."

"That probably explains why they put up with you," I replied. That put me two up on her, which meant there would come a reckoning. I hurried to continue, before she could retaliate. "I was actually surprised that Lane Johnson got carried away like that. He usually has it together better than that."

"I cannot remember him making a mistake," Christine said. "But, I haven't known him long."

"He doesn't make many. I'm not sure this was one. As I said, I do like the idea."

"That relieves me," Avis said. "I really love working in this church. I love the people, and I love working for you. I was afraid you would be upset with me."

I smiled at him. "Oh, I'm not upset with you. I can't imagine you doing something that would upset me. I like your careful approach to the ministry. In fact, if I wasn't convinced we all had a sin nature, I would be hard pressed to find any fault in you."

I looked over at Christine and saw the glint in her eye. I couldn't think of anything to say quickly.

"What a study in contrasts," she said.

I laughed. "I've got to count that as a score. Unfortunately, you are too right. The events of this past fall proved how immature I am. The Lord had to beat me to a pulp to get my attention."

"Begging your pardon, Preacher," Avis interrupted. "I am no angel."

Christine held up a hand. "I can testify to that."

He blushed. "Oh, come on, Baby."

She leaned over and hugged him. "We won't even talk about how I can drive you right up a wall, okay?"

He gave her a shy grin. "You're not like that."

"Okay, it's settled," I said. "We're all sinners. The other thing is I've made up my mind."

"They looked expectant and nervous at the same time, but said nothing.

"If you're going to be a part of the team, then we need to review our plans for this ministry. This is not just a run of the mill country Baptist church, you know."

They both heaved a sigh of relief, and I laughed.

"Thank you, Preacher," Avis said. "I will do my best to make sure you won't be disappointed."

"I know you will, Avis." I stretched out my hand. "Welcome aboard."

"Doesn't the congregation have to vote?" he asked, as he shook my hand.

"Well, yes, but the deacons wouldn't have gotten this far if they hadn't talked to the congregation individually."

"When will that be?" Christine asked.

"I'll probably give Lane a call tonight, and we can schedule the vote for next Sunday night. Sunday morning I can formally announce your candidacy."

"I'll have to give notice at my other job," Avis said.

"That's okay. For all intents and purposes, you're a part of this ministry already. We'll get the vote out of the way, but meanwhile, Lane can talk to you about a formal start date, and give you the salary information."

"He mentioned that there might be a place to live included," Avis said.

"The deacons talked about that," I said. "I think they will try to do it, if possible, but that is really up to the deacons and congregation."

"We've talked about it and would prefer to live close to the church." Christine nodded in agreement with him.

"Let's just keep praying about it," I said. "One thing I have learned is the importance of bathing these major decisions in prayer. Things have a way of not going well when we try do make these changes in our own strength."

"You got that one right, Preacher," he said. "I would tell you about how I messed up our engagement, but I'm still too embarrassed and ashamed of myself."

I looked at Christine with a raised eyebrow. She simply nodded. So apparently he really had messed things up. In the time I knew him, he considered forgetting to button his collar buttons a major failure. I wondered what he had done, but really could not imagine.

# # #

I awakened Monday morning much more relaxed. After my evening with the Brodys, I had talked to Lane. He seemed relieved to have things come together. Since I had a few more calls to make at the hospital in Galesburg, I packed the car, and left Appleton, planning to head to Rockford from Galesburg.

One of my favorite older ladies in the church, Minda Cullen was in the hospital following an emergency gall bladder removal. She was adamant about getting out of the hospital and returning to her home. Her daughter told me that the doctor had given instructions for her to stay someplace where her family could keep an eye on her for about six weeks. Generally, Minda wouldn't listen to the doctor, and she wouldn't listen to her daughter either. I was able to apply enough pressure on her to agree to stay with her daughter during that time. She didn't give in gracefully, but that didn't surprise me, either. She was a wonderful Christian lady, but strong-willed didn't begin to describe her disposition.

A couple of people from the Methodist Church in Oneida stayed in a nursing home in Galesburg and asked me to visit them. I was happy to do so, but privately planned to call their new minister, and let him know about my activities. He seemed like a decent sort and a true believer. I didn't want to cut the ground out from under him. I suspected most of the believers from his church were now attending Appleton Baptist, and the remaining rump would probably not be easy to serve.

The construction crews were pushing I-74 from Galesburg towards the Quad Cities, so I thought I'd try the new road. The straight, smooth concrete arrowed north and was a pleasure to drive on, compared to the tooth rattling ride caused by the frost heaved pavement of the old two lane roads. I was driving the Dart, since it now had the snow tires, and I wanted to keep the winter salt off the good car as much as possible. The things rusted out all too soon as it was. Sort of like this world.

The orange barrels directed me off the new road at Woodhull, and I drove a couple of miles over to US-150 and again headed north. At the Quad Cities, I picked up I-80 and headed east towards Indiana, then turned north towards Rochelle when I came to US-51. I arrived in Rockford during the middle of the afternoon. After throwing my stuff in the apartment, I drove over to my parents' house. Mom would automatically invite me to supper, and I also wanted to see how Nigel was doing. Besides, they were family -- including even Nigel.

CHAPTER TEN

Dad continued to use the former Provost's office in the college Administration Building. He was concerned that he might be sending the wrong message by moving into Nigel's office. Nobody seemed to complain about that strategy, although Ellen had to either walk through the conference room to deliver papers to Dad's desk or walk down the hall. I assumed she would have said something if she thought it was a problem.

There was a small secretary's office on the other side of Dad's office, and he assigned it to me. I had refused to officially become an employee of the college, but I was functioning as a student volunteer to help coordinate the symposium. It was also a handy place to hide and study between classes.

I looked up at a tap on the doorway to the hallway to see Stephen Gardiner standing there.

"Hey, Stephen, what's going on?"

"Hi, Beryl. I heard that you were helping get this symposium thing going. I was just wondering if I could help with anything."

"You certainly can. Come on in and take a load off."

Gardiner had an eminently forgettable visage. He was of medium height, and somewhat paunchy. His medium brown hair blended in, and his face was instantly anonymous in a crowd. Other than his penchant for asking idiotic questions in class, he probably would have passed through Mid-North without notice.

As it was, everyone knew him. Dr. Voysey wasn't the only professor who experienced Gardiner's less than erudite questions, he was merely the one with the most explosive responses. As I had gotten to know him, I discovered Gardiner was actually a very good student. That, of course, made his proclivity to speaking without thinking all the more amazing.

He plopped into the chair across from the desk I was using. "I know who your dad is and all, but I didn't think they would just hand out offices in this building. During my freshman year of undergrad, they had a big fight about some offices in this building. It was big enough that the students heard about it."

I leaned forward. "Oh really? That's kind of interesting."

"The Dean of Religion decided to claim an empty office in the building. It was much nicer than the one he had. So he moved in over a weekend."

"That was Dr. Cliffe?"

"Himself. The provost had other ideas, and I guess the disagreement became loud. It was spring and the windows were open. So what few students didn't hear it personally were informed by the others."

"Huh," I commented. "Odd thing to happen."

"Yes, it was. More interesting, Cliffe was back in his old digs by the end of the day."

"So the provost laid the law down?"

"Weak Richard?" Gardiner asked.

"What?"

"Richard Redlaw was the provost. No. Everyone was amazed at the outburst. Everybody called him *Weak Richard*. Redlaw never seemed to care about anything much. But the board chairman was in the building, and heard the racket. He threw Cliffe out."

"Charlie Bigelow did?"

"You got it."

"So, this Redlaw guy was the provost?"

"Yes. When he retired they didn't replace him. They claimed it was to save money, but the story around campus was that nobody could figure out what he did anyway, so it didn't make any sense to hire a replacement."

"Gardiner, you are a fount of information," I said. "How much of this do you know to be fact?"

"It really happened, Beryl. I mean, the speculation as to why they didn't replace the provost is just that, but everything else is true."

"Come on," I said. "You know the way people gossip."

"Half the campus heard the fight," he insisted.

"Okay, okay. I believe you."

"But it was the most interesting event of the year," he said.

"I can believe that too. Back to the business at hand. You said you wanted to help."

"Yes. I know I'm not the brightest candle on the cake, but I truly believe we have drifted a little from our high view of the Scripture."

"What do you mean?" I asked.

"Oh come on, Beryl. You can't tell me you haven't seen how Dr. Carper dances around on the topic of inerrancy. And Dr. Cliffe is worse."

"Is that so?"

"You haven't taken New Testament Introduction yet. I'm in his class now. You know how I sometimes am incautious in my questions?"

I laughed. "Gardiner that was a masterful understatement."

He blushed. "Yes, well, anyway." He took a breath. "I asked in class one time how we harmonized Christ's statement about not the smallest stroke or letter of the law going away with his teaching on inspiration."

"And how did he answer?"

"He looked at me like I was some kind of insect. He said that if I took that passage literally, I was no better than a brain-dead fundamentalist."

"Apparently he doesn't like fundamentalists," I commented.

"You will want to watch out around him, Beryl. He is not as considerate as Dr. Carper."

"I always watch out," I replied.

Gardiner laughed, then. "Ha! I've seen you in action. I'm surprised Voysey has never thrown you out of class."

"Honestly I'm surprised too, I have to admit."

"But, you understand what I'm saying, though."

"Oh, yes. But I would appreciate it if you didn't talk about this. My dad, in particular does not want to directly challenge the faculty on this. Above all, he has told me the conference cannot be controversial."

Gardiner looked at me carefully. "I think that might be a faint hope, Beryl. Cliffe has already been making snide remarks about the symposium."

I didn't want to tell him what Voysey had told me.

"Okay, Gardiner, here's what I want you to do. Start building a schedule for campus prayer meetings. We need some in the men's and women's dormitories. Then some general group gatherings. We can reserve the chapel for some. I'd like to arrange some small group sessions at the Gutter. Think you can do all that?"

"Yeah, sure. I know a couple of girls who are really interested in the Symposium. I could get them to handle the dormitory meetings."

"Good. And scratch out some ideas on what some posters would look like to announce the prayer meetings."

"What about publicizing this outside the school?" he asked.

"Dad and Nigel... er, President Robart are working on that aspect. I'm focused on the campus."

"If I do all this, Beryl, what will you be doing?"

I grinned at him. I had just shuffled a lot of the organizing off on to him. I was working on ideas for some *pre*-symposium lectures, and rallies. "I could tell you, but then I'd have to kill you."

"Yeah, right. I guess you have plenty on your plate, as well."

"Actually, I do. I have some other ideas to develop. Once you get rolling, I'd like you to identify any of the creative types we could co-opt for some brain-storming sessions."

"I can do that."

"You're sure? We don't have a lot of time to get things ready. The semester ends in two and a half weeks. Once we get into January, we'll be on a death march."

"I gotcha, Beryl. I can do this. This is going to be the best thing that's happened to this place in years."

I certainly hoped so. I kept thinking of Jesus' illustration of watching for the signs. And the signs here portended stormy weather. I really needed to talk to Dad. He was very busy, and I tried to stay out of his way. But, he needed to know what I was doing, and what was happening on campus.

At 11:30 I stuck my head into his office. "I'm going to lunch. I really need ten or fifteen minutes to talk to you sometime soon."

He looked up from the mound of paper on his desk. He hadn't been running his hands through his hair, which I interpreted as his having a decent morning.

"Why don't you eat with me. That'll give us a chance to get caught up on things."

"Sure."

He picked up his phone and punched the intercom button.

"Ellen, call the country club and reserve a private table for two." He paused for a moment. "Okay. Thanks."

He hung up and looked at me. "While I'm thinking of it..."

He opened the drawer under the center of his desk and pulled out a key. "This will open the outside doors of this building. You really need to be able to come and go as you please. Just don't lose it."

"Thanks, Dad."

"Let's go."

As usual, he pointed me to my car and climbed in the passenger seat. I backed out of the space and headed off campus.

"Have you done your upgrades to this yet?" he asked.

Earlier in the fall, shortly after I had bought the Dart, I had purchased the parts to hop up the engine a bit. As usual, my intentions ran ahead of reality.

"No. The parts are still in the trunk of the other car."

He grinned. "Think you'll ever get around to it?"

"I don't know. I may try to talk one of the men in the church into helping me. The farmers aren't *quite* as busy in the winter."

"What did you need to talk about?" he asked, as I pulled out on to US 20.

I busied myself with the lane change to get ready for the turn on South Main Street and also to think. Dad just smiled.

"I think Nigel and I were a trifle optimistic about the reaction of some of the faculty about the symposium."

He frowned. "I can't say I'm surprised. Aside from Alan Carper's visit,

Sancy Pearlman has been feeding me tidbits."

"That woman is plugged in," I said.

"Yes, she is. But she very much wants this thing to go forward. She has been having regular prayer sessions with your mother."

"Really?" That surprised me. Not that my mom wasn't closely attuned to the Lord, but that she and Sancy had become friends. "I guess I've gotten a little out of touch with the family."

"We've all have a lot going on, son."

"Well, Voysey as much as told me things were going to get interesting. I also heard the Dr. Cliffe has been making unfriendly remarks about this."

"I had heard that too. And, that is unfortunate. I hoped we would have the leadership of the religion department behind us."

I pondered as I drove. "So, we have five religion faculty. Two of them are not in our court. We know that."

"What about the other three?" he asked.

"Voysey is behind the conference rather firmly. I've never met the others."

"Could Voysey run the department?"

"I don't know. Are you saying the other two have problems too?"

"Not necessarily. Howard Sternholder is with us, I think. But he's only been here two years, and he's barely thirty."

"Relative youth is not such a bad thing."

"Could you hold a departmental chair, Beryl?"

I snorted. "I see what you mean. I feel like I'm so far behind the curve in Appleton, I can't even see the curve. Especially after last weekend."

"Something there you need to talk about ?" He raised an eyebrow.

"If we have time. I think I've got things sorted out, but it was interesting."

"Anything else for the agenda?"

"I've got to start discipling Sully, and I don't have time."

"You *don't* have time?" Dad's tone of voice said it all.

"Yes, I know what you're saying. I have to make time."

"And you need to listen to what I'm saying, Beryl. You need to make time. This stage of his Spiritual life is when he is most vulnerable."

"Okay, I hear ya."

"And what about your church?" he asked.

I explained to him the deacons' proposal to hire the Brodys.

"The more I thought about it, the more I liked it," I said.

"I believe you and the deacons have made a sensible decision. You have, what, north of one hundred members now? It's probably a good time to consider it."

I pulled up to the doorway of the club, and we climbed out. They were apparently used to my pulling up in my Dodge Monaco. There was a look of barely concealed disdain at the Dart. Dad snorted as we walked through the door.

"It's how they measure status, Dad," I said.

"The world's standards," he replied. "Aren't you glad we aren't into that game?"

"I like to think I'm not. But every once in a while, the Lord kind of rubs my nose into it."

He nodded as we walked across the dark, wood-trimmed lobby. "I was just thinking that my comment sounded an awful lot like pride."

"Now that you mention it."

He elbowed me in the gut as we stepped up to the maître d'.

CHAPTER ELEVEN

"I don't know how many times we can do this," Connie Seabright said.

"Do what?" I asked.

"Mr. Brinker doesn't like it when both Sully and I are out of the office over lunch. It leaves Chester to answer the phone, and Mr. Brinker thinks he's too gruff."

Connie and Sully had met me this Thursday noon at Mel's Restaurant, otherwise known to me as the Diner of the Scrumptious Pork Chop. On my first visit to Rockford I had taken my supper there and was served an unbelievable pork chop. I now returned to the restaurant as often as my schedule allowed.

We sat around a corner table. Connie had ordered the BLT. Sully had a hamburger, and I had the eponymous pork chop. My Bible was open on a corner of the table, and I was careful not to spill anything on it. As we ate, we talked about John's gospel.

"I'm tellin' ya, Mr. Cathcart, I go from highs to lows when I'm reading. It just amazes me how Jesus describes himself. And I don't understand how people refused to believe, even when He was workin' miracles."

"It's a good lesson in comparing God's greatness to the depths of man's sin. Does it help you understand what God saved you from?"

"Oh, yes. An' I tell ya, I don't miss it one bit. I can't thank you enough for tellin' me about Jesus. And I can't thank Him enough for savin' me."

He picked up his burger and took another bite. The burgers at this place were fair sized – bigger than McDonalds, but the sandwich seemed lost in his enormous hand. Sully represented one of the most radical transformations I had ever seen in a new convert. He had been friendly and helpful the first time I met him, but now that was overlaid with incredible joy. And the beery and tobacco aura that formerly surrounded him was gone. Even his body odor was in abeyance.

"Sully went forward at church last Sunday morning," Connie said, suddenly.

I looked over at the salesman. "I just wanted to let people know Jesus saved me," he explained. "The minister said anybody wants to come forward to confess Christ. Well, I wanted to."

"Good for you, Sully," I replied. "Some people get nervous about that."

"I don't know why. Greatest thing's ever happened to me. I'm getting' baptized this Sunday night. I was hopin' you'd be there. I know you have responsibilities downstate, but I would be honored."

He was right. I had responsibilities. And I had a church business meeting coming up on Sunday night. But, Sully was now a child of God, and I had responsibilities toward him. I was going to have to shift things around, and didn't know how I was going to do it. I quickly came to a decision.

I looked him in the eye. "I'll be there, Sully. I wouldn't miss it."

"Thanks, Mr. Cathcart," he beamed at me. "Isn't this wonderful?"

We continued our examination of John's gospel, and the time passed quickly. I glanced at my watch.

"I really need to get going. I don't want to be late for class."

Sully jumped up. He could move quickly in spite of his bulk. "Oh, I am sorry for takin' your time, Mr. Cathcart."

"No, no. I'm glad to be here," I said. "I guess I'll see you Sunday, then."

He nodded with a happy smile. I reached to pick up the check, and he immediately grabbed it.

"Let me get that."

I was out of time. "Okay, thanks. I really have to run."

I had trouble paying attention in Systematic Theology that afternoon, because I was pondering my schedule for the weekend. After class, I threw my things in the car and headed for Appleton. Along the way I prayed for the upcoming weekend and also asked the Lord what to do about Sunday night.

The usual stack of messages was on the spindle when I arrived home at 7 PM that Thursday night. Also, there was a letter from a church in Troy, Pennsylvania, inviting me to preach a four day series of meetings over the Christmas holidays. The evangelist originally scheduled for the meeting had become ill, and Uncle Angus suggested I might be available. It would mean being away from Appleton for yet another weekend, but this sounded like something I would like to do.

In the stack of notes I discovered one written in Mrs. Marsden's small, precise handwriting. The business meeting scheduled for Sunday night was now going to be after the Sunday morning service. And following that was to be dinner on the church grounds. The first thing I did was say a prayer of thanksgiving to God for taking care of my need. Then I wondered what was going on.

I picked up the phone.

"Operator."

"Hi Violet."

"Hey, Preacher. Just get in?"

"Yes. Is Lane home tonight?"

"Sure thing, Preacher. Just a moment, and I'll connect you."

As I listened to the raucous buzzing of the phone ringing on the other end of the line, I thought again about how hard working was the Johnson clan. Lane managed a thousand acres of farm and chaired the deacon board at the church. His wife Liz worked as a nurse for a doctor in Victoria and also managed the household. Lane's mother Violet worked evenings as the phone operator for the district. And she was routinely up at sunrise helping with the chickens, the garden, or around the house. Each was certainly more productive than I, and I didn't know how they did it.

"Hello."

"Hey, Liz, this is Beryl. Is Lane there?"

"Sure thing, Preacher."

I waited for a few moments before Lane came on the line.

"Deacon Johnson, I just wanted you to know I wasn't calling with a problem tonight."

There was a pause. "Uh... Preacher, you caught me off guard."

"That's something we don't see very often. It's not old age creeping up, is it?" I don't know why I say some of the things I do.

"Ha! One of these days you're going to find out just how young I still am."

"Never mind," I said. "I'll take your word for it."

"Right. I guess you got the note about the church meeting."

"Yep. Kind of interesting. What's going on?"

"We've canvassed the congregation, and it looks like the vote for Avis is going to be close to unanimous. We decided to go ahead and have dinner on the grounds to welcome the Brody's aboard."

"That makes sense. Kind of interesting, though."

"In what way?" he asked.

"You remember Sully, the guy I led to the Lord last week? Well, he's getting baptized Sunday night, and he asked if I could be there. I prayed all the way down here about it."

"Preacher, it always amazes me how the Lord answers your prayers."

"It amazes me too. I won't keep you, Deacon, but I wanted to check on that item."

"Nothing sinister, Preacher. Things are going well."

I nodded as I held the phone to my ear. "That's when we need to watch out."

I heard him laugh. "Preacher, I always try to watch out."

"Okay. Thanks for your time."

"Sure thing, Preacher. By the way, are you free to stop over here for dinner tomorrow night?"

"Absolutely. Thanks."

"Good. We'll see you around six."

After talking to Lane Johnson, I sorted through the slips of paper from the spindle. Mrs. Marsden had done a good job of ordering them already. But, by reviewing them, I had a pretty good idea of what my Friday would look like. Or so I thought.

Before I started roughing out the Sunday morning message, I called Avis Brody and assigned him the Sunday evening service. If we, meaning Appleton Baptist Church, were going to put him into the harness, I intended to have him do some plowing. He still had stars in his eyes and was enraptured with the romance of the pastoral ministry. It was time for him to learn of the tyranny of Sundays. I don't know for sure who coined the term – maybe Spurgeon or Martyn Lloyd-Jones, but it was a solid truth. I knew I no longer felt so alone when I read the phrase.

My December messages were mainly wrapping up ideas I had been exploring for weeks or months. In January I intended to start a series on the great doctrines of the Bible. This would serve several purposes. First, our *exodusal* Methodists, as Nigel called them, needed to be taught what Bible believing Christians believed. And I also thought it would be good reinforcement for the rest of the people.

The great challenge was not teaching the doctrine itself, but rather finding an immediate application for each message. The apostle Paul clearly taught the value of the Scriptures in Second Timothy. There should be a natural application of the nature and attributes of God, so that the listeners could use it to make their lives *perfect, throughly furnished unto all good works*.

I normally preached expositional sermons. The effort to dig the basic meaning from each passage and satisfy the context was a deeply ingrained habit for me. Preaching on doctrine would force me into a thematic style, which I disliked. One of the great problems of Biblical Christianity was shallow and insipid preaching. Preachers would tend to select a topic and erect a supporting structure of Bible verses around it. The result was a talk about a particular topic the preacher was at the moment concerned with. Unfortunately, current events with a smattering of Scripture did not produce growth in the believers.

So, I spent the rest of the evening working ahead on January's sermons. By ten o'clock I began to get sleepy. I put my desk to bed for the night and started getting ready myself. The wind had kicked up outside. I glanced out the window, but could not see anything in particular. I brushed my teeth and checked the oil level in the stove in the living room. Since it heated the whole house, it wouldn't do to have it run out one night in December. I had allowed that to happen once a few years previously. Not only was it unpleasant to get out of bed in a very chilled house, I didn't think I'd ever get the place warmed up again.

I awakened on Friday at six o'clock. It was still dark, and it seemed very still. I rolled out, and checked out the window. A heavy blanket of snow covered everything. Under the gaze of the street light I saw a heavy curtain of snow falling vertically. It was too dark to see much, but I suspected nobody in the area would be going far that day.

It may have been my upbringing in New York City that resulted in my antipathy towards snow. Oh, it was lovely to look at through the window of a warm house. But, I had no great desire to go out and play in the stuff. But, if I wasn't going anywhere, I was perfectly happy to spend the day studying. I was glad to have driven down from Rockford on Thursday afternoon. I otherwise wouldn't have made it until late Saturday or early Sunday.

After the shower and shave, I opened the bathroom door, and was assaulted with the aroma of bacon and eggs. Mrs. Marsden had braved the drifts to get my breakfast. I wasn't too surprised. The woman was an elemental force of nature. Compared to her, a mere blizzard would come in second place every time.

"You'll not be going out this morning, Preacher," Mrs. Marsden said.

"Not very far, anyway. I want to clean the snow off the car, but it looks like I would get stuck if I went too far."

"There is wisdom in awaiting the snow plow."

"There is that," I said. "Besides this will give me a chance to get some studying done today."

"Spending time in God's Word is always profitable. I do not wish for you to freeze to death in a snow drift somewhere."

"Believe me, that is my fervent wish as well."

"God has plans for your life, young man. My ministry is to make sure you fulfill them. Right now, Appleton is where God has placed you for seasoning. You will not be here forever."

This was getting a little spooky. I really wondered what she was talking about.

"Whatever you say, Mrs. Marsden. But the here and now is the only place I can focus."

"As you should. But do not forget that God is always preparing us for our next assignment. It is true for you, and it is true for me."

"I'll keep that in mind. Now, if you could refill my cup with your wonderful coffee, I'll go hit the books."

She snorted as she reached for the percolator. "You think the old lady is short a hairpin or two. Just remember what I told you, Preacher."

Oddly enough it stuck in my mind for years. It was surprising how prescient she was. As I look back I still wonder whatever happened to her.

CHAPTER TWELVE

The roads cleared enough so that we had a normal crowd on Sunday morning. As the deacons had predicted, Avis Brody was elected Assistant Pastor unanimously, and the dinner at church went famously. The people were delighted to have him formally a part of the church. I was too. It took some of the pressure off for sermon prep and visitation. On the other hand, I was now in the position of having an understudy, which meant new responsibilities. This required some thought on the right way to mentor him. Brody was very bright, but even with my slim five or six years lead in the pastorate, I was quite a ways ahead of him in experience.

With Brody having been assigned the Sunday night message, I didn't feel so bad about slipping out from the dinner early and getting on the road. The snow plows had covered most of Knox County, but I wasn't sure what to expect heading north. My snowy travel experience two week's previously was still very much in mind. I was delighted to have the Lord rescue me and reveled in the reassurance of God's watch-care. But, I had no desire to repeat the event.

As I drove across the state, I spent the time in prayer. I prayed for the church, and individually for the deacons, and as many of the church members as I could remember. I prayed for Avis Brody. He still had stars in his eyes, but I had no illusions about the ways a young pastor could face-plant – even in a church where the membership was solidly behind the ministers. I prayed for Mid-North, and I prayed for Dad and Nigel. Dad truly had his hands full, and Nigel wasn't bouncing back as quickly as we had hoped. And I prayed for Sully.

The trip was routine, and I arrived in Rockford at about 5:30 PM. The piles of snow here were even higher here than they were down state. I stopped by my parents' house for a quick chat with my family and with Nigel. Mom fixed a sandwich for me. Her leftover roast beef was better than most people's fresh cooked. I sat down at the kitchen table and dug in. Nigel hobbled into the kitchen on his crutches and slid into the chair across from me.

Ruth chose that time to storm into the kitchen carrying the rubber snake.

"There you are, you louse!"

"Hey Cakee, how's it going?"

"Don't try to jolly me, Beryl," she said as she wrapped the snake around my neck and acted like she was going to strangle me. "This stupid snake woke up the whole house."

"Must be a noisy snake," I said as I winked at Nigel.

"Don't be a smart aleck. You're already in enough trouble with me."

"How do you know Nigel didn't put the snake in your bed?"

Nigel held up his hands. "Keep me out of this. I had nothing to do with it."

"Okay, Beryl, I'll get you for this," she said, and stormed out of the kitchen just as quickly.

"I was awake when she found it," Nigel said. He was grinning.

"And the reaction?"

"Spectacular. She screams loud enough to wake the dead. I heard a crash at the other end of the house, and then your dad running down the hall."

"What do you think we should do for a bonus shot?" I asked.

He snickered. "Might be wise to leave it for a bit."

We sat across the table from each other quietly for a few moments enjoying the fun.

"So, how goes it, Nige?"

"The usual. Trapped here while the world goes around."

"Are you getting tired of Mom and Ruth yet?"

"Don't set me up, Beryl. Your folks have been wonderful. I'm really embarrassed about imposing upon them."

I grinned at him. "Mom and Dad are delighted to be involved in a ministry. And believe it or not, Mom views taking care of you as part of her ministry."

"More like purgatory," he grumbled.

I looked at him innocently. "Nigel, according to Catholic doctrine, the Devil isn't in Purgatory."

"Oh, shut up!"

"You keep setting yourself up like that, sooner or later I won't be able to resist the temptation."

"Yeah, yeah, yeah. But, the reason I made the supreme sacrifice to hobble out here was to talk about the Symposium."

"Okay. To business. What do you want to know?"

"What you're working on mainly. Your Dad filled me in on the marketing side. You're supposed to be working on the campus promotions. That's if you haven't fallen into habit of laziness again."

"It's not a habit, Nigel, it's a good management practice."

"Right. In other words, you've shuffled the work off on to somebody else."

"You got it. Remember Stephen Gardiner?"

"Of the stupid questions?"

"You got it. He volunteered to help. So I've got him doing the leg work.

He's arranging campus prayer meetings, and he's going to try drawing some posters."

"You really did shuffle the work off to him?"

"Yes. My time is limited, so I'm trying to leverage all the resources I can."

"Where did you learn that?" he asked.

"It was a tactic of desperation. Dad was the one that told me it was simply good management. Since I now have an assistant pastor, I'm practicing it in Appleton too."

"You are much too young to retire."

"Don't start on my age, now."

He laughed. "I knew sooner or later you would step into a hole."

"Right. You know me too well. Umm. He's also talking to other students about setting up prayer meetings in the dormitories. I really don't know any of the girls on campus, and he does, so he would be a natural for setting things up in the women's dorms."

"That's a good idea," Nigel said. "What else are we missing?"

"I'd like to schedule some chapel speakers to kind of prime the pump for the symposium. First, to set the expectations, and also to get the students and staff thinking about the doctrine of inspiration. That occurred to me after Dad preached on the topic in chapel."

Nigel nodded. "I'm glad you mentioned that. Chapel is one area I've kept my fingers on. I can talk to your dad about that, but I know several people we could bring in as guest speakers."

"Have you settled on the Symposium speakers?"

"Tentatively. I've got somebody from both the graduate schools at Wheaton and Trinity. And Dr. Voysey asked if he could speak."

"Really? I've never heard him preach. Is he any good?"

"Oh, yes. He is probably the most powerful speaker on campus."

"That sounds like a good idea to me, Nige. If we have one of the faculty on board, it won't look like a bunch of outsiders trying to ram this stuff down everybody's throat."

"My thoughts, exactly. Which brings us to the next item."

"Carper and Cliffe?" I asked.

"Exactly. I understand Cliffe has been muttering. Have you heard anything from Carper?"

"You know about Carper taking me to the Gutter and also his meeting with Dad."

"He really is unhappy about this."

"Voysey made a comment to me too," I said.

"Do tell."

"Basically, that I had better expect trouble."

"And he still volunteered to preach."

I thought about that. "Miss Pearlman commented that he was probably the most solid, doctrinally, of all the faculty. I'm glad he's on board."

"He's been here long enough to have credibility too."

I worked my tongue around in my cheek as I thought. "You know, Nigel, even if this goes over extremely well and with no problems, you're likely to lose several faculty."

"I know that. I'm prepared to do that."

"Is Dad?"

"I don't know. I haven't talked to him about it."

I raised my eyebrows. "Do you suppose we should talk to him about it?"

"Probably. I just don't want to start another fight between the two of you like the last time this came up."

Dad chose that moment to walk into the kitchen. "Fight between who?"

Nigel and I looked at each other. "You started it," I said.

Dad looked at Nigel. "What?"

"Actually he started it, Mr. C. But I guess I'll bring this up, since you like me better anyway."

Dad laughed, and pulled out a chair and dropped into it. "Now, I'm sure I don't want to hear it."

"I just to explained to Nigel how he and you should expect to lose several faculty before this is over and done with."

"You're talking about the Symposium?"

"Yep."

"I'm not as dumb as I look, Beryl. Don't say it, Nigel. I had come to the same conclusion a while back. Okay, I accept that. I don't like it, but we have decided to make Biblical authority part of the mission of this school. So, therefore, we can expect a few rough patches, moving forward."

"That's why the prayer meetings are so important," I said. "We really need the Lord's help with this, and we'd better recognize it."

Dad nodded. "That goes without saying. We all need to keep this before the Lord."

"What time do you have to leave, Beryl?" Nigel asked suddenly.

I looked at my watch. "The service starts at seven, so I've got another half-hour, or so. I told you Sully's getting baptized tonight, didn't I?"

"Yes, you did," Nigel said. "I think I'd like to go."

"Are you up to it?" I asked.

"I've been sitting around the house for three weeks, and I need to get out."

I looked over at Dad. "Can I borrow your car tonight? I don't think I can push the seat back far enough in the Dart to get his leg in."

"That's fine. Nigel, are you sure you can handle this?"

"Oh, Beryl is no problem, usually."

Dad laughed again as he stood up. "Let me go get the keys. Plus let me get away from you two. This is supposed to be a day of rest. I'll start Monday all worn out."

So I piloted Dad's new Cadillac across Rockford to the church in Love's Park with Nigel enthroned in the front seat. The car had a bench seat, so I felt like I was sitting across the room from the pedals and steering wheel. Nigel laughed.

"You look like somebody's child driving the car, Beryl."

"Thanks, Buddy. I'll leave you home next time."

"What, and miss out on this? I wish I had a camera."

"Don't you have a camera?" I asked.

He shook his head. "Nope. Nobody to take pictures of."

I didn't follow up. Nigel wasn't exactly estranged from his family, but he didn't have much to do with them. I think this was the reason he was so close to Mom and Dad. They were the parents he never really had. I sometimes thought he merely tolerated me, as a way to be close to them.

We drove along for a while without saying anything, and then he spoke up again.

"Your dad likes to travel in style."

"Yes, he does. You've seen our place in the city, so you know my parents aren't ostentatious. But Dad likes his Cadillacs."

"Is that why you drive Dodges?"

"No. Well, not really. I do like them, but Dad offered to buy me a new Cadillac. Can you imagine me pulling up in the church yard in that? I'd probably lose what little confidence the congregation has in me."

"Nah. That's already happened."

"So I came back to school at the urgings of the original confidence man," I said.

"As I like to say, Beryl," he said with a smile, "you always were a sucker."

"Don't remind me."

Considering the weather, the church was well attended. As I helped Nigel through the door, I saw Ellen Holgate talking to Connie in the church lobby. Ellen glanced over and spotted us, then immediately trotted over to take custody of Nigel.

"What are you doing out on a night like this?" she hissed at him.

"Night like what?" he asked.

"It's cold, and there's snow all over the place. You really aren't recovered yet, Nigel. Let's get you to a seat."

He looked over at me and smiled, as she led him away. Connie and I looked at each other, and I shrugged.

"Need somebody to sit with?" I asked.

"I think so," she replied. "It looks like Ellen has things in hand."

She had eased him into the back pew, and was busily arranging hymnals and Bibles while talking to him. He liked the attention as well as anybody. I just hoped he knew what he was getting into. I smiled at the dark-haired, dark-eyed, and olive-skinned Connie Seabright, and we walked over to the other side of the auditorium to find a seat. We sat quite a ways forward, so we could clearly see Sully's big night.

"I wasn't sure you would be able to get back here with the weather the way it is," she said.

"When I woke up Friday morning and saw the snow, I didn't think I would make it back either. I guess, since they had a couple of days to plow the roads, things were fairly clear. I didn't have any trouble."

"Was there any problem with not being at your church tonight?"

"Actually, no," I replied. I then told her about the recent addition to the church staff.

"That's wonderful that God led someone to help you out at your church."

"It's kind of liberating," I replied. "I don't want to make a habit of being gone on Sundays, but in this case there was a very good reason."

"True. I know Sully will be glad you're here."

"I really wanted to be here."

We had been talking with the pianist playing in the background. The song leader stepped up to the pulpit and introduced the first song. As we sang the last verse of the gospel song, the pastor stepped into the baptistery and faced the congregation. The song leader opened in prayer, and then the pastor spoke.

"Welcome to the services. Tonight we have one new convert to Christ to baptize."

He turned and reached out his hand. Sully stepped down into the water.

"Charles Sullivan, do you believe Jesus Christ is the Son of God, crucified for our sins, and raised from the dead?"

"I do." he said firmly.

"Do you confess Jesus Christ as your Lord and Savior, and that you have given your life to him."

Sully hesitated, then said, "I do... praise God, I do!"

"Then upon your confession, and in obedience to Christ's command, I baptize you in the name of the Father, and of the Son, and of the Holy Spirit. Amen."

Sully was a big man, and the pastor was not. Nevertheless, the pastor eased Sully into the water and brought him up again.

As he performed the ordinance, the pastor said, "Buried with Him in baptism. Raised to newness of life in Him."

As he came up, Sully swung his head to clear his hair out of his eyes, and in so doing sent a spray of water across a very surprised choir. And the congregation yelled, "Amen!"

CHAPTER THIRTEEN

It seemed like life had only begun to settle into a routine again after Thanksgiving, and then we were at the semester break. I received my *A* from Dr. Carper, and fully expected to in spite of our differences. Voysey was more of an unknown. Being mercurial and unpredictable kept the students on their toes, but nobody really knew what to expect on the final grade.

I completed the final exam for Voysey on Wednesday morning and had moved into frantic preparations for my preaching engagement in Pennsylvania starting Friday night. Thursday would be a long day on the road. I hurried back to campus in the afternoon. Gardiner had created some sample posters, and I wanted to drop them by for Dad and Nigel to look at. First of all, I trotted towards the campus mail room hoping that my grade report arrived. I nearly ran over Dr. Voysey as he was coming from the mail room.

"Bit of a hurry, are we, Cathcart?" he murmured.

"I'm sorry, Dr. Voysey. I guess I probably need to slow down."

"No sense in having a wreck right after vacation starts." He gave me a slight wink.

"I'm preaching revival services this weekend in Pennsylvania, and I'm trying to get everything done today. I have to be on the road tomorrow."

"And on what will you be speaking?" he asked.

"I'm going to do a series of messages on John the Baptist. Sort of focus on his message of repentance, but looking forward to the Christmas season."

"A good choice, Cathcart. And, I wouldn't worry too much about my grades if I were you."

"Why is that, Sir?"

"You already have a ministry. Report cards are not going to make much of a difference either way in your church."

"You may have a point, Sir."

"Of course I do," he said as he marched off. "I always do."

I watched him as he moved across campus with his rolling gait and wondered about his cryptic comment. An envelope with the Mid-North College logo and return address was in my box. I quickly tore it open and studied the grade card. I laughed out loud when I saw the A for Old Testament Introduction. Once again, Voysey was adept at pulling my chain. Plus, with the A in Systematic Theology, I wouldn't be letting the Cathcarts down this semester.

I made my way to Dad's office and dropped off the posters. He promised to look at them over the Christmas holidays. I also wanted to ask him about the best route out east. I had pulled several maps and planned a route, and I had asked him with some trepidation, because I knew what he would do – and which he actually did.

"Come with me, Beryl." He pulled me into the conference room adjacent to his office and spread the maps from Illinois, Indiana, Ohio, and Pennsylvania across the conference table, and started plotting routes for me.

"Okay," he said, "probably a good idea taking the turnpikes across. You can stay on four-lane highways all the way into Pennsylvania. Some of the new Interstates are partially built, but you would waste a lot of time hopping on and off them."

"So," I wondered, "I should head north out of Harrisburg on US 15?"

"That's probably your best bet. I've never been on that road, though. Where are you staying?"

"Probably the Holiday Inn in Elmira."

"The church is putting you up there?"

I shook my head. "All I got was the invitation to preach. I talked to Uncle Angus about it, and he said to just stay in Elmira."

Uncle Angus was Angus McKisson, the president of McKisson University where I attended college.

"Sounds like an odd situation," Dad commented.

"I said something like that to Uncle Angus, and he didn't argue with me. It's liable to be an interesting weekend of services."

"I'll pray for you, son."

"Thanks, Dad. Any other thoughts on the route?"

"You should have called Triple-A. You had plenty of time."

The American Automobile Association provided preplanned routes and maps to its members as part of the services.

"I'm not a member."

"Well, you ought to join," he said, shocked.

"Never needed to."

"The first time you need a tow truck will pay for the services for a long time," he said.

I could see he was getting into his lecture mode. "Dad, I really need to run. I'm leaving in the morning, and there's still a lot to do."

"Don't let me keep you, son," he replied.

That was exactly what I was trying to avoid. My dad was usually pretty sensible, but sometimes he would get the bit in his teeth and charge. I could have been sitting there for hours. Taking advantage of the opportunity, I gave him a quick hug and got out of there.

And there was one more thing I wanted to do before I left town. I had arranged for a dinner with Connie Seabright. We had been together on a number of occasions, but had yet to have a formal date. She readily agreed, and I would be picking her up at her home at 6 PM. She had given me the address, but six o'clock in the evening in December was dark, and tracking house numbers could be a chancy thing. So after finishing my business on campus, I hopped into the car and headed over to find her place. The early afternoon was a good time for exploring, and I found the street. It was a working class neighborhood, but not as down-in-the-heels as some I had seen. The houses were the old, narrow, two-story clapboard designs so common across the mid-west and northeast. I spotted the house. It seemed as anonymous as the rest, but I carefully located myself from the nearest corner, and counted the houses in. One could never be too careful.

I then gassed up the car and went back to my apartment. I suspected I would not have a chance to do so later in the evening, and I planned an early start the next morning. I actually had a couple of hours for sermon preparation before I had to dress for dinner.

Hank Seabright was of medium height and very thin. His dark brown hair was starting to grey. We shook hands and I noticed the line of grease under his fingernails. Here was a man who worked with his hands for a living. I had met him at the church in Love's Park, but we had not had an extended conversation.

"Connie tells me you're a pastor, when you're not going to school."

"Something like that. I've pastored a church in Appleton, Illinois for the past five years or so. The president of Mid-North is an old class mate, and he convinced me to take some seminary training at his school."

He nodded. "Connie'll be down in a minute. Where are you planning to take her tonight?"

"I thought we would have dinner at the Rockford Country Club. They have a Tuesday night buffet that's really good."

"That's a pretty expensive place to eat," he said.

Once again I hadn't thought ahead. I knew from some of Connie's comments, that her family worked hard to make ends meet. Not expecting the interrogation from her father, I had decided the food and atmosphere at the club was just right for a first date. I could feel things slipping off on the wrong foot.

An elegant middle-aged woman with a Mediterranean complexion came down the hallway, and held out her hand.

"I am Contessa Seabright, Mr. Cathcart," she said with a slight Italian accent. "Connie has told us much about you."

I took her hand. "An honor to meet you. I hope she just related the good things."

Contessa responded with a melodious laugh. "Although she does look on the bright side of things, she has a high opinion of you."

"Well, thanks. I can't say as I know her well, but I have yet to hear her say anything bad about anybody."

"She gets that from her mother," Hank said with a smile. "I tend to be a little more... judgmental."

"I think Connie actually described you as being careful," I said, thinking I sounded lame.

"I understand your parents have recently moved to Rockford?" Hank asked.

"Yes. Dad originally came out here from New York City to help Nigel Robart with some issues at the school and ended up getting deeply involved. Plus, he saw some business opportunities here, although I don't think he has had time to follow up on that very much."

Hank nodded. I could tell he was busy putting the pieces together in his mind that would form his opinions of me and my family.

He canted his head slightly, and stared at me. "What time are you expecting to bring Connie home?"

"It'll be before nine," I said. "I have to get on the road early in the morning, so it'll be an early night for me."

"Travelin' back to Appleton? Just where is Appleton anyway?"

"It's about twenty miles due east of Galesburg, and directly south of Oneida. I'm not going there, though. I have a preaching engagement in Troy, Pennsylvania this weekend. I'm driving out there tomorrow."

I saw Connie coming down the steps behind her dad. She was wearing a deep blue dress and a lighter blue sweater. The combination looked very nice on her.

"Daddy, quit giving Beryl the third degree. He's quite trustworthy, you know." She walked up, squeezed his arm, and laid her head against his shoulder.

"Ah, sorry, Baby. I just can't help it."

I was seeing another instance of Daddy's little girl having her daddy wrapped around her little finger. As I thought about it, I decided that some day I would like to be on a little girl's short list of favorite people.

"You look nice tonight," I said.

"Thanks. I heard you tell Daddy we are eating at the Country Club."

"Yes, if that's all right with you."

"That would be fine. It's a nice place."

"Don't forget your coat, young lady," Hank said. "It's December."

"I know, Daddy. I didn't forget."

As I helped her on with her overcoat, Hank spoke again. "Well... you two have a good time."

"Thank-you, Sir. It was nice to meet you." I looked over his shoulder at Connie's mother. "And you too, Mrs. Seabright."

He gave me a quick, curt nod, and then walked over to open the door for us.

"I'm sorry about that," she said as we walked to the car. "Daddy is very protective."

"Oh that is no problem. He impressed me. I enjoyed meeting your mother as well."

"Oh, good. Mama is very curious about you."

I opened her door for her.

"Got the snow car, I see."

I walked around to my side carefully. The snow in the driveway was packed into an uneven frozen surface. I opened the driver's door and started to get in when I felt my feet slide out from under me. I hung there suspended by one hand on the roof of the car, and the other on the door frame, while the rest of me slid about halfway under the car.

It's an awkward position. I was wearing good clothes, plus my new overcoat, so I didn't want to just drop into the snow. I managed to pull myself back up, through sheer brute force, and then dropped into the seat. I looked over at Connie, who had her hand over her mouth. Devilish merriment danced in her eyes.

"That's a cute trick. Can you do it again?"

"There's something about this car," I said. "It's just the right height. When I bend over to get in, my feet want to slide under the car. It's happened a couple of times before."

The look on her face told me she was convinced I was simply clumsy. "That's an interesting explanation."

I laughed. "Yes, and you'll probably see it happen again."

"Sully fell down in the lot this morning," she said. "He was trying to get a car out for a customer to drive."

"He didn't hurt himself, I hope."

"No. he just laughed and brushed himself off. It scared everybody, though."

I got the car out of the driveway and headed across Rockford, without further incident. The country club was busy, which surprised me. But in 1965 northerners gave no real thought to the weather. If they could plow through the snow drifts, the weather was fine.

The buffet at the club was excellent, as usual. After loading my plate with the laced potatoes and the green beans almandine, I stepped over to the next table where one of the kitchen staff sawed a massive piece of prime rib off the roast for me. I knew I would regret the heavy meal when I went to bed, but it looked so good.

"Are your parents staying here for Christmas?" Connie asked, as we worked on our meal.

"No, they're flying back to the city for a week or so. They're going to stay with Grandma. They moved out here in such a hurry, I think they have a lot of things to catch up on in New York."

"Ellen told me that Nigel was going to stay at her house while your parents are gone."

"Nigel told me that too. Ellen's parents are fine people, and I'm sure they'll make him welcome."

She nodded. "Yes, they will." She paused for a moment. "Ellen wasn't happy when I told her we were going out tonight."

I thought about that. Connie and Ellen were best friends. Connie had apparently decided it was best to just tell her what we were doing.

"I worried about that," I said. "I don't want you to break a friendship."

She looked troubled. "I don't want to either, but I also can't manage my life to Ellen's desires. She can be unreasonable at times."

I didn't know how to respond to that, so I cut a piece of the prime rib and began chewing on it. Connie grinned at me. I don't know why I was so transparent to people. It could be exasperating.

Even though my parents had taught me not to talk with food in my mouth, I pushed the piece of meat into one cheek and replied. "I simply don't know what to say to that."

She laughed softly. This girl seemed understated in everything she said and did. I kind of liked that.

"I don't want you to worry about it. Ellen is my friend, but I have my own life to live. Mama has often told me I am too tolerant of Ellen's behavior."

"Does she treat her friends like she does her boyfriends?" I blurted out.

"Worse. But, I can handle her," she said. "When things start to get out of hand, I just stay away from her for a while. She doesn't like that."

I took a bite of the potatoes, and then wiped my mouth with my napkin. The food was very good. I'm not sure it was worth what they charged for it, but I was paying for the ambiance that evening.

"Our... former relationship was interesting," I said.

"I saw some of it," she said. "It was typical. I'm sorry."

"No need to be. There were some things that God needed to teach me. Sometimes that involves pain. I think I'm pretty well past it, though."

"It seemed to me it was just one thing after another this fall,"

I snorted. "Seemed like that to me as well. I just didn't know what was going to happen next. I'll tell you though, there is nothing like the certain knowledge that God has His arms around you, and He's in control."

"I'm not sure I would want to go through what you did to find that out," she said.

I laughed. "I know I wouldn't have made the choice to go through it. Aren't you glad God doesn't allow us to see the future? We would die from the sheer terror."

"I never thought about it that way, but you are right."

The waiter stepped up to the table to refill our water glasses. I didn't want to fight the caffeine high the coffee would give me. I had to be up early in the morning.

"What does your dad do for a living?" I asked.

"He runs a Sinclair gas station over on US 51."

"He's not afraid to work on cars, then."

"Oh, no. He told me he makes more money from car repairs than from selling gas."

"And you have three brothers, right? That's how many I've met at church."

"Three brothers. Cayle, Carlo, and Corey. Daddy calls them his Triple-C."

"And they're all older than you?"

"Right. I'm the baby of the family."

"So I need to watch out for your brothers, then," I said.

"If they thought you were mistreating me, your life would get interesting."

"I will certainly bear that in mind," I said. "And I understand. I'm very protective of my sisters... when they're not driving me crazy."

"And what about your sisters?" she asked.

"I have three sisters, but they are younger than me. Ruth is still at home. The other two, Hermione and Martha are at Gordon College."

We had both finished eating and had enjoyed the conversation in the club dining room. The waiter had quietly left the small portfolio with the check at the table. I looked at it, added a tip, and signed at the bottom.

She looked curiously. "Don't you have to pay?"

"I'm a member of the country club. They send me an invoice at the end of the month for any of the services I use here."

"This is something I'm not familiar with," she said. "Ellen told me you were rich."

"Does that bother you?"

"It makes me a little nervous."

"I'm really not rich. Dad is wealthy. He provides for me what he calls mission support, so that I don't starve in my small country church."

"He must give you a lot," she said.

"It's not a huge amount. It's more than I want to spend in Appleton. I don't really need a lot of money. Nigel actually makes more than I do. Plus, Dad taught us kids to accept that he could leave everything to the Lord's work, if he felt that was the right thing to do."

She nodded. "The time I met your dad, I was impressed."

"He actually paid for my membership here. He expects me to help him with his business meetings occasionally. I'm glad to do so."

"You have a really interesting life, Beryl."

"The Lord has allowed me to do some interesting things," I replied. "I would be just as happy to be a country preacher and minister to the farmers in western Illinois. God seems to keep finding other things for me to experience."

"That's what I mean," she said.

I looked at the Bulova watch on my arm. "And I'd like to sit here all evening with you, but I have a very long day tomorrow."

She jumped to her feet. "Oh, I'm sorry. I completely forgot. I'm sorry if I kept you."

"No need to be in a panic." I stood up. "But it's probably a good time to leave."

We continued our conversation as we drove across Rockford again. It had turned into a cold evening, but the heater in the Dart was up to the task.

The conversation seemed warm too. I walked her to the front door of her house and said good night. To put a cap on the evening, I slid most of the way under my car, when I tried to climb in. I laughed to myself, and also hoped she wasn't looking out the window.

CHAPTER FOURTEEN

The singing sounded a little flat. Well, I felt a little flat too. Some clown in the room next to me at the hotel in Elmira had kept his radio on loud until about four in the morning. This was after a fourteen hour drive from Rockford. Since I was awake anyway, I used the opportunity to spend time on my knees. I prayed for the meetings. I prayed for Nigel. I prayed for my church in Appleton. And I even prayed for the inconsiderate fool next door who had probably gone to sleep with the radio blaring. Then I had to pray about my lousy attitude.

After about four hours of sleep, I had carefully dressed, and headed over to the campus of McKisson University for my appointment with Uncle Angus. He stepped out of his office and apologetically told me that something had come up, and could we meet the next day for lunch. Having seen the way events could wreck Nigel's and Dad's schedules, I guessed the challenges of running a Christian college were universal.

I spent an hour walking the campus of McKisson. Little had changed since I had graduated six years before. Like Mid-North, the students had left earlier in the week for their Christmas vacation. I perused the campus bookstore and picked up a couple of interesting tomes to add to my collection. The dining hall was open, so I indulged in nostalgia and had lunch there. While the campus was in good repair, it was old. Nobody attended McKisson University because of the facilities. On the other hand, Uncle Angus set a good table. The cartwheel-sized hamburger patties were served with the jumbo buns. The French fries were almost perfect, which was hard to achieve in an institutional kitchen.

Few students were around, but several of the faculty were eating their lunches, and I knew most of them. I caught up on what they were doing, and they listened with interest as I told my stories of the pastorate in Appleton. I didn't say much about my graduate work at Mid-North. While Uncle Angus had blessed it, there was little point in raising unnecessary controversy. In 1965 the wounds from the rupture of conservative Christianity into evangelicalism and fundamentalism were still fresh. I had no doubt where my loyalties lay, but there was no point in raising questions in the minds of others.

So here I sat in that auditorium in Troy, Pennsylvania, on a cold Friday night, listened to the unenthusiastic singing, and wondered how the message was going to go. Having fifty people show up for special services on the weekend before Christmas was a very good start. But my initial good feelings sagged when the attendees slunk to their seats without the usual good-natured buzz of the pre-game fellowship. After listening to the singing, my optimism decreased further. Uncle Angus had told me he thought there were problems in this church, and it seemed he was correct.

The pastor had greeted me perfunctorily when I arrived, and then disappeared to wherever he normally retreated. I sat in the front row, and reviewed my notes as the people drifted in. After the insipid song service, the pastor introduced me as *our special speaker.* Apparently he couldn't remember my name. I decided I needed to draw on whatever reserves of energy I had, and at least seem to be dynamic.

"Hi there, I'm Beryl Cathcart. I'm the pastor of the Appleton Baptist Church in Appleton, Illinois. I'd like to thank... your pastor for the kind invitation to speak this weekend." I realized I didn't remember his name either. This was not a promising start.

"Let's turn in our Bibles to Isaiah chapter forty and get started."

I launched into the voice crying in the wilderness and preached about preparing the way for the Lord. I felt like I was preaching to the wax museum. The people looked at me. They had their Bibles open. But they were not interacting. They seemed frozen. This was unnerving and scary. I needed some way to wake them up.

"How many of you are glad Jesus saved you?" I asked suddenly.

There was a half-hearted raising of hands. Okay, I got a bit of a reaction there. This was getting to be a challenge to me. I dropped back into the sermon.

"The prophet is calling the people to prepare the way of the Lord. He says to make straight the highway in the desert."

I continued a while with the introduction. I knew from past experience that if I didn't have the audience with me before I hit the first main point I was in trouble. I was in the fugue of maintaining progress on the sermon, while praying frantically on another channel, and furiously thinking of ways to capture the people. It was time for a snap change of subject.

"How many of you have heard the story of the religious horse?"

Okay, while wax dummies and manikins did not react, I detected some slight movement with this group. I thought they were, now at least, listening. There were some curious looks.

"A preacher walks into the stable, and says to the stablemaster, 'My horse has died. I need a new horse.'"

"The stablemaster says, 'Well, preacher, I have just the ticket for you. It's a religious horse.'"

"Now, the preacher is used to being teased by people, but decides to play along. 'Religious horse? How can that be?' he asks."

I could see the people starting to sit up a bit straighter. Everybody likes to hear a joke, even if it's a dumb one.

"'Yes Sir, preacher, this is a religious horse,' the stablemaster says. 'If you say *Praise the Lord*, the horse will start moving. If you say *Amen*, the horse stops.'"

"The preacher is now intrigued and says, 'This I need to see.' So the stablemaster saddles the horse, and the preacher climbs on."

The fish was nosing at the bait. There were even a couple of smiles of anticipation in the audience.

"The preacher says, 'Giddyap,' and the horse just stands there. He shakes the reins, 'Come on, horse, let's go,' and the horse just stands there. Finally he says 'Praise the Lord,' the horse starts walking. He then says, 'Amen,' and the horse stops."

I smiled at the congregation. I had them on the hook, now. They were beginning to wake up.

"So, the preacher buys the horse. Later that day, he needed to ride out to visit a church member in the country. After he saddled the horse, he climbed into the saddle, straightened himself, and said, 'Praise the Lord!' The horse began walking. So he said, 'Praise the Lord,' again, and the horse eased into a gallop. He said, 'Amen,' and the horse stopped."

"The preacher is getting more comfortable with the horse, and let me tell you, he was thrilled to have a religious horse. He couldn't wait for to Sunday to come, so he could tell his congregation about it. I suppose I should mention to you that my car is *not* religious."

That generated a slight positive rumble in the church. I continued with the joke. The key with these things was to draw it out enough so that the listener begins to get anxious to see where the story is going.

"As the preacher rode his religious horse across the countryside, he began to wonder just how fast this horse could run. 'Praise the Lord,' he called, and the horse broke into a canter. 'Praise the Lord,' he called again, and the horse was in a full gallop. This was exciting, and he yelled 'Praise the Lord,' again. The horse was in a headlong rush."

Okay, everybody was with me, and it was time to slap them with the punch line.

"The preacher and the religious horse are plunging across the countryside, and the preacher sees the edge of a cliff ahead. Did I tell you this took place in Pennsylvania? The preacher yanks the reins, and yells, 'Whoa!' The religious horse, of course, keeps running. The preacher is in a full panic. 'Stop, horse!' he screams, and the horse doesn't even slow down. He sees the cliff edge coming, and he is sure he is going to die. What to do? 'Whoa!' he yells with all his might, and to little effect."

A couple of the listeners in the congregation have actually grasped the back of the pew in front of them in suspense. I've always enjoyed telling this joke.

"Finally, the preacher experiences that clarity of mind we always discover during one of those life or death situations. He yells, 'Amen!' and the horse digs in its hooves, and stops right on the edge of the cliff. The preacher looks down at the front hooves of the horse, a few mere inches from the edge of the cliff. He leans out and looks over the edge at what he thought was certain death."

Here it came. I had them primed, and ready for the punch line.

"The preacher leaned back, pulled out his handkerchief, took his hat off, and mopped his head in relief. He then looked up at heaven, and yelled a heartfelt, '*Praise the Lord*!'"

Laughter exploded from the congregation, probably in relief. I sensed they were a little more relaxed, now. I slipped back into Isaiah and helped to prepare the way of the Lord. Next week was Christmas, and I wanted everyone to understand how all the tracks of history pointed to Christ's work on Earth. In 1965, the commercialization, and eventual debasement of Christmas was in the future. But we had grown casual about it. We had a tendency to accept Christ's birth and eventual death and resurrection, and then get on with our busy lives. I wanted them to stop and really think about it.

It seemed to me like the sermon had come together well. After my initial theatrics, they were probably wondering what the strange young man from Illinois was going to do next. Things seemed to warm up considerably in that little church in northern Pennsylvania during the sermon. But when I got to the application at the conclusion of the message, the cold pall settled over the room again. It was positively frosty during the invitation. I nodded to the pastor to step up to the pulpit to close in prayer. I slipped to the back of the church, where I could greet the members as they left.

Most of the people shook my hand as they left. Few seemed to want to look me in the eye. A few mumbled platitudes about the services. Eventually, they filed out, and the pastor stood with his hands on his hips, as he scanned the place.

"Well, I guess that's it," he said. "See you tomorrow night, Brother," he said.

"Would you like me to go with you tomorrow to call on anybody in the church or community?"

He seemed to ponder the question before replying. "No. Probably not necessary.... Thanks, though."

I grabbed my coat and headed for the car. I drove the dark, winding road back to Elmira. I pondered and prayed over the evening's services, and puzzled over the deadness I saw in that church. What ever could have happened to get a church in such a condition?

I found a diner in Elmira, and stopped for a toasted cheese sandwich and a Coke. After that, I made my way back to the hotel in the eighteen degree night. I draped my clothes over the chair in the room and slipped under the covers. I don't remember lying awake for any length of time. If the lout next door was still there, or had his radio on, I didn't notice.

CHAPTER FIFTEEN

"So have you discovered any more problems with Alan Carper?" Angus McKisson asked.

We were in the Executive Dining Room at the university. Lunch with Angus McKisson was usually an interrogation session. The Executive Dining Room was served the same menu as the main Dining Hall, but the privacy allowed conversations that didn't need listening ears. Although I had been away from school long enough that I no longer viewed its president and professors as demigods, it was still flattering to be invited to lunch with the school's founder.

"Nothing new, really. After Dad announced the Symposium, he collared me for a question and answer session."

"Was he belligerent?"

"No, but he was very intense. I stopped by Dad's office one evening, and Carper was bending *his* ear too."

Uncle Angus paused in spooning the soup into his mouth. "Have you spotted any more doctrinal problems other than his Bibliology?"

"Not really," I replied. "we are using Berkhof in the Systematic Theology class. He doesn't seem to deviate much from that."

"I suppose that's good," he sniffed, "although there are a lot of things about Berkhof I don't like."

He was referring to Berkhof's Calvinistic viewpoint, which he loathed. I had no desire to get into a discussion with him over that. Fundamentalism in 1965 was in the thrall of Dispensationalism, as taught in the Scofield Reference Bible. Theological systems were, to me, frameworks on which to hang doctrine for study and comparison. One was nearly as good as the other, depending on your current emphasis. Reference Bibles were generally useful, but the little old ladies in the pews tended to uncritically accept Scofield's notes as holy writ.

"I think that the Symposium on the authority of Scripture will have the effect of smoking out heterodoxy. I mean, beyond just people who have problems with inerrancy."

Uncle Angus picked up a piece of fried chicken and crunched through the crisp skin in bliss. It was very good, I thought. I knew for a fact the kitchen used a recipe acquired from Bob Jones University. I don't know if Uncle Angus begged, bribed, or simply stole it from Dr. Bob, but the fried chicken served in the dining hall at McKisson University had no peer north of the Mason-Dixon line.

"You are assuming, of course, that anyone with heretical beliefs will simply pull up stakes when they are faced with your Symposium," he said, waving his piece of chicken in the air.

"Well, yes. It'll back them into a corner."

"What's to keep them from lying about it, Cathcart? I mean, if there are people on the faculty of Mid-North with Liberal or Neo-orthodox views, they are in fact already breaking the school's statement of faith, are they not?"

"I guess that's true," I admitted. "But if they have been teaching false doctrine, sooner or later someone is going to call them on it."

"And have you identified anyone else of questionable beliefs?"

"Based upon some things I have heard, I wonder about the Dean of Religion."

"Who is..."

"William Cliffe."

"Okay, I don't know him."

"Another student told me he was making overt remarks about the Symposium, and they weren't complimentary."

Uncle Angus had taken a bite of the squash casserole, and then pointed his fork at me. "You cannot go after this Dr. Cliffe on the basis of hearsay. That's gossip, Cathcart. Moses said that by the mouth of two or three witnesses is every fact confirmed. Remember that. Too many fundamentalists get caught up in witch hunts. It does great damage to the cause of Christ."

"I understand. I will be taking one of his courses next semester. I expect I will find out first-hand."

"That's the easy part. You have good judgment about these things. But pinning them down will be very difficult."

"Carper is slippery."

"Right. They will look you in the eye and tell you they support the reliability of Scripture. And they will rationalize what they believe as actually fitting the doctrinal statement. They will use the same words, and attach different meanings."

"It's hard to believe someone could get away with that."

"Believe it!" he snapped. "That is why I am so vigilant here. The Devil is subtle, and so are his servants. Not only are people like that fully convinced they are orthodox, but their orthodox friends will agree."

I thought about what he was telling me. "Have you ever had anybody like that here at the University?"

"1955," he said. "I had a couple of boys graduate in '51. They wanted to get doctorates, and come back here to teach. They were good boys."

To Uncle Angus, any ministerial students who were loyal to the Lord first of all, and to Angus McKisson were good boys. I nodded to let him know

I was following him.

"They went to graduate school at Wheaton. Wheaton was a good school – a little overly intellectual maybe, but solid. Someone there, I don't know who, suggested they go to Princeton for doctoral work. They stayed in touch, and I thought they were doing fine."

"What happened?" I had never heard this story, and I was fascinated.

"I hired both of them to teach Bible. Midway through the semester I had Howard Summy in my office telling me I had a problem. You remember Howard?"

I remembered Dr. Summy. A great teacher, but he had a tendency to see liberals in every corner.

"I see you do. And you know he was a bit excitable. So I took what he was saying with a grain of salt. My faculty *must* be faithful to the Scriptures, and to the Lord Jesus. But I also want honest exposition of the Scriptures. For example, the Gap Theory in Genesis chapter one is a crock. I want people brave enough to point out where a century of tradition got it wrong."

"I take it they went a bit farther than that," I commented.

He nodded. "A couple of ministerial students asked to see me. They were terrified about questioning one of the faculty members, but a teacher questioned the traditional authorship of Isaiah, and this bothered them."

"That would bother me."

"Right. It bothered me, too. And I figured that since one of them had gotten this at Princeton, the other had too. So I sat them both down, and we had a little conversation."

I could imagine the tone of that little conversation. Angus McKisson had developed the reputation of being a harsh, mean old man. Much of that came from his ferocious defense of the integrity of the Bible and the divinity of the Lord Jesus Christ. When it came to pure doctrine and the person of his Lord, Uncle Angus was implacable, unyielding, and whatever else you wanted to say about him.

"So they admitted it, then?" I asked.

"No, and that's what I am trying to explain to you. So quit interrupting."

I realized at the moment that Uncle Angus had a bit of Clarke Voysey in him. I had never noticed the similarity before.

"So I sat them down," he continued, "and asked them who wrote Isaiah. They both immediately said Isaiah wrote the book. What they meant was that it really didn't matter who wrote it. Church tradition says Isaiah wrote it, and that's good enough for their purposes, although it clearly had two or three actual writers."

"Did they say that?" I asked.

He glared at me for interrupting again, but his glare did not frighten me as much as it did when I was a student.

"Not in so many words. It took about an hour of beating around the bush, before I could nail them down. For all practical purposes they were neo-orthodox. That's why it was so hard to figure out what was going on."

"They use the same language we do, but change the meanings."

"Exactly, Cathcart. So, I fired them on the spot. Told them to clear out of their offices by the end of the day."

"Good," I said.

"But that wasn't the end of it. The next day I received a deputation from the religion department. They wouldn't come right out and challenge me, but they questioned my commitment to academic freedom. I told them they had freedom to teach as they saw fit, subject to good sense and fidelity to the Scriptures. If they didn't like it, they were free to leave too."

"Did they?"

"I had several quiet resignations at the end of the school year."

"I've never heard this, Sir," I said.

"Well, it's not something you like to talk about. The bad thing is not just the doctrine, but the way people like this spread poison around their peers. And I'm sure they thought I was being reactionary, and they were perfectly orthodox. I could see it in their faces."

"That's scary."

He snorted. "Why do you think I worry so when my students go somewhere else for advanced work. The Devil is a liar, and he's gotten very good at it over the past six thousand years. If you are not absolutely grounded in your faith, places like Princeton are extraordinarily dangerous."

"I understand."

"Do you really, Beryl?" he asked. I was a little surprised. He had never used my first name before. "I've never told anybody this, but you are one of the most intellectually gifted graduates we have had at McKisson University. If you ever forget this is how you were gifted by God, and start trusting in your own intelligence, you are in grave danger."

The conversation had taken a turn I had not anticipated. "I don't know what to say."

"God has also gifted you with humility. You don't take yourself too seriously."

"God has a way of allowing me to make a complete fool of myself on a regular basis," I said. "It's never fun, but apparently I need it."

Uncle Angus laughed. "I've had a taste of that myself from time to time. But listen to me carefully, Cathcart," and he grew serious again. "Satan desired to sift Peter like wheat. Think about that. Peter was not an idiot. Far from it. The Lord Jesus surrounded himself with twelve very capable men. They were the ones He would use to build His church. Even Judas was very, very smart. For three years, Jesus taught those men, and he regularly humiliated them. Yes, they were smart, but that was not a candle to God. And Peter promised Jesus he was willing to die for Him that night. And there was no question he was absolutely committed to that. And he failed miserably. Do you see the lesson, Cathcart?"

I nodded. It had been while since I had been personally preached to by a man I admired nearly as much as I did my father. It was both uplifting and humbling. But Uncle Angus wasn't finished.

"You are taking courses in a place that tolerates, in some fashion, heterodoxy. If it wasn't for your father and Nigel Robart, I would do everything possible to drive you away from that place. It's just too dangerous to sit under men who would corrupt the doctrinal purity of young people. But Cathcart, you must be very careful. Satan desires to sift you like wheat."

I shivered at his last statement. And I was frightened. I was comfortable in my faith and doctrine. When I thought about the apostle Peter, I realized, once again, how easy it would be for me to go over the edge.

"Uncle Angus, could we pray? I don't want to do anything to cast shame on the name of Christ."

He smiled then. "Of course, we can, son."

We bowed our heads, and he prayed for about five minutes. We then continued our lunch.

"You know, Cathcart, I try to pray for all of my boys and girls. It just breaks my heart when they fail. I wept after I fired those two. But think of how Jesus must feel when we fail Him."

"I try to remember that always."

"Good. Now tell me about last night's meeting in Troy."

It always amazed me how Uncle Angus stayed on point. It would seem as though he was meandering around the countryside in his conversation, but he had a reason for everything he said. I related my experience at the church, and he carefully questioned me as he dissected the evening.

"So what do you think is going on there?" I asked.

"Clearly, there is some kind of un-confessed sin that the whole church knows about," he said. "Whether it's an individual or corporate sin is hard to tell. But one thing is true, until you can break it open, the meetings are not going anywhere. Neither is that church."

"But how I find out what's going on?"

"You've got to drive it out into the open. You won't be able to do that until some of the church members decide their loyalty to Christ is more important than their membership in that place."

As usual, Uncle Angus had given me much to think about. I returned to my hotel room to study for the evening's service, and spent time on my knees asking the Lord to blow things open so He could deal with the sin in this church.

CHAPTER SIXTEEN

I was thoughtful after my lunch with Uncle Angus. As always, he gave me a lot to think about. I had my Bible and books with me, and the university snack shop was open, so I parked there for the afternoon and prepared for the evening message. The manager remembered me from my days at school and kept my coffee cup filled all afternoon. That kept me awake and alert, and also afforded me the opportunity to exercise the facilities next door.

The crowd at the church was about the same size or maybe even a little larger that Saturday night. This surprised me as Saturday night was usually the worst night for attendance for these kind of meetings. Whatever the problems this church faced, and I thought they were probably serious, the core members clearly believed in being in the building whenever the doors were open and the lights were on.

As the song leader, and I finally learned his name was Oliver Heckel, led the listless singing, I reviewed my message and prayed. Since I couldn't figure out the problem with this place, I left it in the Lord's hands. That is always a good strategy, and I nearly always adopted it on the second or third try. The pastor then opened in prayer and made a few perfunctory announcements.

"I won't take up any more time," he continued. "Brother Capeheart, will you come speak to us again?'

"Thank you, Pastor Knerr," I said as I stepped up the six inches or so to the raised platform. I knew I had gotten his name right, because I had carefully studied the sign in front of the church. As far as he was concerned, I was glad he made the attempt on my name. It was certainly better than what Sully's boss had called me.

"Turn in your Bibles to Luke chapter seven. I want to read just one verse – verse 20

> "**When the men were come unto him, they said, John the Baptist hath sent us unto thee, saying, Art thou he that should come? or look we for another?**"

"What we have here is an example of prophetic impatience. John knew who Jesus was. How could he not? While the Scriptures say little about the early life of Jesus, and none about John, it is entirely possible they played together as children. They were distant cousins. And, I think we could argue that they were aware of their ministries from a very young age."

I looked at the congregation. Although I had not told any silly jokes, they were attentive. A good sign, I thought. I decided to improvise just a bit.

"What do you suppose the two six year old boys talked about? We know that the twelve-year-old Jesus told his parents, *I must be about my Father's business*. Much of what they did prior to the formal beginning of their ministries remain a mystery, and properly so, I think."

The normal background noise of an audience was gone. There was not the rustling of Bible pages, the clearing of throats, or even the whisper of children. They were with me.

"While I prefer, and most often do preach expositional messages, I hope you will permit me to make a thematic variation tonight. As we come into this season, and ponder the nativity of our Lord, I would like to pose the question: Is Christ truly the Lord and Savior, or do we look for another?"

There was almost a gasp in the room. My question bordered upon the absurd, but also jerked them out of the comfort of listening and not participating. I wanted them to have that desire to tell me the question was nonsensical, as it was.

"I think everyone in this room wants to speak up, and say, 'This is the Christ child! He is the Lord!'"

I began pounding on the pulpit in time with my words. "Then.why.are.you.serving.other.gods?"

I rarely get very physical in the pulpit, but my frustrations were starting to boil over. I looked down, and there was blood on a knuckle where I had caught the corner of the pulpit. I paused after the question, and the room was dead silent. Everyone was staring at me.

"I want to commend you on your attendance at these special meetings. Not every church would dare call meetings on the weekend before Christmas. And yet it seems a majority of the congregation is in attendance. But also," and I knew I was stepping out where the ice was very thin, "you cannot deny that there is something very wrong with this church. You sneak in here like you are afraid someone will see you. You slip out after the services without any greetings for your fellow believers. Brethren, this ought not to be."

They were now staring at me like I was some kind of apparition. I suppose calling attention to a problem in the church was just not done. Well, I had gone and done it.

"I don't expect to be invited back. In fact, you may decide that after tonight, you won't allow me back in the pulpit here again. Be that as it may, while I am here, I *will* preach the Word of God."

I calmed down a bit, and shifted back to the main track of the sermon. The fear that showed on everyone's face gradually faded, and normalcy returned – to quote Calvin Coolidge. I worked my way through the message, and this time I managed the invitation myself, rather than turning it over to the pastor.

I had little use for the emotional theatrics Charles Finney introduced along with the mourner's bench. But I have always thought the concept of an invitation time in the service was Biblically sound. From Isaiah's *Come and let us reason together, saith the Lord* to the reaction to Peter's sermon at Pentecost – *men and brethren, what shall we do?* The Bible always ends specific teaching with what I call a decision point. I was always very careful to question any individual who came forward, and I tried not to prolong things. At a certain point, you simply must let God do His work.

But tonight, I wanted to hold their feet to the fire. "I am not an advocate of running to the altar for every little sin. If you have sinned against someone, go ask their forgiveness. Then go ask God's. But I fear many of you have placed something ahead of Christ in your hearts. Remember, if you are Christ's, He will have *all* of you. One way or the other. What will it be?"

Following the close of the service, I again stood at the door. Remarkably, many of the people thanked me for the message as they shook my hand. Once again, Pastor Knerr stood with his hands on his hips, but this time he stared at me.

Finally he shook his head. "I really don't know what to say, Brother Capeheart."

"Cathcart."

"What? Oh." He shook his head again. "I'm sorry. I've had some kind of a mental block about your name."

"Don't worry about it. People have problems with my name all the time."

"It seems they had no problem listening to you tonight."

"I certainly hope that was the case. I trust you are aware of the problems you have here."

He swung his head. "I think you could say so."

"Could I bother you to explain what is going on?"

"I don't even know where to start, brother," he said. "I've been here for a year, and I haven't figured it out."

"I don't envy you."

"I guess the Lord is teaching me a lot through this," he said. "But it is frustrating."

"I'm sure it is." I paused. "I suppose I'd best get on my way."

"I'll see you tomorrow, Brother Cathcart."

Once again, I was exhausted. Preaching is hard work. I had eaten before the services, so I drove to the hotel and climbed into bed. Sunday would be a long day. I was encouraged that the people hadn't simply thrown me out. I was going to have to be patient and let the Lord work.

Sunday was more of the same. I focused on different areas of John the Baptist and pointed to Christ. The people were attentive, but completely unresponsive. Sunday night I was so frustrated that after the invitation, I gave the closing prayer, and then just stood in the pulpit and watched the people file out. I guess I was praying, mainly for patience. I believed God's Word did not return void, but I was used to seeing results. I thought about Adoniram Judson, who labored in Burma for eight years before seeing a convert. Certainly these people could not be that stubborn.

I noticed a white haired gentleman about halfway back in the auditorium studying me. Finally, he seemed to make up his mind, and then marched forward. Since he was obviously coming to see me, I stepped off the platform and waited for him. As he got close I was able to study him. He was one of these ageless men who could have been sixty or seventy-five. I didn't know. His face was not heavily lined. I saw his hand, when he reached out to shake mine and decided seventy-five was closer to the mark.

"I just wanted to thank you, Preacher," he said with a soft, clear voice. "This is some of the best preaching we have heard here in years."

"Thank-you," I replied. "I really try to give the Lord credit."

"As well you should. Pastor Knerr is a good sort, but he is not... dynamic." He managed a low, quiet laugh. "But we love him anyway. God called him here."

"I honestly have not had a chance to get to know him."

"Nor anybody else, from what I could see," he said.

I merely nodded. I wondered if he would make some comment that would unravel my ignorance of what was really going on in the church.

The old man smiled again. "Not much response to your messages, is there?"

"You might say that. I've never had an experience quite like this."

"Would you like to know why?"

I looked at him, carefully wondering where this was going. "If you could enlighten me, I would thank you, Sir."

He swung his head across the auditorium. "Take a look at the carpet. Notice anything?"

The carpet was new. The unmistakable odor was the first thing I had noticed when I first walked into the church building. The crackle and snap of static electricity, when I touched a door knob, told me it was wool carpet. And the gray floor covering was obviously of very high quality.

"It's new," I said. "Very nice."

"Look closely."

I wasn't sure what he was getting at, but I examined the carpet closely. I shook my head.

"Step over here, brother Cathcart." He took my elbow, and guided me to the center, in front of the communion table. "Now look closely."

I stared at the carpet. What in the world was he talking about? Then I saw it – a faint line up the center aisle of the church auditorium. I looked again to make sure.

"There's two different colors of carpet in here," I blurted out. The difference was so subtle I hadn't noticed it, and I had been in the building for three days.

He patted my arm, as if congratulating a particularly dimwitted child. "And why do you think that is the case?"

I stared at the carpet, bewildered at the abrupt change of perspective. I am sometimes slow to pick up on things, but this time the pieces of puzzle slammed into place with almost a physical impact.

"The people got into a fight over which color of carpet to pick," I said.

I suppose he could have said something like, "Congratulations." That would have really rubbed salt into the abrasions caused by my lack of perceptiveness. But he merely nodded.

I said, "They couldn't come to an agreement, so they decided to physically split the church over it."

"That is pretty much it, Preacher."

"Wow! How long has this been going on?"

"Oh, they have been arguing off and on for six months. The carpet was finally installed last week."

I looked again at the carpet, and then back at his kindly, smiling face. "I don't know what, if anything, I can do about this. But it sure clears up a lot of things for me. Thanks for telling me."

"I just couldn't watch you continue to preach your heart out, and see these... fools carry on with their bickering. It's shameful. Our pastor has tried his hardest, but hasn't gotten through to them."

I nodded. "Well, Sir, I can say some things he can't say. I can leave town after tomorrow night. He has to stay here."

"I just thought you would want to know."

"Thank you," I said. I shook his hand again. "God bless you, Sir."

CHAPTER SEVENTEEN

I woke up in the hotel room Tuesday morning, December twenty-first with two or three inches of light snow on the ground. It was eight o'clock, and I had pretty well slept off my weariness. A thought popped into my head – a spur of the moment idea, and I rolled over in bed and picked up the phone.

After placing the call, I heard the operator speak when the receptionist at Dad's office answered. "I have a collect call for anyone from Mr. Boris Cathcart."

The receptionist quickly accepted. She was used to people having problems with our names. I got a little tired of it at times.

"How are you Beryl?" she asked. "This is Mindy."

Mindy was the sixty-something grandmother who had ruled Dad's office with a rod of iron for as long as I could remember. And my memories extended back to Dad carrying me into the office when I was a toddler.

"Fine, Mindy. And you?"

"Oh, the usual. Keeping this office the way it should be gets to me sometimes." That was her usual complaint, which meant she was doing well.

"Family coming in for Christmas?"

"Jack and Carol will be here Thursday and stay for a week. I'm taking some vacation."

"Good for you," I said. "As hard as you work, you deserve it." And she did work hard. Although she was not a thing like Mrs. Marsden, after I landed in Appleton I quickly decided she was Dad's keeper.

"Tush!" she said. "Making coffee and answering the phone isn't hard." Her flat New York accent lent emphasis to her words.

"Well, anyway, is Dad in the office this morning?"

"For the past hour, Beryl. I keep telling him to slow a bit."

"Like that works."

"For sure. Just a moment, let me get him on the line."

I didn't have to wait long.

"I suppose I need to bail you out of something," he said without preliminaries.

"Do you think you could get me a flight out of LaGuardia on Friday morning through Chicago to Galesburg?"

"You're still in Elmira?"

"Yes, I finished the meetings last night."

"How'd they go?"

"Interesting."

He was quiet for a moment. "I take it Uncle Angus dropped you into an unusual situation."

"You got it. I'm going to see him in about an hour. I thought I'd drive over and spend the rest of the week in the city."

"I assume you want to fly out sometime after Christmas to pick up your car?"

"Probably Monday or Tuesday. Then drive home on the thirtieth."

"Your mother and the girls will like that," he said. "Okay, let me get somebody on this. If there is any problem, I'll leave a message with Angus McKisson's secretary."

"Great, Dad. Thanks."

I heard the click of him hanging up while I was in the middle of my sentence. Dad was not one for long goodbyes. Chuckling, I rolled out of bed and headed for the shower. The pressure of the services in Troy was off. I didn't have to worry about homework for another couple of weeks. I had four perfectly good sermons in the can from Troy that I could reuse in Appleton the next weekend. It was a liberating feeling. I considered myself on vacation.

As I attempted to lather myself up in the shower with one of those tiny hotel soaps, I sternly reminded myself I was not on vacation from the Lord. It would be easy to coast. I planned to spend my usual time in prayer during the next couple of weeks, and use the opportunity for what I called free Bible study. I wanted to just read the Bible for enjoyment and blessing, without the pressure of sermon preparation. I had told Lane Johnson and Avis Brody I would be back for the Christmas weekend. We would have a Friday night Christmas Eve service and then the usual Sunday meetings.

After I started the car, I used one of those sticks with a brush on one end and a scraper on the other to brush the snow off the windows. It was in the low twenties, and the snow was fluffy – and had not frozen to the glass. The car had barely warmed up during the short drive over to the McKisson campus. I wished I had my big Dodge for the trip. I had a persistent back ache from the bench seat in the Dart. The buckets in the Monaco were much more supportive. On the other hand the Dart was sure-footed in the snow and drove well.

"I see you survived the disobedient believers and hordes of the mixed multitudes," Uncle Angus said as he ushered me into his office.

"It was actually one of the most passively rebellious groups I've ever seen," I replied. "I did finally discover the immediate cause of the problem."

He sat me down across from his desk, and then dropped into his chair with a sigh. "Immediate?" He raised one bushy eyebrow. I was struck, once again, how much he looked like a much older Billy Graham – although I would never tell him that.

"Believe it or not, they had a fight over what carpet to buy for the auditorium."

He snorted. "It's often something like that which lights the fire."

"I didn't even notice, but there was a dividing line down the middle of the room with different carpet on either side."

"People do some foolish things, sometimes."

"Well, it seems the congregation is split right down the middle. I don't think the pastor really knew what to do."

"I've met Jethro Knerr a few times," he said, "but I can't say I know him well."

"He's not one of our graduates, then?"

"No, he went to Tennessee Temple," Uncle Angus sniffed.

For some reason Uncle Angus had a low opinion of the Baptist college in Chattanooga. I wasn't sure why – I had heard Uncle Angus had a falling out with that school's president. But, the graduates I had run into seemed like solid people.

"Well, I changed my approach last night, and preached from Joshua 24:15."

He nodded. "'Choose you this day whom ye will serve.' No sense in beating around the bush."

"That's what I thought."

"Any reaction?"

I shook my head. "Nope. They were polite and thanked me for coming. The love offering was generous too. Incidentally..." I pulled the check out of my pocket and handed it to him. I had endorsed it. "Here. For the school."

"I can't take this, Beryl."

"Why not? I don't need it."

He laid the check aside on his desk and didn't argue further. I knew he wouldn't.

"Thank you for your generosity. You know, the carpet in that church was probably not the root cause."

I thought about what he said. "I see what you're saying. It had been building up for a while."

"That's the way it usually works, Cathcart. The carpet was the spark that touched the whole thing off. I would bet there have been some hard feelings in the church for quite a while. I talked to Knerr last year when he was up here for Evangelism Outreach. He said that the church seemed kind of dead, and he couldn't figure it out. No surprise there." Uncle Angus could be cruel if he thought somebody was an idiot.

"He seemed pretty helpless this weekend. But to be honest, I didn't do much better."

"Don't underrate yourself, Cathcart. You planted the seed. Sometimes you just have to let God's Word do its work."

"I'm taking some comfort in that. I have to say they seemed to listen, once I got their attention."

"And how did you get their attention?"

"The religious horse," I replied.

I could tell he was trying not to smile. He was not big on humor in the pulpit, but I had actually heard the joke from him.

"I guess sometimes the Lord... just works."

"I certainly hope so, Sir."

"What are your plans, now, Cathcart?"

"I'm going to drive over to the city today and spend a few days with my parents."

He gave me a withering glare. "I mean with your graduate work."

I tried not to quail. "Oh. Assuming Mid-North survives, and we don't get thrown out, I'd like to finish a Master of Divinity. At two courses per semester, it'll take years, though."

"You should push through and do a doctorate."

He surprised me. "Uncle Angus, I don't need a doctorate for a pastoral ministry. I think the M Div will be useful in making me more effective."

"Listen to me, son, I don't want you to pass up the opportunity. Mid-North is not a large school, but a doctorate from there will be valuable."

I wondered what he was aiming at, but it didn't make sense. But Uncle Angus never said or did anything without a reason.

I shrugged. "Okay, I'll see how things go. That's a long ways away in any case."

"Are you planning on taking courses in the summer?"

"No. Not really. I don't like being away from my church that much."

"Take the summer courses, Cathcart."

The president of McKisson University was one of the few people who could make me do things I really did not want. I still didn't see where he was going with this, but I could see my summers consumed with classes, just like the rest of the year.

Later, as I wound my way through northern Pennsylvania and New Jersey, I pondered our conversation. Like my weekend of special meetings in Troy, it was enigmatic. I had a lot to think about. I really wondered what Angus McKisson wanted from me.

Dad was correct. Mother was delighted I had come out to the city. Hermione and Martha were full of stories of the first semester at Gordon College. Ruth competed with stories from her high school classes in Rockford. My grandmother was delighted to have everybody home.

Mom's mother had come to live with us when Grandpa died, not because she had to, but rather she wanted to. She in her mid seventies and looked about sixty. When my parents had moved to Rockford so Dad could involve himself heavily in the college, she had decided to stay in the city. This worked well, because the house would not be empty, and she could maintain her activities with friends there. Dad had hired a housekeeper to do the cleaning and kind of keep an eye on Grandma.

I wondered how Dad could manage the firm from Rockford. In those pre-Internet days, communications were slow and expensive. Travel was still fairly arduous. He took things in stride, as usual, using the Christmas hiatus at Mid-North to concentrate on things related to the family business. He never took vacation, unless it was with the family. Since we were all home, I expected him to be around somewhat.

After one of our riotous dinners, Dad and I retreated to his den. He was carrying a glass of water, and I had a cup of coffee.

"Sometimes it's good to get away for some peace and quiet," he said.

"It got pretty loud there at the table."

Dad smiled. "Did you notice how happy your grandmother was tonight?"

"Do you think she would move out to Rockford?" I asked.

Dad shrugged. "I've invited her. I guess she will have to make up her own mind."

"I'd have to hide the rubber snake, then." Grandma hated snakes.

Dad winced. "I'm still sore from that night?"

"Huh?"

"When your sister screamed, I fell out of bed."

I laughed then. "Nigel mentioned hearing a crash."

Dad sighed. "I keep hoping you will grow up, Beryl."

"I am as grown up as you."

Dad just smiled. He reached into his desk and pulled out a leather-bound binder.

"This is for you, Beryl."

My name was embossed in gold letters on the cover, along with the name of a private bank in Manhattan.

"What's this?"

"It's a trust account for you. Merry Christmas."

I opened the binder and looked at the summary page at the front. I looked at the total amount and pursed my lips in a soundless whistle.

"What's this for, Dad?"

"I've been giving a lot of thought to my estate."

"Is something wrong?"

He laughed. "No. Not that I know of, anyway. But each day is one day less."

That made me nervous. Dads are supposed to be around forever. Losing my father was something I knew would happen eventually, but I tried not thinking about it. It scared me.

"No," he continued, "your mother and I have been talking about the best way to handle our estate, so that we can take care of you kids and still support the Lord's work."

"So you're doing this for the girls too?"

"Yes. I'll be talking to them individually this week."

"This is a lot of money, Dad."

"The bulk of my estate is still going to the Lord's work. This trust is designed to provide income, so that you are not dependent on your churches, and so that you won't have to worry about retirement. Also, if you should become disabled, this should carry you, plus most of your medical expenses."

"Thank-you," I said quietly.

"There's more," he said. "I want you to direct the charitable trust. I may do something else later, but this seems the best solution to me. Also, if something happens to your mother and me, I want you to keep an eye on the arrangements for your sisters."

"I understand. Is managing the trust going to be a full time job for me?"

"No, you'll have to meet with the bank several times per year, but all you should need to do is give general directives."

"I'm honored that you gave me the responsibility."

"The estate is a moving target, Beryl. I may ultimately decide to staff it as a separate organization. Or I may just divide the money between several organizations and then dissolve the trust."

"I guess we'll need to talk about this on a regular basis," I said.

"Oh, yes. I want you completely up to speed."

I paged through the binder. The arrangements had been put into place, and it meant I was now truly wealthy. I didn't feel the elation that I might have felt for winning the Reader's Digest sweepstakes. I guess it was because my parents had carefully schooled me on Biblical stewardship. What I did feel was the responsibility.

Dad chewed on the inside of his cheek as he watched me. "There is one other thing, Beryl."

"Yes?"

"I also set up a trust for Nigel."

"Dad that is wonderfully generous of you."

"No, it was something I had to do. I am convinced I was responsible for his injuries. And it is entirely likely he will never completely recover. You must know that there is a good chance he won't come back to work."

"I try not to think about that," I replied. "He's not doing that well, is he?"

"No. I talk to his doctor regularly. He thinks Nigel will probably never be free of the pain."

"Nigel doesn't blame you, you know."

Dad shook his head. "Some of the most foolish decisions of my life I made during that week when Roland Fordyce and Charlie Bigelow were running around Rockford with guns."

"You can't say that, Dad. God was working through this."

"Well, I believe He worked in spite of us, Beryl."

As I sat in the chair in Dad's study and fingered the hand tooled leather binding of the trust document I learned something else. My father wrestled with challenges every bit as tough as what I faced.

CHAPTER EIGHTEEN

Friday was a long day. I rode a Transcontinental & Western Constellation out of LaGuardia to Midway in Chicago, then rumbled along in a noisy Ozark Airlines DC3 from Midway to Galesburg. It seemed like the pilot flew only about five hundred feet off the ground, and it was bumpy. A winter storm was on its way, and I was worried about beating it to Appleton.

Avis Brody picked me up at the Galesburg airport in his ratty '57 Ford. Christine opened her door and slid over to the middle. I tossed my suitcase into the back seat and climbed up front with them. My heels skidded on the floor of the car when I climbed in. I looked down, and saw a piece of plywood on the floorboard.

"What's this?"

He looked over as he backed out of the parking space. "Awww, the stupid floorboard is rusting out."

"The whole car is a rust bucket," Christine added helpfully.

"It sounds pretty good," I said.

"It runs good," he replied. "It's only got forty-thousand miles on it."

"So it'll turn into a pile of rust before you wear out the drive-train."

"That's about it," he admitted. "But the price was right."

"No complaints, there," Christine said. "I think the salesman felt sorry for us. We were getting ready to offer him $125 for it, and he told us he'd take $75."

"Sounds like he just wanted to get it off his lot," I said. "I guess the Lord was looking out for you."

"Very true," he said. "It's a piece of junk, but we haven't had any trouble with it."

"Well, if you need to do any traveling, I'll let you use one of my cars."

"Oh, Preacher, I couldn't let you do something like that."

Christine slapped his leg with a rifle-like report. "Hush, Avis. Let the man talk."

"How did the special services go?" he asked. "We prayed for you."

"Thanks, Avis. It was the strangest thing you ever did see. I walked into the middle of a church split, I think. They were fighting over the color of the carpet in the church. They had one color on one side and another color on the other. The seam ran down the center aisle."

"That's one for the books," Christine said. "What did you think when you saw it?"

"The difference in the color was so trivial, I didn't notice it until a kindly old gent pointed it out to me."

"And they were fighting over that?"

"I talked to Uncle Angus about it. He thought there was some other underlying issue, and the carpet touched off the fight."

The Bodys were quiet for a few moments as they considered what I had told them.

"So, how did the services themselves go?" Avis asked.

"As I said, it was strange. They were quiet and respectful, and after I got their attention the first night, they pretty much stayed with me. The altar call got a bit lonely, though."

Christine asked, "So you were up there all by yourself, and everybody just stared at you?"

"That was it exactly. I didn't find out what was going on until Sunday night after the services. So I unloaded on them on Monday. I figured I probably wasn't going to be invited back anyway."

"Where was the pastor in all this," Avis asked.

"Ha," said. "Like a non-person. He got up to introduce me the first night and couldn't remember my name."

"That's not too surprising," Christine said. "You have such an anonymous name. You know, like Smith, Jones... Cathcart."

"Thank you very, very much. Santa Claus told me about you."

"What?" they both asked.

"Oh, yes. When Christine was a little girl, Santa used to leave her a lump of coal on Christmas. Her parents felt badly about it and made sure to collect the coal, and then they'd set out gifts for her. But, they carefully taught her that there was no such thing as a Santa Claus."

Christine looked back and forth between me and Brody, obviously waiting for the punch line.

"Go on," she said.

"The fact of the matter, Christine, is that there really is a Santa Claus. And he hates you."

Avis surprised everyone by bursting into full-throated laughter. Christine glared at me.

"Thanks a lot, Buster! Where did you hear that one, anyway?"

"Believe it or not, I came up with that one all by myself. I was tormenting my sister."

"It's a wonder they'll even admit to being related to you," she muttered.

I looked at my watch. It was late afternoon. "Have you had anything to eat?"

"Mrs. Marsden ordered us to bring you directly to the parsonage. She said she was preparing an early supper for the three of us."

"And Mrs. Marsden is not to be trifled with."

"Avis is scared of her, but I think she's great!"

"I am not," he said.

"Why does that not surprise me?"

She looked over at me with her patented glare. "You'll find out who Santa Claus really hates," She said darkly.

Avis started giggling. She slapped his leg again. "Stop that, Avis. You're only encouraging him."

I think Avis was half-terrified of Christine, too. I could see him biting down on his lower lip to keep from smirking.

Mrs. Marsden, true to form, had prepared an enormous Christmas Eve feast. There was a buffet with baked ham, roasted potatoes, squash, green beans, and cranberry sauce. Along one side was a pumpkin pie, and a pecan pie. Since she was very careful not to make something I didn't like, there was no mincemeat pie.

The Christmas Eve service was only a couple of hours away, so I was careful not to overdo it. I had enough trouble with getting my shoelaces tied together in the pulpit, without losing control over an enormous belch. I had learned that the congregation derived a lot of entertainment from my (fortunately) infrequent *faux pas*, but I did my best not to encourage them. That I lived in terror of making a fool of myself in the pulpit was not an exaggeration.

"Preacher, are you going to be in town for the rest of the season?" Mrs. Marsden asked.

I shook my head. "No. I left my car at my parents' house; I'm flying back there on Monday. I'll be home here on Thursday night sometime. After that, I don't plan to go anywhere until the start of the new semester at school."

"It'll be good to have you home for a bit," she said.

I felt a twinge of guilt over having taken advantage of the patience of these good people. They had tolerated my being gone during the week, and sometimes even missing Sundays. I resolved to spend more time in Appleton.

"Are you going to visit your parents, Avis?" I asked.

"Oh, no," he immediately replied. "I just started here, and we can't afford to take the time off."

I suspected he couldn't afford the gas to drive to Council Bluffs, Iowa to see his parents. I knew what we were paying him, and it wasn't much. I was going to have to talk to Lane Johnson about sending him home for a few days, and putting some extra money in his pocket for the trip. Meanwhile, I enjoyed Mrs. Marsden's exquisite meal.

Christmas had always been a magical time for me, in the Christian sense. The members of Appleton Baptist Church took delight in decorating the building for the season. Evergreen branches graced the windows, and a decorated tree stood on one corner of the platform. The lights were turned down, and candles lined the aisles and the rail behind the platform. The air was perfumed with the scent of fir trees, and it awakened memories of childhood.

I was once again reminded that this place was home for me. While it was pleasant to spend time with my parents and sisters, this was where I belonged. I was with the church members, whom I loved. To varying degrees, they were all my friends. I was rapidly getting to know the migrant Methodists that were now a part of the congregation. Several had already joined the church, and many more were taking the new members' class. Our little church building was comfortably full this Christmas Eve.

Roland Klegg, the new pastor in Oneida was holding Christmas Eve services for the first time in years. Our expatriates therefore invited their friends from the Presbyterian church in Oneida, which was *not* having services this night.

I had planned to preach one of the John the Baptist messages I had used in Troy, suitably tuned for Appleton. But when we finished the song service, and Larry Smith looked down at me, indicating it was time to preach, I stood up.

"Let's sing some more, friends. This has been wonderful.," I said. And it was.

As we sang the old familiar carols, I was filled with that bright anticipation the shepherds felt as they made their way to Bethlehem to see the Christ child. We sang every Christmas carol in the hymnal, and Larry looked at me again. I looked at my watch, and we had been at it for about fifty minutes. So, I simply got up and read the Christmas story from Luke, then closed in prayer.

We didn't need to think about John the Baptist this night. We needed to see the Christ child. We needed to behold our King. Our new members and visitors were open-mouthed at the experience. I don't think they had ever been to a service like this one. I fervently prayed that God would bless them richly over the Christmas weekend. And nobody was in any hurry to leave. We stood around in the auditorium and shared fellowship and blessings. It was a wondrous time. The Spirit of Christ was with us, and several times I had to blink back tears.

Several of the members pressed small wrapped packages into my hands. I noticed that they had not neglected the Brodys. Christine had a small stack of presents on the pew next to where she was standing. Once again I was touched by the thoughtfulness of the people and felt guilty for not treating them better.

We stood around for another hour, and finally people began easing out the door. I touched Lane Johnson's arm.

"A word with you, Brother Johnson?"

"Sure thing, Preacher."

He followed me back to the small office behind the platform. Since I did all of my studying at home, we just used this for prayer meetings, and the like.

"What's on your mind?"

"I'm flying back to the city on Monday. I left my car there. I'm planning to drive back on Thursday."

He nodded.

"If it's alright with you, I'm going to tell Avis to take off for his parents' house next Thursday and be gone for a week. He felt uncomfortable about leaving so soon after he started ministering here."

"I think that's a good idea, Preacher."

"And I'm going to give him the keys to the Monaco and order him to take that. I'd hate to see him go all the way out there in that wreck he has."

"That's very generous of you, Preacher."

I shrugged. "And there was one other thing."

"Yes?"

"Could we could quietly pass the hat for a little Christmas bonus for them. I don't think he has the money to drive out to Council Bluffs."

Lane looked abashed. "I should have thought of that. I don't know what's the matter with me."

I pulled my wallet out. I was flush from the cash I normally carried when I traveled. I pulled a pair of twenties out, and handed them to him. "Here, let me prime the pump a little bit."

"That's mighty generous of you, Preacher."

"God has been good to me. But I don't want Avis to think I'm directly subsidizing him."

"I understand. Let me talk to some of the other people, and we'll get this done."

"Thanks, brother. And Merry Christmas."

"Thank you, preacher. And Merry Christmas to you. I assume you're coming to dinner tomorrow."

"Only if I'm invited."

He grinned. "Oh, I think we can consider you invited."

Since I had come to the church six years previously, I had made it a practice to always be at the church over Christmas. This was the most important season of the year, and I felt I should be there for the people. So it had become something of a tradition for me to have Christmas dinner with the Johnson's. I thought it would be especially important for me to be there, since Lane's father had passed away earlier in the fall.

"Thanks. I always enjoy the meals at your house."

"Liz invited the Brodys too, but they've already made plans to eat with Christine's parents in Galesburg."

"That makes sense. Well thanks again, Brother Johnson."

"Sure thing, Preacher. We'll see you tomorrow."

He clapped me on the back as we left the small prayer room. The building was nearly empty by this time, and we stepped out into a cloud of heavy, fat snowflakes. I thought once again, about my dreams of sitting by the fire on Christmas Eve with someone special and looking at the snow. But, it wasn't going to happen this year.

CHAPTER NINETEEN

I was about traveled out for the season. The winter air was boiling up a major storm again when I flew back to New York City. This made for a rough ride in the DC6 between Chicago and New York. Then, I had to turn around three days later and drive back to Illinois through the same storm.

It was nice to finally stay in one place for a while. It was still the holiday season, and things moved at a slow pace. I decided to spend the better part of the day visiting our members in the nursing homes.

"And how do you like your new home?" I asked.

"Just fine, Preacher," Gracie Hollander said. "It is nice not too have to cook and keep house anymore. And I have a good roommate." She looked over at the other elderly woman, Abbie Martie, and smiled.

"So it worked out well."

"It did. I was sad to leave my house and garden." She paused, and I could tell she was slipping into her memories. "But God has a new ministry for me, and I'm so excited about it."

Gracie had failed alarmingly in the past six months. Her little house in Appleton had been ideal. She could putter around her garden and yard to her hearts content, and there were friends and neighbors close by to keep an eye on her. For someone to wander through their retirement years, it was close to idyllic. I had fully expected her to carefully ease up to the century mark without fuss.

But, in such cases, God had other ideas. Sometime during the summer of 1965, Gracie Hollander had grown frail. It happened almost overnight. When I began traveling to Rockford in the late summer, I noticed distinct differences just in the week I was gone. Her husband having been dead for a decade or more, the woman's children had reluctantly decided it was time for other arrangements.

The Knox County Nursing Home was a decent place. It was largely staffed by middle-aged people from the community, and there were a lot of long term friendships between the residents and the employees. They didn't warehouse the old people. Oh, there were the residents who were far gone into dementia that required physical restraints. And, to be honest, the building didn't smell all that great. But, I guessed that was common to most of these places.

"I'm glad you came to see me today, Preacher," she said.

"Does your family get in to see you?"

"Oh, yes. They come several times each week." Her side of the room was plastered with pictures of sons, daughters and grandchildren. Little gifts and trinkets littered the dresser top and window sill. This lady was revered and loved by her family.

"I'm glad to hear that. I would think the days could get kind of long around here."

"Oh, no, Preacher. There is plenty to do. But your visit is the highlight of my week." She reached out and patted me on the knee.

There was something humbling about visiting these elderly saints in their time of decline. I hoped I would be as accepting and gracious when I had toddered down this road.

"Well, if you have time, I would like to share some thoughts from a message I preached in Troy, Pennsylvania last week."

"Oh, yes, Preacher, that would be wonderful. I hope your meetings went well. I prayed for you."

I was convinced that the only reason I had any effectiveness at all in the pulpit was because of these folks who spent their days praying for me. I viewed that as a side-blessing of my ministry to the retirees at Appleton Baptist Church. I supposed I spent too great a proportion of my time serving these folks, but to tell the truth, I just really loved the old people. I would have been completely content to spend my entire day working with them.

After reviewing John the Baptist with Gracie Hollander, I drove north from Knoxville on the East Galesburg road. This brought me to US 34 between Galesburg and Wataga. I drove through Wataga on to Oneida, where I was to have lunch with Dennis James's mother. In contrast to Gracie, Flo James was well into her nineties and still energetically keeping house on her own.

"And now, Reverend Cathcart, just you sit yourself down at the table. I have our lunch all prepared." Flo James was of medium height, and stocky. Her hair was still mostly a lustrous deep brown with just flecks of gray. She didn't look any older than her son, Dennis.

I parked myself at the indicated place at the table. Lunch consisted of fried chicken, mashed potatoes with what looked like a half stick of butter forming a pool in the bowl, corn on the cob, and homemade bread. I had spotted a pie on the rack when I walked in, so I assumed the feast extended to dessert. The fried chicken was not quite to the standard of Mrs. Marsden. *Not quite.*

My mother was a good cook, I had always thought. But, there was something about the mid-western farmhouse wives. I had yet to meet one who could not cook. They were all very good. The best had to be experienced to be believed. I was convinced that if I still lived in western Illinois into my middle age, I would be facing a massive weight problem. These people liked to feed me, and I liked to eat.

"I had a visit from Reverend Forsen," Flo said suddenly. She had been chattering on about Denny and his family. I wasn't expecting the change of subject.

"Did you now?"

"Well, yes. I didn't really expect it."

I wouldn't have either. Since his conversion, Edgar had not lay claim to his ordination. He mainly focused on learning the Word and growing in the faith.

"Did he call, or just show up?" I asked.

She had taken a bite from a chicken leg and had to finish crunching the crisp skin. She carefully wiped her mouth with the paper napkin before speaking.

"He just showed up and knocked on my door. Surprised me."

I'll just bet it did. Prior to his conversion, Edgar Forsen had been the minister at the United Methodist Church in Oneida, Illinois. Increasingly slack in his visitation responsibilities, his sloth had been the cause of the church members calling me to visit their sick and shut-ins. I was glad to do so, but worried about how this would be perceived.

Things came to a head when he was quoted as saying he didn't see why he should bother to visit these old bags, who were on their last legs, and one step from the grave anyway. This precipitated what my friend Nigel Robart had described with his gift for alliteration as the Mass Methodist Migration to Appleton Baptist Church. It also resulted in Forsen's firing by his bishop, and led directly to my doorstep, where I led him and Eileen to the Lord.

What was interesting was that, although her son Dennis James had come to my church with the rest of the group, she had remained in the Methodist Church in Oneida. She had explained that she was too old to be trekking clear down to Appleton every Sunday, and she knew the Lord would understand.

"So, what did he have to say?" I asked.

"He apologized." She had a shocked look on her face. "He even asked me to forgive him."

I finished a bite of my chicken before I could speak again. I nodded. "I guess you heard that he recently came to know the Lord."

"I heard that, of course, Reverend. But let me tell you, I was surprised. I have never had anyone apologize to me before."

I'll bet she was surprised. Mid-westerners were among the most warm and generous people I had ever met. But, they also could carry grudges to the grave. Asking forgiveness was something alien to the culture here. It was a source of amazement in my pastoral counseling. When confronted with the Scripture, people would freely confess their sins to the Lord and repent. But going to someone they had wronged to beg forgiveness simply was not done.

If a repentant individual went forward during the invitation at church, even the wronged parties seemed to accept that and move on. It was strange, and I didn't understand it. But there you are. I looked at Flo James.

"What did you do?" I asked.

"I forgave him, of course. But why would he do that, Reverend Cathcart?"

"I guess the Holy Spirit convicted him about his former life, and he wanted to make things right."

She shook her head. "I just don't understand people sometimes."

I didn't either. Edgar had told me he wanted to make things right with the people in Oneida, and I encouraged him. The reactions he received were interesting.

I was thoughtful as I drove home that afternoon. Many of the people were very private about their relationship to God. From her comments, I wondered if Flo James was really saved. Her son Denny assured me she was. During the lunch I had again shared some thoughts from my messages on John the Baptist. She listened politely, but said little.

The temperature had drifted up into the lower forties, and the sun had dried off the roads during the afternoon. When I arrived home, there was another stack of notes on the spindle in my kitchen. Mrs. Marsden had come and gone during the day. The house smelled of cleaner and dusting polish, and she had left a note reminding me of dinner in the refrigerator.

I glanced at the notes. Avis would be back that evening, and I planned to assign them to him, so I could spend most of Friday in sermon preparation. I walked into the living room and checked the oil level in the heating stove. I tended to forget about it, when the weather warmed up. I walked out to the road and checked the mailbox. Two envelopes came that day – one from Uncle Angus and one from Connie. That was interesting.

I opened the garage and grabbed the five-gallon jerry can of fuel oil, so I could top off the stove while I was thinking about it. A lot of people kept their extra fuel oil in the basement. I had grown up with central heating and was a bit afraid of the stoves. So I kept the combustibles away from the house as much as possible. I had no desire to wake up in the night in the middle of a raging oil fire.

I sat down at my kitchen table with a cup of coffee and opened the letter from Uncle Angus. I made a conscious decision to save Connie's letter for last. Uncle Angus reminded me to work hard on my additional degrees and encouraged me to stay true to our shared convictions. I wondered why he paid so much attention to me. I knew he regularly corresponded with other graduates, but I felt like he had singled me out for some reason.

The envelope from Connie contained a chatty letter, which was interesting because I was the chatty one when we were together. There was nothing of significance in the note other than the note itself. As I sipped my coffee, I pondered the relationship. My heart didn't flutter, and I didn't think I was infatuated. But a feeling of warmth and peace slipped over me as I reread her letter. It was pleasant.

My relaxing reverie was interrupted by the sound of a car pulling into my drive way. I glanced out the window and saw that Avis and Christine had arrived in the Monaco. I pulled on a jacket and grabbed the keys to their Ford from the counter.

"How was the trip?"

"Oh, it was wonderful," Avis said. "We had a very nice time with my family."

"Thank you so much for letting us use your car," Christine said. "Everyone thought we were coming up in the world."

"Oh, but you are," I said. "Is there any other way to describe working for me at Appleton Baptist?"

"And he starts already," she said, rolling her eyes.

"Um, we washed the car, Beryl," Avis said. I had been coaching him to address me by my first name. I was pleased to see him doing that without the reminders. "It was warm today and the roads were clear."

"Thanks, but that wasn't necessary."

"It was covered in salt," he said. "I couldn't bring it back looking so awful. I know you like to keep it clean."

"That was thoughtful of you," I said.

I helped them move the luggage to their car. With happy smiles and waves, they backed out of the driveway and headed to their cottage. I was glad I had thought of suggesting their vacation. It obviously had done them a lot of good. But spending the week as a dedicated pastor in Appleton had done me a lot of good, too. I was beginning to understand the difference between happiness and contentment.

The phone rang. It was Lane Johnson.

"Hey Preacher, I was wondering if you could give me a hand tomorrow?"

"No problem. What's going on, Brother Johnson?"

"I gave the farm hands the weekend off, and I just bought a field of hay. Could you help me pull the bales out of the field?"

"Sure. What time do you want me there?"

"Breakfast at 6:30AM, if that's not too early."

"I'll be there."

"Thanks, Preacher."

"See you tomorrow."

I hung up thinking about the capacity for life to change in an instant. Instead of spending my Friday drinking coffee, and digging in the Word, I would be stacking bales of hay with Lane Johnson. From previous experience I knew that the hay would be soaked with rain and snow melt, and then frozen again, so they would weigh about twice as much. It would be a long nasty job. But for some reason, I looked forward to it.

About 9:30 that night I was in the middle of The Doctrine of God and struggling to put together an outline for the Sunday morning service, when I remembered the Monaco was in the driveway. The temperature had been dropping during the evening, so I put on a winter coat and went outside to put the car into the garage.

It was a struggle to pull the doors of the garage open as they dragged in the snow and ice. It had started to melt during the day, and it was now frozen again. I hadn't put on any gloves on, and my fingers were numb by the time I fished the keys out of my pocket and unlocked the car door. The button on the door handle popped as I pushed it in. That didn't sound good. Then I slipped on the ice and nearly fell, when I pulled on the door handle and the door didn't move. I braced myself against the car and yanked again. The door was frozen shut. After Avis and Christine had washed the car that afternoon, it had not entirely dried before the temperature dropped below freezing. If I tried to force the door open, I would risk tearing the rubber seals away from the door. Okay, the car would sleep outside tonight.

I went back in the house, poured another cup of coffee to fold my frozen hands around, and finished the sermon outline.

CHAPTER TWENTY

"Hi Mom, is Nigel around?"

"Oh, hello, Beryl," my mother said. "Are you back in town?"

"Yes, I just got in."

"Nigel actually went home on Monday. He decided he was imposing on the Holgates."

"So he didn't come back to your place?"

"No. I am concerned about him in that house of his too. The only bathroom is upstairs."

"I'll stop over and check on him," I said. "I see you made it back from the mad, mad city."

"Oh, yes. I never thought I would say something like this, but I'm glad to be back in Rockford."

"I never thought I'd hear you say it either."

"Well, the town grows on you," she said. "Plus your father and I are getting more enjoyment working with the school than we ever did in real estate."

"That's good to hear, I guess. What's Grandma think?"

"Oh, Mother thinks we've lost our minds."

"She sort of told me that one time when she cornered me last week."

Mom laughed. "I heard her start in on you. I decided not to enter the room right at that moment."

"My own mother. Wouldn't even come to rescue me."

"You seemed to be defending yourself quite well. I think, deep down, she's glad we are working in a ministry. She just wishes it was in New York City."

"It is a bit of a hike out here," I said. "It was a long drive."

"I think next time we'll try taking the train. Flying is quicker, but the train would be more relaxing."

"And you don't have to worry about the weather."

"It was a bit bumpy coming back here. Are you coming over for dinner tonight?"

"Am I invited?"

"Stop that! We will probably eat at seven. If I don't make it later, it gets cold because we're waiting on your father."

"Dad loves that office," I said.

"He really does, even though he complains about it all the time."

"I'll probably be there by six, Mom. I have to run a few errands this afternoon."

"See you later then, Beryl."

"Bye, Mom."

It was 11:30 Wednesday morning. I had gotten up early to drive to Rockford that January fifth, in this new year of 1966. I needed to register for classes that afternoon. Classes started on Thursday, although the two courses I needed to sign up for were Monday-Wednesday-Friday courses. That put an enormous crimp on my schedule since I needed to be in

Rockford by 8 AM on Mondays for New Testament Introduction. Fortunately, Hebrew I was at 9 AM, so I could get on the road back to Appleton by late Friday morning. There was no question Avis Brody would earn his meager pay this semester.

The duties of a faithful son out of the way, I trotted back out to the car and pointed it towards the Chrysler-Plymouth dealer. Connie Seabright and I had exchanged a couple of letters over the holidays, and we had arranged for a lunch date. I was tempted to think things were looking up, but my recent experience with Ellen Holgate kept me cautious.

I met the owner of the dealership as I was walking in. He was apparently headed to lunch and was in the process of opening the door to a new Imperial when he saw me.

"Hey Burdle, I'm disappointed you didn't trade for that Belvedere a while back."

He was now on a first-name basis with me, although he still had difficulty getting it right.

"Sully told me he made full list on it, when he sold it. That's a bit more than I would have paid."

"Yeah, but I really wanted your trade. That Monaco of yours is a nice car."

"Thanks, but after I thought about it a bit, the Monaco makes a lot more sense for me."

He grinned. "You're right. I always worry about selling things like that. I'm afraid some kid will go out and kill himself in it."

"Could happen. I imagine that car could get to be a hand full if you didn't pay attention."

"Ain't that the truth. Well, have a nice day, Birdie."

"Thanks."

I was proud for managing a straight face as I walked past him into the showroom. Sully leaned against the counter and was chatting with Connie.

"Hey, Stranger," he said. "How did your special meetings go?"

"A long story, Sully. I promise to tell you the next time we get together for Bible study. There are some lessons in it."

"I'll look forward to that, Beryl. Don't let me keep you." He grinned at Connie.

"Thanks for covering the phones for me, Sully," Connie said. "Can we bring you anything from the restaurant?"

He shook his head. "No. But, thanks. It's tuna salad for me. I've got to get some weight off. I went soul-winning with the church Monday night and nearly walked myself into the ground. It made me realize I couldn't serve the Lord well if I was a fat slob."

"That's really good, Sully. I think the Lord wants us to take good care of ourselves. Although, I don't think I would view you as being overweight."

He suddenly grinned, and I heard Connie snicker. I quickly reviewed what I had just said, and then felt the flush creeping across my face. "Uh, sorry, Sully, That just didn't come out right."

He laid his hand on my shoulder. "That's okay, Beryl. You just made my day."

"I'm glad something is going right."

"Oh, a lot is going right. I didn't know life could be so satisfying until I found Christ."

"Well Amen, Brother." I looked at Connie. "Hungry?"

She got a wicked gleam in her eye. "So are you now suggesting *I'm* overweight?"

"Oh, for pity's sake!" When people learned I was an easy target, they tended to be unmerciful. The day was not going well for me.

She laughed and came around the counter. "Let's go Beryl. See you later, Sully."

He waved as we walked out into the January day. The temperature had climbed to about forty, so it was relatively pleasant outside. The company was even better. Connie directed me to a small diner that was near the dealership. She ordered tuna salad. I had the pattie melt. I knew I would be breathing onion fumes on somebody that afternoon, but I liked the things too much.

"Mr. Brinker doesn't know what to make of Sully," Connie said.

"Has he been witnessing to him?"

"Mr. Brinker doesn't want to hear it. But a lot of Monday mornings Sully used to show up late with a hangover. And you know the way he used to smell."

"I'd say there has been a change for the better."

"Very true. Sully is now always on time. He goes out of his way to be helpful. And the customers...."

"Has he had problems?"

"Oh, no. I mean, the customers have always liked him. But now they love him. He won't sell them the junkers, and that makes Mr. Brinker mad. But, he closes more business now than he ever used to. Mr. Brinker was talking about bringing a second salesman aboard, but now he really doesn't need to. And people come in asking for him."

"I would think that would be hard for Brinker to complain about."

"Oh, it is. I heard him tell one of the brokers that he was just going to start wholesaling the stuff Sully didn't want to sell. He said his business was better than it had ever been, and it was worth his while to keep Sully happy."

"That says a lot for Sully's testimony."

"It does. I'm just a little embarrassed that I never witnessed to him before."

"Sometimes what you do is more important," I said. "He knew you were different, and church was important to you. He's very observant."

She used her fork to toy in the salad. "I apologized to him, you know."

"He told me. You impressed him."

"You taught me a lesson, Beryl. I've always been afraid to bring up the gospel."

"Me too. I just have to force myself to do it. And as it turns out, very few people get really nasty about it."

"Oh, I know. We passed out tracts downtown on December twenty-third. People thanked us."

I nodded. "I suppose some day, people won't be as appreciative. That's why we need to make the most of the opportunities."

"Did you do any witnessing down state this past week?"

"Actually I'm getting a little rusty. I was in New York last week and spent most of my time at the house. When I got home, I had to push hard just to catch up on the pastoral calls. I did manage to leave a few tracts. I tend to forget to ask the Lord to give me the opportunities."

"I know what you mean. Is it because we are selfish?"

"Probably. I had a conversation one time with one of my old professors out at McKisson. I asked him if there was a root of all sin."

"What did he say."

"He immediately said, *idolatry.*"

"Really?"

"Yep. Essentially, anything that takes our eyes off of God is idolatry, because it places something in the way of that relationship. But it is most often expressed in selfishness. If Christ summarized the law and the prophets as Love for God, and Love for Man, what else is there? Love for self."

"I don't think I've ever thought about it that way."

"This guy was a strange old bird. He had this habit of speaking evangelistically."

"What's that mean?" she asked.

"Umm. He tended to exaggerate, sometimes excessively. Less polite people would call it lying."

"Why would he do that?"

"I think he couldn't remember the details of the stories he told, so he would make things up to emphasize the importance."

"That sounds like you're being generous."

I shrugged, as a snagged another French fry. "We all have our besetting sins, I think. His were just more glaring."

"Did no one ever talk to him about it?" she asked.

"I think Uncle Angus sat him down, every once in a while – usually after he had said something particularly outrageous."

"I guess we really need to confess our sins every day."

"You got it. At least, I need to. I don't know about you."

She giggled. I kind of liked the sound. "You intimidated Daddy, you know."

"Me?"

"Yes, you. You didn't back down or try to make excuses when he was giving you the third degree."

"I was just trying to be polite." I was learning a lot of new things today.

She gave me a warm smile. I kind of liked that, too. "I'm glad that you're not self-important."

I rolled my tongue inside my cheek as I considered her statement. "I'm not naturally humble, Connie. It's just that every time I start thinking highly of myself, the Lord beats it out of my with a great big stick."

"At least you learn from it."

I was uncomfortable when she talked to me like that. I wasn't special, and I knew it. I also knew what a louse I could be at times. And there was probably nobody in my family who was as stuck on themselves as I. On the other hand, I was definitely enjoying the lunch.

The lunch was pleasant, but over all too soon. I dropped Connie off at the dealership and drove back across town to the campus. I swung around the circle in front of the Administration Building, and drove down the perimeter street; then pulled into Nigel's driveway. The stately president's mansion reflected the ambivalence that reflected the rest of the campus. It looked impressive, but under the skin it was neglected and outdated.

I tapped on the door and turned the knob. It was unlocked, so I opened it. "Nigel, are you there? Nigel?"

"Up here," he called.

He had an upstairs study, just like I did before my house got burned down. I assumed he was there. I walked down the upstairs hallway and looked into the study. He wasn't there.

"Where are you?"

"I'm in here." The voice sounded disgusted.

I walked back down the hall and looked in the bathroom. He was lying on the floor between the toilet and the wall. His crutches were tossed across the room.

"Are you alright?"

"Yes, I am alright. Help me up, Beryl."

I got a hold on his arms and levered him to his feet. "What happened?"

He hopped on one leg as I retrieved his crutches. "I was trying to pull up my pants, and one crutch slipped out, and then the other one did. I couldn't pull myself out of where I fell."

He arranged his clothes in place and buckled the belt. "I'm sure glad you showed up." He reached around to flush the commode.

"How long had you been laying there, Nige?"

"Not long. But I had no idea how long the wait would be. I was starting to get cold."

"Well, let me help you. Where do you need to go?"

"Just get out of my way, so I can get back to my study. Knowing you, you would probably pitch me down the stairs."

"Only if I had a good reason."

I kept up the joking with him, because I didn't want him to see how shaken I was.

"Yeah, I know. You'd get rid of me so you would end up with my record collection."

"Naah. Yours have to many scratches on them. Do you have anybody looking in on you?"

"Ellen drops by periodically. And your mom brings in meals."

"And Ellen was here at lunch time?"

"Uh. Yes."

"Cripes, Nigel, you could have been on the floor there all afternoon."

"I've got a room-temperature IQ, Beryl. I figured that out all by myself."

"It looks like you haven't figured out just yet, that you don't need to be living here all by yourself, until you are more motile."

"Is that a word, Beryl?"

"Motile?"

"That one."

"Yes. Look it up."

He just waved his head as he clumped down the hall to his study. He collapsed into his easy chair, where he had everything close at hand.

"Okay, I'm back together again. What's on your mind, Cathcart?"

I rolled my eyes. "Does this mean you aren't going to listen to me?"

"And you're not going to tell your mom either."

Maybe it was because we were like brothers, but our fights were as entertaining as everything else. I think we liked to argue just to score points. I slipped out to sign up for my course, but then spent the rest of the afternoon at his house. I couldn't bear the thought of him falling again and just lying there.

CHAPTER TWENTY-ONE

"Come into my office, please, Beryl," Dad said over the intercom.

I stood up and glanced out the window, noting the black '66 Imperial parked next to Dad's Cadillac. In his office were four bulky men in suits. They were arranged in chairs around Dad's desk.

"Gentleman, this is my son, Beryl Cathcart. He is assisting me with my business interests in Rockford."

One of the men stood up and stuck his hand out. "Giovanni D'Amato. A pleasure to meet you, Mr. Cathcart."

"Sit down, Beryl. These gentleman have brought us some interesting information."

I turned the side chair next to Dad's desk around and sat down facing the guests. I quickly studied the four men and started putting the pieces together in my mind.

"You are from New York City, Mr. D'Amato?"

"Correct. We have some business in Rockford that needs sorting out."

I had seen his type in the city. I was ready to bet money the mob was sniffing around concerning the late Roland Fordyce.

"Why don't we take this from the top," Dad said. "That'll keep Beryl from having to ask unnecessary questions."

"We really hate to bother you," D'Amato said, "but we have made a significant investment with a business partner for a project here in Rockford. He is now dead, and we are concerned about recovering that investment."

What was interesting to me was that the man really did seem deferential. I wondered if it was because he was not on his home turf, or because he was visiting a Christian organization.

"Roland Fordyce," I said.

D'Amato nodded. The other three men were stone faced, and seemed satisfied to let him speak. "Mr. Fordyce seems to have left things in an unsettled state following his untimely demise."

I was sure D'Amato didn't normally talk that way. New Yorkers of his variety were normally more colloquial. It took me a moment before some more pieces of the puzzle fell into place. I looked over at Dad, who was wearing his negotiating face. It was unreadable and expressionless, except for the slight grin he carried when he was thinking hard. Then the next piece dropped into place – D'Amato was intimidated by Dad. I had the almost uncontrollable urge to giggle. But somehow I managed to keep my poker face pasted where it belonged.

"If you have seen the papers, you will know that Beryl and I were present when Roland Fordyce was killed. It was unpleasant."

D'Amato shook his head. "It is always unpleasant when these things happen. As it happens, my investment company is holding the paper on the properties Mr. Fordyce purchased here in Rockford. As such, it will be just a matter of time until we can take possession of them. There was, however, a substantial amount of cash that is not accounted for."

I looked over at Dad. The water was deep here, and the sharks were circling. Knowing what these men represented, I was frightened.

"I think we know what happened to the cash," Dad said.

D'Amato leaned forward. "If you could help, Sir, this is a matter of some concern to us."

"To put it baldly," Dad said, "Roland Fordyce was scammed."

"And who did that?" D'Amato asked.

This was something he understood. In his mind, he was probably already fitting somebody with cement overshoes.

"You understand, of course, I came in after the fact," Dad said.

"No, no," he replied. "We know about you. Everybody knows you're the most honest developer in the city. That's why we thought to talk to you. I am mainly interested in getting these things sorted out."

Dad nodded. "Roland Fordyce was working with the former chairman of the board of Mid-North College. Fordyce wanted to build an industrial park near the airport. This campus is right in the middle of his plans. The chairman, Charlie Bigelow, claimed to represent the school, but kept the board and the president in the dark on what he was doing."

"The school didn't know about this?"

"He told the board he had an offer on the property and was working on it, but gave them no details. There was no vote taken to proceed."

"So what happened?"

Dad sighed. "Roland Fordyce gave Charlie Bigelow the earnest money to close the deal. Charlie talked him into giving it to him in cash."

D'Amato nodded. I was sure he negotiated deals like this all the time in the City. If you shook hands with Giovanni D'Amato, he would enforce the deal.

"We have a copy of the sales contract," he said.

Dad nodded again. "I have a copy as well. It's fraudulent. There was no vote of the board, and the president did not sign it."

"I see."

I could see too. The wheels were turning in Giovanni A'Amato's head. He was wondering if he could enforce the contract, either in the courts... or otherwise. I knew the cards Dad was holding, and I was fascinated to see how he was going to play them.

"So... where did the money go?" the mobster asked.

"As far as we can tell, Charlie Bigelow lost it at the tables in Las Vegas."

Something like a sigh escaped from Giovanni D'Amato.

"I might also add," Dad continued, "Charlie Bigelow embezzled a considerable sum of our money as well."

"So then we both have a problem."

"I offered to help Fordyce work out his problems. I think he had a viable project here in Rockford. He refused."

"My money man has looked at it as well," D'Amato said. "It's a good project. I don't suppose you would be interested in taking over the development project for us?"

"I can't do that," Dad said. "I'm sure you already know the biggest reason. But, I also have my hands full here."

The man from New York grimaced. "Just to set your mind at ease, I have no desire to move in on your turf, either here or in the city. I have bigger problems. I just want this one to go away."

I could imagine what those problems were. President Lyndon Johnson had declared war on organized crime. The crime bosses were now facing the resources of the United States Justice Department, and they were all scrambling for cover.

"To be honest," Dad said, "this campus was the only piece remaining for Fordyce to get the project rolling. He was not offering anything like what we would need to replace the physical plant elsewhere. With your... other problems..." and he was searching for a term.

"I understand," D'Amato said. He stood up, and the other men did also. "We won't take any more of your time, Mr. Cathcart. I appreciate your help."

Dad nodded, and the four men slipped out of the office, quietly. Dad looked over at me and then picked up the phone.

"Ellen, see if you can get me the United States Attorney in Rockford."

He set the phone down, and looked at me. "I want you to recognize, Beryl, how very dangerous these men are."

"It didn't look like he was getting ready to kneecap you or anything."

"Pay attention, Beryl," Dad said. He was starting to look stern.

I raised an eyebrow as I looked at him.

"The federal government is looking at all the angles on bringing these guys to justice. Mr. D'Amato was ready to send in a proxy to buy the campus, and it would probably be a generous price."

"So," I replied, "I know I don't understand a lot about this, but why shouldn't we do just that?"

Dad snorted. "It's tempting. I'm concerned that if the Feds can find a way to seize the mob's money, they could follow the chain back to us. I don't think they could grab the school property, but we might spend years in court."

"Is that why you want to talk to the federal attorney?"

"That, and also send him a message that I'm not dirty."

"What are you talking about?"

Dad folded his arms across his chest. "Think about it, Berl. When somebody like Giovanni D'Amato gets on a plane to go somewhere, the law enforcement people usually know about. I'd be willing to bet that the local U.S. Attorney knew within minutes of when D'Amato hit town – and who he came to see."

"Oh." I hadn't thought about that. "You don't want the FBI going on a fishing expedition in your pond."

"Exactly. So, we tell them who stopped by to say hi and describe the conversation."

Dad's phone rang, and he picked it up. "Yes, Ellen?"

He listened for a moment. "Thanks. Put him on."

He looked at me and nodded.

I listened to his side of the conversation. Presently he hanged up and turned to me.

"Can you hang around long enough tomorrow to have lunch with me and Ronson Hyde?"

"That's the fed?"

"Yes. I'll reserve the private dining room at the country club."

"Sure. I'm always up for a free meal."

"Just so you don't end up with three square meals and a warm bed."

"Yeah. Do you think there's any danger from them?"

"Potentially, yes. It's like swimming with sharks. Chances are they would just ignore you, but do you really want to find out?"

"I think I would just as soon stay in the boat," I said.

"Exactly. There is a certain risk in our meeting with the government. But I feel the risk is worse if we don't."

"Now you really are starting to scare me," I said.

"Don't lose sleep about it, Beryl," he said. "First of all, we are in God's hands. Secondly, D'Amato knows me by reputation. He probably expects me to talk to the government. The situation would be different if we actually did business together. By his lights, D'Amato is an honorable man, and he expects the same from his business partners. If I rolled over on him, my life wouldn't be worth spit on a griddle."

I studied Dad carefully. He never lied to me, but this bothered me. I had been terrified when that tow truck had tried to run me off the road. Being in Charlie Bigelow's study when he was waving his gun around had me beyond terror. I was not panic stricken at the moment, but this low grade fear was beginning to gnaw at my vitals.

"What are you thinking, Beryl?" Dad asked.

"That I had enough terror this past fall to last a lifetime."

He smiled. "Honestly son, it's like working with electricity. You have that constant awareness that if you touch the wrong thing, you would get zapped. You just pay attention to what you're doing. I've run into these people a few times in the city. I recognize the potential danger. I'm just very careful."

"What do we tell Nigel?"

"We tell him everything."

"By the way, Dad, I wanted to tell you something about Nigel. I didn't want to say anything last night in Mom's hearing."

"A change of subject, Beryl?"

I shrugged. I wasn't aware I was even doing it. "I stopped by his place yesterday after lunch. He had fallen in the bathroom and couldn't get up."

"Why didn't you tell me sooner, Beryl? That could've put him back in the hospital?"

"He ordered me not to tell Mom. We had quite the argument about it, after I got him back on his feet."

Dad picked up a pencil and tapped the eraser head on the desk. "I wasn't happy when he decided he could go home, but he wasn't getting up and about as much as he should have with your mother and Ellen waiting on him hand and foot."

"The only thing that's changed is that Mom and Ellen now spend every spare minute at Nigel's house."

"Not necessarily, Beryl. Nigel threw Ellen out earlier this week."

"Why didn't I hear about this?"

"Think about it. Nigel probably wouldn't say anything about it to you. And you are not exactly communicating with Ellen anymore."

"Okay. I understand. How did you find out about it?"

"Ellen told me."

"Okay. Is there anything we can or should do?"

"I don't know. I just hope Nigel can get back on his feet."

"He's starting to make noises about coming back to the office."

"That's not a bad idea," Dad said. "We would just have make sure he didn't overdo it."

Dad had started gazing at the work on his desk. I took the hint and stood up.

"Was there anything else?"

"No, Beryl. Thanks for your help."

"That's what I'm here for."

I stepped through the door to the secretary's office, where I normally hid out. I needed to have a long conversation with Nigel. But the one thing I needed to talk to him about was his developing relationship with Ellen, and for obvious reasons, he and I both tiptoed around that. I wondered if our friendship would survive if he married her. It then occurred to me that the friendship between Ellen and Connie would probably be strained if she and I progressed further.

I spun a pen on the desk as I thought about the permutations of human relationships. I resolved to spend some extended prayer time on the subject and went back to work on the plans for the symposium.

CHAPTER TWENTY-TWO

William Cliffe was a portly man and looked to me like Sigmund Freud. He wore a charcoal colored pin-striped suit and complimented his full beard with gold wire-rimmed glasses. Full beards were unusual in those days, and in the *pre-hippie* era, wire-rimmed glasses were merely anachronistic. In small schools like Mid-North, academic deans were not exempted from teaching duties, and so I landed in Cliffe's New Testament Introduction course.

He marched ponderously into the classroom about three minutes after the bell. Setting an alligator skinned valise on the desktop, he extracted a three-ring binder and laid it on the podium. Judging from the level of polish on the valise, it was either new, or his pride and joy. Or both. The binder also appeared to be leather covered and had bright brass-work around the edges.

I had met the man briefly at a reception for new students back in the fall, but there had been no opportunity for me to form an opinion. I had heard he was strongly against the idea of the Symposium, but he had not spoken to either Nigel or Dad about it. Therefore, I expected the class to be interesting.

"I am Doctor Cliffe. That is spelled with two F's and an E. This class is New Testament Introduction."

He spoke with a deep voice and measured cadence.

"Twelve people registered for this course, and there are twelve here in the room. That satisfies me in terms of attendance. The bulk of the course material is in the lectures. Therefore, your class attendance is essential to completing the course."

Okay, so far, so good.

"Most of you noticed, I assume with joy, that no text was specified for this course. I have not been able to find anything suitable. There are several Neo-orthodox authors who bring a fresh approach to the topic, but I find their theology abhorrent. Most of the Evangelical works in use today are far too restrictive in their treatment of the underlying text of the New Testament."

Things were beginning to get interesting.

"One of the well known rejoinders in less polite society goes something like, 'If you're so smart, how come you ain't rich?' In a similar vein, I have decided to write my own text for New Testament Introduction. The content of such is contained in my lectures. I, in fact, hope to complete the first draft of the book this next summer."

Stephen Gardiner raised his hand. I felt my stomach clenching. He was getting ready to ask one of his famous questions. Cliffe pointed imperiously. "Yes?"

"Would it be possible for us to use an early draft during this course?"

"Ahhh, the estimable Mr. Gardiner. Your reputation precedes you. You are obviously still learning that skill of thinking before speaking, I see. And no, there will be no early draft available for the students this semester, since I have not finished it yet."

I heard somebody in the back of the room mutter, "Gosh Gardiner." And that pretty much reflected my thoughts as well.

Cliffe cleared his throat and continued. "As I was saying, the contents of my lectures form the basis for my new textbook. As such, you all will be assisting me in the formative stages by your feedback, and questions raised in the coursework."

I saw what he was doing, then. This was a well known gambit by published professors everywhere. By careful design of the assignments, the students would provide much of the research for the professor's work. This was not considered unethical by the education establishment, and Cliffe was upfront about it. The students tended to have other opinions.

"Just to give you background to the course," he continued, "I grew up in Ames, Iowa. I completed my undergraduate degree at Bethel College, and then completed my doctorate in 1948 at Princeton. I then spent six years teaching at Fuller Seminary before coming to Mid-North as the Dean of Religion."

I wondered what had precipitated his move to the mid-west. While taking a dean's position was nominally a move up for a professor, a teaching post at Fuller was prestigious. Mid-North was a backwater, comparatively. Maybe he just hated California.

Cliffe went on to list the monographs he had written, as well as the two books he had published. He continued with a detailed listing of his academic accomplishments. At the fifteen minute mark I began to wonder how long he could continue to talk about himself. I detected a certain restlessness in the class. After about twenty minutes he wound down his *I love me* lecture, and began talking about the class requirements.

The semester would consist of two papers, and bi-weekly quizzes. It would conclude with a final exam. That was not a heavy load for a graduate level course. I wondered how he would succeed in getting feedback and research from the students, if this was all the work he required. Maybe he was planning to coast through the class, so he could focus on his manuscript.

Halfway through the class he finally launched into a discussion on the authorship of Matthew. Funny, I always thought Matthew had written his eponymous book. Cliffe not only explored the cultural backgrounds to the book, but also discussed the various documentary theories.

I scribbled notes as he lectured. I didn't know if Cliffe's thoughts were further to the left of Dr. Carper, but his means of tossing them out to the class meant that they were definitely more incendiary. I was assembling the pieces in my mind when Gardiner raised his hand again. Somebody in the back of the room said, "Uh oh."

"Yes, Mr. Gardiner, what is it time?" Cliffe sounded as thought he struggled to maintain his patience.

"Sir, it seems you are saying that the origins of Matthew are somewhat murky."

"That may be one way to phrase it, Mr. Gardiner. What is your point?"

"How can we be sure of the inspiration of Matthew if Matthew did not write it?"

Perhaps I was too quick to write off Gardiner. He asked precisely the question I wanted to ask. But, I had decided to keep my mouth shut for a lot of reasons.

"Mr. Gardiner," Cliffe said with a hint of exaggerated patience in his voice. "The origin and inspiration of the Gospel of Matthew are two different questions. We have the universal testimony of the church to Matthew's inspiration."

"But doesn't the church testify of Matthew's authorship?" Gardiner persisted.

"That presents a very weak argument, Gardiner. That is the reason you are in this class. Now, may I go on?"

Cliffe took a deep breath, than began lecturing again. He was erudite, and carefully examined various views on the history of Matthew. I had to be careful to pay attention. I kept trying to analyze what I was hearing and would miss a sentence of the lecture. I had studied some of this material on my own over the past several years. It was superficially attractive. How could we not understand the Scriptures better by studying the background and authorship? However, I strongly felt we needed to keep in front of us the overriding purpose of studying the Scriptures -- to gain a better understanding of Christ, and through him, God. This was as true of the seminary student as it was of the layman in the pew.

Discussions of the cultural backgrounds of the New Testament were valuable in helping us understand passages that were obscure to twentieth century readers. I was convinced that discussions on the cultural backgrounds, which were used to raise questions about authorship, were ultimately a tactic used by Satan to break the Scriptures, whatever William Cliffe personally believed. This first day of classes led me to conclude Nigel had a bigger problem than he thought.

Going from New Testament Introduction to the next class was another kind of a shock. Elementary Hebrew was badly misnamed. There was nothing elementary about the language. I had thought to study it while at McKisson University and bailed out a week into the semester. I didn't have that option here. It was a requirement for my degree program. I wasn't looking forward to the slog.

On the other hand, the Hebrew teacher was none other than Dr. Voysey. I knew he would not make the course any easier, but I also would not have to constantly filter what I was hearing against orthodox thought. After sitting through a semester of his teaching, I was familiar with his quirks – and they were legion. But I was comfortable he would teach me Hebrew, or I would die trying. The workload was going to be amazing.

As I was leaving Voysey called to me. "Cathcart! A moment of your time?"

I walked over to where he was packing up his things. "Yes, Sir?"

"I understand you are taking New Testament Intro?"

"Yes, Sir."

He squinted at me, as if he was sizing me up. "Be careful around William Cliffe."

"I understand," I replied. And I did understand.

Voysey studied me some more. "Yes, I believe you do. He is a dangerous man."

I raised an eyebrow, and nodded. "More than just his doctrine, then?"

Voysey grunted. "In addition to his doctrine."

"Thank you for the advice."

He shrugged, and then turned his piercing look upon me again. "And don't think you can slack off in Hebrew, Cathcart. This is an unforgiving course."

"This is my second try at the language, Sir. I intend to finish."

"See that you do."

Without another word, Dr. Clarke Voysey launched himself out of the classroom. I followed more slowly, pondering the conversation. As I had learned from the pastorate, any Christian organization was vastly more complex than appeared on the surface. It was true of Mid-North College, and I had forgotten. I was thankful that Voysey reminded me.

Normally, the college did not hold chapel on Fridays. But since this was the second day of classes, the administration scheduled a chapel session. As I walked across campus towards the chapel building, Sancy Pearlman stepped up beside me. Sancy was a middle-aged English professor and unmarried. She also acted as the unofficial counselor for the women employees at the college.

"So, Beryl, how are you finding your classes this semester?" she asked as she walked beside me. She was nearly my height and matched my stride. She wore what would later be called a granny dress, and it swirled about her ankles.

I said the first thing that came to mind. "I merely walked to the class room building, and searched until I found a room number that matched my schedule."

"You recent experiences have done nothing for your mouth, young man!"

I grinned at her. "Purely self defense, Miss Pearlman. Having been skewered by you in the past, I was instantly on my guard."

"Ha! Just be glad you are not taking remedial English."

"Oh, you don't know *how* glad."

She walked along with me for a few more paces before she spoke again. "Seriously, Beryl, what do you think of your professors?"

"I've got Voysey for Hebrew, and I think I'm glad."

She snorted. "Such ambivalence. Still, you probably have the right sentiments. Are you taking any other courses?"

"New Testament Intro."

She glanced over at me with a raised eyebrow. "That would be taught by our Dean of Religion, I suspect."

"Correct as usual," I said. "An interesting course and an interesting class session."

"I took that course, once upon a time," she said.

"And what was your conclusion?"

"It did not end well," she said.

"Is that so?"

"Come by my office, sometime, Beryl. We'll talk."

"I believe I shall," I replied.

When we entered the double doors to the chapel, she peeled off to sit near the front with some of the other faculty. I selected my usual seat near the back and along an aisle. I hated standing in the middle of a crowd of students taking their own sweet time leaving the building. Besides, I had a lunch appointment.

CHAPTER TWENTY-THREE

"Mr. C, when the Mafia was visiting, if Beryl had acted as he usually does, he might be on crutches today, too," Nigel said.

"Believe me, Nigel," Dad said, "that was at the forefront of my mind. We don't need two gimpies around here."

We were on our way to the Rockford Country Club for our lunch meeting with the U.S. Attorney. I had managed to place the events of the morning in the back of my mind, so I could focus on the lunch meeting. Dad was driving, and Nigel had wedged himself into the front seat. Dad had moved the seat all the way back to accommodate our friend, and I had been needling him about looking like a child behind the wheel.

"Maybe we could drop Nigel off at the rescue mission. Then we wouldn't have to worry about any gimpies."

"That's just a couple blocks off Main Street, isn't it?" Dad asked. "It would be no trouble at all."

In the months since Nigel had gotten shot, and through his multiple surgeries, he had developed his martyred sigh to a high art-form, and he used it then.

"Just no appreciation for the brains of this outfit. Here, I drag myself from my sick-bed to lend the benefit of vast expertise..."

"And I'm just the chauffeur, right?" Dad asked.

"I would never suggest anything like that," Nigel said.

"Hey, Nige," I interrupted, "the glare from your halo is bothering me."

"Probably because you are under conviction about something," he replied.

I leaned forward and popped the back of his head with my hand. "You can't be that sick."

"And violence is the last refuge of the incompetent."

"That's pretty good, Nigel," Dad said. "Did you just make it up?"

"I think so."

"Wait a minute," I yelled. "You didn't just make that one up Nigel. Let me see... okay. Salvor Hardin said that."

"Who's he?" Dad asked.

"He's a character in one of Asimov's books. *Foundation*. You're plagiarizing, Nigel."

"Nonsense. You are simply being too critical," he replied.

"Dad, I think we're going to have to call Funder College and ask to see Nigel's doctoral dissertation. It's probably a complete fraud. We'll save the school an enormous embarrassment."

Dad shook his head. "I don't know, guys. I think I'm going to need to take a stick to see if I can find the bottom of that mud hole before I wade in."

"Just use one of Nigel's crutches. There is no doubt they have been used for that before."

We drove up to the front entrance of the country club, and I was a bit disappointed. I was on a roll and had seldom run up the score against Nigel to that extent. When in that mode, I could keep the zingers going for a long time. One of the parking attendants moved around to open Dad's door for him. I got out of the back and opened Nigel's door to help him out.

Another parking attendant waited along the drive, and saw Nigel struggling to swing his bad leg around to get out of the car. He trotted over.

"Can I help you, Sir?"

In that instant, Nigel's face twist into a snarl. "No! I am not a child!"

Just as quickly it smoothed back over, and Nigel was his normal, affable self. "I'm very sorry. I got impatient there. Yes, I would appreciate the help."

We levered him out of the seat and got his crutches attached. The attendant carefully walked with Nigel up to the door. Dad followed and gave me a puzzled look. Nigel stopped, and fished in his pocket, pulling out a money clip. He peeled out a couple of dollar bills and handed them to the startled attendant.

"Here you go. Thanks for your help. And once again, I apologize for yelling at you."

We made our way into the lobby of the club house, leaving a bewildered parking attendant in our wake. I was surprised too. After a few moments, I leaned towards him.

"Did you skip your pain medicine this morning?"

He looked disgusted. "Yes. I thought I would try to start easing off of it. Apparently, I was wrong, and I took it out on that poor fellow. I feel like a louse."

Dad stepped up next to us. "Would you like us to take you back home? If you're hurting that badly, there's no need for you to be here."

"Thanks, Mr. C, but I'll be alright once I sit down."

"Okay then, let's get you to the dining room."

That was one of the things I always liked about my dad. If he thought you were being stupid, he would quietly make a suggestion to help you retrieve the situation. If you didn't follow his advice, he would step back and let you learn your lessons on your own dime. It was sometimes painful, but it taught me to listen to him more.

The U.S. Attorney was tall, chunky, and had graying blond hair. He looked like he might have been an ex-football player. He also seemed to have more energy than any human being should be allowed. He was standing in the corner of the private dining room when we walked in. He bounded over to us.

"Hi, I'm Ronson Hyde."

"Daryl Cathcart," Dad said. "This is Nigel Robart, the President of Mid-North College. And, this is my son Beryl."

"Glad to meet you," He said. He pumped each of our hands in turn. "I'm glad you called me. I did not know our friends from the city were in town."

"So, you don't watch for those things?" I asked.

He looked at me like I had stepped in the mud and tracked it across the room. "He's a private citizen, Mr. Cathcart. While we certainly have suspicions about his business activities, I cannot start an investigation without authorization from Washington."

"So why are we here today, then?" I asked.

"Beryl," Dad warned.

"No, wait a minute," I said. "When you talked to him yesterday, Dad, he fell all over himself to set up a meeting. And I'll bet you will be picking up the tab for the lunch."

Hyde straightened himself, almost to a position of attention. "Perhaps there was a misunderstanding. I'm sorry for taking up your valuable time."

Dad held up a hand, and Hyde stopped speaking. "Beryl sometimes speaks a bit bluntly. I will be happy to cover the lunch. But, he did have a point."

I could see the federal lawyer wilting under Dad's gaze. The old Daryl Cathcart intimidation was alive and well.

"Perhaps I spoke hastily, Sir."

Dad gazed at him for a bit longer; then stretched out his arm. "Please, let's be seated."

After Hyde stepped past him, Nigel looked over at me and pursed his lips in a silent whistle. I wasn't sure what it was I said that set the government man off, but Dad wasn't having it. And I was mentally keeping score. Over the course of two days, Dad had managed to stare down an organized crime boss *and* a federal employee. I don't know how he did it.

The lunch meeting seemed inconclusive to me. Hyde asked questions, and he was skillful. He was non-committal though, when Dad asked for suggestions on what the Justice Department thought about the situation. And, he ordered the most expensive item on the menu.

The parking attendant brought Dad's Cadillac around to the front of the clubhouse, and we wrestled Nigel back into the front seat. I leaned against the upholstery in the back seat and marveled at the smooth, stately quiet of the DeVille as Dad drove across the city streets of Rockford. I could get used to something like this, but I didn't want to say anything. Dad would, once again, lecture me on how I should be driving a proper automobile. I thought about the strange meeting.

"So, what was it I said that set Hyde off?" I asked.

"Just your innate natural talent," Nigel suggested. I had stung him pretty well on the ride over to the club, and I knew he was itching to get even.

Dad jumped in to forestall another match between Nigel and me. "I think maybe he thought you were a lot younger than you are and was annoyed."

"Annoyed at the smart-mouthed youngster, you mean."

"Something like that."

"But, why didn't he tell us how to deal with D'Amato?" I asked.

"I was kind of curious about that, too," Nigel said.

"One thing he said that was probably true," Dad replied. "He is probably calling Washington for guidance on how to answer us. I expect he is afraid to do anything that might get him into trouble."

"Like going to the bathroom without permission," I said.

"You do that all the time," Nigel said. "One of these days we have to get you housebroken."

Dad groaned. "I don't think I can take this anymore."

Nigel wanted to spend some time at the office, so we drove back to the campus. Dad and Nigel spent the afternoon reviewing the school finances, and I worked on plans for the Symposium. Finally, at about six o'clock, we drove Nigel around the corner to the president's residence. There was a white Mustang convertible parked in the driveway when we arrived at Nigel's house.

"Looks like your dinner arrived, Nige," I said.

"Can I come home with you, Mr. C?" he asked.

Dad laughed out loud. "I suspect Ellen would not look lightly upon you missing one of her dinners."

"It's not that I mind the dinners, it's just that she won't let me stop eating."

During my brief dating relationship with Ellen, I had learned she was a wonderful cook, but the quantities were huge. Nigel had always been slightly plump, but I noticed he was bulking up a bit.

"You *are* getting a bit pudgy, Nigel."

"Shut up!"

I climbed out of the back seat and opened his door. "Come on. Let's get you in the house so you can face your just desserts."

"Oh, very funny, Beryl." He had a sour look on his face.

I walked along side as he worked his way up the steps to the porch with his crutches. He was actually getting more accomplished with them. He let himself in the door and waved me on.

"See you tomorrow, Beryl."

"'Night, Nige."

Dad had moved the car seat up again, when I climbed in. "How about that – you can reach the pedals."

He looked over at me. "You know, if you weren't my son, I could be persuaded to leave you on the sidewalk."

"Naaah," I replied. "You love me too much."

"Don't push it, Beryl."

"What are we going to do about D'Amato?"

"I'm going to let it ride a couple of days and then give Ronson Hyde another call. Presumably, he will have heard from Washington by then."

"I don't mind telling you, Dad, that those guys scared me."

He nodded as he guided the car off campus. "I don't much like it either. But, there are certain rules everybody follows in these games. As long as you stay within the sandbox, there is no great risk."

If that's the worst thing that happens this week, I'll be happy," I said.

"Optimism is good," he said. "I may have even found a finance man for the school."

"Did you, now?"

"Yep. Accounting grad from Mid-North about five years ago."

"What's he doing now?"

"He's on the staff of a Christian camp over near Chicago. He's looking for another ministry."

I thought about that for a few moments. "At least he's used to not making much. This would be a step up. If he was working for Arthur Andersen or something, he probably wouldn't be able to afford to come here."

"I thought much the same thing," Dad said. "He is not very busy during the winter, I guess. He agreed to drive over here for a couple days next week."

"Good. I'd like to see you get some of the load off you."

"I need to Beryl, but honestly? I'm having the time of my life. And I think I'm closer to the Lord than I've ever been."

"It has been an interesting ride, Dad. I just hope we can make something of this."

He drove back around to the front of the Administration Building and swung in next to my car. He tapped his fingers on the steering wheel as he thought. "You know, I don't think the Lord will let His ministries be shut down while they are effective. We have students. We have some dedicated faculty. We are getting a handle on the financial problems. No, I think Mid-North is going to be around for a while."

CHAPTER TWENTY-FOUR

It didn't seem like I had a weekend. Or, it seemed like I spent it in the car. When I got home Friday afternoon, Mrs. Marsden had left a list of calls on the spindle in my kitchen. Some of our migrant Methodists were getting restless. They had been attending the new members' class and were anxious to start contributing to the ministry. I was anxious for them to work their way into the congregation as well, but was chary about rushing things. Lane and I spent Friday afternoon and evening visiting some of the families, and picked it up again Saturday morning. I was thankful I had used the Christmas vacation to get ahead on my sermon prep. It certainly didn't happen that weekend.

Lane and Liz had me over for dinner Saturday night and also invited Avis and Christine. It was an opportunity for good fellowship over a good meal. We spent some time brainstorming about ways to put our new members to work, especially since they were so anxious to get started. We ended the time with prayer. I went home, glanced at my sermon notes, then buried myself in Hebrew for the rest of the evening. Sunday flew by.

So it was Monday, and I again found myself in Dr. Cliffe's NTI class. Once the man settled into the content, he was not bad. He wasn't a great teacher, but his lecture material was solid. Cliffe had spoken in chapel once during the first semester, and he was capable there too. He knew how to modulate his voice as he spoke, and the sermons were well constructed. I hadn't realized, until Gardiner told me, that Cliffe also taught homiletics.

Stephen slipped over next to me at the end of class. "Beryl, we're having a prayer meeting tonight in the chapel – for the Symposium."

I glanced at him as I tried to arrange my notes in the correct order. "What time?"

"Nine o'clock. Can you be there?"

That was right in the middle of my evening. I expected to be submerged in either homework or sermon prep at that time.

"Bad time, Gardiner," I said. I saw the disappointment on his face and reconsidered. "But, I guess if I take time off for worship in prayer, I believe God will honor me in my studies."

He brightened again. "That would be great if you could, Beryl. Everybody knows you are leading the effort."

I wasn't sure that needed to be common knowledge, but it was probably too late now. "Okay, nine o'clock in the chapel. Is it okay if I bring a friend?"

"Sure. That would be great."

"I'll see you then."

We turned to leave, and Cliffe was still standing at the podium rubbing his chin as he studied us.

"You know, Gentlemen, I am all in favor of investing time in prayer. It is a great way to draw near to God. But, I have some real reservations about holding a conference dedicated to a questionable concept." He frowned. "Oh, I suppose it is harmless enough, but people will resent having this rammed down their throat!"

His last sentence ended with some real venom. We watched as he shoved his papers in the pristine valise and marched out of the room. Gardiner looked at the door for a few moments, then turned to me.

"Do you suppose we are going to have trouble there, Beryl?"

"Do hens lay eggs?"

"I think I'll pray for him while I'm at it," Gardiner said.

"Stephen, you shame me. We ought to pray for all our teachers. Thanks for the reminder."

"I'm not... sure that's what I meant."

"I think that's what the Lord meant. Listen, I've got to run. If I arrive late for Hebrew, Voysey will have my head."

"Don't let me stop you," he replied quickly. "I'll see you tonight."

"Sure thing."

I had plenty of time to get to Hebrew – it was right down the hall. But there was something else I wanted to do. I trotted to the lobby of the classroom building, and dropped a nickel into the pay phone.

"Brinker Chrysler-Plymouth." Connie's voice had an interesting timbre. It was almost furry, with a slight lilt that sounded like her mother's accent.

"Prayer meeting tonight on campus at nine. Are you interested? Maybe we could get a cup of coffee afterwards."

"Sure."

"I'll pick you up at about twenty till."

"I just got my new car this morning. How about if I pick you up at ten till?"

"Fine with me. I'll look forward to seeing what you bought."

"Great. See you then."

"Okay. I gotta run. Hebrew is next."

My day somehow brightened. It was probably a mistake for me to make the call right before Hebrew. I was now seriously distracted. I walked into the classroom pondering the difference in my feelings now, compared to when I was dating Ellen.

With Ellen I had been firmly in the grip of infatuation – the heart-pounding, palm-sweating, back-tingling rush that resembled an unending roller-coaster ride. After talking to Connie, I felt like I was on a boat, gliding across a deep, still pound. The theme was one of quiet contentment, I thought.

I took a firm hold of my thoughts and carefully placed them into an inner closet. Connie and I had been out less than a half dozen times, and my experience with Ellen made me cautious. Besides, Dr. Voysey had just loped in the room and any inattention would be lethal.

I got a good look at the '55 Plymouth when Connie pulled up under the street light.

"Where did you get this? It's beautiful."

"Mr. Brinker has been telling me I needed something so Mama wouldn't have to bring me to work each day. He took this in trade and offered it to me. Sully said it was a great deal."

I noticed the seat belts and buckled up. "This thing looks brand new."

"Little old lady, believe it or not. Daddy looked at the car and told me I'd be crazy not to buy it. He did order me to have the seat belts installed."

"From personal experience, I can tell you that's a very good idea."

"I agree, and I hope to never find out," she said sincerely.

"I hope you don't, either."

She slipped the clutch and eased away from the curb. I heard the low moan of the flat-head six as we accelerated.

"I didn't know you knew how to drive a stick."

"Daddy made all us kids learn before he would let us get our driving licenses."

"Your Dad must be one smart cookie."

She looked over with a smile. "I know he is hard to get to know, but he's really a good guy."

"He takes good care of his girls," I said.

I could see her eyes sparkle in the evening lights. "Mama and I think so. I was surprised he let me out of the house by myself tonight."

"He seems pretty careful."

"I think he trusts you, Beryl."

I thought about what she said for several moments before I replied. "I will do my best to be worthy of that trust."

"I know you will."

"How's Sully doing?" I asked. I was a little uncomfortable with the conversation and changed the subject.

"He's always been a good salesman, but I think his sales have gone up a lot since he got saved."

"Is he working harder then? He seemed to have a lot of hustle when I first met him."

"He doesn't seem to. He spends his spare time in his office with his Bible. But he keeps closing the sales."

"That's got to make Brinker happy."

She chuckled. It was a low sound, deep in her throat. I kind of liked it. "Mr. Brinker doesn't know what to think of Sully. He's making more money for him than he ever has before, but Mr. Brinker is scared to walk into Sully's office."

"What do the other people think?"

"Chester doesn't care. He told me that if it took religion to get Sully on the wagon, more power to him."

"Is Chester a Christian?"

Connie shrugged. "I don't know. I've tried to talk to him a couple of times since Sully got saved. He says he's doing just fine."

"I'd guess that's a *no*," I said.

"That's what I think too. But, I've started to pray for him and the other guys in the shop. I have a whole mission field there and never thought about it."

"That's the way it is with most of us, I think. I mean, I'm a pastor, so people just naturally think I'm going to preach at them. But I get out of the habit of talking to people about their souls."

"I don't want to get out of that habit again," she said, fervently. "I was really glad when you led Sully to the Lord, but I was embarrassed, too."

We drove on to the campus. A few snow flurries drifted past the street lights as we rolled past the dark buildings. The chapel was well lit, and we found a parking space in front.

"Stephen Gardiner was pretty excited about having the prayer meeting tonight," I said.

"Is he the one who asks the stupid questions?"

"The one and only. He has really pitched in to help with the preparations for the Symposium, though. If he can learn to think a little before asking questions, I think he will do well."

"He must be entertaining," she said.

"Most of the time he's just a nice person. He's even nice when he's being dumb."

The college kids were ten years younger than we were, and I was instantly aware of the relative immaturity. Gardiner had recruited heavily from the dormitories, and there were nearly one-hundred young men and women at the meeting. While they were full of giggles and inconsequential discourse, they were clearly serious about the prayer meeting.

I guess memories fade, but being around these eighteen to twenty-year-olds reminded me of the earnestness with which they approached these things. Everything was, for that moment, of the utmost importance. So, they were focused on their prayer.

Gardiner had recruited several other graduate students, so we broke into several smaller groups, with the older students leading, and had some serious prayer. And their sober prayer impressed me. I was then convinced that we would indeed have a Symposium on the Reliability of Scripture, and God would bless it with great success.

Following the prayer meeting, everyone trooped over to the *Gutter*, which I still thought was an unfortunate name for the campus snack shop. Connie and I sat together and talked quietly, surrounded by the undergraduate magpies. The coffee was really not very good, but the company was pleasant.

We did not stay long. After about fifteen minutes, I excused myself to visit the restroom. I was washing my hands when Stephen Gardiner slammed into the room.

"Hey Beryl, where in the world did you find the babe?"

"What?"

"Connie. She's gorgeous."

"Huh?" I was apparently not making very much sense.

"Really, Cathcart, I don't know how you do it. She's a knockout."

"She's a friend of a friend. We were introduced, and we've sort of gone out a few times."

He grinned as he punched me on the shoulder. "You rascal, you."

I left the restroom as he headed over to the urinal. I was kind of bemused. It occurred to me that I had met Connie when I was in the thrall of Ellen Holgate, who I still thought of as the blond goddess. In the reflected light of Ellen, my initial impression of Connie was that she was... pleasant looking.

Now, as I walked across the main room at the *Gutter*, I really looked at Connie for the first time. My knees nearly buckled, and I felt my pulse racing, and I distantly hoped she did not notice the silly smile on my face. She was... beautiful. I had not noticed that before. How had I missed it? I stepped up to her and took a deep breath.

"All set?" she asked.

I nodded, not trusting myself to speak without a quaver. We stepped out into blowing snow, and I followed her to the car. I somehow managed not to drag my knuckles on the sidewalk. It seemed she carried the conversation for the ride back to my apartment. I think I managed monosyllabic replies, through my emotional turmoil. She pulled over to the curb across the street.

"Beryl, what happened back there?"

I looked at her dark eyes and felt myself falling into them. What was the matter with me? After Ellen, I had learned not to act this way. Or so I thought.

Sometimes when you can't think of anything else to say, just blurt out the truth. "I don't quite know how to say this without seeming the complete idiot... but, tonight before we left, I just realized how beautiful you are."

She just gazed at me with those beautiful eyes for a long time. That deep, still pond turned into Niagara Falls – my emotions were roaring. Finally, she placed her hands on both sides of my face, then leaned forward and kissed me chastely on the lips.

"I had a wonderful time tonight, Beryl. Thank-you."

A distant part of my mind, where the sane Beryl Cathcart lived, decided it was a good time to get out of the car. I looked through the windshield at the blowing snow.

"You'd better call me when you get home," I said, pointing outside.

She nodded. I managed to clamber out of her pristine Plymouth without falling on my behind. I watched as she drove off; then walked into my apartment. I walked directly to the phone and dialed her number.

"Hello."

"Mr. Seabright, this is Beryl Cathcart."

"What is it, Beryl?"

"Connie just dropped me off, and I thought you might want to watch for her. The weather is getting kind of wintry."

There was a pause. "I see." His voice was much warmer now. "I will. Thank you for calling, Beryl."

"Yes, Sir. Good night, Sir."

"Good night, Beryl."

CHAPTER TWENTY-FIVE

I awakened to a chilly apartment – it had gotten cold overnight. This made for good sleeping, but I had to sternly override my body's demands to stay under the covers and sleep in on that Tuesday morning. I got the percolator started, and took a hot shower. I resisted the temptation to trot over to the Diner of the Scrumptious Porkchop for breakfast. I had started to gain a little weight, and didn't like where that might lead. This semester would involve a lot of sitting -- either in the classroom, the car, or at my kitchen table studying. I made do with a piece of toast.

Everything was laid out on the table for studying. I had rented a furnished apartment after the fire gutted my house. I didn't want to through the hassle of furnishing a place until the house was rebuilt. So... no desk. I ate at one end of the table, and used the other end as my office.

Dragging myself out of bed gave me the morning to study. Based upon a few days' experience, I estimated I was going to spend twenty hours per week on Hebrew. My personal knowledge of the New Testament would get me over the rough spots in New Testament Introduction. I hoped. William Cliffe was a wild card, both in his course content, and what seemed like a slightly erratic personality.

So, at the table, I started scratching Hebrew words on small memory cards, and struggled to focus my mind totally on this archaic and complex language. My mind wanted to slip over to the church in Appleton, and next Sunday's messages. If not that then, it was the problems Dad faced at Mid-North. Most of all my mind wanted to swirl around the previous night's date with Connie Seabright.

I had firmly made up my mind that I didn't have time to fall in love again. Once in a year was plenty. I had only recently recovered from the emotional tatters of the failed relationship with Ellen. There seemed to be a slight thaw developing there, which I hoped would develop into a friendship, if not just toleration. She and Nigel seemed to be drawing closer to one another, and that meant I would be seeing a lot of her. I wondered if she and Connie had discussed the complex web which events wove about us.

As I plowed my way through the homework, and Dr. Voysey did not stint on assigning work to his students, I gradually became aware of the squeak-rumble on the floor above me. Once it had intruded into my consciousness, there was no ejecting it. With a sigh, I shoved my chair back, and stood up. If I was going to continue to live in that place, I needed to do something about the noise.

As I walked up the stairs to the second floor of the apartment building, I wondered who I would meet. I didn't remember seeing anyone coming or going from there, but my hours were a little odd as well. I could clearly hear the rhythmic noise from outside the apartment in the hallway. I tapped on the door, and the noise stopped. The door was opened by a frail, white-haired lady, who looked to be about half my height.

"Yes, young man?"

"Hi, um, I'm Beryl from downstairs. I just wanted to introduce myself."

"Well, don't just stand there. Come on in."

I followed her across the room, and noticed she had wrapped herself in an afghan. If anything, her apartment was even more chilled than mine. She walked over to a wooden rocking chair and slipped into it.

"Don't just stand there, have a seat, young man."

I sat down in a lumpy easy chair across from her. She bent over and picked up a hot-water bottle from the scarred hardwood floor, and placed it in her lap. On a side table next to her was a well-worn Bible, and a cup on a saucer. A Lipton's tag was hanging from the cup. Now that I was there I didn't know what to say. She began rocking in the chair, and I then

216

identified the source of the noise that was so annoying in my apartment below.

"I suppose you will want to complain about all the racket up here."

"Oh, no. You don't make *that* much noise."

She cackled. "Used to have a young feller next door. Parties every night. Had to call the police a couple of times. Finally the landlord threw him out."

"I will keep that in mind," I said. "No wild parties."

"So, what do you do, young man?"

"I'm a student over at Mid-North College, and I also pastor a church downstate."

"I must be forgetting my manners," she said. "My name is Jessie Pearlman."

"I'm Beryl Cathcart."

She nodded. "And what brings you to Mid-North?"

"The president is a friend of mine, and he suggested some graduate work would be good for me. Twisted my arm, actually."

"A good education goes a long ways. My husband and I graduated from Mid-North in 1902."

"Are you a believer, then?"

"Oh, yes. We served on the mission field in Bolivia. I decided this was as good a place as any to retire after Thomas passed away."

I made the connection, then. "You have a daughter working at the school?"

Her smile warmed up. "You have met my Sancy, then. We sent her to school here, hoping she would meet a man who would serve the Lord with her. Instead, she fell in love with the school."

"I can see why you would like to live here."

"That, and being near the school. I cannot get out as much as I used to, but I try to visit over there."

"I see." I looked around. "It's a bit chilly in these apartments. Yours may be even colder than mine."

She nodded as she continued to rock. "I spend a lot of time in my chair here. With the afghan, the water bottle, and my tea, I get along."

I noticed she wore heavy woolen socks under her slippers. The poor thing must be freezing up here. I stood up.

"I suppose I should be getting back to my homework. I'm taking Hebrew, and it looks like it is going to be tough."

She smiled, now. "I remember taking Hebrew. It was difficult. Well, don't let me keep you, young Mr. Cathcart. Be sure to come visit again, though."

"I will."

I left her apartment and returned to mine. I now had a mission for the day, and Hebrew was forgotten. Well maybe not forgotten. I simply decided I had something more important to do, even though there would be an eventual accounting from Voysey.

I put on my coat, scraped the frost off the car and drove over to the offices of Property Management Partners of Rockford. I had not been there before, but I sent the monthly checks to the address. Darlene Swanson was not in the office, but the receptionist immediately led me to the president's office once she found out who I was.

"How can I help the Cathcart's today?" Ken Sweeney asked.

"More of a minor complaint, really," I said.

He folded his hands and leaned forward across his desk. "Please, what can we do?"

"The apartment I'm renting seems to be unusually cold."

He frowned. "Unfortunately, I'm too aware of that, Mr. Cathcart. We bought the building several years ago, thinking the price was right. We discovered the oil furnace mainly burns money. We've talked about replacing the whole heating system there, but the economics just don't make sense, right now." He held his hands open.

"I understand. Dad's been in the business, as you know. I am mainly concerned about Mrs. Pearlman."

"Oh, yes, the widow that lives above you. She has lived there for fifteen years."

"I visited her this morning. She was wrapped in an afghan, and was sitting with a hot-water bottle."

"Oh, my." He shook his head. "We really would like to help her find a warmer place to live. We approached her daughter, who keeps an eye on her, to find a warmer place, but the old lady won't leave."

"She seems to be a real character," I suggested.

He grinned. "She certainly is. Said she had gotten by for forty years in the mountains of Bolivia. A few cold days in Rockford wasn't going to hurt her."

"Have you ever given any thought to carpeting the apartments?"

"That may happen at some time in the future. We need to get through a few years on the depreciation schedule first."

I thought about my own objectives. The sound of her rocking chair was driving me crazy. "How about if I cover the cost of putting carpet in her living room? At least she wouldn't have a cold floor to walk on."

I left the property management offices with one goal accomplished. I felt guilty about helping out an old lady merely to take care of my own annoyances. But Ken Sweeney seemed to think the carpet was a wonderful idea and decided that if I was willing to pay for one room, he could certainly see that the rest of the place was carpeted as well.

Since the Pearman family was on my mind, I decided to swing by the campus on the chance my visit would coincide with Sancy's office hours. As it happened she was in her office with the door open.

"Come on in, Beryl," she said. "You look like a bewildered freshman out there."

"I hope that's not what I look like," I said as I walked into the office and dropped into the proffered chair.

"Has anybody ever told you you look young for your age?" She had a wicked grin now.

"All the time. When I get to be sixty, I'll probably be glad of it."

"It's about time you decided to come by for our talk," she said.

"Uh huh. And, by the way, I met a friend of yours this morning. In the apartment upstairs from mine."

"Oh, really? I do not have that many friends."

"This is an older lady named Jessie."

"Oh. You live downstairs from Mother?"

"Seems that way."

"How very interesting."

"She apparently insists she copes fine with the cold."

Sancy shook her head. "I'm just afraid I'll stop by there sometime and find her frozen body. Nobody has been able to talk her in to moving."

"She likes it there."

"Other than the inadequate heating, it is a nice place. The owners have been very pleasant to Mother."

"Now that I have met her," I said, "I will try to keep an eye on her."

"She does not abide well people who want to look out for her." Sancy said.

"Including you, I presume?"

"Exactly, Beryl. I spend a lot of time biting my tongue when I visit her."

A thought occurred to me and I chuckled.

"What?"

"It just seems that the acorn didn't fall far from the tree, Miss Pearlman."

"I have ways of getting even you know."

"Somehow, I suspect you do. Now tell me about Mid-North."

She sat back in her chair and looked at me. "I can only relate my experiences and perceptions, Beryl. But let me try to tell you what I have seen."

I nodded. "I would like to hear it."

"I came to school here in the fall of 1936. My parents were on the field, of course. I had grown up in Bolivia, and really did not know anyone here. At the time, Mid-North was smaller than it is, even now. So, we all knew each other – the students and the professors. It reminded me of the times the missionaries would get together. Everyone able to make the trip would gather in LaPaz. We would have worship services, and Bible studies. And lots of fellowship. There were missionaries from Peru, Chile, even Ecuador."

"I was dreadfully homesick. I had only been in the states twice before. There were other missionary kids, we called them MKs, at Mid-North, so I was able to rather immediately make some friends. Once I settled in it was wonderful."

"You majored in English, then?"

"Yes. I graduated in 1940. I had carefully noted to a few people of my interest in staying here. I, of course, prayed long and hard about it. The Provost suggested that if I were to earn a masters degree, there would be an appointment to the faculty. He recommended Beloit College. It was right up the road and had been a pioneer in admitting women students. He felt I would do better there than someplace like, maybe, the University of Chicago."

"You are uncomfortable in large cities?" I asked.

"I grew up in LaPaz, which was fairly large. No, the culture still bewilders me, however. I'm happiest to just stay on campus."

"I see. So you returned here to work, then?"

"Yes. I managed the Master of Arts in a year and came right back. I have been here nearly twenty-five years now."

"When did things begin to change?" I decided to be blunt about it, and see how she reacted.

"When President Weathers came to Mid-North in 1950, I think, was when the stage was set. He was a friend of Harold John Ockenga, and Charles Fuller. He was not unorthodox. Far from it. His dream was to make Mid-North a center of Evangelical scholarship in the mid-west."

"That can be a challenge," I said. "You don't get that reputation by just announcing it."

"Correct, Beryl. And with Wheaton and Trinity just down the road, as it were, the competition for both students and teachers was fierce. And those schools have much deeper pockets."

"So what happened?"

"President Weathers had to reach down into the second tier for talent. He brought in John Osmo as the Dean of Religion. Almost immediately there were problems. The religion faculty did not appreciate being passed over for the position. And it soon became apparent that Osmo was *not* Evangelical. He lasted for three years before the rest of the faculty managed to drive him off. Weathers resigned in disgust."

"That would seem to be the end of the problem," I said.

"Not at all, Beryl. You see the other faculty hated Osmo because he wasn't from here. It did not have anything to do with his doctrine."

"So they did the right thing for the wrong reasons."

"Exactly. And God does not often reward that kind of behavior. William Cliffe was one of Osmo's students."

"Light dawns. And since Cliffe went to school here, he was one of *us*."

"Yes. He went to Princeton for his doctoral work, and came back with what I call the infection."

"So he is not an Evangelical?"

"What is an Evangelical, Beryl?" she fired back. "Bill Cliffe is more conservative than was Osmo. On the other hand, he certainly drank from Osmo's fountain."

"How long has Cliffe been here?"

"Ten years now. He has had time to insinuate several of his favored friends into the faculty."

"Who are those friends?"

"I think I am not going to tell you that," she said. "This is something you must find out for yourself."

"Voysey probably won't tell me," I said.

"Clarke might just surprise you. He is easily the most conservative professor we have here. However, he wants to stay here. So he will not rock the boat."

"Can he be engaged in private conversation?"

"Probably."

She didn't elaborate on her reply. She seemed to delight in letting me find out things for myself. While that was not a bad thing to do to encourage learning, it did leave me exposed. I guessed that was the teacher in her. I drove home pondering what she told me. As usual the background to any story is much more complex than most people would realize. I had some thinking to do.

CHAPTER TWENTY-SIX

My conversation with Sancy Pearlman really started the ball rolling for me that semester. The aura of doom hovering over the pile of homework and sermon preparation drove me back to my apartment that day. Now knowing the resident upstairs, I resolved to endure the rumble of her rocking chair and for the most part succeeded. It was like being caught in an avalanche.

I survived Hebrew on Wednesday, anyway. And, there was a sense of popping to the surface again on Wednesday afternoon. I felt confident enough in my progress to go to church Wednesday night with Connie. But even that produced mixed feelings. It was comfortable being with Connie, but Ellen sat across the aisle from us, and I endured her blistering glare through the services.

I drove over to the office on Thursday morning to talk to Dad. Nigel's Buick was in the parking lot, so I walked into his outer office.

Before I could say anything, Ellen spoke to me. "I saw you in church last night with Connie. I am not sure whether I like that."

I was rarely at a loss for words. Dad says it never happens. But, I didn't know what to say to that. My normal defense mechanism sprang into gear, and I changed the subject. "I saw Nigel's car out front. Is he available?"

"You're not going to answer me," she said. She put her hands on her hips as she sat behind the desk. "I don't know why you think you have to mess up my life like you have."

"Is there any point to arguing about this, Ellen?"

"Ignoring the problem will not make it go away."

"What do you want me to do," I asked, "roll on the floor and beg for mercy? For Pete's sake, Ellen, breaking up is never very pleasant, but it happens all the time. You need to get over it."

She glared at me for a long time. I heard the chair squeak in Nigel's office and wondered if he was listening.

"Oh, I'm sorry, Beryl. After you broke up with me, I thought a lot about it, and realized the same thing you did – we weren't right for each other. It just wasn't very much fun at the time."

This was something new: Ellen apologizing. I wondered if the Lord had been working on her.

"It wasn't a lot of fun for me either," I said. "Apology accepted."

She nodded, and picked up the phone. "Beryl would like to talk to you."

She set the phone down. "Go on in, Beryl."

"Thanks, Ellen."

I shut the office door and sat down across the desk from Nigel. He cocked his head, and waited until we could hear the rapid, machine-gun style typing in the outer office.

"Okay, we can talk, now. When she's typing she doesn't pay attention to anything else. She usually doesn't even hear the phone."

"She just apologized to me," I said.

"You'll pardon me for eaves-dropping, but I heard."

"Are you and Ellen getting serious?" I asked.

He sighed. "I don't know. Probably. We argue about everything, though. What about you and Connie?"

I shrugged. "Who knows."

He looked at me closely, then started laughing softly. "You've got it again, don't you?"

"I don't know what you're talking about."

"Uh huh. When did Cupid strike?"

I tried to glare at him, but couldn't make it stick. "Monday night," I said quietly. "But I don't want to talk about it."

"You don't need to."

"If we could get back to the topic of this meeting..."

Nigel laughed louder. "I hate to say this, Beryl, but you're hopeless."

"I was thinking pretty much the same thing."

"Since you're in that mood, I would come around and kick you, if my leg was up to it."

"How is your leg?" I asked.

"Still hurts. The doc is wondering if there is an infection in there somewhere."

"Because of the pain?"

"That and I've been running a fever when I get tired."

"So what are you doing in here anyway, Nigel? If you're not feeling good, you should stay home."

"Would you?" he asked. "I seem to remember somebody who rolled a car five times and was determined to go to class the day after he got out of the hospital."

"But I didn't go."

"That was only because we hid the car keys," Nigel said. "I suppose I could be accused of not having any good sense about my health. But, you don't need to go about calling the kettle black."

"Okay, okay. But at least I was on the mend. I think you need to be careful."

"I am being careful, Beryl. I will probably go home at lunch time and have a little nappy this afternoon."

"Good boy."

Nigel rubbed his hands together. "Now that I have sufficiently stroked my best friend, what brings you to the office?"

"I had a meeting with Sancy the other day, and she gave me the low-down on your doctrinal problems."

"Is that so?"

"Most of it seems to trace back a decade ago or so."

"Before you launch into your stem-winder, how about if we include your dad in the entertainment."

"Once more, my friend, you are misusing the word."

"What? *Entertainment*?"

"No. You know what I mean."

"Ha. Since I knew you would be in the neighborhood, I am forearmed." He spun around and pulled Merriam-Webster off the credenza behind his desk. He quickly paged through the dictionary and then slid his finger down the line of words. "Uh huh. That was the meaning I intended. I was right. You were wrong."

"I think you're lying."

"Ahhh. Retreating into your small-mindedness again. When you can't win an argument, you resort to slurs."

"Right. Your nose is growing longer."

"Since you are obviously going to be difficult, we might as well go see your Dad. At least there is *one* reasonable Cathcart around here." He dragged himself to his feet and reached for the crutches, which leaned against the desk.

I quickly jumped to my feet and pulled the crutches out his reach. "Now, who was right and who was wrong?" I asked with my most evil grin.

"Give me the crutches, Beryl."

"Say, *pretty please.*"

"When you were little you probably pulled wings off flies and stole candy from babies."

"Naaah, I just stepped on the flies."

I heard Dad's voice behind me. "Beryl, *what* are you doing?"

"Oh, I just wanted to prove that Nigel was malingering."

"Give him the crutches! Good grief, Beryl. I don't understand you sometimes."

After returning them, I turned around to face Dad. "We were just coming to see you." Then, Nigel clipped me on the back of the head with a crutch. "Ow!" I whipped back around, and he was leaning on both crutches and looking innocently at the ceiling.

Dad decided to ignore the further byplay, evidently deciding it was the safest course. "Well, I'm here. What do you two want to talk about?"

"Let's go back to your office, Mr. C." Nigel said. "I need to move around a bit."

I stepped aside, and motioned Nigel ahead. "After you."

"No, you go first. I'm afraid you'll trip me."

"And you'll probably try to run that crutch through me."

Dad finally lost patience and walked quickly from the office. Nigel and I

229

grinned at each other.

"I know it's not very respectful to your dad," Nigel said, "But it's fun to push him over the edge like that."

"But, you don't want him getting even with you, Nige. You know what they say about payback."

"You don't scare me."

"We'd better get down to his office, before he leaves the building or something."

Nigel launched himself into motion. "Right. Let's go."

Both Nigel and Dad listened carefully as I recounted the meeting with Sancy. I included the part about meeting her mother and then the narrative about the previous president and Dean of Religion.

Nigel looked thoughtful. "It's funny how the formal records of the school say nothing about things like that."

"Places like this never want to air their dirty laundry," I said. "Can you check to see if Cliffe hired Carper?"

"He did," Dad said. "I already checked."

"So, you're ahead of me, then" I said.

"Not really. When Cliffe started making snide remarks about the Symposium, it occurred to me to check. The employment records confirmed the hiring, but, once again, no details."

"Sancy gave me enough to fill in the blanks then. I wonder why the rest of the faculty tolerated Cliffe's views?" I asked. "He is pretty outspoken."

Nigel held up an index finger. "Have you heard him say anything that was clearly heretical?"

"Not yet."

"You probably won't. At least not in a clear way. The Bible professors are afraid of him. I've heard he has fired professors on the spot."

"Why has the school let him do that?"

"You remember the way things were when I took over?" Nigel asked.

I nodded. "Okay, I understand."

The previous board chairman, Charlie Bigelow, had arranged the appointment of Nigel Robart to the presidency of Mid-North College as a way to maintain his control over the place. Nigel had not only experienced Bigelow's heavy-handed control, but the faculty would also go around him to the chairman, anytime they thought they could get away with it. Nigel originally invited me to take some classes at the college as a way to help him track down some of his problems. In the past, it seemed Cliffe could get away with quite a bit.

"Did Sancy identify anyone else with suspect views?" Dad asked.

"No. She told me that was something I needed to figure out on my own."

"The woman has her own way of doing things," he said.

"I'm glad she's on our side," Nigel said.

"For some unfathomable reason, Nigel, she really likes you."

"Now, don't start that, again," Dad said.

"I'm so glad there's a voice of sanity in here," Nigel said.

"I probably shouldn't tell you this," Dad said, "but I received a resume in the mail from somebody who thinks I ought to appoint them to the presidency of this school."

Nigel shut his mouth with an audible click. I laughed and clapped my hands.

"I told you he would get even."

Dad looked at me. "I'll deal with you later."

We talked a while longer, and then I left to get back to my studies. I had to get through Hebrew for Friday, and I was not anywhere near having the Sunday messages ready to go. I was glad Nigel felt well enough to bat words around with me, and I think Dad was happy to see him feeling better. I worried about his continued recovery though.

I was getting tired of making sandwiches at home, so I drove over to the McDonald's on U.S. 51 and picked up lunch. The fries were cold by the time I got home, but I still enjoyed the meal. I resolved to drop in on my parents for supper. I hadn't talked to Mom or Ruth that week anyway.

About midway through the afternoon, I grew weary of Hebrew and pushed it aside. The sermon outline felt like an old friend, and I was able to rapidly flesh out my continuing message on the attributes of God. I was once again forced to recognize His greatness and how small I was. That reminder drove me to my knees, and I spent an hour in serious prayer. God was indeed great. Horror at the sin of the old self, and gratitude at his mercy filled my heart. I hoped I could communicate some small measure of what I felt to the congregation that Sunday.

On Friday, I packed the car before classes and planned to get on the road right after Hebrew. That was assuming I survived New Testament Introduction. Dr. Cliffe walked into the classroom and dropped his valise on the desk. He pulled out his notebook and slapped it on the lectern. Okay, he was in a bad mood. I resolved to keep my mouth shut. It didn't help.

"I fail to understand the absurd literalism of the Fundamentalist mind-set," he began. "God has given us His Word. He has also given us a brain. I believe we should use it. Or attempt to do so, given the mentality of some in this classroom."

He glared at me during the last sentence. So keeping my mouth shut wasn't going to help.

"Don't you have anything to say, Cathcart?"

"No, Sir."

"I just don't understand how this Fundamentalist slime thinks it can invade this campus and turn everybody into little robots that march to Angus McKisson's tune."

There was no question in anyone's mind who he was attacking. I was more sure than ever that the smart thing to do was to just keep quiet. But, this was a no-win situation.

"I also think it is quite cowardly not to stand up for your beliefs, eh Cathcart?"

"Yes, Sir."

"Then why are you not speaking up?"

"Sir, my purpose here is to get an education, not to stir up trouble."

"And you have caused nothing but trouble since you arrived."

He took a deep breath and scanned the class. I'm sure the rest of the students showed varying degrees of terror, fear, or concern. But I dared not look around. I resolved to let the storm blow itself out. *Maybe* things would not spin out of control.

"Very well," Cliffe said. "I believe we were outlining a harmony of the Gospels."

The relief in the room was palpable. At the same time I was severely rattled. I managed to take reasonable notes for the class session, but was thankful when the hour came to a close. Without a word, Cliffe packed up and left the room.

"Jeepers, Cathcart, what set him off?" one of the students asked.

"I don't know. I guess he just doesn't like Fundamentalists."

"I don't like Fundamentalists, either," he continued. "However, I am willing to make an exception in your case."

"Oh, thank you very much."

Several of the other students chuckled. Gardiner walked over to where I was sitting and studied me carefully.

"What?" I asked.

"I don't see any blood or broken bones. You will probably be all right."

"Thanks, Gardiner."

"Don't mention it."

In addition to the verbal attack in NTI, I had to get into the zone to handle the Hebrew class. I just hoped Voysey didn't call on me that day. Cliffe's outburst was not something I anticipated on a Friday morning, and it cast a pall over the entire day.

After class, I made my way to the Administration Building. Dad was out somewhere, but Nigel was in his office. I told him what had happened.

"And you didn't say anything to set him off?" Nigel asked.

"Nope. He walked into the classroom and immediately went on the attack."

"Not good, Beryl. Cliffe is rapidly becoming unglued."

"What should we do?"

"You've got to leave for Appleton, right?"

I nodded.

"Let's get together with your dad on Monday. I believe someone needs to have a word with William Cliffe."

"Sounds good to me, Nige. With that, I need to hit the road."

I knew there would be a stack of messages on the spindle, and I wanted to get my boots on the ground in Appleton. Heading down U.S. 51 through Rochelle, I glanced at the site of my accident. There was nothing at the place indicating the horrid aftereffects of my losing battle with the tow truck, except my memories. I was thankful to be alive, and I told the Lord that.

I sipped on a Coke as I drove – to soothe a slightly scratchy throat and a mild headache. I hoped I wasn't catching cold. Being in the pulpit with the voice of a frog, and drainage plowing a furrow down one's upper lip, was torture for both the speaker and listeners. One hundred miles later I was convinced that I was *not* catching a cold. But, I was not thankful. Instead, the mild headache had turned into one of those monsters that felt like it was going to squash my eye-balls and explode my head. I hurt all over and knew the fever was climbing. This was going to be bad.

When I arrived in Appleton, I didn't bother to gather my things from the car. I staggered into the kitchen with the last of my strength. Mrs. Marsden had arrived earlier in the afternoon to warm up the house. As I came through the door, she slid a plate with a piece of fresh apple pie on the table.

"Preacher, are you alright?"

"No. I am as sick as a dog. I'm going to bed."

I made it down the hallway and into my bedroom; then rolled into the bed with my clothes on. I had not even taken my coat off. She followed me into the room and put her hand on my head.

"Preacher, you're burning up."

"Tell me something I don't know."

She walked over to the dresser, pulled out a pair of flannel pajamas, and came over to the bed.

"Let's get you into these."

"I don't think I can."

"Yes you can. I'll help."

In hindsight, I was embarrassed to have a seventy-five-year-old woman undress me and put me into my jammies, but at the time I really didn't care. I vaguely remembered telling her that I slept in my underwear, but she deftly rolled me into the bed and covered me up.

A few minutes later she came back into the room with a glass of water and a couple aspirin.

"Here, Preacher, take these."

She plumped the pillows and tucked me in. "Get some sleep preacher. You've got the flu, and it's a good thing you made it home."

She snapped the light switch off as she walked out. I drifted off to sleep thinking I had never heard anything quite like the long, drawn-out echo of the sound of that light switch.

CHAPTER TWENTY-SEVEN

If you have suffered the flu, you have probably blotted it from your memory as too unpleasant to even recall. If you have not, it's something to be avoided at all costs. I have always been healthy. The occasional cold or headache was about all I ever suffered. It sounds kind of lame to explain how rotten I felt. It was just that I never experienced anything like this. The newspaper articles about the flu pointed to the serious nature of the illness, and I began to wonder if I was going to die.

Sometime during the night the pressure on my bladder finally overcame the desire to not even move. I levered myself to a sitting position and was amazed at how much everything hurt. About five hours later – it seemed like five hours, but was probably only thirty seconds – I dragged myself to my feet. I was reminded of the local farmers trying to move rusty machinery for the first time in the spring and understood how the machinery felt.

I negotiated my way to the bathroom, somehow. It helped that Mrs. Marsden had left the stove-light on in the kitchen. There's no telling where I would have ended up otherwise. I turned the light on in the bathroom and quickly turned it off again. Even the light hurt. I made a successful start to taking care of business, but about halfway through, I lost my balance and toppled against the wall. I vaguely hoped I hadn't left a mess for Mrs. Marsden to clean up, but really didn't care at that point.

The wan light of the winter dawn was streaming into my bedroom, and I awakened when Mrs. Marsden walked in. Even when she was being quiet, her footfalls tended to shake the room. She set a pitcher and glass on my nightstand. Liz Johnson followed her in to the room.

"Here you go, Preacher. I made you some iced tea. You need to start drinking as much as you can. It'll help the fever to go down."

"Uhhhh." I was being profound.

Liz stuck a thermometer in my mouth. She was a nurse and worked for a doctor in Victoria. I guess she had appointed herself as my physician.

"And here is some more aspirin," Mrs. Marsden said.

"Preacher, you are down for the count," Liz said. "Don't even think about trying to get back on your feet for a while."

Like I had that in mind. I still didn't want to move.

"Lane called Brother Brody, and he will take the Sunday services."

That was fine with me. At some point during the journey the day before, I had ceased thinking about the church, and Sunday, and everything else. I had focused on getting home before I died or wrecked the car or both.

I drifted off again. Sleep was a blessing, even though the dreams were unpleasant. I awoke again sometime in the afternoon and sipped some of the iced tea. Mrs. Marsden brought in a cup of chicken broth. The work of taking about half a cup of the broth was exhausting, and I slept more. This seemed to be the pattern of my life for the weekend.

Sunday afternoon I eased to wakefulness in a quiet house. Mrs. Marsden did not seem to be about. Lying in bed was silly, I thought. I really felt much better. And there was homework waiting for me. I visited the bathroom, and then walked into my study. Someone had brought in the things from the car. I slid into the chair and de-stacked the books on the desk. I kept a bookmark in the Hebrew grammar and began studying in the current chapter.

About fifteen minutes later the page came back into focus. I had been staring. Maybe it was a good time to go back to bed. There was a problem, though. I couldn't seem to stand up. Okay, getting out of bed was a bad idea. The only possible solution was *not* to stand. I made my way out of my office, across the living room to my bedroom on hands and knees. The floor was cold.

Several hours later, I awakened once again to Mrs. Marsden coming into the room with Liz Johnson.

"Is it still Sunday?"

Liz shoved the thermometer into my mouth and held my wrist as she looked at her watch.

"Preacher, I brought you some stew. You need to keep your strength up."

What strength?

Liz looked at Mrs. Marsden. "The fever is up again. I don't like that."

"Perhaps I should stay over tonight," Mrs. Marsden said.

"I'll be fine," I croaked out.

"No, you stayed last night. I can stay tonight," Liz said. "Tomorrow is my day off."

"I'll be fine," I repeated.

"I'll be back in the morning, then," Mrs. Marsden said.

I didn't know why they were ignoring me.

Liz looked at me. "Preacher, just try to rest. You were doing better earlier."

It was probably better that I said nothing about my mid-afternoon adventures. It was obvious to me that the perambulations had not been smart. I didn't need them telling me that. Besides, Liz would probably bring Lane in to lecture me. I really did not feel up to that.

It was Tuesday before I felt well enough to attempt taking a shower. Mrs. Marsden looked askance at me as I trudged by her in my bathrobe. The actions required for a shower included turning on the water, standing under it. Using the washcloth was beyond my abilities at that point. The shower completed, I successfully dressed in clean underwear and got back into the flannel pajamas. I made it back to my bedroom and rewarded myself with another long nap.

By Thursday, the fever had run its course. I was now capable of lucid thought, although still very weak. It was time to rejoin civilization. I made my way to my study and picked up the phone.

"Operator."

"Hi Violet. I need to call my Dad at the school in Rockford. Do you have the number?"

"Hey Preacher, are you feeling better?"

"I'm getting there."

"Well, we're all praying for you."

"Thanks."

"Why don't you let me make the call, and I'll ring you back."

"That would be fine, Violet. Thanks."

"You're welcome. It's good to hear your voice."

About two minutes later the phone rang, and I picked it up.

"Have you rejoined the land of the living, Beryl?" Dad asked.

"Getting there. I've never had anything quite like this."

"The flu is nasty stuff. You don't want to mess with it. Lane Johnson called me to let me know about you. I figured we wouldn't see you for a week."

"That's about it," I said. "I just wanted to check in and see what's going on."

He paused. "It's been an eventful week."

"What happened?"

240

STORM SWEPT

"Nigel is in the hospital. The surgeon had to go into his leg again to dig out an infection. He is not feeling too spry, either."

"I'm sorry I couldn't be up there, Dad," I said. "How's Nigel doing?"

"He's doing about as well as can be expected. And don't worry about not being here. You couldn't help getting sick. Maybe the Lord decided you needed to be on the shelf for a while."

"It wasn't a lot of fun." I was whining. I needed to get a grip. "How are things at the school?"

"Interesting," he replied. "William Cliffe gave the chapel message yesterday and launched into a major attack on the Symposium."

"Man, oh man. How did that go over?"

"The faculty who were willing to comment were outraged. I think some of the others were quietly cheering him on."

"How did the students take it?"

"They seemed to mostly be confused. It helps that the students don't seem to like him very well."

"That's unfortunate. I mean that they don't like him. I wonder if he knows that."

"I don't know. But, it puts me in a terrible spot. I am going to have to take some kind of official action. Openly criticizing the school administration during a chapel message is kind of hard to sweep under the rug."

"I can see it hasn't been your week."

"Are you ready for the next item?" he asked.

"There was something else?"

"Our friends from New York dropped in for a visit again."

"Oh, no. Were there any threats?"

"Actually, no. It was very civil. I explained that my legal counsel was investigating the possibilities, but I didn't have anything to tell him at that point."

"What are we going to do, Dad?"

"I called Ronson Hyde, and told him I would appreciate it if he could get me some advice from Washington."

"We're going to get backed into a corner, aren't we?" I asked.

"Just remember we have the Lord in our corner with us, Beryl. I'd be lying if I told you I wasn't concerned. But, we just have to pray things through."

I was starting to feel very weary again. I didn't know if it was because of what I was hearing.... Well, I guess it was. But my body was telling me it hadn't fully recovered yet.

"Tell Nigel I'm thinking of him."

"You don't sound so great yourself."

"I think I need to go lie down."

"Okay, son. Take care of yourself."

And he hung up. Once again I said goodbye to a dead phone. This time I was able to walk to my bedroom, but I slept another couple of hours. I was just stirring when I heard Mrs. Marsden come into the house. She appeared in the doorway.

"I brought you a chicken pie. I thought maybe you were ready for some solid food."

"Oh, that sounds wonderful, Mrs. Marsden. I really appreciate your help this week."

She sniffed. "With you gone all the time, Preacher, it's about time I had a chance to keep an eye on you."

"I'm glad you were here. It's been a rough week."

"I suppose you are planning to head back north this weekend." She sounded a bit grumpy.

"I really have to. I've missed a whole week of classes. If I don't get back in the saddle, I'll have to drop out for the semester."

"You will want to be careful, Preacher. If you try to do too much before you completely recover, you could have a relapse."

"I'll be careful. I'm feeling a lot better than I did the other day."

"Hmmph." she sounded dyspeptic. "You don't take good care of yourself, Preacher. This might be the Lord telling you to slow down a bit."

"I took a week off at Christmas time."

"No you didn't. You were busy shuttling back and forth from New York. When you got back here, you spent your days on the go. I don't think you know how to relax."

I wasn't sure why she was picking at me. I felt guilty about lying around this week. True, I was weak as a kitten. But, I *should* have been doing something.

I felt well enough after supper to make another phone call.

"Where have you been?" Connie asked.

"Trapped here in Appleton. I came down with the flu."

"Are you alright?"

"Getting there. It's been a rough week."

"Do you want me to come down. I can get a few days off work, I think."

"No, Connie. I have a whole church full of people down here who have made it their mission to nurse me back to health."

"You poor thing. Are you getting enough rest?"

"I seem to spend every spare moment sleeping. I don't mind telling you this took a lot out of me."

"My brother, Sam, had this last year. It took him weeks to get back to his old self."

I felt a wave of fatigue wash over me. This was getting old.

"I think I need to go lie down again."

"Then, don't feel obligated to stay up. I'll pray for you, Beryl."

"Okay. Thanks." I felt my voice trail off.

"Go to bed, Beryl."

"Okay. Bye, Connie."

I was flattered she had offered to come down to take care of me. It was nice having her *poor dearing* me. I dragged myself back towards the bedroom, waving to Mrs. Marsden as I trudged past the kitchen. I had just climbed into bed when I remembered the Lord. I had tried to keep up with my parents and Connie. I didn't want to neglect Him. I rolled back out on to my knees and got caught up with the Lord. I thanked him for taking me off-line. I didn't know the reasons, but I trusted Him to know what was best for me. I crawled back into bed and seemed to feel His loving arms around me. There is nothing like being a child of God.

The fever came back. I awakened Friday morning burning up. My lungs felt like they were on fire. I was racked with fits of coughing and couldn't catch my breath. Mrs. Marsden came in and touched my forehead, then immediately went to call Liz. I felt even worse than I did the previous Saturday. I fell back asleep. I woke up again, briefly, in the back of a vehicle. A white-coated man looked at me with concern and held a mask over my mouth. The cool air was soothing as I inhaled. I heard a siren in the background. Nothing made sense.

CHAPTER TWENTY-EIGHT

Being in the hospital is not a pleasant experience, though I remembered little of the first week or so. Periods of questionable wakefulness interspersed with nightmarish sleep filled eternities. Even lucidity was infrequent. So my life was a series of vignettes, capturing those brief moments in time. It was odd how vivid the memories were afterwards.

Awareness came when a nurse was drawing blood from my arm. I looked behind her, through the window, and saw snowflakes dancing against a night sky. Another time, I awakened to a blizzard of bats fluttering around in my room. I screamed and tried to wave them away until the nurses ran into the room. I dreamed of standing transfixed on a railroad track, while the single headlight of the locomotive bore down upon me. The light halted and backed up to reveal a doctor peering into my eye with his scope.

The worst was the dream where I was walking across a pond on the ice and fell through. I plunged into incredibly icy water, and when I tried to extricate myself, a group of doctors and nurses pushed me back in and tried to drown me. I don't know what was worse, the shock of the cold water, or the sheer panic the drove through to my inner being. I was dying, and I knew it. But, I didn't know what to do about it. All I could do was cry. I wept, and I begged God to help me.

Sensibility returned, and I awakened in a darkened room. The curtains were drawn, and it was night again. In the corner was a floor lamp, and my mother sat in a chair reading her Bible. It seemed peaceful, and that feeling of peacefulness drifted over me. I started a long consideration about speaking to Mom, when I drifted off again.

I felt like I had been on a long trip. They told me it was nearly a week before they got control of the pneumonia. The periods of wakefulness were now longer. I opened my eyes one morning to see Mom standing by Lane and Liz Johnson in my room. Lane twisted his stocking cap in his hands, as they looked at me.

"How are you doing, Preacher?" he asked.

From somewhere I summoned the energy to speak. "You should'a given me that raise."

I had so responded to him once before, another time, when he visited me in a hospital. It wasn't very funny this time either. He gave me his one-sided smile.

"You must be feeling better."

"Than what?"

"Good point, Preacher. Don't try to talk. We just wanted to come in and let you know we're all praying for you."

I managed a short nod. It was suddenly more effort than I could manage to continue the conversation, and I drifted off to sleep. The next time I opened my eyes, Mom started spooning Jello into my mouth. I thought it was the most wonderful thing I had ever eaten.

"The doctors want to get some food into you, Beryl," she said. "You need it to regain your strength."

She continued the one-sided conversation as she worked the spoon. My contribution was in swallowing the red stuff and managing the occasional *m-m-m-m*.

"We are so thankful to see you coming out of this. Your father and I were concerned. When Liz Johnson called with the news you were in the hospital, I got in the car and drove down here."

I managed to raise an eyebrow. I certainly wasn't capable of raising an arm.

"Your father is using Nigel's car. Ruth said she could do the cooking."

"Thanks," I managed.

"Oh, Beryl, we were so frightened." I saw her eyes fill up with tears.

"Sorry, Mom."

She put her hand on my forehead and ran it back through my hair. "We know it wasn't your fault. But, you were very ill. You nearly died."

"What day is it?"

"It's Saturday."

My thoughts were starting to make sense, but the process was slow. The curtains were open and the blue sky contrasted the bare tree limbs. The room was bright, and I was comfortable. It was nice to be able to maintain conversations. I felt well enough to be tired of lying in a bed.

Mom turned as someone tapped on the door, and Connie slipped into the room.

"Hello, Connie," Mom said. "You're a long ways from home."

"I got off work at noon today and decided to drive down."

She stepped over to the bed. "Everybody at the church has been praying for you all week, Beryl."

"Thanks," I said. I stared into her dark eyes and felt dizzy again.

"He's doing much better," Mom said. "It was touch and go for a while, there."

"Sully said to tell you he was praying for you. Even Mr. Brinker was concerned."

That was nice of Brinker, even if he couldn't get my name right.

Mom stepped to the side. "Connie, why don't you sit down right here and talk to Beryl. I want to step down to the cafeteria."

Connie slipped her coat off and hung it on the back of the chair. After she had sat down, she folded her hands in her lap and looked at me. *Okay, here it comes,* I thought. *She's going to tell me that she loves me as a brother in the Lord.* That was a favorite line when girls wanted to let me down easy.

"I was frightened, Beryl," she said. "I don't know what I would have done if you had died."

I couldn't think of anything to say, so I didn't say anything.

"I have been praying all week. I didn't know what the Lord was going to do. I called and talked to your mother every day to find out how you were."

Okay, she wasn't going to throw me in front of the train just yet. Seeing her in my hospital room seemed to confirm, in my mind anyway, that I really did not want to let this one get away.

"Thanks for coming down," I croaked out.

She patted my hand and gave me a soft smile. "Don't think that you can keep me away that easily."

"I don't want to keep you away."

"How do you feel?"

"Very weak. I think the worst of it is over."

"Just rest then, and I'll tell you what's going on in Rockford."

I had been awake for a little while and grew increasingly weary. But I really wanted to stay awake and listen to Connie. I closed my eyes for just a second, and when I opened them, Mom was back in the chair.

"Connie?"

"Don't worry Beryl, I sent her down to the cafeteria. She will be back in a bit. She hasn't had anything to eat since this morning."

I considered what she said.

"I'm glad she came."

"I thought maybe you would be," she said. "I invited her to stay over with me."

"Where?" I was getting good at the single word communications.

"Oh, I'm staying at the Holiday Inn. It's a very nice hotel. There's an extra bed. The girl doesn't have much money, Beryl. You will need to be careful not to make her feel obligated to spend anything."

"Give her gas money?"

"That was my thought. I think she gives most of what she earns to her parents."

Another thought slipped unbidden into my head. "How long will I be here?"

"Oh, the doctor thought maybe another week. He thinks you're out of the woods, but you are still very sick."

"Never been this sick."

"Your father and I were surprised this hit you so hard. You have always been healthy. Apparently a nasty strain of flu is going around. The doctor said he was going to tell you not to leave the house for six weeks after you get out of here."

"That's it for school."

"Your father has already withdrawn you for the semester. I've got two boys to take care of, now."

It sounded like she assumed I would be staying with her and Dad in Rockford. That couldn't happen. I needed to be near my church.

"I can stay in Appleton."

Mom looked at me curiously, but at that moment Connie slipped back into the room.

"If you would like to get away for a bit, Mrs. Cathcart, I can sit with Beryl this evening."

Mom looked back and forth between us. "You know, the hospital food gets wearing after a while. I think I'll go out for something and come back later."

"I won't run away," I said.

"I suppose I should warn you, Connie, that my son has a terrible lip on him."

She chuckled. I really liked the sound of her low laugh. "I think I can deal with it. He's right. He can't escape."

I really didn't want to escape. I felt much better, although I was tired and weak. I was perfectly happy to lie in bed and listen to Connie for as long as she wanted to talk. So after Mom left, Connie caught me up on the events in Rockford. It seemed that Ellen kept her up to date on campus happenings. I heard the latest on Sully's spiritual growth and what was going on at her church in Love's Park. These were the most interesting things I had ever heard.

Nigel was in the hospital too. The doctors decided they had to operate again to deal with the infection in his leg. The poor guy couldn't catch a break, it seemed. Ellen was wearing herself out, taking care of the office and shuttling to hospital to be with Nigel. That relationship still puzzled me. Reading between the lines, I thought Connie was puzzled too. And she had known Ellen for a lot longer than the rest of us.

A little while later there was a tap on the door, and Avis and Christine Brody walked in. Connie stood up and immediately introduced herself, as did the Brodys.

"Beryl, we are so glad you are back on the mend," Christine said.

"I think Avis is going to be preaching for me for a while."

"That's fine, Beryl," he said. "Everyone at the church is praying for you. I understand you are going to be laid up for a while."

"That's what I've been told."

Christine turned to Connie. "I don't know him very well. My husband and

I recently joined the ministry at Appleton. But, the universal consensus is that Beryl does not follow direction well."

Connie's eyes twinkled as she glanced over at me. "I have noticed that in Rockford as well. Do you suppose we could work on some solutions to the problem?"

"What a wonderful idea, Connie. I am sure that between the two of us, we could introduce some discipline into the pastor's life."

Avis surreptitiously rolled his eyes. That told me I was having a good influence on him, at least. There was, however, a more immediate problem.

I groaned theatrically. "I think I'm taking a turn for the worse."

"Poor baby," Christine said. "Connie, we definitely have our work cut out for us."

"I believe we can salvage the raw material, though," Connie replied.

Christine rubbed her chin with her fingers and cocked her head. "Yes. He may have some possibilities."

It was delightful to see Christine and Connie hit it off like they did. But, I was definitely concerned about the consequences. Christine could be unmerciful, and I wasn't sure it was a good idea for Connie to fall under her influence.

Christine glanced over at me, and her eyes narrowed slightly. "Come on, Avis, we probably should let the preacher get his rest. If he's determined to lie around the hospital, we should not interrupt the fun."

The energy level dropped when the Brodys left the room. The emotional kick was fun, but it reminded me that I still had no reserves. Connie slipped back into the chair next to my bed, and leaned over to adjust the blankets around me. The slight essence of the perfume I associated with her drifted by.

"I like her," she said. "You have really nice people in your church."

I started assembling a reply, when my eyes closed on their own accord.

CHAPTER TWENTY-NINE

One surprise about a lengthy illness is that the world does not stop, while the patient recuperates. Several times I found myself looking at an event, and wondering when did that happen? The doctor determined I could be trusted out of his sight, so Mom packed me into the Cadillac and drove me to my little house in Appleton.

I was anxious to get back into the saddle. During the trip across I-74 and US 150, I planned my activities. There would be mail to go through, the spindle on the kitchen counter would be overflowing with notes from Mrs. Marsden. I had sermons to prepare and church members to visit.

"Oh, preacher," Mrs. Marsden said, "it is so good to have you home again."

I stood in the kitchen and looked around. Things were the same, only different. The kitchen looked quaint and small.

"Thank you, Mrs. Marsden. It's good to be home."

"Maybe you should go lie down for a while," Mom said.

"I'm fine." But I wasn't. During the ride in the car, I felt the energy draining from me. But I had to get some work done.

"Why don't you go rest for a bit, Preacher?" Mrs. Marsen said. She phrased it as a suggestion, but her authority made it an order.

Mom guided me to my bedroom and helped me ease into the bed. "There now, Beryl. Nobody is expecting you to do everything this afternoon."

I lay back in my pillow, hoping to rest for a bit. I could hear my desk calling to me. When I opened my eyes again, the room was dark. I sat up and switched on the lamp so I could look at my watch. It was a quarter til six. I hoped it was still in the afternoon and not the next morning. A certain amount of noise filtered through from the kitchen, so I assumed it was still the same day.

Mrs. Marsden prepared a light meal for me. Beef stew and toast, and it tasted good. The best thing that could be said about hospital food was that it was bland. I had fully planned to spend the evening in my office, but following the supper, I drifted back to my bed and slept through the night. Apparently the half hour trip from the hospital to my home was exhausting.

The next morning after breakfast, I made my way to the office and lifted the phone off the hook.

"Operator."

"Hi Violet, can you dial Mid-North College for me?"

"Oh hi, Preacher. It's good to hear your voice."

"Thanks. It's good to be home again."

"Let me make the connections and call you back."

"Thanks, Violet."

A voice I didn't recognize answered in Nigel's office.

"This is Beryl Cathcart. Is my father in?"

"Yes, just a moment please, Sir."

In just a few moments, Dad was on the line. "My wayward son reports in."

"Hi Dad. I wanted to see how Nigel is doing... well, and you too."

"Thanks. I'm glad you qualified that."

"One must always respect his parents," I said.

Dad sniffed. "I know about your so-called respect, Beryl. Nigel expects to get out of the hospital tomorrow. They think they have the infection under control, and he seems to be on the mend."

"That's good news. Was he very sick?"

"Sick enough to be in the hospital," Dad replied. "They couldn't seem to knock the infection out with drugs and had to open up his leg again. It was definitely a setback."

"I'm sorry to hear about that. Poor Nigel hasn't had a break lately. Is he communicable?"

"I don't think you would catch anything from him, Beryl." Dad's voice took on a dusty quality.

"No, I mean can I talk to him?"

"He's in room 313. Give him a call. I think he'd be glad to talk to you."

"Okay. How are plans for the Symposium?"

"The plans are going well. But, there is some kind of undercurrent among the faculty. I haven't been able to track it down. We may see some fireworks there."

"And we don't need that," I said.

"Right. Just last week we finally got through all the financials. The books are now something we won't be ashamed of."

"That's good news. Any progress on finding a controller?"

"Actually, yes. Mr. Jay Larke starts with us next week."

"Is he the guy from the camp over by Chicago?" I asked.

"Yes. He came over for an interview, and I hired him on the spot."

"He must have impressed you."

"He did. I don't often make decisions that quickly," he said.

"I sure hope it works out."

"Me too. I sometimes get concerned. I have hired people in the past where I spent more time trying to manage them, than if I just did their work myself."

"I believe you said something like that about me, when I worked for you one summer."

Dad was silent for a moment. "I don't believe I remember that."

"Let's just forget I said anything, then."

Dad was quiet again. I knew he was frantically trying to remember the conversation with me from ten years previously.

I picked up the conversation to let him off the hook. "So... how goes the life of the acting president, Dad?"

Dad paused. "You know, this school runs pretty well all by itself. It isn't any wonder the former provost had a reputation for being a do-nothing."

"But, is that a good thing?"

"Therein lies the rub. What it means is that the deans and department heads hold the balance of power. I do not think that is necessarily a good thing."

I thought about what he said. "When Nigel first approached me, he said something about the faculty doing end-runs past him to the board."

"Exactly. I don't know if they were running to Charlie Bigelow, or if there is somebody else on the board with lines of communication to the faculty."

"Based upon past experience, I don't think you want to assume all is sweetness and light on the board."

"I think you have that one right," he said.

"When is the next board meeting?"

"We are going to meet right after the Symposium. Most of the board is planning to be here for that. I've got a meeting to go to, Beryl."

"Okay, Dad. Bye." I spoke my final words to a dead line. Dad was like that. When he was done talking, that was it.

Dad didn't give me the number for the hospital, just Nigel's room number, so I spent the next half hour working Violet Johnson to track it down. Lane's mother had been the switchboard operator for twenty years. She effortlessly juggled the multiple calls coming from the neighborhood, as well as tracking down my odd requests for phone numbers. I wondered what she would do when the phone company finally introduced direct dialing in the area.

"Hello."

"I can't seem to leave you to your devices without your getting into trouble."

"I wasn't the one at death's door, Beryl," Nigel said.

"Not this time."

"I suppose you are bouncing around, the very picture of health."

"Of course."

"So why won't Mrs. Marsden let you come out and play?"

I leaned out of my chair towards the doorway. "Mrs. Marsden, Nigel wants to know why you won't let me come out and play."

I heard her heavy foot-fall as she walked from the kitchen into the living room, and then to my door.

"You tell Dr. Robart that I know of two young men without enough sense to come in out of the rain!"

"Did you hear that Nigel?"

"I'm just glad I'm on the other end of this phone line," he laughed.

"I heard that," Mrs. Marsden said.

Nigel got very quiet. Mrs. Marsden gave me one of her patented ferocious scowls, but the twinkle in her eyes spoiled it. She turned and marched back to the kitchen.

"Okay, Nige, the coast is clear."

"Not for me," he laughed again. "I think she would come up to Rockford just to make sure I behaved."

"She probably would."

"So, when are you coming up again?" he asked.

"I have been told I am to convalesce for the next six weeks. Then I will make my triumphant return to Mid-North."

"Yeah. Right. They're letting me out of here tomorrow."

"Dad told me."

"And my instructions are to remain off my feet for three weeks."

"That shouldn't be a problem for you," I said. "You've been skating on your backside for years."

"You wound me, Beryl. After all I have done for you."

"When have you ever done anything for me?"

"I introduced you to Ellen..."

"Which led to the great disaster of the twentieth century."

"...who introduced you to Connie."

"Okay, okay. But that was accidental on your part."

"I can still take the credit." I could hear his smirk over the phone.

"With your lack of modesty, I can believe that."

"Hey, I got to grab recognition where I can."

"Seriously, how are you doing, Nige?" I asked.

"Seriously, I am getting very tired of this leg. It hurts all the time, and the docs seem to want to keep tinkering with it. I am seriously considering having them just take the thing off, and be done with it."

"You don't want to do that, Nigel."

"I know. I know. I talk to the Lord about it. A lot. He keeps taking me back to Second Corinthians."

"Paul's thorn in the flesh?"

"Right. I think the Lord is telling me that I need to learn what He's trying to teach me."

"And what is He trying to teach you?" I asked.

"As soon as I figure it out, I'll let you know. No, I can't lie to you. I know what it is. I'm way too casual in my spiritual life. If something needs to be done, then I just jump in and do it. I've discovered that the Lord will keep you from doing things in your own strength if He takes your strength away from you."

"Maybe that's been my problem," I said. "I've kind of been tied down here recently."

"Tell me about it," he said. "All I could do was lie here and stare at the walls of the hospital room."

"At least you weren't battling hundreds of bats flying around you."

"What?"

"There I was, minding my own business, and opened my eyes to find all these bats swarming about the room. It was terrifying."

"Eh? I'm not following you," he said.

"Fever dream."

"Oh. I don't think I got to that point, Beryl. Sounds horrible."

"Waking up when they dropped me into an ice bath to get the temperature down was no picnic either. I think I slugged one of the nurses."

Nigel began laughing. "It just proves what I have believed all along."

"I'm not even sure I want to ask."

"You're a cold fish, Beryl."

"Oh, thank-you very much. I'll get you for that, buddy."

"In your dreams."

"Let's not go there."

And he responded by laughing. We continued chatting for several minutes, then called it quits for the day. His doctor had stepped in the room to see him, and a freight train load of fatigue came barreling through my door. I staggered to my room and tumbled into the bed. A couple of phone calls, and I was wasted. I wasn't this tired when I spent an entire day on the hay wagon with the local farmers. The three hour nap was nice, though.

I was proud of myself for keeping my priorities straight. After Mrs. Marsden prepared tomato soup and a toasted cheese sandwich for my lunch, I repaired to my office once again and picked up the phone. This time I had the number ready for Violet.

"Brinker Chrysler-Plymouth." That voice was beginning to have an effect on me.

"Uh, yes. I'd like to order a tow truck."

The response was immediate. "Would you like one configured to run preachers off the road or to pull you out of a ditch?"

"I'm stuck down here in central Illinois, and I can't seem to get myself shifted into gear." I was going to say something about needing to get my motor running, but decided that sounded a bit suggestive.

"Sir, you don't need a tow truck. You just need a little encouragement,"

Connie said.

"By George, I do believe you may be right."

"Let me go get Sully."

"No. Wait."

"You don't want to talk to Sully?"

This girl was good, but I wasn't sure I liked the trend.

"I can talk to Sully when I get back to Rockford. I mainly wanted to talk to you."

"Aren't you worried about hurting Sully's feelings?" She wasn't going to let me off the hook. I could hear the smile in her voice.

"Sully's a big boy. He'll understand. Besides, he doesn't know I'm on the phone with you."

"He's standing here by the counter."

Oh, man! She had really sandbagged me. But two could play this game. "Let me talk to him."

I heard his gravelly voice come on the line. "Mister Cathcart? How are ya doin?"

"It's Beryl, and I'm doing a lot better than I was a couple weeks ago. I've got a ways to go, though."

"Well, we all have been prayin' for you, since we heard you were sick."

"Thanks, Sully. I think it was people praying that pulled me through."

"I've been studying my Bible."

"That's good. Are you learning things in Sunday School?"

"I sure am. The more I study the Bible, the more amazed I am that God saved me. I just don't understand why He reached down for me, but I'm glad He did."

"I'm glad he did, too, Sully." I got a lump in my throat. "You are a trophy of God's grace."

"It's His trophy, not mine. When I think about all those years of drinkin' and swearin' an' such. Well, I was a sinner for sure. But God saved me. Isn't He wonderful?"

"He sure is."

We chatted for a couple of minutes, and I had an idea. "Sully, don't say anything, but I'd like a favor. Say something like *nice talking to you*, and act like you're going to hang up the phone. See what Connie does.

Sully was nobody's fool, and immediately figured the game out. "Well, nice talkin' to ya, Mister Cathcart. We'll keep prayin' for you. Have a good day."

I heard a strangled *wait*, and then he really did hang up the phone. I leaned back in my chair and laughed out loud. I then picked up the phone again.

"Operator."

"Hi Violet. I just got disconnected. Can you dial that last number for me again?"

"Sure thing, Preacher."

I waited for the buzz on the other end.

"Brinker Chrysler-Plymouth."

"I still need that tow truck."

"Beryl!" Connie was laughing now. "I don't know who is worse: you or Sully."

"Me? He's the one who hung up."

"Uh huh. He's standing over there giggling like a fifth grader. I sort of figured out who put him up to that."

"You cut me to the quick."

262

"Your mother warned me about you, Sir," she said. "You were there. She said you had an awful mouth."

"I don't remember that. I was sick and in the hospital. Besides, you seem to be holding your own."

"Purely a defensive move."

I stopped to take a deep breath. I was thoroughly enjoying the banter, but I discovered it required more energy than I had at that moment.

"Are you all right, Beryl?" She asked.

"I'm fine. I just wanted to thank you for coming down to Galesburg last week. You didn't have to do that."

"Yes I did. I didn't want you lying in the hospital all alone down there."

I was not anywhere near being all alone in the hospital, but her concern really felt good.

"I just wanted to thank you. It was kind."

"Beryl..." It sounded to me like she gulped. "I'm just glad you survived. I don't know what I would have done..."

"Connie. Hey." I said softly. "The Lord saw me through. I'm going to be fine."

"I'm sorry. I didn't mean to come apart like that. Now I've got Sully looking concerned."

"I know Mr. Brinker probably doesn't want you taking personal calls, but I wanted to talk to you."

"Can you call me tonight?" She asked. "No, wait a minute. I'll be at church."

"I'm really not much good in the evenings, right now," I said. "Will you be home Saturday?"

"I'm going to be out of town on Saturday."

"Oh." I thought frantically, but my brain seemed to be slowing down. "Umm. I'll think of something."

We chatted for a few minutes longer, but then I reluctantly had to hang up. The phone call was followed by another three hour nap. I wondered about my ability to get twelve or fifteen hours of sleep in twenty-four. But, I really enjoyed talking to Connie.

CHAPTER THIRTY

I have never seen a cat after it had eaten a canary. In fact, I knew no one who was silly enough to let their canary get within range of a cat. Therefore, I did not know what a cat would look like after so partaking. But there was no other way to interpret the look on Mrs. Marsden's face that Saturday morning. I wondered what was up.

My minder had quit spending twenty-four hours per day at my house. She was always there to prepare my meals and clean, but she increasingly trusted me by myself. She did actually make me promise not to go outside. She was an old bat sometimes, but on the whole, she was an amazing example of Christian grace – when she wasn't plotting something.

I polished off the Eggs Benedict she had prepared for my Saturday breakfast. It was excellent, by the way. Whenever she thought I wasn't looking, I noticed a very un-Mrs. Marsden-like smile on her face. Something was definitely up. I wondered what it was, but knew that I wouldn't pry the answer from her. I often wondered if her husband Harvey was as intimidated by her as was everyone else.

After breakfast, I retreated to my office and started studying my Bible. My fellowship with the Lord had suffered during my illness, and I was anxious to resume my walk. It's surprising how hard it is to reestablish Bible study and prayer habits. My naps had been growing shorter, but after a couple of hours of concentrated study and prayer, I crawled into the bed for a morning nap.

Wakefulness does not come quickly for me. Most mornings I preferred to lie in bed for fifteen minutes or so before getting up. That allowed time to fit together the pieces of coherence and logical thinking into a functioning personality. The sounds of people talking in the kitchen of my Appleton home wove their way into an interminable dream about the church, and Mid-North, and McKisson University. I snapped awake and immediately decided to investigate the source of the disturbance. I pulled on my trousers, and stumbled, barefoot and tussled into the kitchen, where I dropped into one of the chairs, and stared owlishly at Mom, Dad, and Connie. Mrs. Marsden leaned against the counter with folded arms and an amused expression.

"What are you doing here?" Since the neurons in my brain were not really firing, I said the first thing that came to mind.

"We were in the neighborhood, and just thought we would stop by," Dad said, wearing his trademark smirk.

Mom looked concerned. Connie looked... entertained, I guess.

I shook my head, trying to clear the cobwebs. "I just woke up, and I heard voices."

Boy, that came out wrong. Dad raised an eyebrow. Connie slipped her hand over her mouth. The corners of her eyes crinkled, which was bewitching, but also meant she was enjoying herself.

"Perhaps we should find you some professional help," Dad said.

Mom's snort turned into a guffaw, and Connie started shaking. I still was not far enough spun up to offer a riposte, although seeing Connie aided the process. Her deep brown hair and dark complexion contrasted her peach colored turtle-neck sweater. I thought she looked splendid.

Mom slapped Dad on the arm. "Daryl, go easy on him. We just woke him up from a sound sleep."

"I have recovered to the point where I only require two naps each day." That sounded lame, even to me.

"Are you feeling better?" Connie asked.

"Yes. Much. Thank-you."

"We decided to come visit you this weekend," Mom said, "and it seemed like a good idea to invite Connie along."

"I'm glad you did," I said. "Although I don't know how much I'll be able to contribute."

"You're doing just fine, so far," Dad said.

"That's what I'm afraid of. Please don't hold anything I say against me; I'm still trying to wake up."

"I was just getting ready to put lunch on the table," Mrs. Marsden said.

The preparations for a full meal were on the stove and counter. This confirmed my suspicions about her participation in the conspiracy. She knew I was going to have company. I honestly did not have any complaints.

Lunch was a pot roast with potatoes and carrots. The apple pie crowned the effort, and Mrs. Marsden's efforts were outstanding, as usual. Following lunch, my parents left to drive to Galesburg to check into the Holiday Inn. Dad had reserved two rooms and insisted on paying for Connie's. While Mrs. Marsden busied herself in the kitchen, I gave Connie a quick tour of the house. There wasn't that much to see. I didn't use the upstairs of the house, but I showed her the two small bedrooms there. They were empty and dusty, and the low ceilings constricted the space.

We spent time in my office. She carefully examined the books on the shelves.

"Oh, you have the International Standard Bible Encyclopedia," she exclaimed. "Daddy has that set. It is really useful."

"The ISBE is useful," I agreed. "It's great for background information."

She ran her fingers along the books and pulled out one of the volumes of Shaff's History of the Christian Church.

"I'm interested in history, but this is awfully fine print."

"I haven't managed to get all the way through it," I said. "It's heavy reading. And I was a history minor too."

"What was college like?" she asked. She had a wistful tone to her voice.

"It was fun. I met a lot of interesting people. A lot of them are still my friends. I think the most interesting was the chance to just ask questions of the professors. Many of them seemed to have a bottomless well of knowledge."

"I wish I could have gone," she said.

"Why didn't you?"

"No money." We had a family meeting, and decided we would all work and try to put my brothers through school. I've worked since I was in high school."

"You would have done well, I think. Sully has a high opinion of your abilities."

"Oh, Sully is a sweetheart."

We eased back into the living room and settled on the sofa. I sat on the end nearest the oil stove and soaked up the heat. I had a tendency to get chilled.

"This is a pleasant home you have, Beryl," she said. "And the village is charming."

"Thanks. Over the past several years it really has become home for me. The people here are great."

"I like your Mrs. Marsden," Connie said. "She really loves you."

"She scares me, too."

"Oh, poo, Beryl. She's really a softy."

I had heard Mrs. Marsden described in a lot of ways, but this was a first. "There is no question she rules here."

"As well she should. Your mother said that you have never been good at picking up after yourself."

I saw the glint in her eye. I was beginning to realize she had a subtle way of teasing that was a perfect reflection of her personality.

"It's just that I carry a heavy weight of responsibility here. Because I am preoccupied with these weighty thoughts, I often do not concern myself with minor matters."

A comment like that was usually enough to set Nigel off. I wondered how Connie would react. She picked up a throw pillow and threw it at me.

"Has anyone told you that you are insufferable?"

"All the time."

"They are right."

"I know."

She picked up the other pillow and threw it at me. We continued picking at each other for a while, until Mrs. Marsden rumbled into the room carrying a tray. On it were two cups of coffee, and a plate of cinnamon rolls. We continued conversing as we worked our way through the coffee and rolls.

"She really looks after you."

I had to agree. "I don't know what I'd do if she wasn't here."

"Does she live near here?" Connie asked.

"Two houses down the street, she and her husband Harvey. He's a real estate broker."

"Has she lived here long?"

I thought about the question. "She was here when I moved in. Somebody said they came to Appleton about six months before I did. She said she came from upstate New York, but has never said much about her past. She is very much in the present."

"Interesting."

"I think she is the most *others* focused person I know."

We sat in companionable silence for a while.

"Let's read together," Connie said suddenly.

"Okay. What would you like to read?"

"Could we start with the Bible?"

"Sure. Just a minute."

I stepped into my office and grabbed my study Bible. I sat down again at my place on the sofa next to the heater, and Connie slid over next to me.

"Where shall we begin?" she asked.

I looked over at her as she sat there in her peach sweater and gray flannel pants. I felt myself getting short of breath. "How about if we start with the Psalms?"

"Sounds good to me."

I opened to Psalm One and began reading. For me, the first Psalm has always been special. It has been an anchor for me life. Not walking in the counsel of the ungodly, and taking delight in the Law of the Lord was a wonderful set of phrases to mediate upon. I was reminded, once again, how much I loved God's Word.

Following the six short verses of that passage, I briefly expounded upon the passage. I had a rapt student, and she asked penetrating questions. We talked about the passage, and what God was teaching through it, then we prayed together. Other than at meals, this was the first time Connie and I had prayed together. It occurred to me that Ellen and I had never prayed together like this, when we were dating. Yet, here in the living room of my little house in Appleton, I felt a special closeness to this girl as together, we stepped before the throne of God.

I didn't want the afternoon to end. When we finished praying I picked up my coffee cup.

"Let's get some more coffee."

She poked me in the chest. "You, Sir, are going to go lie down. You just turned pale."

I was hoping she hadn't noticed. I wanted to spend every moment of the afternoon with her, but my batteries were running down. I tried to think of something witty to say, and even that became an effort.

"Go," she said. "I will go talk to Mrs. Marsden. She's a dear."

I wouldn't have described Mrs. Marsden as a dear, but I was rapidly loosing ability to reason. I stumbled into my bedroom and stretched out on the bed. She closed the door and left me in the cool afternoon twilight of that February day. I wanted to replay each moment of the afternoon in my mind, but the sleep quickly stole over me.

After the heavy lunch, Mrs. Marsden prepared ham and swiss sandwiches on homemade bread for supper. The four of us sat around the table, as my keeper served us.

"Are you coming here for church tomorrow?" I asked.

"We haven't decided," my mother said. "Do you think you really need to go out already?"

"Sure. I'll be fine. I want to hear Avis preach, anyway. Besides Dad, if I fall asleep, I can just lay my head on your shoulder."

"Not on mine, you won't."

"Don't you love me anymore?"

"Let's not get started, son," he said.

"I knew it," I said. "You really do like Nigel better."

Dad looked at Mom and shook his head. "Where did we go wrong?"

Connie chose that moment to join the exchange. "My Dad always says that some children need nurturing, and others need to have the devil whipped out of them."

She didn't continue through to the conclusion, but I could follow the dotted line as well as anyone.

"I'm starting to feel unloved. I think I'm having a relapse."

Mom looked over at Connie. "I don't know if you've noticed this, but Beryl is very good at pouting."

"Does he do it a lot?" she asked.

"All his life," Dad said, as he picked up his coffee cup. "I never quite knew what to do with him."

"Maybe Daddy could help."

Dad choked on his coffee.

CHAPTER THIRTY-ONE

"How come this car has so many gears?" Connie asked.

She had taken the train to Galesburg and stayed with Avis and Christine Brody for a couple of days, before accompanying me on my first trip back to Rockford. With the first hint of spring in the air, I had pulled the big car out of the garage for the trip. The Dart was a good car, and served its purpose well in the snow and mud around Appleton, but I was happy to get back behind the wheel of the Monaco.

"A lot of people talk about having the extra gears so as to better match the speed of the car with the power band of the engine," I said. "That is true, probably, but I mainly ordered the car this way because it was fun."

"But you're shifting all the time."

"Right. It's fun."

She looked out the window at the brown stubble of the corn fields as they flowed by. Though it was early March, it was a typical Illinois winter day. A gray featureless overcast muted the brown shades of the countryside. The roads and fence boundaries were marked by the remaining snow drifts, as they slowly retreated in the forty degree weather.

Connie and I differed in our views of automobiles. I loved them and tended to anthropomorphize them. She viewed them simply as tools or appliances to convey her about her business.

"Besides, I said, you have just as many gears in your car."

"I do not. My car has a three on the tree," she said, referring to the column shifter.

"But, it has over-drive."

"That's different."

"Well, yeah. Sorta. But if you think about it, since you can use the overdrive in both second and third, you actually have five gears to choose from."

"I can use over-drive in second? I didn't know that."

"Yep. Get up around thirty or so in second, let off the gas, and it'll kick in."

"Why would I want to do that?"

"Flexibility. The car would be more responsive in the thirty to fifty mile-an-hour range than third-prime. It would be useful in heavy traffic."

She pondered for a while as we drove north on US 51 towards LaSalle-Peru.

"I don't drive that aggressively," she said finally. "My brothers all have four on the floor in their cars."

"See? It's not just me."

"Exactly."

"So where do you want to eat?"

She slowly turned her head to look at me. "Was that a change of subject, Sir?"

"I think it might have been. We're coming up on LaSalle-Peru, and it's about 11:30."

"Why do you call it LaSalle-Peru?"

"Because that's the name of the place," I said.

"But that's two towns."

I shrugged as I drove. "That's what everybody calls it. I'm just following the accepted practice. Anyway, do you have a preference?"

"Not McDonald's."

"But they have great French fries."

"You seem to have this habit of just looking for an argument, Sir."

She had recently become enamored with the Peanuts comic strip, and mimicking one of the recurring characters, frequently addressed me as *sir* whenever we tormented each other – which happened often.

"Not me," I said. "I'm just my usual, lovable self."

We crossed the bridge over the Illinois River and drove into the outskirts of the town.

"How about that place?" she said, pointing to a roadside diner.

"Why not?" I swung off the road into the gravel parking lot of the Alluvial Cafe. Maybe a dozen cars graced the lot, and I eased the car into an area next to the grassy border.

"There are places closer to the door," Connie said. As we had gotten to know one-another, she was quicker to speak her mind.

"True," I said. "But over here, maybe some clown won't open his door against the side of the car."

She didn't comment further, but opened the door when we stopped. "With this many cars on a Monday morning, the food must be good."

"Could be. Shall we see what's on the menu?"

The place looked like a typical greasy spoon, but the food *was* a bit above average. I ordered the patty melt, and she had a cheeseburger. We slipped into easy conversation. She had recently visited a Christian bookstore and stumbled across a commentary on Habakkuk. Ironically, I had recently purchased the same book. We discussed the wealth of teaching in that most minor of the prophets. There was depth to this girl's spiritual perception, and it impressed me. The depth of my attraction to her was increasing as well, although we had not kissed again since that snowy night in Rockford.

I had felt completely recovered, after my enforced rest in Appleton. But when we walked out of the restaurant, a wave of fatigue washed over me.

"Um... Do you think you could drive?"

She looked over at me quickly, and her eyes widened. "That just came over you, didn't it?"

"Just as we walked out here."

"Of course I can drive. You should not. You're not as recovered as you think."

"Tell me about it."

I pulled the keys out of pocket and handed them to her. She followed me around to the passenger side, unlocked the car, and made sure I was safely embarked. She bent over and pulled the seat belt buckle out of its retractor.

"Here. Make sure you get buckled in."

"Yes, Mommy."

"Hush, Beryl!"

When she got to the point she was losing patience with me, she usually told me to hush. At the point I recognized her irritation with me was beginning to exceed her concern.

"Sorry."

"You should be." And she closed the door.

As I got to know Connie, I understood that while she would bat words back and forth with me, she grew tired of it more quickly than I. Courtship is intended for couples to test the limits of their patience, and learn each other's likes and dislikes. So far, though, I had yet to discover anything about the lady that I did not care for. I wondered if that was infatuation.

I studied her as she slipped into the driver's seat, then slid it forward. She carefully adjusted the mirrors and looked around to study the sight lines.

"This car is as big as Daddy's station wagon."

"Probably so."

She turned the key to switch on the ignition and pushed the clutch peddle in with a grunt. "That's a stiff pedal."

The Chrysler four-speeds of that era were derived from truck transmissions, I think, and everything was heavy duty to handle the torque of the engine.

"That surprised me when I got the car," I said. "I had kind of forgotten about it."

She fed it plenty of gas, so it started with a roar. She studied the shift pattern on the top of the knob, and shoved it to the left and up.

"Are you sure you're in reverse?"

"Yes, I'm sure I'm in reverse," she snapped.

I pointed ahead of the car. "I don't want to go for a ride into the river."

She looked down and pulled it out of gear. She wiggled the lever back and forth and shoved it into gear again.

"Wait," I said. I reached over and pulled the lever back to neutral, then shoved it against the spring and into reverse. "There you go."

She colored slightly, but didn't say anything. She fed it the gas, and started easing off the clutch. I really hadn't thought about how stiff that clutch spring was, because I saw the pedal pop up, pushing her leg back, and then heard the sound of gravel cascading against the sides and underside of the car as the wheels spun. I tried not to cringe. We whipped backwards out of the parking space, and she quickly spun the wheel to turn the car. She hit the brakes, and the car slid to a stop with a dead engine.

"Sorry."

"Don't worry about it."

She got the engine started again and shifted into first gear. We carved a furrow in the parking lot from the madly spinning tire. She stopped at the edge of the highway without killing the engine again. She flipped the turn signal lever and looked to the left at a row of oncoming trucks. A hole in the traffic opened, and she took it. I saw the unforgiving clutch pedal drive drive her leg back again, and the car tried to dig a hole in the gravel. The right-rear tire generated a long shrill shriek when we got onto the pavement, leaving a cloud of blue smoke and a long black strip. I burst into laughter, even though I knew it wouldn't help matters. She shifted to second and chirped the tires again. I looked over to see her biting her lower lip, and the edges of a smile were showing through.

By the time she had fought her way through the traffic in LaSalle-Peru, she had begun to master the controls. Back on the open highway, she relaxed, and so did I.

"You know, this is a really nice car... except for the clutch."

"You're doing fine, Connie."

"Uh huh. I should have insisted you bring your other car."

I studied her as she drove. She sat upright in the seat with both hands on the wheel in the prescribed ten and two o'clock position. She watched the road carefully and periodically glanced down to watch the gauges. I leaned against my door and drifted off to sleep, lulled by the motion of the car. I awakened once when she barked the tires starting from the traffic light on the north side of Rochelle and drifted back again.

I awakened to find us sitting in the street in front of my apartment.

"I was planning to drop you off at your house."

"You're going to go to bed right now, Beryl. I'll come back and pick you up at five. We are going to have dinner at my house."

"You sure you can get the car over there okay?"

"I've made it this far, haven't I?"

"Let me get the apartment key off my keyring."

"Oh, yes. You probably will need that."

"And I should get my stuff out of the trunk."

She blushed. "I forgot about that. I'm sorry. I'm still a little stressed from driving your car."

"Seriously, Connie, I can drive you home."

"No. I'll be fine."

She shut off the engine and got out to walk back to the trunk. By the time I got there, she already had it open. I reached in and pulled out my one small suitcase. I planned to spend only a few days in Rockford. I took the keys and slipped the apartment key off the ring.

I looked at the dark-eyed girl standing before me. I was struck again how attractive she was.

"Well, thanks for being my minder," I said.

She reached up, and clasped her hands behind my neck and gave me a long, solid kiss. "It was my pleasure, Sir."

After the kiss, I was not in much shape to communicate.

"I'll be here at five, Beryl."

I nodded and picked up the suitcase. As I walked towards the apartment building, I heard her start the engine. She managed to get moving with only a slight chirp of the tires. She was improving.

The apartment smelled musty after being unoccupied for two months. I set my suitcase down on the bedroom floor and toppled into bed. I awakened at 5:15 to an insistent knock on the door.

"You're not awake, are you?" she said when I stumbled to the door.

"Of course I am."

"I'll wait in the car while you get ready."

I changed into something less rumpled, brushed my teeth, and trotted out to the car. She remained behind the wheel. I was still a little woozy, so I climbed in on the passenger side. Connie was a quick learner. I wondered if she had spent the entire afternoon practicing in the car, because she was now driving it smoothly.

"Once I figured out this clutch, it's not so bad."

"Good. I thought maybe you had been practicing."

"Nope. I've been helping Mama get dinner ready for tonight."

"I'm looking forward to it," I said. "I'm interested in seeing if there is anything you don't do well."

"Give over," she said. "You act like I'm perfect or something. And we both know full well I'm not."

I wasn't prepared to concede the point. "I have watched carefully and have not discovered any faults."

"I have a terrible temper, Beryl. I'm frightened do death you will catch me losing it."

"If you didn't lose it today when you were fighting with the car, I wouldn't call it terrible."

"That was nothing. Just a little challenge. As Daddy told me one time, it doesn't do any good to lose your temper at a piece of machinery. It can't help being the way it is."

"Your Dad has a point. So when was the last time you lost your temper."

"In sixth grade."

"That was what, twenty-five years ago?"

"It was terrible, Beryl."

"What did you do?"

"I hit my brother in the head with a frying pan."

She saw my reaction. "It's not funny. He fell to the floor. I thought I had killed him. All I could think was that I had killed my favorite brother, and they were going to put me in the electric chair."

"Whatever did he do?"

"I was helping Mama in the kitchen, and he put a spider on my arm."

"I would've hit him too," I said. "I hate spiders."

"I saw that spider and swung the pan around without thinking."

"What did your parents say?"

"Mama screamed. Once Daddy decided Carlo was okay, he gave him a whipping. He said he heard the clang of the frying pan clear out in the front yard."

We were sitting at a stop light, and I could see her clenching and un-clenching her hands on the steering wheel. I struggled not to laugh, because I could see how traumatic it had been for her.

"What did your dad do to you, then?"

"He sat me down and explained to me that I had to learn to control my temper."

"I don't know, Connie, but I don't think that was temper."
"You don't?"

"No, it was sheer terror. And given the provocation, they probably wouldn't have sent an eleven year old to the chair. They would have just put you away for life."

She glared at me. "Oh, you are just so funny. You're as bad as Daddy. When he was trying to talk to me, he kept having to stop, he was trying so hard not to laugh."

I reached the conclusion that as intimidating as Hank Seabright was, he was not a bad fellow.

CHAPTER THIRTY-TWO

"Look Ma, no hands!" Nigel exclaimed as he walked carefully around his bedroom without his crutches.

"Okay, so the exhibition game works for you," I said. I leaned against the dresser and folded my arms. "You still gotta get up and down the stairs."

"One accomplishment at a time, Beryl," he shook his finger at me. "This time I recovered much faster than you. In fact," he hesitated and shook his finger again at me again, "I am more than halfway convinced you faked the whole thing to get attention. I mean, your dad has been paying a lot of attention to me lately."

"I wish. Do me a favor, Nige, don't ever get what I had."

He stopped his pacing and faced me, with hands on his hips. "I detect a certain *deja vu*. We've had this conversation before – when you got out of the hospital the last time."

I thought about it for a few moments. "I guess we did at that. Different context, though."

He grimaced. "I guess that's enough exercise for one day." He eased himself into the wheelchair and beamed at me. "Am I great, or what?"

"Do you suppose, Nigel, that Mom and Dad regretted coming out here to help their black sheep son and their black sheep *adopted* son?"

"They haven't said so, but the two of us have been a trial, haven't we? Let's reach an agreement between ourselves for a bit of quietude, right?"

"I think we've had *this* conversation before," I said.

"I think we need to get better at keeping our New Years' Resolutions."

"Amen, brother."

He paused as he leaned back in the chair and breathed deeply. "Phew, that takes more out of me than I like to admit."

"I had to switch off and have Connie drive on the way up here yesterday. I can't believe how long it's taking me to shake this."

"A good thing she was with you."

"Sure was."

"Umm. Did your dad bring you up to date on what's happening on campus?"

"He said, changing the subject. Only in the most general terms. I understand there is some kind of an undercurrent against the Symposium."

"Dr. Cliffe has become a bit... outspoken in his opposition."

"What's Carper doing?" I asked. Dr. Alan Carper had been my Systematic Theology professor the previous semester, and I had discovered him to be deficient in his view of the Scripture.

"Carper has been quiet," Nigel said. "I'm not surprised about Cliffe, considering his pedigree."

"I thought Carper would have been in Dad's office again, like he did with you that time."

"I think he's scared of our board chairman and acting president."

I laughed. "Sometimes *I'm* scared of our board chairman and acting president. Dad does that to people."

"Nevertheless, Dr. Carper has been uncharacteristically quiet."

"How are the students treating this?"

Nigel looked down at the floor and smiled. "Your friend Stephen Gardiner has become quite the hero with the students."

"Gardiner of the stupid questions?"

"One and the same. When you got sick, he took over the organization of the prayer meetings, and they are happening two and three times a week. They are heavily attended."

"Good for him," I said. "I've prayed with him a few times. I think God listens to him."

"Not only that, but it seems our Dr. Cliffe made some caustic remarks in class about the Symposium. Gardiner asked a couple of questions about his views of Scripture, and Cliffe jumped all over him."

"Uh oh."

"The other students in the class rose to Gardiner's defense. It seems Dr. Cliffe was rather taken aback."

"From what I have seen, everybody likes Gardiner," I said, "even if they do get impatient with him at times. They didn't stand up for me when Cliffe jumped all over me."

Nigel raised an eyebrow. "I suppose I should never let a straight line like that go by. I guess I could say that you are a lot like your dad in that regard. The other students are a little afraid of you."

"Afraid of me?"

"Well, you definitely intimidate them. In terms of your knowledge of the Bible and theology, you can hold your own against any of the faculty."

"Oh come on, Nigel. I'm not that smart."

He began slapping his forehead. "Got to stop letting these great opportunities go by. Anyway, that's what I heard."

"A lot of the graduate students are less hesitant about speaking up. It's not just me."

"I remember you telling me one time that the graduate students are not quite the sheep the undergrads are."

I looked over at my friend perched on his wheelchair. "It seems Dr. Cliffe was rather forcibly reminded of that fact."

"I wonder if that is why he has never tried to confront your dad. Having the students no longer regarding you as the oracle must be disconcerting."

"Makes sense." I looked at my watch. "Are you up to a little fresh air?"

"What do you have in mind?"

"How about if we go over to the country club for lunch? Since neither of us is up to a long hike, the valet service will be useful."

"Good idea."

He wheeled over to the nightstand and picked up the phone. He dialed a number and listened.

"Hey. I'm going to the country club with Beryl for lunch."

He listened some more.

"Come on, Ellen, I can't stay cooped up here forever."

He looked over at me and rolled his eyes.

"Okay. Okay. Alright. Yes, you can come by tonight."

He looked over at me after he hung up. "We gotta take the wheelchair."

"That's probably a good idea."

"That's why I get so annoyed," he said. "She's always right."

Nigel managed to get down the stairs under his own power. I followed carrying the wheelchair. I unfolded it at the base of his front porch and pushed him to the car in it. After opening the passenger door for him, I refolded the chair and put it in the trunk.

"Ah, you brought the hot rod up this week," he said when I climbed into the driver's seat.

"I missed driving it, and the weather was decent this week."

"We'll probably get another blizzard."

"The thought crossed my mind."

He looked carefully at the passing landmarks as we drove up South Main street in Rockford. It was a bright, sunny, forty degree day, and he drank in the scenery.

"You don't know how good it is to get out of the house, Beryl. I had a bad case of cabin fever."

"I shouldn't have to tell you this, but if you don't behave in the restaurant, I'll lock you in the basement again."

"Boo Radley," he laughed delightedly.

We had both read Faulkner's *To Kill a Mockingbird* and would sometimes toss each other lines from the book. One of the unique characteristics of our friendship was that we could go from perfectly serious to cutting up and back again within a single conversation.

The valets at the country club watched curiously as I pulled up and then headed for the trunk. One of them had immediately opened Nigel's door for him and was puzzled as to why he didn't get out. When the other saw the wheelchair in the trunk, he immediately sprang into action.

"Excuse me, Sir. I can take care of this."

I stepped back as he lifted the chair out of the trunk. I was just as glad. The thing was heavy. He carefully unfolded it and made sure all the latches were in place. Nigel then climbed out of the car and eased into the chair. The valet pushed him into the club, and I walked alongside.

"Will you be dining with us, Sir?"

"Yes."

The maitre'd snapped his fingers, and one of the staff trotted up.

"Please show Mr. Cathcart and his guest to table twenty-two."

"Yes, Sir. If you will come with me, please."

I thanked the valet for his help and pushed Nigel into the dining room. Ahead of us, the wall was lined with French doors on to a veranda. One story below the veranda was the entrance to the locker rooms for the golf course. I leaned over so I could speak softly.

"Do you suppose we could gain enough velocity to launch you through the doors?"

"No thank-you," he replied. "I am not confident of my ability to control this thing in a glide."

The waiter apparently heard, because he turned and gave me a crooked grin.

"Here you go, Sirs. I trust this will be satisfactory."

"This looks great," I said. "Do you want to switch to one of the chairs, Gimpy?"

"Of course."

He slipped over to one of the chairs, and the waiter helped him slide in. He reached, and moved the wheelchair out of his way and studied it critically.

"You know, Beryl, I have discovered that if you don't get the latches on that thing just right, it will pinch the fire out of you."

"That sounds painful," I said.

"You wouldn't believe the welt I have on my right cheek."

I reached out and grasped his chin and tried to turn his head. "Let's see."

"I don't believe you would want me to show you the welt here in the restaurant."

"I don't believe I would want you to show it to me *anywhere*."

The waiter returned a few moments later to fill the water glasses and leave the menus. Nigel picked up the menu, then gazed out the windows at the winter-browned golf course.

"I'm really glad you suggested this," he said. "I definitely needed it."

"Last fall Dad and I talked about getting you a membership in the club. Has he said anything to you about it?"

"No, but that would be too much, Beryl."

"Not at all. It's a great way to see and be seen here in Rockford. For someone in your august position, it would be a good thing. I'll remind Dad. He has probably forgotten in the crush of events."

"You and your dad are too generous," he said.

"Nonsense. It's Dad's way of supporting the ministry. Plus, you really are like family, all kidding aside."

Nigel picked up his water glass and twisted it, studying the reflections from the lights. "Your dad surprised me recently."

"The trust fund?"

"Yes. That came out of the clear blue. Not that I don't appreciate it. I have wondered how I will support myself if I am unable to stay on here at the school. This eases my mind considerably."

"All things considered, Nigel, I would just as soon see you get well."

He picked looked at the lunch menu. "If you don't mind, I do like the steaks here."

The subject was changed.

"No problem. I do too."

After we ordered, we sat and looked outside, and also around the dining room. The Tuesday lunch crowd was light, and the waiter was therefore attentive. Once the club factotums had figured out that there was money in the family, they had fallen all over themselves to be helpful. I enjoyed the service enough that I could mostly ignore the fawning.

The luncheon steaks were up to standard, as were the baked potatoes. They did things right here, and I enjoyed the meal. It was good to see Nigel relaxing. There was one topic that had bothered me for quite a while, and I wasn't sure how Nigel would react.

"There was one thing I wanted to ask you about, but if it's none of my business, just tell me," I said.

He gave me his best blackjack dealer's smile. "You wanted to talk about Ellen."

"Well, yes."

He snorted. "This has been driving you crazy for months. I could tell."

I wasn't sure if I wanted to admit that, so I quickly carved another piece of meat and popped it into my mouth. He laughed.

"You are so easy, Beryl."

Fortunately the steak was tender. I was able to chew the bite and help it down with a swallow of iced tea.

"I'm just concerned about you, Nigel."

"I know, and I appreciate it. Remember, I have known Ellen longer than you have."

"True. It just seemed odd to me that she picked up with you so quickly after we dated."

"Caught me on the rebound in other words?"

"Well, yes," I said. "She's a complex girl."

"I'm not sure what to tell you, Beryl," he said. "Other than the hubris you are showing."

"Oh, come on."

"Seriously."

I thought about that. I didn't *think* I was guilty of hubris. On the other hand, would I recognize it if I did?

He grinned at me again. "I'm really not offended, Beryl. I think her feelings for me had been developing during the time she worked for me. She got caught up with you, but when I got hurt, it immediately brought her focus back."

"I wondered if that might be the case," I said. "But that was not what concerned me. What are your feelings towards her?"

He looked down at his plate and set his fork down. He pulled his napkin out of his lap and wiped his mouth. I could tell he was trying to formulate a response. He shook his head.

"I really don't know. Sometimes I'm head over heals for her. Other times, it's just like I'm an actor in a play."

"I'm surprised you let her run your life like that," I said.

"There are limits to what I am willing to put up with, in that regard."

"And?"

"Then I put my foot down."

"What happens then?"

"We fight."

"I can imagine."

"I guess you can," he said. "We fight a lot."

"Where is the relationship going, Nigel?"

"I wish I knew. Ellen seems to have it all planned out."

"A word of advice?" I asked.

"Sure. Why not?"

"Don't let yourself get too far down the road before you figure out where you're going."

"What's that supposed to mean?" he asked.

"Ellen takes compliance for agreement. You may find yourself halfway down the aisle at the church and wonder how on earth you got there."

"Naaah. I have managed to keep her pruned back, so far."

"Nigel, listen to me. It almost happened to me. You really need to be careful."

He sat and stared at me for a long while. I began to get uncomfortable.

"Okay," he said finally. "I know you really are trying to look out for me, so I'll forgive the meddling."

"I won't say any more."

He swung his head back and forth. "Listen, Beryl. I really do appreciate it. Especially since I haven't figured out what to do myself."

"I know I've upset you," I said, "and I'm sorry. I won't say anymore."

"Don't worry about it. Ever since I've known you, you have managed to say something truly offensive about once per week."

"Gee, thanks!"

"Think nothing of it," he said smugly.

CHAPTER THIRTY-THREE

Dad was at some meeting or another that afternoon, so I slipped into the office adjacent to the one he used. I thought of it as my office. There were several small stacks of papers neatly arranged on the desk, and I examined them. One was a series of promotional materials for the Symposium. Another outlined the plans and agendas for the sessions. It looked like somebody had been keeping up with things in my absence. I was gratified to see that.

I heard a light tapping on the door, and Stephen Gardiner stuck his head in.

"Man, am I glad to see you," he said.

"Come on in, Stephen and plant yourself. I need you to bring me up to date."

"I feel like I have been wandering around in the dark, Beryl. Your dad has been so busy, that I've had to do a lot of the organizing myself."

I waved my arm over the desk. "Is this your work?"

"Yes. I've come in a couple afternoons per week to work on it. The promotional company has been doing the external publicity stuff. Nobody else seemed to be doing anything about the internal materials."

"This looks great. You've really put a lot of effort into it."

"Thanks, but I wasn't sure I was doing the right thing."

"It looks fine to me. Has Dad looked at it?"

"He looked in the office a few times to say *hi*, and that was about it."

"We've got two weeks before the conference. We need to get this to the printer."

"I don't know how to do that."

I picked up the phone on the desk and punched a button.

"Yes?"

"Ellen, this is Beryl."

"Oh, hi Beryl. How are you doing?"

"Much better, thank-you. Listen, Stephen Gardiner has prepared most of the schedules and agendas for the Symposium. Would you be able to proof them and get them to a printer?"

There was silence over the phone for several long moments. I wondered if she was getting ready to tell me she didn't work for me or something.

"You know, it never occurred to me to have something like that," she said. "It might be helpful if he could bring the materials to me and explain what each of them are."

"Right," I said. "I'll send him down in a few minutes. Thanks."

"No problem."

I looked over at Gardiner. "Did you get that?"

"You were talking to Miss Holgate?"

"Yep. When we get done here, we are going to take this down to her. She's going to proof it and have it printed. And, if I know her, she will probably retype some of it."

He looked relieved. "I'm just glad to have somebody working on it that knows what they're doing."

"Once again you underrate yourself, Gardiner. I would suggest you pay attention to what Ellen does with this. Once you get into a ministry, you will be doing it again."

"I'm just glad you're back. I was so worried about this stuff, I nearly threw up."

"Take it easy. It's pretty hard to mess up something like this. By the way, I've been hearing good things about the prayer meetings."

"God really has blessed the meetings," he said. "We keep getting more and more people to show up for them. I think we're going to have a great conference, Beryl."

"I sure hope so."

The change in Ellen was astonishing. After our breakup, she had been cool, nearly hostile for a long time. I had noticed she was gradually warming up again, but expected she would never be truly friendly. In fact, I was afraid she would use her growing relationship with Nigel to drive him away from me.

"Did you get Nigel safely home from lunch?" she asked as we walked in the door.

"I had to threaten to push him down the stairs in his wheelchair, but after that he settled down and behaved."

She snickered at my comment. "I'm glad you thought of taking him out to lunch. He needed to get out."

"He said that. He seems to be doing much better."

She looked over at Gardiner. "And you have the conference materials there?"

"Yes, Ma'am." He walked over and laid them on her desk.

"I'm not *ma'am*," she said. "I'm just Ellen. Why don't you pull that chair over, and we can go through this."

"Yes, ma... uh, Ellen."

I looked at him. "Well, Stephen, I'll leave you in her capable hands. I'm supposed to be at my parents for supper tonight, and I really need to go lie down for a while."

She looked up at me. "I'm glad you are on the mend, Beryl. We were all badly frightened when you went to the hospital."

"Thanks. I do feel much better. Not something I want to repeat. Ever."

I managed a two hour nap that afternoon, and I guess I needed it. I could tell I was getting stronger, but I wasn't nearly back to one-hundred percent. I was being careful not to over do it. I was going to have to drive back to Appleton Wednesday morning, and Connie wouldn't be along to help me drive. I got ready to leave to pick up Connie, and go to my parents' for supper. I stopped outside my apartment door, then impulse I trotted up the stairs and knocked on the door of the apartment above mine. Old Mrs. Pearlman opened the door.

"Well, I thought maybe I had managed to run another neighbor off," she said.

"I've been sick," I said.

"So my daughter told me. Said you were in a bad way. Come on in."

"I can only stay a minute. I was on my way out, and thought I'd say hello."

I stepped in on the new wall to wall carpet.

"This is nice."

"The people at the property management firm had this installed. I wonder, did you have something to do with this, young man?"

I grinned. "I suggested that they do something, since they couldn't fix the heat."

"My rocking chair is a lot quieter too." I saw the glint in her eye. She had read me pretty well.

"Is that so?"

"Young people who mislead their elders often come to a bad end."

"I would never lie to you," I said.

She sniffed. "But you sure know how to use the English language, don't you?"

I shrugged. "I guess it's part of my job."

"Since you are in an all-fired hurry, I don't suppose you would like a cup of tea?"

"Thank you, Mrs. Pearlman, but I'm due at my parents' house for dinner in a half hour, and I need to go pick up my girl-friend."

"Don't let me keep you. You have a young lady waiting for you. Much more important than an old biddy." She started pushing me to the door.

"But I like the old biddies, too."

"Ha! Sweet talk doesn't work with me, young man. Now, on your way. Stop by again when you have more time to visit."

"Oh, I will."

She actually slammed the door behind me when I walked out of the apartment. I laughed as I walked down the stairs. It was clear where Sancy got her personality. Old Mrs. Pearlman must have been formidable when she was on the mission field. In fact, she was formidable now.

Hank Seabright opened the door when I rang the bell.

"Beryl. It's good to see you recovered. Come on in."

"Thanks."

He looked over my shoulder as I walked in.

"Did you trade cars?"

"No. I use the other car on the roads around Appleton because I don't want to mess up the good one."

Once again, I was on the wrong foot with Hank. My *mud car*, the '64 Dodge Dart, was nicer than the Seabright family station wagon, a '59 Ford. And that was their *only* car. Connie's mother drove Hank to work every day, and picked him up.

I hadn't considered myself as wealthy. I mean, it was Dad who had the money. But the allowance Dad gave me – he called it mission support – was probably more generous than the salary Hank Seabright made as a mechanic at the Sinclair station on US 51 in Rockford.

"I see. That's a nice looking Dodge."

"Thanks." I felt compelled to justify myself. "I probably bought a more expensive car than I really needed."

He tilted his head. "When I got out of the service I bought a new '49 Mercury. With a wife and five kids to support, it was a stupid thing to do, but I fell in love with the car. I'm glad you were able to pick up something nice." He grinned. "Connie didn't care for the clutch."

His comment caught me by surprise. I bent over and snorted.

"Once she got used to it, she did all right."

"She said she figured everyone in the restaurant was staring at her when she threw gravel all over the place."

"They were."

"I heard that, Beryl," Connie said as she came down the stairs.

She walked over to her father and kissed him on the cheek. "I won't be too late, Daddy. Beryl has a long drive tomorrow."

The look he gave her told me, without a doubt, who his favorite child was. He patted her on the shoulder.

"Have a good time, Princess."

"Thank you, Daddy."

I walked her out, and helped her into the car, then climbed in myself.

"Did you get some rest today?" was her first question.

"A two-hour nap this afternoon. After I took Nigel to lunch."

I backed out of the driveway and headed across town to my parents' house.

"I'm glad to see Daddy loosening up around you," she said.

"Believe me, I am too. I was sure he was going to disapprove of the car."

"In most ways, you are a modest man, Beryl."

Okay, where was this going? I didn't know how to respond, so I said nothing.

"You don't throw money around, but you are generous with your friends. I think Daddy is glad that I am seeing you. Especially after today."

"Why today?" I asked.

"They closed the gas station where Daddy works. He has been there for fifteen years. As of tonight, he doesn't have a job."

"Oh, man. What a terrible thing to happen. What is he going to do."

"When he got home, he got Mama and me around the kitchen table, and we had a prayer meeting. He said that God was going to take care of us. We just needed to talk to Him about showing us the way."

"Wow. I am really sorry to hear about this."

"Mama cried. But he said that this was God's way of showing us that he had something new, and we needed to trust Him."

I pulled into the parking lot of a grocery store.

"Why are we stopping here?" she asked.

"We are going to pray for your parents right now."

I stopped the car, put it in neutral, and set the parking brake. I reached across and took her hands, and prayed for Hank and Contessa. Following my prayer, Connie prayed. Afterwards I pulled back into the street.

"Thank you, Beryl."

"We simply need to pray. Your dad is right. It's in God's hands. But we still need to pray."

"I know God will take care of us."

"He always has. He always will."

We stepped into Mom and Dad's house to the heady aroma of lasagna. Mom made great lasagna. After the greetings, I immediately stepped into the living room and over to the phone. Ellen answered.

"Hi Ellen, is your Dad home?"

"Just a minute, Beryl."

Mac Holgate picked up the phone swiftly. "Hey Beryl. What's going on?"

"Hank Seabright lost his job today."

"What happened?"

"The gas station closed, I guess. I just wondered if you were looking for a good mechanic in the shop?"

"Believe it or not, I had somebody quit today. I've been wanting to hire Hank for years."

"Here's your opportunity."

"I need to call him."

"Don't let me get in your way," I said.

"Don't worry about that, Beryl," he laughed.

"Okay. Talk to you later."

"Right. Thanks for calling."

Dad had stepped over to the phone, while I was talking.

"Was that Mac Holgate you just called?"

"Yep. Connie's dad lost his job today. We prayed about it on the way over in the car, and it occurred to me that Mac might know of something. He did."

"He's going to hire him?"

"I think so."

"Are you going to tell Connie?"

She was in the kitchen talking to Mom. While Mom liked Ellen, she and Connie had become good friends over the past month. Something about spending that time sitting at the hospital, I guess.

"I don't know. I guess I probably should. I'll tell her on the way home."

"Tell her now."

Dad seldom gives me direct orders, but he did that time. I was not prepared to debate him on it, either. I walked over to the kitchen door and motioned for Connie to join me.

"What is it?"

"I just talked to Mac Holgate. He wants to hire your dad."

She immediately threw her arms around me. I was glad I was able to help them. I also enjoyed the warmth of her embrace. It occurred to me that this was our first hug.

CHAPTER THIRTY-FOUR

It was nine o'clock that Wednesday morning, and I was on the road again. While at my parents' the night before, Dad had the television on for the evening news, and I happened to catch the weather. The National Weather Service was predicting a spring snow storm, and it would begin its sweep across central Illinois on Wednesday afternoon. Driving through the snow would do vile things to my endurance, and coat the car in salt.

With the 65 MPH speed limit in Illinois, you could drive 70 in most places without worrying about the state police. I eased up to 75 betting that US 51 wouldn't be heavily patrolled on a Wednesday morning. If I didn't pay attention, the car liked to settle in at about 85 MPH, but I didn't want to risk it here. First of all, any cop that spotted me would surely pull me over. And it wasn't really safe on a two lane highway. The farmers liked to pull out onto the road in the pickup trucks or tractors without checking, or even caring who was coming. Having had one major automobile accident in my life was a great plenty, thank you very much.

I pulled into the driveway in Appleton at 11:30, and by then my arms and hands were shaking. Mrs. Marsden knew I was coming and was sliding the plate with the sandwich onto the table when I walked through the door. I dumped my things in the bedroom and office and went back to the table.

"Good to have you home in the middle of the week, Preacher." she grumped.

"I kind of like being here for the prayer meetings, especially since I'm speaking tonight."

"You look a little pale," she said.

"After I eat, I need to switch the cars in the garage. Then I'm going to lie down."

The look on her face told me that I didn't need to be worrying about the cars. But I had arrived ahead of the storm and was not going to waste my efforts. A thin skein of clouds had already swept across the sky.

"I'll take care of the cars for you, Preacher."

"Do you know how to drive a four speed?"

She just looked at me. I then remembered her driving her husband Harvey's ancient Studebaker truck. If she could drive a crash box, she could drive anything.

I took a bite of the sandwich. "Where did you get the turkey?"

"I had some in the freezer after Christmas," she said. "Decided it was a good time to use it."

"This is a great sandwich."

"I'm planning to work at getting your weight back on you. You're nothing but skin and bones, Preacher."

"I was getting a little pudgy before. This is not so bad."

"Hmpph. As thin as you are, you'll be getting sick again."

I wasn't prepared to argue with her – it was usually futile anyway. So I dug into the sandwich, which was wonderful, by the way.

I spoke out of First Corinthians ten that evening at church. To me, it is one of the most subtle chapters in the Bible – if you don't consider the entire book of Hebrews, of course. The subtext of First Corinthians is Christian Liberty. As believers, we have an astonishing degree of liberty. Paul carefully points out that our liberty is subject to our love for God and our love for our neighbor. And, in chapter ten, he shows how believers will use their liberty as a cover for idolatry and licentiousness.

I knew Avis had been hammering the topic of holy living. Whenever we met, he gave me summaries of his messages. This was fine, and Avis Brody was a careful expositor, but I wanted to temper things just a little bit. I believed in hewing a cautious line in my walk with Christ. I was not prepared to argue about some of the things other believers did in the name of liberty, but most were simply things I had no desire to participate in. On the other hand, there was probably more latitude for Christians in personal behavior than most Fundamentalists were prepared to admit in 1965.

It was good to be back in my pulpit and among my people. After the prayer meeting, they crowded around me, to shake my hand, pat me on the back, and generally congratulate me on my recovery. I noticed Lane Johnson waiting around for the others to leave, and wondered what he wanted. Avis and Christine had already left. I would be meeting with him the next day.

"A word, Preacher?" he asked.

"Sure thing, brother Johnson. Why don't you come over to the house. I need to sit down."

"If it's not too much trouble."

"No trouble at all."

I drove through the blowing snow back to my little house. I had turned on my television prior to church, and the weather man predicted six inches. It was already that, and it didn't look like it was slacking off much. Mrs. Marsden had preceded me, and plugged in the percolator and set an apple pie on the table. She was convinced I needed to put on weight, and the prospect of pie and coffee after church was attractive.

"Grab a seat at the table," I said as he followed me into the house. I threw me keys on the counter and walked into the living room to throw my coat on the couch. There was a row of hooks inside the back door, but somehow I never thought about using them. I had lived there long enough, that Mrs. Marsden had finally given up nagging me about it.

I pulled a couple of dessert plates and forks out and set them on the table. Then I set two mugs and the percolator down. We each cut ourselves a piece of pie, poured a cup of coffee, then dug in.

"So what's on your mind, Brother Johnson?" I asked after my first mouthful.

"Edgar Forsen."

"Okaaay. Is there a problem?"

"Yes. Well, maybe not. I don't know, Preacher."

It wasn't often he seemed confused. "It's been a long day?"

"No." He wasn't going to take the bait. "It's just that Edgar wants to preach."

I had just forked a bite of the pie and was in the act of raising it to my mouth. I set the fork back down again.

"Well, he was a minister before he got saved. It's probably a part of his personality to be in that kind of work."

Lane nodded. "I agree. As I have gotten to know him, I think he would make a good preacher."

"So what's the problem?"

"He's not ready. He thinks he is, but he's not."

"He's been saved for what, six months?" I said. "He spends a lot of time in the Word."

"I know that. But have you heard him talk?"

"I haven't been around a lot lately, Brother," I said. "Tell me about it."

"As far as I can tell, Preacher, his theology is running straight. I think he has trash-canned everything he learned at Vanderbilt."

"That was my opinion, too."

Lane hesitated, and I wondered what was bothering him.

"It's just that I don't think he has his politics straight just yet."

I grinned at him. "I think I get it, now. He thinks Lyndon Johnson is only one or two steps removed from the throne of God, right?"

"Probably not quite that bad, Preacher, but you get the idea. He's got a bumper sticker for the Democrat that's running for the statehouse from our district."

"Come on, Brother Johnson, I'll bet there are a half-dozen farmers in the congregation who will vote Democrat this fall."

"I don't think so, Preacher." He hesitated for a moment. "Okay, maybe a couple."

"You've never asked me how I have voted," I said.

He stopped chewing on his pie, and his mouth dropped open. Then he visibly shook himself, and continued working on the pie. It was a moment before he spoke.

"Okay, you got me, Preacher. So you voted for LBJ in '64?" I guess he decided to play the game.

"Are you kidding? Dad would have skinned me alive. He's a personal friend of Barry Goldwater."

"Back to Edgar," he said. Lane must've been tired that evening. Normally we would have volleyed three or four more times. "I'm a little uncomfortable letting him in the pulpit this soon."

"Oh, I agree with you. He gets so enthusiastic about the Lord, I get nervous about what he's going to say."

"Sort of like Apollos."

"Right," I agreed. "And you and Liz probably don't have the time to ride herd on him like Priscilla and Aquila."

"Plus, Liz and I are not in the same league with those two."

I sat there for a moment and debated whether to send a fast ball over the plate. I hated to not take advantage of straight lines like that. But, I felt myself starting to get very tired, and I would have been in trouble if he swung at it. Plus, I could see his tongue start to wander around inside his cheek – he was waiting for me to try something.

"Two suggestions, Brother. Have somebody take him over to North Creek next Sunday."

North Creek was a swimming, fishing and camping club at the end of the Fremont Road, and south of Victoria. Even this early in March, some hardy souls would spend the weekend camping. Once a month, Appleton Baptist was responsible for a Sunday afternoon services in the log chapel at the camp. The deacons usually split the duties among themselves.

"That's a good idea, Preacher. If he puts his foot in his mouth, it won't be quite as embarrassing."

"As someone who has an occasional taste for shoe-leather," I said, "I wouldn't quite put it that way."

"I know," he grinned.

"Okay, you got me."

"What's the other thing?" he asked.

"I think I might give Uncle Angus a call, and see if he could work Edgar in as a post-graduate special student. That would immerse him in the culture for a couple years, and also help him get firmly planted."

"That's really a good idea, Preacher," he said. "Do you think Dr. McKisson would do that."

"Oh, I think he probably would. The question is whether we could talk the Forsens into it."

"I see what you mean."

"I kind of like having Edgar around here. I mean, he's a trophy of God's grace. But, we may not be doing him any favors."

"I agree. When will you talk to Dr. McKisson?"

"I can probably call him tomorrow," I said. "No, I should write a letter. He's probably out speaking somewhere, and a letter would catch up to him sooner."

"Whatever you think, Preacher."

I yawned, and stretched. "I think this preacher needs about forty winks."

"You looked like you were starting to fade a bit there, Preacher."

"I am starting to fade a lot."

He finished his coffee, and stood up. "Thanks for the dessert and the time, Preacher. Let me know if you need anything."

"Thank you for paying attention," I said. "You have a good record of catching things before they turn into real problems."

"I have to give the Lord the credit for that," he said. "The minute I start thinking I'm doing it, we'll be in trouble."

I knew I needed to remember that, myself. After he left, I locked up and headed for my bedroom. I had enough energy to spend about fifteen minutes on my knees. I really didn't regret being a full time pastor again, although it complicated Dad's life. I really loved my little church in Appleton.

CHAPTER THIRTY-FIVE

A few years previously I had attended a Bible Conference in South Carolina in March. Angus McKisson had been invited to join the group of speakers, and I took the opportunity to visit the place. Spring in South Carolina amazed me. Everything was in bloom, it seemed. And anything not in bloom was a verdant oasis. It was the middle of March in Rockford, and we were digging out from about fifteen inches of snow deposited by a late winter storm. The skies were again in the grip of the gray winter haze, and everyone seemed afflicted with chronic depression. I could easily envy the southerners.

The Symposium was next week, and I was spending the week in the office next to Dad's, trying to pull things together. I had a check list of stubborn details that resisted my efforts, and I did not feel I was winning. Nigel had wheeled down the hall from his office and was helping me in the struggle.

"How did you manage to leave this so late, anyway?" he grumped.

"I was otherwise occupied this winter, if I need to remind you," I said.

"Yeah, yeah, yeah. Always making excuses for getting out of work."

"As I understand it, you haven't been seen much in the offices this winter."

"That's different. My management genius ensured things would continue unimpeded in my absence."

I snorted. "And that's why we have the high-powered and very expensive management on retainer from New York City." I nodded to the office next door.

"It's a mark of my massive brain-power and leadership capability that I have even the wealthy running to do my bidding."

I started to stand up. "I'll bet you wouldn't say that to his face."

He paled. "You wouldn't."

"Gotcha."

He shrugged. "Okay, let's get back to this mess you caused."

"I guess the two biggest pieces we need are the chairs and the public address system."

Since we could not fit the entire student body into the chapel at one time, it was a foregone conclusion we needed another venue for the conference. We had selected the gymnasium as the best, or rather least worst alternative. We planned to slide out the bleachers, and then place folding chairs along the gym floor. But, there were not that many folding chairs on campus.

"Let me see your phone book," Nigel said.

I handed it over and continued scanning the list. He ruffled through the yellow pages and slid an index finger down the open page.

"Okay, here it is. Bryson Rentals. I think we've used them before. Give me a slip of paper."

I tore a strip off the bottom of my legal pad and handed it to him. "You want me to call them?"

"No. Ellen will do that. I think these people will have a PA system we can rent. I'm sure they have chairs. Now, what's next on the list?"

"Food. We really don't know what attendance is going to be. I don't want to buy a bunch of food for the dining hall and have it go to waste."

He leaned back, and rubbed his chin. "I'll put this one on my plate, so to speak," he grinned. "Our food service distributor has contributed to the school before. I'll see if I can arrange for consignment deliveries. He's not that far away. He can run a truck over here every day if I twist his arm a little bit."

"And maybe suggest he attend and fatten up the offering plate."

"That too. Next item."

I looked down at the list. "Lodging."

"You should have taken care of that back in December, Beryl," he said.

"I did. We're getting a bunch of last minute requests. People can't find places to stay. I have a stack here on my desk."

"Cripes, Beryl, can't you think?"

I just looked at him, and he glared back. Finally he sighed.

"This one is on your plate."

"So, what am I supposed to do?"

"Start calling the local pastors. See if they can ask the congregations to open their homes to visitors. You're going to have to stay on top of this. Get lists of homes and start matching them to people. Most of these congregations are used to hosting missionaries and the like. I think they'd be glad to help out."

I scratched my head. I thought they would too, and wondered why I hadn't thought of it. To give credit where it was due, Nigel did have a genius for working down through details and driving to solutions. I had learned a lot just that morning from his guidance.

"Okay, I can do that."

"Of course you can. That's why we pay you the big bucks."

"You haven't gotten my bill yet."

"That's what scares me," he said. "The way you run the meter up, you're worse than a New York City cabbie."

"Hey!"

He just grinned. He knew he had scored.

The side door opened, and Dad stuck his head in. "At the risk of getting into the crossfire, I'll say that you two fight worse than a couple of kids. How do you expect me to get anything done?"

"I'm sorry," Nigel said. "I'm in here having to do Beryl's work for him. And I must say, he is not being gracious about it."

I thought quickly. In the interests of getting ahead in the game, Nigel was apt to just turn his wheelchair around and roll back to his office, leaving me with this mess. I needed his help too much. So, I just threw my hands into the air and rolled my eyes in surrender.

"What, my son with the big mouth has nothing to say?" Dad asked with a grin.

"I'm a desperate man. This thing is just not coming together."

He looked over at Nigel. "Then I admire your forbearance."

"Gee, thanks, Dad."

"Think nothing of it, son" he said. "The reason I interrupted this on-going civil war is that our friends from New York called from the airport. They want to come see us."

He stood and looked back and forth at us. "What? You have nothing to say?"

"What's it mean, Dad?"

"I don't know. They will be here in an hour.

"Did you call Ronson Hyde?" Nigel asked.

"First thing. He thanked me for keeping him informed."

"So, Giovanni could spray the room with bullets, and Ronson would wipe his forehead with his handkerchief and look sorrowful," I said. "And what kind of a name is Ronson, anyway?"

"Sort of like Beryl, only different," Nigel said in apparent mirth.

"Hey!" Dad and I both said at the same time.

"And stop giggling, Nigel," I said. "It's undignified."

Dad rolled his eyes. "If you two could settle down a little bit, I could use your help in this meeting. Giovanni D'Amato is sitting on a pile of property out here he doesn't know what to do with."

"Why should we even be talking to him?" I asked. "I mean, it's not our problem. Roland Fordyce and Charlie Bigelow set fire to great big batches of Giovanni's money. He should have known better."

"Yes, he should have," Dad said. "He's under a lot of pressure to get his money into legit businesses. I think that is what probably caused his lack of judgment where Roland Fordyce was concerned. So he's sitting on a major investment here in Rockford. He can't move forward, and he can't back up. My main interest is his soul. I feel some obligation to see if I can help him out."

"Dad, if you do business with him, doesn't that tie you to the same string that the Feds will use to reel in D'Amato? The money is tainted."

"That was very much what I was worried about," Dad said. "Not to mention doing business with the mob."

"It sounds to me like you are working on a solution," Nigel said.

"I am. I've been picking at it since Giovanni first came to see us."

"And do you have anything you would like to announce?" I asked.

"I've been looking at Fordyce's original project plan, and I don't think the local economy is ready for an airport industrial park. But I think we could put several housing developments in the area and actually come out better."

"The smaller you subdivide, the bigger the profit," I said.

"And you thought you didn't understand the real estate business."

"I guess some of it soaked in."

"So, are you going to buy out Giovanni and develop the area?" Nigel asked.

"No, I am not."

"Why not?" he probed.

"Because it would logically include the campus property. If we are going to do this, I want use it as an opportunity to build Mid-North a new campus. I can't do that and stay on the board here. It would be a conflict of interest. Plus I wouldn't have time."

I tilted my head as I considered what Dad was saying. "So, do you have someone in mind for this project?"

"Lyle Wagar."

"He's a local guy, isn't he?" I asked.

Dad nodded. "I've been talking to him over the past couple of weeks. He's about as leery of Giovanni as I am. But, he's had a lot experience turning over distressed properties. He and I had lunch with Hyde the other day. We think there's a way to put together a deal that will be financially and legally clean."

"Risk?" Nigel asked.

"Right," Dad said. "I am not about to do something to put the school in jeopardy. We've already seen what could happen."

"That was frightening enough, thank you very much," Nigel said.

"Exactly," I said. "But, if you're talking to these people, it must mean you think it's doable."

"I've also spent a lot of time on my knees," Dad said. "This is the most complicated deal I've ever put together."

"Should we start looking for another piece of property for a new campus?" Nigel asked.

"Don't get your motor revved up just yet, Nigel," Dad said. "We've a long way to go. But just to ease your mind, I've been quietly asking around about available pieces. Lyle has some leads too. But that doesn't leave this room."

"So, how do you want to handle the meeting with Giovanni?" I asked.

"I'd like you both in the room. I'm planning to tell him that I'm making inquiries to see if I can help him shift the properties. Then I'm going to share some things from the Bible with him."

I nodded. "Okay. Nigel, why don't you help me get this wrapped up before our friends arrive."

"I'll leave you two to your battle," Dad said with a smile as he eased back into his office.

An hour later, we sat in Dad's office as Ellen ushered Giovanni D'Amato in. This time he had left his goons in the car. I guess he felt secure on campus. Or, he wanted to appear non-threatening. I didn't know. I suspected his muscle was as much a part of him as his necktie.

"Thank you for allowing me to visit your lovely campus again," he said. His New York accent was incongruous with his attempt at cultured speech.

"You are always welcome here, of course," Dad said. "I would like you to feel you are among friends."

D'Amato looked surprised. "How can you say that, knowing my organization?"

Dad leaned forward and smiled. "That would give me no justification for treating you poorly. You and I stand before God with much the same problem."

The visitor looked uncomfortable now. "What do you mean?"

"We are all sinners and under judgment from God. In fact, God would probably judge me more harshly if I were tempted to look down upon you."

"I know I am not a good man... but I really try to be honorable."

"Would you consent to my showing you some verses from the Bible?"

"The Bible?"

"Yes. You do believe the Bible, don't you?"

Giovanni twitched slightly. "I expected to talk to you about a property deal, Mr. Cathcart."

"And so we shall."

Dad started to speak, and he was interrupted by a heavy thump outside the door. D'Amato whirled around in his chair, started to rise, and the door slammed open. I'm sure he thought Dad had arranged for the police to sweep in and arrest our mobster. In fact, I wondered if he hadn't.

In to the room lurched William Cliffe. "You are ruining my career, Cathcart." he shouted.

"Dr. Cliffe, whatever are you talking about?" Dad asked. I could tell he was completely surprised.

"This... this so-called Symposium is driving the students into blind Fundamentalism. I can't even teach without some young jack-ass challenging me on every point."

"Dr. Cliffe, you are interrupting an important meeting."

Dad stood and walked over to the academic dean. He reared back when he got close.

"What have you been drinking?"

"Just something to settle me down. I've been watching as you and your son have been destroying this place."

Dad looked over at me. "Can you and Nigel handle this?"

"Sure," I said, though I wasn't sure I could. But I wasn't sure a college president in a wheelchair was going to be any better.

"Come on, Nigel."

I walked over to Cliffe. As I got close I was nearly overcome by the fumes emanating from him. He hadn't just been drinking. He smelled like he had fallen in the barrel.

"Come on, Dr. Cliffe. Let's see if we can help you."

"You broke it. How can you fix it?"

"We can talk about it," I said. I was sure any further conversations would be short and to the point. Our inebriated Dr. Cliffe had happened upon one of those crash landings that would get him fired as quickly from an Evangelical institution as from a Fundamentalist school.

CHAPTER THIRTY-SIX

Nigel and I were sitting in his office later when Dad walked in.

"Sheesh, what a day," he said. "Did you take care of our errant dean?"

"Dr. Voysey drove him home," I said. "He hates me and doesn't trust Nigel."

"Not that any of that is going to matter in the morning," Nigel said.

Dad raised an eyebrow as he moved over to a chair and dropped into it. "Meaning what, Nigel?"

"I told him to be in my office at 8 AM tomorrow morning showered and sober."

"Showered?"

"After Beryl and I dragged him out of there, he threw up all over himself."

Dad winced. "And Clarke drove him home?"

"I didn't know who else to call," Nigel said. "He was rather belligerent, as you may have noticed."

Dad snorted. "Not exactly what I needed at that moment."

"And it wrecked your meeting?" I asked.

"No. Not really. Giovanni was understandably curious. I told him we had some problems getting all of the faculty on the same page. He told me he understood. He has the same problem."

"Maybe we could fit Dr. Cliffe out in cement overshoes," I immediately said. "Or maybe Giovanni owes you a favor, Dad."

"That's really not funny, Beryl."

I had learned that when Dad slapped me like that, it was usually smart just to change the subject and move on. So I did.

"Well, did you accomplish anything?"

"I gave him hope," Dad said, "which may not have been a good idea. I carefully explained that I was a long way from putting a deal together, but there was a chance that I could reduce his losses."

"How did he react?" Nigel asked.

"He lunged for it. He must be under more pressure than I thought."

"Does he understand your limitations?" I asked.

"I think so. Giovanni D'Amato is no fool. He recognizes that polite society views him and his cohorts as sewer rats. That fact that you and Nigel are routinely polite to him impressed him greatly."

"I'd just like to see him get saved," I said.

"I would too. We will just have to pray to that effect. Now Nigel, what are you planning to do about Bill Cliffe?"

"When he gets here in the morning, I will have his final paycheck ready. Dr. Voysey and the campus security officer will escort him to his office and assist him in packing everything up. He will then leave campus for the last time."

"Who is covering his classes?"

"Voysey is convening a departmental meeting at eleven. There's no chapel tomorrow, remember. He said they would decide among themselves how to portion out the workload. Although at that point, he was hardly speaking to me."

"Because you made him drive Cliffe home?"

"No. He readily agreed to help with that. No, I just appointed him acting dean. He was really mad at me about it."

I snickered. "He was really inventive. He took you apart verbally without using a single bad word."

"You might say that. It didn't help that you were obviously trying not to laugh."

Dad groaned. "Sometimes I am despair of your ever growing up, Beryl."

"What can I say? I'm my father's son."

"I've got to call my lawyer while there's still time to cut you out of my will."

Nigel laughed. "Then we can drop him off on a street corner in Chicago where he can sell pencils for a living."

Dad shook his finger at Nigel. "And don't think I'm going to leave it all to you either. You're still on probation, even if I do like you better."

It wasn't often we could convince Dad to participate in our silly games, but it was fun when we did. He didn't unbend often, but Mom told me one time that before I was born he used to get unwound a lot like I did. I guess having kids made you think about being an example or something.

Dinner that Tuesday night was a little different. I had already planned a date with Connie, when Nigel started complaining about being cooped up. So I arranged a double date with him and Ellen. It was a weak moment on my part, and I worried about it all afternoon. Nigel and Ellen were enthusiastic, as was Connie. I decided I was being overly cautious.

Nigel was getting around on foot fairly well, but we decided to take the wheelchair with us to the country club. The waiters were much more attentive when we wheeled our recovering invalid into the dining room. Ellen and Connie were animated and excited about being together at the country club. I think Nigel was eagerly anticipating the possibility of my putting my foot in my mouth – something I was fully capable of doing. I resolved to be especially careful, knowing I would receive no mercy or sympathy from that group.

While we were waiting for the staff to get a table ready for us, Nigel asked me to push him to the men's room. The expansive, white-tiled privy was empty when I eased him through the door.

"This is as far as I'm taking you, Nigel. From this point you're on your own."

"Don't worry, Beryl. I'll try not to wet all over myself."

"That would be an accomplishment."

"And I have a proposal," he continued.

"What would that be?"

"Simply this," he said with a grin. "Just between the two of us, you understand. But, which ever one of us cracks up first owes the other five bucks."

I considered his offer carefully and decided it was a worthy challenge. "Okay. Deal."

"You poor sucker."

"I don't know, Nigel, you would probably never pay up anyway."

"I won't need to."

"Ha!"

"What's going on?" Ellen asked immediately when we rejoined them.

"What are you talking about?" I asked.

"Nigel has that look he gets when he has put something over on someone."

"I have no idea what you are talking about," Nigel said.

Connie made no comment, but her faint smile worried me. I had discovered she was perceptive. And I was learning that, in her quiet way, she could more than hold her own with me. I was starting to wonder if I had made such a great deal with Nigel in the men's room.

The maître d' stepped over to us. "Your table is ready, Mr. Cathcart."

"Thank you."

The pastel décor in the club dining room set a nice background for the meal. We were again at the table by the windows and a bit separated from the other diners. We managed to order our beverages without mishap.

"Quite the day today," Ellen said.

"How so?" Connie asked.

"I don't believe we've ever had a faculty member throw up in the president's office before."

"What?" Connie obviously did not see that one coming. "Was somebody sick?"

Ellen suddenly looked over at Nigel. "Should I be talking about this?"

"Yes, Nigel," I jumped in, "should she be talking about this?"

Nigel rolled his eyes. "Okay, you've already started the tale. But it doesn't go beyond this table."

"Dr. Cliffe and Nigel were comparing surgery scars," I jumped back in, "and it made Dr. Cliffe sick."

"Will you stop?" Ellen said.

Connie gave me a warning look, and upon reflection I decided I was pushing things just a bit.

"I'm sorry. That was not as funny as I thought it was going to be."

"His dad tells him that all the time," Nigel said. "He never seems to learn."

"Could we get back to the story, please?" Ellen asked. She had the *I'm not kidding* tone in her voice that I remembered well.

"Oh, very well," Nigel said. "Dr. Cliffe was upset about the changes the Symposium is bringing about. Our new emphasis on inerrancy has resulted in some of the graduate students challenging him in class. He interrupted a meeting we were in with Dr. Cathcart. He was pretty deep into his cups."

"He was drunk!" Ellen explained. "Nigel and Beryl got him out of the meeting and into Nigel's office."

Connie's hand was over her mouth in shock. "But he's a member of the faculty. He was drinking?"

"He smelled like a brewery," I said. "He wasn't quite falling-down drunk, but he was pretty unsteady."

Ellen jumped back in again. "I had to call the janitor in to clean up Nigel's office."

"And the janitor brought in that stuff they sprinkle on the floor when somebody gets sick," I said. "It made things smell even worse than Nigel's office usually does."

I felt Connie's shoe tapping me on the side of my ankle, and I looked over to see her warning look again. She hadn't seen me and Nigel misbehave, and she clearly didn't like it. Maybe I would be smart not to push it at that moment. As it turned out, it wasn't necessary for me to provide the entertainment.

The waiter materialized at our table again.

"What would the ladies and gentlemen like to order tonight."

Ellen ordered the trout, and Connie decided she would like the chicken cordon bleu. I selected the filet mignon with a baked potato and salad. Nigel had been scanning the menu and looked up when the waiter stepped over to him.

"I'll have the twelve ounce sirloin. And you had the potatoes.. um"

"Au gratin?" the waiter supplied helpfully.

"Yes, yes, that's it. And the last time I was here, I had a truly outstanding macaroni and cheese dish. Do you happen to have that tonight?"

"Nigel!" Ellen hissed. "You don't need all that."

He kind of waved her off and looked at the waiter again. "If you have that, I would really like some."

"Yes, Sir. The manager's wife actually makes the macaroni and cheese for us. It's a specialty of the house."

"Oh, very good. And you also have a very nice cauliflower and cheese dish, I believe."

"Nigel!" Ellen was getting a little more pointed.

"Yes, Sir," the waiter said.

"I'll have some of that too."

"Very well, Sir. Will there be anything else for anyone?"

"Just a minute," Ellen said. "Nigel, you need to take something off that order." She looked at the waiter. "He doesn't need the macaroni and cheese. And make that an eight ounce sirloin."

"Ellen, give it a rest," Nigel said quietly.

The waiter was starting to look confused. I didn't know what to do. When I was growing up, my Dad had counseled me that when two dogs start fighting, just stay away from it. Otherwise you were liable to get bit. Connie seemed content, or maybe resigned to see how things were going to play out. She definitely had more patience than I.

"I'm very happy with what I ordered," Nigel said. He looked at the waiter. "Leave things as they are, please."

"Yes, Sir." And the waiter quickly vanished, which was a good tactical move on his part.

Ellen swung on Nigel. "It isn't any wonder you are putting on weight the way you are. If you keep eating that way, you are going to turn into the Gospel Blimp!"

"Hey, Ellen, I don't get out very much right now, and I want to enjoy my meal. Besides, you're the one who has been trying to get me to eat."

"That was before you started piling on the weight."

"Just give it a rest, Ellen."

"You were here yesterday noon with Mr. Cathcart. What did you eat then?"

"That's neither here nor there. It was a business meeting."

"And you probably had the macaroni and cheese yesterday, too."

Nigel didn't say anything. He just stared straight ahead across the room.

"I knew it. We are going to have to get a handle on your diet, Nigel."

"Ellen, this is not the time or place," he said.

"Oh, I think it is."

"We will talk about it later. Okay?"

I had seen it a few times before when Nigel adopted the tone of voice which indicated he was not going to be pushed any further. I think Ellen recognized it too, because she subsided. I think I had a slightly hysterical tone in my voice when I clapped my hands together and picked up the conversation. The look on Connie's face told me she was enjoying my discomfiture.

"So... anyway... After Dr. Cliffe finished... unloading himself all over Nigel's office, I stepped out and called Dr. Voysey."

Ellen decided to pick up the tale. "So, Dr. Voysey came right over to help. He's such a dear man."

Nigel flashed me a look of thanks, as well as his amusement.

"Dear man?" I asked. "I mean, I have a lot of respect for Dr. Voysey, but *dear man* is just about the last way I would describe him."

"Oh poo, Beryl," she said. "You just don't know him well. He's really a sweetheart."

"Whatever. But anyway, he was pretty quick to help us out. He drove Cliffe home, leaving Nigel to deal with the results of that industrial accident in his office."

"It did kind of take the wind out of his sails," Nigel replied. "After the little incident," and he held up two fingers on each hand to indicate quotation marks, "he settled right down."

"That I can understand." I glanced over at Nigel, and it looked like his good humor had returned. I began calculating for maximum effect. "It kind of reminds me of Balaam."

"How, so?" Nigel asked. He must have been a little behind the curve after his brief fight with Ellen because he handed me that straight line on a platter.

"Because when Dr. Cliffe opened his mouth, he had no idea what was going to come out."

Nigel bit his lip and struggled not to laugh. Now was the time to close the deal. "On the other hand Nigel, do we really know who was speaking? Was it Balaam, or was it the dumb ass?"

And Nigel exploded into laughter. The other diners were looking curiously at us. I grinned at him and rolled my tongue around in my cheek.

Then Connie slapped the table with her hand. "Now that's just about enough, Beryl!"

She wasn't loud, but she definitely carried authority. I felt that thrill of fear in the pit of my stomach. My big mouth had gotten me in trouble again, and I really didn't want her mad at me. I quickly looked over at her to see her struggling to maintain a stern face. But, her eyes were twinkling. And Ellen was laughing too. Okay, I had skated past that one, but it was probably a good time to call the game. I was way ahead on points, anyway.

Then Nigel made a ceremony out of extracting his wallet from his pocket. He pulled out a five dollar bill, and slid it across the table to me.

"Would somebody like to tell me what is going on?" Ellen asked.

"To the victor," I said. "The vanquished can explain."

"Explain what?" Connie asked.

Nigel looked sheepish now. "Well, Beryl and I made a bet as to who could make the other laugh first."

Ellen looked back and forth between us for a few moments before she spoke. "That's just not funny. I wish I had my car here tonight. I would take Connie, and *we* would go to another restaurant."

The waiter arrived then with our dinner salads, and that probably prevented open conflict. I did enjoy the meal, however.

CHAPTER THIRTY-SEVEN

Connie was quiet for a time after we dropped Nigel and Ellen off at his house. I was nervous because I thought she was mad at me, and I didn't know how the evening was going to end.

"Ellen and Nigel fight all the time," she said suddenly.

"Nigel has told me about it. It doesn't surprise me."

"I hate that. My older brothers fought all the time while we were growing up. I would go sit in my room, so I wouldn't have to hear it."

"I don't have any brothers to fight with, unless you put Nigel into that category. He and I rarely argue, other than to pick at each other. And my sisters weren't so much into fighting as pushing for the quick kills. Plus, Mom and Dad were pretty intolerant of fratricide."

"Ellen always knows exactly what she wants," Connie continued. "I suppose you discovered that."

"I did. That was why we re no longer dating. I'm just as glad, though."

She was quiet again for a bit, and then spoke again. "I'm glad you said that."

"I thought maybe you were mad at me."

This girl was a deep thinker and did not speak quickly. "You're a very funny guy, Beryl. And you're very smart. I think you are just about the smartest person I've ever met. You should not have to descend into the gutter for your humor. I think you could come up with more... mature jokes if you really wanted to."

Ouch! That kind of hurt. But, I really could find little to disagree about. She was right. I was quick to dive into juvenile jokes. She made me look in the mirror, and I really didn't like what I saw. I thought of the times I had soiled my testimony, because I couldn't resist that verbal candy of the off-color humor.

I thought about this for a few moments. "I guess I should apologize to you for the way I behaved."

"Is that all you have to say?"

Wow. I felt like a tuna on the gaff hook. She wasn't going to let me wiggle free. She had a lot of skill as an angler. I knew what I had to do, and if I didn't do it immediately, I wouldn't be able. I pulled the car over to the curb and slipped it into neutral. I turned to face her.

"Connie, I behaved poorly tonight. I knew you didn't like it, but I didn't let that stop me. Plus, I know it was not the way a Christian should act. Can you forgive me?"

"Of course I can forgive you."

"I need to ask God to forgive me. Would you pray with me."

"Of course I will."

After we prayed, and without another word, I put the car back into gear and accelerated away from the curb. After I dropped it into fourth, she leaned across the console, grasped my arm, and laid her head on my shoulder. I loved the closeness. I smelled her clean hair and once again her slight perfume. In my experience though, I don't think I ever felt as close to another human being as when we prayed together that evening.

A little later we stood under her porch light, facing each other, and holding each others' hands. I regretted the end of the evening. The air was crisp, though not really cold. I could have stood there with her for the rest of the evening. Then the front door was yanked open, and Hank Seabright stood there. I think we both jumped.

"You two want to come inside for a moment?" he said through the screen

What was this?

"Yes, Sir," I said.

He pushed the screen door open for us, and I briefly wondered at the incongruity of the screen door being mounted through the winter, and came to the conclusion they probably didn't have the money for a storm door. We walked into the house. He closed the door and motioned us into the living room.

The three of us stood there in the dim light of a lamp next to the sofa, Hank with his hands on his hips.

"I understand, Beryl, you had something to do with Mac calling me with a job offer."

From his body language, I decided he was getting ready to read me the riot act for interfering with his personal business.

"Yes, Sir. I guess maybe I did."

"I just wanted to thank you for helping out. When I came home that day, I had no idea what we were going to do. We don't have enough saved up for me to be on the bricks for any time at all. We just decided we were going to have to leave it in the Lord's hands, since... well, you know. But, thanks."

As I shook his hand, I reflected on how I had once again misread Connie's dad. It was getting to be a habit. And at the moment, Connie was unreadable too.

"Well, I won't keep you two. There's no sense in freezing out on the porch. Why don't you just sit in here?" And he turned and walked out of the room.

I sat down at one end of the sofa, and Connie sat right next to me and grabbed my hand.

"You thought Daddy was going to tear into you."

I snorted. "Once again Beryl sticks his nose where it doesn't belong."

"It was an answer to prayer, Beryl, and Daddy knew that too."

"I'm glad I was able to help out."

She squeezed my hand. "You don't need to worry about Daddy. He really likes you."

I sensed her gentle amusement. I had begun to consider spending the rest of my life with this very mature young woman. She had said I was smart, and I was not so humble that I would disagree. But, I also thought she was probably more intelligent than I. She was certainly more perceptive.

When I arrive back home at my little apartment that evening, I grabbed my Bible, spread it open on my bed, and got on my knees to renew my acquaintance with my Lord Jesus. I had almost gotten myself into real trouble on that evening, and I needed to work on my priorities.

# # #

Wednesday morning came, and I threw my things into the car in preparation for driving back to Appleton. Since I didn't have any classes to attend, I had intended to be back at church for as many of the services as I could. On the way out of Rockford, I swung down the cul-de-sac where a basement and foundation was the only remainder of my house. Dad had hired the general contractor who was building the development to rebuild my house. Since Dad was the *de facto* lien holder on the property, I was happy to allow him to negotiate with the builder.

In our discussions, Dad and I had decided on a few improvements to the design, which Dad suggested to the builder. He was happy to incorporate the changes into the project. He assured me I would be in the house in sixty days. I mentally added up additional time to compensate for his unreasoned optimism, and figured I would be in the house by the time classes began again in the fall.

The carpenters had laid stringers across the foundation, and were busily setting them in place for the floor. The contractor was working too, and immediately walked over to the car when he saw me.

"Morning, Beryl."

"Hey, Dave. How are things looking?"

"Fair to middlin. The repairs to the foundation didn't take as long as I thought they would. At this point, we are a couple of days ahead."

"You're putting the extra days in the bank, I assume."

He laughed. "I keep forgetting you've been in this business. Yeah, we'll get some rain and eat up the time we're savin' now. Iffn' I can get the roof on in a week, we'll be home free."

"Then I'll pray to that effect," I said. And I believed he could do it. Getting the exterior structure and roof up was the quickest part of any homebuilding project. The thousands of details to completing the inside are what chewed up the time.

"Thank you, Beryl. I think God will help us."

Dave Howe attended Nigel's church, and Dad had met him there. Mom and Dad had purchased their house in the same development and were pleased with the quality of the work.

"I need to get on the road, but I'm looking forward to seeing the house come together."

"Sure thing. A pity about the old house. It was one of my nicer ones."

"Oh, I agree," I said. "It really was a nice house. Except for the doorbell."

Howe studied me closely. "You didn't like Big Ben?"

"We are going to install a simple *bing bong* doorbell."

I could see him start to roll his tongue around in his cheek. I don't know why people felt obligated to tease me, but he clearly thought I was a worthy target.

"But Beryl, the quality of my work demands distinctive features."

"You know, Dave, I had always assumed that Roland Fordyce set fire to the house. Now I wonder if somebody over the next county got tired of hearing that doorbell and burned the place down."

"You have wounded me!"

"Yeah, yeah, yeah. Listen, I gotta run," I said. "If anything comes up that requires a decision, just call Dad."

"I'd better get back to it," he said. "These guys can't drive nails straight if I don't keep an eye on them."

"I heard that, Boss!" one of the carpenters called out.

He yelled back, "Hey watch where you're dropping that hammer. You're going to end up with a flattened thumb."

"In your dreams."

He turned back to me. "Have a good trip, Beryl."

"Thanks, Dave. See you later in the week."

I eased off the clutch and swung the car around the curve of the cul-de-sac, and headed back out to Route 20. I was glad we had found a Christian builder. Of course, Dave would pay attention to the bottom line – otherwise he would not stay in business. But I was comfortable he would not take overt advantage of us.

Lunch time found me sitting down to a toasted cheese sandwich at my little house in Appleton. Edgar Forsen sat across the table from me.

"Thank you for inviting me to lunch, Beryl," Forsen said. "We don't get a chance to talk much."

"I'm glad you suggested it. I haven't had a chance to talk to you much lately. You're looking well."

"Thanks," he said.

And he did look better. I'm sure getting saved had helped a lot. Certainly he had picked up weight since he had quick smoking. His skin didn't have the pallor it did when I first met him.

"How are things at work?"

He nodded. "I used to look down my nose at factory workers and farmers. I've since learned they are people just like the rest of us. And they have needs too. I also have more money than I ever have had in my life."

"I'm a little surprised that second shift at Butler pays better than your church did."

"It doesn't, actually. We never seemed to have any money before. But now we're putting money in the bank, even after our tithe."

"I think the Lord is helping you to manage your money better," I said. "And you're not spending money on cigarettes."

"And booze," he said. "I'm sure that's part of it."

I took a bite of the sandwich. It was lightly toasted on the outside, and the combination of cheddar and American cheese inside were just slightly melted. Mrs. Marsden may have been a terrifying old bat, but she had the golden touch where cooking was concerned.

I just then thought of something, and snapped my fingers. "I forgot."

"What did you forget, Beryl?"

"After lunch we are going to go into my office and give Uncle Angus a call."

"Okay," he said. "Who is Uncle Angus. It sounds like something McDonald's would serve."

"Right. Do I miss my guess, or did you come today to convince me to let you start preaching again?"

He colored slightly. "I suppose I had that in mind. Now that the Lord has saved me, I have the burning desire to teach people the gospel."

"You've done well in your personal witnessing," I said. "We've talked about finding places to get you into a pulpit somewhere for some practice."

"You have?"

"Yes. And I had a suggestion. Angus McKisson is the president of McKisson University. It's where I graduated. Anyway, I'm going to ask him to see if it would be a good idea for you to attend his seminary for a couple of years to help you get your theology screwed together solidly."

"I already have a seminary degree." He sounded slightly hurt.

"How many of your professors at Vanderbilt believed the Bible?"

"Okay, you have a point."

"Before you get to settled anywhere, I think you ought to take the opportunity to get a couple years of solid fundamentalist training under your belt. I think you probably already have the basic skills. We just need to get your foundations solidified."

"Do you really think they would take me there?"

I bit my lower lip. "That's why we're calling, but I think so, yes."

He set his sandwich down. "I really appreciate everything you and the church here has done for us. Eileen cries just about every night because of some kindness done for her. She's never had anybody be that nice to her before."

That I could understand. Before they got saved, the Forsens were just mean people. That irascibility had gotten them thrown out of the United Methodist church and parsonage in Oneida. The change in their character was remarkable.

A little while later I was able to introduce Edgar to Uncle Angus over the phone. Edgar was wide-eyed afterwards. McKisson had that effect on people.

CHAPTER THIRTY-EIGHT

This was the week. Or something like that. The Symposium would begin on Monday March 21. I had arranged for Avis Brody to cover the pulpit for me that weekend, and I drove up on Friday. In spite of the planning, there were last minute details. And there were things none of us had thought of. I was glad of my devotions on Saturday morning, because we were being stretched.

Sancy Pearlman breezed through the office on Saturday morning, wearing her normal subdued smirk.

"In here to help us out, Miss Pearlman?" I asked.

"In your dreams, Baptist Boy. I'm just supervising this morning."

"So in your manager's tour of the facilities, is there anything you need to call to our attention?"

"There's a lot of snow on the sidewalks."

I slapped my forehead, and yelled. "Hey Nigel!"

From down the hall I heard, "What?"

"Snow removal!"

The building was quiet for a few moments, and then I heard Nigel groan. "Ellen, call Roger Dellums, and see what's going on with the snow."

We had received another six inches of snow on Friday night, along with an ensuing cold snap. It was in the low twenties that morning when I arrived at the Administration Building. I was not happy about that as I had spent part of Thursday thoroughly cleaning up the Monaco, which is not fun in forty degree weather. The exterior of the car was now again covered with salt and slush.

I looked up to see an apparition float by in the hallway. Roger Dellums had arrived. The man was stooped by age, yet still stood over six feet tall.. When he wasn't talking, which was seldom, he moved around more quietly than anyone I knew. I left my desk and followed him down the hall to Nigel's office.

I stepped into the outer office right behind him. Ellen had the phone handset to her ear. She looked up, and seeing Dellums, she hung up the instrument.

"I was just trying to call you, Mr. Dellums."

"It seems I got here first," he said. "Everybody looks busy."

"The Symposium starts Monday," she replied. "We need the snow off the sidewalks."

"It'll melt off the sidewalks by Monday," he said. "Besides, I don't have time."

"What else do you have to do?" she asked.

"Well, we have a broken pipe in the gymnasium."

"What?" Nigel yelled from his office.

A few moments later he rolled from his office in his wheelchair. "What happened?"

"We have a broken pipe," Dellums patiently explained.

"Did you get the water turned off?"

"No."

"No?" I heard Dad yell from his office. Next came the sound of him shoving his chair back – the squeak was distinctive.

I didn't wait around to hear Dad's follow-up. I was out the door and down the hall. I slammed through the center doors of the building and ran across campus, probably faster than was wise, considering none of the snow had been shoveled. For running in snow, leather soled shoes are about the worst thing to wear. However, I only fell twice in my mad dash to the gym. The small voice that often accompanied me in my adventures told me I was likely to have a dandy bruise on the side of my left hip.

I stepped into the lobby of the gym building, and saw a steady stream of water bubbling from under the doors into the gym proper. The water ran across the lobby and enough was going down the stairs to create a series of small waterfalls. I pulled open the door into the gym to see what looked like a glistening lake. Standing in the middle of the water park were the six hundred folding chairs we had rented, and set up for the Symposium.

Following the sound of running water, I made my way across to the opposite side of the room, where a valve on one of the radiators had failed, and was merrily spewing its contents. I was surprised there was that much water in the heating system. But I really didn't know anything about hot water heat.

I made my way back across to the lobby. By that time, Dad had made it to the building.

"Looks like one of the radiators sprung a leak," I said. "I'm going looking for the furnace room."

I headed to the stairs and he followed. "A lot of water for a heating system," Dad said.

"Seems that way to me too."

At the bottom of the stairs I was standing in ankle deep water, and it was very dark. I was not anxious to touch any of the light switches since I was not in any mood to complete a circuit. Dad pulled a penlight out of his pocket. He always carried one for some reason, and I had forgotten that.

"Let's start trying doors," he said.

We made our way through the maze of corridors, checking each door for the heating system. Water was beginning to drip from the ceiling. It was unpleasant.

"I think we're going to have to look for a new venue," I said.

"Tell me about it. We really did not need this right now. Ahhh, here we go."

He had tried a door, and found the equipment room. We stepped into the room, and Dad shone his penlight around. I could hear the knocking of the meter as water flowed through the system.

"It's coming through the water main, somehow," I said.

"There must be some kind of an automatic valve that kicks in if the water in the heating system gets low," Dad said.

"Follow the knocking noise," I said. "Wherever the water meter is, there should be a master cutoff valve."

Dad swung the light around again, then splashed over to the corner. "Here we are."

He reached down and grasped the arm on the shutoff valve. It wouldn't budge for him.

"Here, hold the light, Beryl."

I stepped past him. "No, point it down here."

I got down on my knees in the water and whatever muck was floating around, and grasped the valve with both hands. It really didn't want to move. I looked around and spotted a length of one-inch iron pipe standing against the wall in the corner. Okay, we had a persuader.

I slipped the length of pipe over the end of the handle on the valve, and pulled hard. The leverage helped. I slowly eased the pipe, and valve around ninety degrees. I heard the flow of water through the pipes gradually stop.

"Okay, that's done," I said.

"Thank-you, Beryl," Dad said. "I'm glad you were thinking."

I stood up and wiped my hands on my pants, since they were soiled from the knees down anyway. "I'm afraid we just accomplished the easy part. What are we going to do next?"

"First thing is I'm going to call the insurance adjuster, and see if we can get him out here today. At the very least, the whole floor of the building is ruined."

"Is the building even worth repairing?"

"That, son, is a very good question. And the three of us are going to have to get on the phones and see what we can line up for the Symposium." He looked around the room. "Let's get out of here. This place gives me the creeps."

Niagara was beginning to taper off as we climbed the stairs. We got to the lobby just as Ellen helped Nigel wrestle the wheelchair through the doors. Nigel scanned the lobby, then pushed himself over to the doors to the gym itself. He stood up and pulled one open to look in. He gazed for a long moment at Lake Mid-North, and then said a bad word. I had heard far worse than his pungent observation, but I had never heard *him* use gutter language.

He hauled back with his bad leg, and I opened my mouth to warn him. Things happened quickly, then. He swung his leg to kick the door, and he was very angry. I heard the impact of his shoe against the door, and then the sickening crunch of his leg breaking. He shrieked and collapsed on the floor.

"Nigel!" Ellen screamed as she rushed over to his side.

Dad and I both ran over to where he lay on the floor, writhing and screaming.

"Beryl, go call an ambulance," Dad ordered.

I trotted across the lobby to a door with the word *Athletic Office* stenciled on the frosted glass. It was locked. I looked around, and saw a fire extinguisher on the wall. I grabbed it and pitched it through the window. The result was just about as spectacular as you might imagine. I reached through and opened the door from the inside, and got to the telephone on the desk.

# # #

I sat at the desk in my little office struggling to focus on the task at hand. All I wanted to do was idly spin my Bic pen on the blotter. The octagonal shaft of crystalline plastic with the core of black ink was memorizing as it caught and reflected the light from the desk lamp. Nigel was in surgery, and we were waiting to hear how it went. I was sickened by what Nigel had managed to do to himself. Ellen and her parents were waiting at the hospital. Dad and I came back to campus to attempt to salvage the Symposium.

Dad was over at the gym with the insurance adjuster. I wondered how we would get through the rest of the semester without a gymnasium. Fortunately, the weather was beginning to warm, and the phys-ed classes could be held outside. Dad had tasked me with locating a facility in Rockford where we could hold our sports events. More importantly, I was walking my fingers through the Yellow Pages searching for a new venue for the Symposium that was two days away.

The phone rang, and since I was alone in the office, I answered it.

"Mid-North College Administrative Offices, Beryl Cathcart speaking."

"Ah... yes. This is the Right Reverend Julius Friessen. I am the rector of the Pike Memorial Episcopal Church here in Rockford."

"Yes, Sir. May I help you?"

"Certainly. Word has circulated about the unfortunately event in your college gymnasium."

Okay, I wondered which unfortunate event he was talking about. I tried to think of a way to tease that knowledge out my caller without him thinking I was the compleat idiot. Nigel would have just laughed, and said that my mental state was apparent to everyone.

344

The Episcopal priest or rector, or whatever he called himself, broke back in. "Am I correct in that you suffered major water damage?"

"Yes, Sir. The building is unusable."

"That is unfortunate. I was looking forward to attending your Symposium on the Reliability of Scripture."

"If we can find a location to hold the meetings, they will go on, Sir."

"I see. I thought I might like to speak with your President Robart, if he is immediately available."

"You will pardon me, Sir, if I sounded a bit slow on the uptake. We two unfortunate events at the gym today. Nigel, I mean President Robart was inspecting the damage and broke his leg."

"Oh my. That is really sad news. Was it his injured leg that was broken?"

"Yes. He is currently in surgery. We have not heard the results."

"I must pray for him. President Robart is a friend of mine."

I tended to forget that Nigel had spent several years in Rockford before I arrived upon the scene, and that he had developed contacts in the community. I was also reminded that I was less cosmopolitan in my outlook than he.

"Thank-you, Sir. I will tell him you called."

"There was one other thing. I realize things are in a confused state at the moment, but I would like to offer my church sanctuary for your meetings during the week. We have substantial seating capacity."

"Sir, that is very generous. Our acting president is over at the gym with the insurance people. As soon as I see him, I will let him know of your very generous offer. Do you have a number where I can reach you?"

He dictated his phone number to me. "Am I correct in assuming you have not yet located an alternate facility?"

I wasn't sure how to answer his question, and he jumped in again. "Of course, you would have told me immediately if you had already procured an alternate venue. I shall await your return call. Please do not tarry. There is a lot to do before Monday."

Boy, that was the truth. Just as soon as we nailed down the location, I would begin calling all the churches in Rockford so they could announce the change. I had the numbers of the hotels and private homes where attendees would be staying, and I would need to begin calling them. Somebody would have to get an announcement out to the students as well.

I looked up as Ellen stepped into the office. She had dark circles under her eyes, and her makeup was not up to her usual standards.

"What are you doing here?"

"I was driving everybody at the hospital crazy. After Daddy yelled at me, I decided I would be of more help here."

"What news of Nigel?"

"He's out of surgery and in his room. The doctor said he will probably not come out of the anesthesia for several hours. And we have a symposium to get up and running."

"And his leg?"

She shook her head, and tears welled up in her eyes. "Too early to tell. There's a good chance he will lose the leg."

I looked down at the Bic pen lying on my desktop. I picked it up and threw it across the room. "Of all the things to happen. That poor guy just can't catch a break!"

"It was after the doctor told us that, that Daddy threw me out."

"I wouldn't have blamed you for staying with Nigel," I said, "but I'm glad you're here?"

"What in the world are we going to do about the gym?" She looked like she was on the edge of crying.

"Do you know the Right Reverend Julius Friessen?" I said it with the same lilt the Episcopalian used, and that earned me a brief smile.

"Oh, yes. Nigel lunches with him often. A strange little man, but very kind."

"He offered the use of his church for the meetings."

"Oh, Beryl, that's wonderful."

"I'm waiting for Dad to get back over here to run it past him. I told Friessen Dad would call him back."

"And we will have a lot to do."

I chewed on my lip and looked at her. "Are you going to be here for a little while?"

"Yes. Why do you ask?"

"I think I'll go over and find Dad. We need to get a decision made as soon as possible."

"I'll hold the fort," she said.

I grabbed my coat and headed over to the gym. The sidewalk was now clear, and in the distance I could see Roger Dellums driving a small tractor with an attached snowplow. I wondered if Dad had said something to him.

Dad was standing on the front steps with the insurance adjuster. In the fading afternoon light, the insurance man was scribbling on his clipboard. Dad looked up as I approached.

"Beryl, can you get some signs made for the doors here that say the building is closed until further notice."

"I can take care of that."

"Mr. Cathcart, I will have a crew here on Monday morning, to pump the basement out, and to start drying the floor. At a guess, though, the building may be a total loss."

347

"I understand, and thank you getting over here so quickly this afternoon."

"That's part of what we do." He touched the brim of his hat. "Until Monday, then."

Dad nodded, and turned to me.

"We had a call from the... pastor of the Pike Memorial Episcopalian Church. He offered his building for the Symposium."

"Did he? I've met him. That church is fairly close."

"I told him you would call him back."

He nodded. "Fine. Let's get back to the office. Heard anything about Nigel."

"Ellen just came in. He's out of surgery, but still out of it. The doc said he could lose the leg."

He shook his head as we walked. He looked over at me. "I know God's plans are never thwarted, but I don't mind telling you that I am just about at the breaking point, Beryl."

"We'll get through this, Dad. I started making a list of things to do. I can call some people in to help."

"You probably should do so. It's going to be a long evening."

And it was.

CHAPTER THIRTY-NINE

I had always viewed Episcopalians as liberal apostates. I mean, I knew there were some Low Church people who were great people and believers. But, the denomination as a whole was just about hopeless theologically. When I stepped into the Pike Memorial Episcopal Church that Monday morning, I saw some things that challenged my assumptions.

On the book table in the foyer were works by C. S. Lewis, and J. I. Packer. I had read both and liked them. There was a banner hanging in the lobby along the wall of the... sanctuary. The terminology was different here. The banner – *Bringing the Gospel of Jesus Christ to a Lost and Dying World.* That says a lot about a church.

I got to the church a couple of hours before the opening meeting of the Symposium. A little man quickly walked over to me. I wouldn't have called him gnome-like, rather cartoonish. He had a shock of red hair spraying at all angles from his head. His mouth was too wide for his face. You could almost miss his pug nose because of the expanse of his face.

"Ahh, Beryl Cathcart. I am so glad to meet you. Our mutual friend Nigel has told me about you."

"I wanted to thank you for offering your church building for the meetings. I don't know what we would have done otherwise."

"I am so glad to be of some assistance," he said. "I have watched for an opportunity to help Mid-North College. We have actually sent some of our young people there for their undergraduate training. We of course, have other recommendations for divinity school."

"I could understand that."

He studied me briefly. "Yes, I guess you would. Tell me, Beryl, how does it feel to be standing in the camp of Christ's enemy?"

I could see the twinkle in his eye as I attempted to mimic the gulping fish.

"I can see you weren't expecting me to be so gauche as to say something like that," he continued.

I was slow to recover my wits. But then, I hadn't gotten much sleep over the weekend. Not only did we have the frantic rush of calling the churches and the lodgings to announce the change in venue, we also had to quickly rent enough buses to transport the students to the meetings.

Friessen chuckled. "I really must apologize for putting you on the spot. My sainted wife has despaired of my cruel sense of humor."

Something finally clicked with me. "The girl I am dating recently said much the same thing to me. I seem to be lacking in Christian maturity. The way I dish it out, I suppose I'd better be prepared to take it."

"Nigel has shared some of your mutual witticisms. I must confess I enjoyed them hugely, which probably says little for *my* Christian maturity. Nonetheless, welcome to the Pike Memorial Church. Be warned that I plan to do what I can to convince my Fundamentalist guest that at least some Episcopalians are not the spawn of Satan."

"But the jury is still out on you personally," Good. I was recovering.

"Oh, very good. I like that. I believe I shall enjoy this week. And as I heard it, this Symposium was your idea."

I shrugged. I was still wary of identifying too closely with Evangelical endeavors. "Nigel and I put the basic concept together. Along with a lot of input from my dad."

"Just so. Let me tell you how pleased we are to have a conference in Rockford on Biblical inerrancy. Unfortunately, many of our Evangelical brethren have been trimming their sails of late on this topic. I know you have serious reservations about my church, and I don't blame you. But there are many of us who recognize that if you break the Scriptures, the rest of our faith soon follows."

This guy was solid. I really didn't know there were people like this.

"So, pardon me for asking – what are you doing among the Episcopalians?"

He laughed then. "A very good question. Because some of us take the thirty-nine articles seriously. We believe God's true church is descended from Saint Peter. The English Church was an attempt at purifying it. Obviously it is not a perfect church. But humans are not perfect people."

"But you tolerate false teachers."

"I do *not* tolerate false teachers. I cry out against them. Christ died to save sinners. He built his church with redeemed sinners. When he returns some day, he will separate the wheat from the tares. That's His job. My job is to preach the Gospel and rescue sinners."

My world-view was undergoing a seismic shift. I knew this guy had it wrong on a fundamental basis, pardon the pun, but I didn't think I would be able to change his mind immediately. Nigel and I had spent several long evenings arguing about Biblical teachings on association and separation, and I hadn't changed his mind either.

"I suppose I would be out of line in turning this meeting into a theological argument," I said.

"Oh, I apologize," he said immediately. "I just couldn't resist the opportunity to bait you. It was really unkind on my part."

"Another time," I replied. "We ought to have a discussion."

"Ahhh. He throws down the gauntlet. We must meet for dinner sometime soon."

"I accept. Today however, I think we need to make sure all the arrangements are ready for the Symposium."

"Indeed. Shall we begin by visiting that most critical part of a pastor's domain: the coffee urn?"

I ran my tongue around the inside of my cheek. "Maybe you are not the heretic I expected to find here."

"Oh, that's a relief, thank the Lord. So Fundamentalists, when they are not pulling the wings off flies, actually drink the stuff?"

"Absolutely. As you just said, we all have a carnal side."

He led me to his office, where a gleaming chrome coffee urn steamed in the corner. He handed me a mug.

"I think this one is clean. I'm pretty sure Miava cleaned it up."

"Would Miava be your wife, or secretary?" I asked.

"Miava is my golden retriever. She likes to lick out the coffee cups."

"Well, in that case, it should be fine."

The rector brewed a good cup of coffee.

"Have a seat, Beryl. There is not much left to do. You saw the sign out front?"

"Yes, it worked out well."

"We can walk into the sanctuary in a bit. I had the pulpit replaced with a lectern. I thought that might be a good touch."

I nodded. "That sounds very good."

I looked around the office. The man was a bibliophile. It looked like his library was more extensive than mine, and I had a lot of books. Three sides of the office were ringed in mahogany shelves, crowded with volumes. The large desk was in a corner and angled towards the door. He looked like a child perched in the high-backed leather chair. He pulled a drawer out and rested a foot on it.

"So, Beryl, tell me about yourself."

"Not much to say, Sir. I grew up in New York City, went to McKisson University, and ended up in a pastorate in Appleton, Illinois."

"Please, call me Jules. And, somehow, I suspect there is more to your story. And where the devil is Appleton?"

"It's about twenty miles east of Galesburg. It's a small farming village. Appleton Baptist Church."

"Small church, then?"

"We have about one-hundred in attendance. Sometimes a little more."

"That's a bit larger than the average for a country church, then."

"We had about seventy-five members, when one of the other ministers in the area made some ill chosen remarks. We had about fifteen or twenty of his former church members show up one Sunday morning."

I thought back on the excitement of that Sunday morning, when the arrival of that many new people was only one of the signal events of the day.

He winced. "We all worry about saying the wrong thing at the wrong to similar effect, I suppose."

"My unfortunate remarks usually generate hysterical laughter in the congregation."

"Nigel has so told me." His eyes twinkled. I decided he really was a gnome. "What was the effect upon the ministry of that benighted minister?"

"I later had the opportunity to lead him and his wife to Christ."

He smiled. "I just love it when God maneuvers people into these impossible situations, and He works it all to his glory."

I nodded. "It really was in this case."

Friessen now had a sly smile on his face. "I suppose this minister was one of those liberal apostates – I believe those were the words you were so glibly tossing around."

"Actually, Jules, I believe *you* used those words."

"Did I?" He waved his hand in a tossing motion. "No matter. Could we talk a bit about the speakers for the Symposium? And I must say I really approve of the format."

"As you saw in the circular, we have speakers coming from Moody, Wheaton, and Trinity. They are all strong inerrantists."

"And you have your own Dr. Voysey speaking too, I see."

"Yes. We felt it would be good to have one of our own speaking, since we were hosting the conference."

"And no one doubts where Clarke Voysey stands."

"I think you could say that," I replied.

He snorted. "I must confess I am delighted to see William Cliffe swept from the board. He not only had doctrinal issues, but he consistently failed to contain his abrasive personality. He had a poor testimony in the community."

"I wasn't aware of his reputation," I said. "Some of my interactions with him were not pleasant. On the other hand, Dr. Voysey is colorful too."

"Yes, but surely you recognize that much of Clarke's *colorful* demeanor is just his classroom personality."

I took a sip of the coffee as I considered Friessen's comment. "It took a while for me to figure that out." If I ever did. "I guess you have known him for a while."

"For thirty years, near enough. He and I have the Thursday night services at the Rescue Mission. We trade off between preaching and soul-winning."

It always surprised me how I consistently misjudged people. I guess learning is good.

He tapped on the circular lying on his desk. "You have Nigel scheduled to speak. What are you going to do about that?"

"Barring a miraculous recovery, you mean?"

"Exactly. I don't see Nigel going anywhere in the next month, if that."

"Poor guy."

Friessen recognized my delaying tactics. "I suppose you could tell me it's none of my business."

"It's not that. Dad and I talked about it. Nigel wanted me to speak. He thought it would be great to have one of our graduate students contribute to the conference."

"The idea has merit. I understand you are a careful student of the Word. Nigel tells me you usually acquit yourself well in the pulpit."

"I was tempted," I said. "It would be fun. But I decided it wouldn't be a good idea."

"Because of what your Fundamentalist brethren might say?"

"That's not a problem." At least I didn't think it would be. Uncle Angus and I had finessed the issue of my taking classes at Mid-North, and I *thought* I could extend that to an occasional appearance in the pulpit.

"The issue is," I continued, "that there are stories going around about the Fundamentalists taking over Mid-North. I don't want to give those stories legs."

"Would you not like to see Mid-North in the Fundamentalist orbit?" he asked.

"In the first place, it's simply not true. As you know, my Dad is the board chairman and acting president. He's a committed Evangelical. If I were going to take the school fundamentalist, it would be only if I was the president, and I was clear up front about what I was doing."

"Do you play with snakes at your church in Appleton?"

"Give me a break, Julius!"

"Sorry. I could not resist. So, you are telling me you haven't selected another speaker?"

An idea occurred to me, and as usual, I just blurted it out. "I suppose you could do it."

He looked shocked and then embarrassed. "Oh, no, no, no. I really wasn't angling for a speaking opportunity. Please don't misunderstand me."

"Why not? After you called on Saturday, I asked around. You have a good reputation in the community. I don't think you would put up a banner like that in the lobby as some kind of a joke... well, maybe you would."

"I guess I deserved that."

"Seriously, let me talk to Dad about it," I said. "The more I think about it, the more I like the idea."

I quiet knock on the door intruded on the scene, and a tiny middle-aged woman walked in. The term *elfin* came to mind.

"There you are, Jules," she said. "People are starting to arrive."

He looked at his watch. "They're early."

He stood up, and I did so as well.

"Beryl, please allow me to introduce the light of my life. Beryl Cathcart, this is my wife Miava."

My immediate judgment was that this was a gracious lady. I quickly composed my surprise and shook her hand.

"Pleased to meet you."

"I can tell by the look on your face that my husband has once again spun his tale about a golden retriever." She reached over and slapped his arm.

"Does he often have these lapses?" I asked.

"Far too often," she immediately replied. "I sometimes fear taking him out in public. You can imagine my terror each time he steps into the pulpit."

I thought about the opportunity that straight line afforded, and decided to pass. "With my history of slips of the tongue in the pulpit, I believe I will forgo comment. I have my own terror of moments like that."

"With that," Julius Friessen said, "perhaps we should inspect the sanctuary."

CHAPTER FORTY

I was much relieved after my introduction to Julius Friessen. We had solved the venue problem. We had arranged transportation for the students. We had contacted most of the attendees. A sign was posted at the entrance to campus and in front of the gymnasium directing people to the Pike Memorial Church, as Friessen called it. Ellen was standing by in the office to direct any visitors who were hopelessly confused, and to cover the phones.

Dad covered the platform and made the introductions and welcomes. I stayed in the lobby and managed logistics. The messages were on point and very good. We got through the first day, and I went home and collapsed.

Tuesday I was much more refreshed and more prepared to enjoy the services. Connie had wangled a day off and joined me for the services. I didn't know she was coming and turned around when she touched me on the shoulder. I turned around to face her small smile and almost melted.

"I didn't know you were coming."

"Mr. Brinker wasn't too happy, but I promised to work extra hours to make up the time," she said.

"You're going to end up having a long week."

"It's already been a long week."

She had come over to the office on Sunday afternoon and helped with the final preparations. That was one of the bright spots of the weekend for me, but it must've been a real drudge for her.

"I guess it has. If you could grab a spot on the aisle at the back and save me a place."

"Sure. I guess that means you still have things to do." She smiled to pull the sting.

"Yes, unfortunately."

She touched me on the shoulder again. "I"ll keep a spot open for you."

"Thanks."

Then I turned to the next guest, who had questions about ordering prints of the messages. I was once again reminded how few people truly paid attention. The circular for the Symposium had described the procedures for purchasing content, and how to get further information from the school. They would walk up to me, point to the circular, and ask me what it meant. Patience is a wonderful thing when you have it.

After the morning services, we had the opportunity to slip away to a nearby diner for lunch. The food wasn't great, but the company, on the other hand, was.

"It seems a little strange to be conducting services in a liberal church," Connie said.

"Did you notice the banner in the lobby?" I asked.

"Yes, and I'm surprised the people there let you put it up."

"It was there when I arrived."

"Was this something your father arranged?"

I smiled at her. "Nope. That sign was hanging there before there was any idea of holding the Symposium there."

"I don't believe I understand."

"The *Pike Memorial Church*, as the people there call it, is Evangelical. The pastor is a solid Bible believer."

She put her fork back on her plate as she stared at me. "I'm sorry, Beryl. You must think I'm slow. I've just never heard of anything like that."

"Going over there and meeting Julius Friessen impacted my world-view somewhat, too. I mean, intellectually, I knew there were some Anglicans and Episcopalians who were believers. I just never expected to find an entire church like that."

"Beryl, does my pastor even know what he is talking about then?"

"In the main he does. You have a solid pastor. But, I'm embarrassed to say that we have picked up some assumptions about other churches that are not true. I mean, there is no question that many, if not most, mainline churches are liberal and dead. It seems there are exceptions to everything."

"But how can those people stay in a denomination like that?"

"Friessen spun me a rationale about his church being descended from Saint Peter. Apostolic succession and all that," I said. I don't buy it, but he was serious about it."

"I don't understand how people can believe that. It's not in the Bible."

"He asked me if I handled snakes at my church in Appleton."

"Was he serious?" Her eyes opened wide.

"No, he was picking at me. But he made his point. I do know that a whole bunch of people have false assumptions about Fundamentalists. When I thought about it, I had to concede that we probably have the same problem."

She was thoughtful now. "I guess I need to think about that. I mean, I'm comfortable with what I believe being Biblical, but when you stop and think about it, people in other churches must feel the same way."

"It's a good lesson for us to make sure what we know about other groups are not based upon hearsay," I said. "I think we sometimes are too quick to believe the worst about others."

"That seems to happen a lot."

"Yes, and it's unfortunate, too."

It got quiet for a while as we worked our way through our lunch. It was a bit before she spoke again.

"How is Nigel doing?"

"He is in a lot of pain, right now. The doctor wanted to take the leg off. Nigel refused. He is determined to get back on his feet."

Connie shook her head. "That poor man. Will his leg heal?"

"The doc didn't think so. He was shaking his head when Nigel threw him out."

"Nigel threw him out?" she asked.

"Yep. I was there on Sunday night. The doctor came in to look at the incision. He told Nigel to be prepared to lose the leg. Nigel told him that if he couldn't do any better than that, he would find another doctor."

"What did the doctor say?"

"Not much. Honestly though, if it were me, I wouldn't be anxious to have them cut off my leg."

"Talk about a tough decision."

"You got it, " I said. I looked down at the table. "Are we finished? I don't want to rush you, but I really need to be back at the church."

"Oh, I'm sorry if I kept you."

"No, Connie. I have a tendency to lose track of time when we're together. My fault."

"I think I like your faults."

I shook my finger at her. "Don't speak too quickly. I have some major faults."

"I will try to remember that, Sir."

We paid at the register and got back to the church. There were a few early arrivals who either wanted to find a good place to sit, or to ask me more inane questions. I reached the conclusion that the Evangelicals were as bad in that regard as the Fundamentalists. As I was patiently explaining things to them for the fifth or sixth time, a hand grasped my arm. I nodded to the old couple and turned to see who now needed my attention. I must have looked surprised, because Giovanni D'Amato smiled.

"Mr. D'Amato, how good to see you."

"Ah, young Mr. Cathcart. I decided to take up your father's invitation and attend one of the meetings."

"That's wonderful, Sir. Do you have a preference on where to sit?"

"Oh, I do not want to be a nuisance. I'll find a good place. I heard you had some problems with a building on campus."

"Yes, Sir. We had a water pipe break. The people here were very generous in offering their building for the Symposium."

"Any idea on the damages?" he asked.

"No, Sir. We may have to tear the building down."

He grimaced. "That is sad. Well, thank-you for your time."

I nodded as he walked away and into the sanctuary. Once again the power of the Gospel was manifested. Dad's words to the mafioso were used by the Spirit apparently. I said a silent prayer for God to continue to work in D'Amato's heart.

A moment later Dr. Carper walked past me into the sanctuary. I had forgotten until that moment that he and Dr. Voysey were friends.

Dad walked up to me. "How are things going?"

I pointed to the slightly stooped figure walked down the center aisle.

"Is that Giovanni D'Amato?"

I nodded.

Dad whistled softly. "Praise the Lord. And Dr. Voysey is speaking."

He sure was. Following a brief song service, Voysey walked to the lectern. His manner was completely devoid of his classroom antics. He opened the Bible and soberly began to expound from John 1. He used the message to compare the perfection of the written Word to that of the incarnate Word. I used a doorstop to block the door to the sanctuary open slightly, so I could listen as I kept an eye on the lobby. I had a spiral notebook and Bic ready. I had briefly thought of asking Voysey for a copy of his notes, and was sure he would have excoriated me for not taking notes on the message.

There was no question in my mind that D'Amato heard the most powerful exposition of the Gospel that had been preached in that church, Julius Friessen notwithstanding. There was no debating that our guest was squarely faced with the question that God puts before all men: *What will you do with My Son?* When God's Word is expounded in that manner, it impacts every soul within hearing. I stepped around the corner and dropped to my knees to confess my coldness of heart.

There was a hush among the listeners at the conclusion of the message. The usual gabble of conversation was missing as the people filed out. Most seemed to be in a somber mood as they considered what Dr. Voysey had said. Giovanni D'Amato's face was pale as he walked slowly up the aisle. He definitely was on the receiving end of both barrels of the Gospel gun. He gave me a short, sharp nod as he walked by. His normal loquaciousness was in abeyance.

The Imperial was waiting at the door as D'Amato left the church. One of the muscle got out and opened the door for him. He got in, and the car eased away. Dad walked into the lobby and looked at me.

"All I can say is wow!"

"One for the books," I said. "Did you see our friend?"

"That arrow hit the heart," he replied.

Dad then walked across the lobby, and looked outside through the picture windows in the front of the lobby.

"Well, crud!" he said with evident disgust.

"What?" I walked over to the window. "I don't believe this," I said.

Across the parking lot marched William Cliffe, carrying a sign. In the middle 1960's, public protest was something of a fad. The importance and seriousness of the civil rights movement was diluted, I thought, by imitators who felt obliged to take the streets for any minor grievance. In this case, it was simply embarrassing. The sign said, *Mid-North Cheepens God's Word.* Cliffe was not even capable of proper spelling.

I looked at Dad, hoping he had an answer. I didn't. People were staring at Cliffe as they walked out of the church. From the triumphant look on his face, I think he was sure he had scored a major coup. I suppose he did, but not in the way he thought.

"Beryl," Dad said, "I suppose I can confess that I have now seen everything." He then giggled.

Dad rarely giggled. It usually happened when he was taken by surprise, or if he was unable to contain himself. He thought it was unmanly to giggle. I was forced to agree. But, if Dad could see the humor in the situation, maybe things weren't so bad.

Sometimes you lose situational awareness at times like this. I was so focused on Cliffe's production in the parking lot, I paid no attention to anything else until the black Imperial screeched to a stop next to Dr. Cliffe. The trunk lid popped open, and the two muscle stepped out of the car.

"Oh, no!" Dad gulped.

My heart stopped beating, I think. Giovanni apparently was not able to tolerate an insult to his friend Daryl Cathcart, and was going to stuff William Cliffe in the trunk of his car, and dispose of the body. The scandal would wreck the school.

One of the bodyguards eased the sign from Cliffe's unresisting hands and tossed it into the trunk. After closing the trunk lid, he opened the back door. The other guided Cliffe to climb into the back seat. The two climbed back into the front of the car, and it quietly motored off. The Symposium attendees in the parking lot watched open-mouthed as the Imperial silently rolled out into the street and drove away.

I shook myself out of the trance. "Maybe you'd better call the Police," I said to Dad.

"Where are you going?" he asked.

"I'm going to follow them. Maybe I can talk Giovanni into letting him go."

"Let's go," he said.

We ran past an open-mouthed Connie on our way out of the building. She was just coming out of the sanctuary and hadn't witnessed the drama in the parking lot. I didn't have time to stop and explain. My Monaco was parked along the drive outside of the church building. I hadn't wanted to put it in the parking lot where it would suffer the indignities of having people open doors against it. My obsession paid off in this case.

I got us out into the street without leaving significant rubber on the pavement of the parking lot. The Imperial was moving at a sedate pace a block ahead of me. I accelerated hard to catch up.

"Don't get too close," Dad said. "I don't know how excitable Giovanni is."

"If we don't stop them, all we'll see is him pushing Cliffe's body out of the back door."

"I don't think he would want to mess up the upholstery," Dad said. "Plus, I want to see where they are taking him."

Dad was awfully cool about the whole thing. I had no great love for William Cliffe, but I didn't think he deserved a bullet. I just couldn't see a good ending to this.

Giovanni's car turned to a side street and made its way three more blocks before rolling to a stop next to the curb.

"Now what?" I asked.

Dad said, "Just stop here, Beryl."

I eased to the side of the street, and we waited. I didn't know what was going to happen, but I was sure it was going to be dramatic. A door opened, and I held my breath. Then William Cliffe got out and walked unsteadily up the walk to a house. He opened the door and walked in. Then the Imperial eased away from the curb.

I looked over at Dad. "Is that it?"

"It seems Giovanni wanted to have a quiet word with Dr. Cliffe."

"You knew."

He continued to gaze out the windshield at the house. "Not specifically, no. D'Amato had heard somehow about Dr. Cliffe, and asked me if I thought he should do something about it."

"Really?"

"Really, Beryl. I told him that wasn't necessary, and that things would sort themselves out. He told me that he would have a quiet word with the man, if the opportunity presented itself."

"I'll bet ol' Cliffe was terrified."

Dad turned to me with a grin. "That was the whole idea. Let's get back to the church."

MARVIN REEM

CHAPTER FORTY-ONE

"Your dad said we covered the cost of the conference from the offerings on the first day," Nigel said.

"Yeah, I had heard that," I said. "That's far better than anyone expected."

Connie and I had concluded a celebratory dinner on Friday night with a visit to Nigel's hospital room. Ellen was spending most evenings with Nigel and was sitting close to his bedside.

"There's a lot of talk about campus about Dr. Cliffe," Ellen said. "The students were buzzing."

"You know, I didn't even think about the students when D'Amato picked him up," I said. "I was sure I was witnessing an abduction that would end in Cliffe's murder."

Connie rolled her eyes. "And I didn't know what was going on until afterwards. Beryl ran past me outside and took off in his car. I thought he had forgotten about me."

"I came back," I said.

"I figured you would remember sooner or later," she said.

"Probably later rather than sooner," Ellen said.

She was getting more relaxed around me again, and was willing to cut up a little bit. I took it as a positive sign. I guess she had decided if she was going to stick with Nigel, I was a part of the bargain. Apparently Nigel had laid down the law on that topic, at least from what he told me. From what he had said, this precipitated one of their regular bomb throwing contests.

"The Symposium went well, in spite of everything that happened," I said.

"Including the major train-wreck by yours truly," Nigel said.

"I was too polite to say anything," I replied.

"No you weren't. You were just waiting for the chance to pile on."

"It's probably a good thing you weren't there, Nigel. You might have been the one to get thrown in D'Amato's trunk."

"No I wouldn't. Giovanni likes me."

"He's just measuring you for cement overshoes."

"Will you two stop?" Ellen said with some asperity. "You go after each other all the time."

"Nigel started it," I said.

"Stop!" she said.

"How's the leg, Buddy?" I asked him.

"Kicking that door ranks pretty high on the list of stupid things I have done."

Both Connie and Ellen gave me warning looks, so I decided it wasn't worth investing in that one.

"When you hauled back to kick it, I couldn't believe what I was seeing."

"I was already committed when it occurred to me that it was possibly not a smart thing to do," he said. "Man!"

I cringed again at the memory. "One of those things I hope I never see again."

Nigel stared into the distance. "My fears that it was just about as bad as it could be were amply rewarded."

"How long are they keeping you this time?"

"Another week at least," Ellen interjected. "And the cast will be on for six weeks this time."

"But we solved our William Cliffe problem," Nigel said.

"Amen to that," I responded. "I haven't heard of him talking to anybody on campus after Tuesday."

"Humiliation can be a wonderful thing," I said. "Speaking from personal experience, of course."

Nigel snorted. "Probably not to the extent our friend William did."

"That was pretty spectacular. Now the students are all running around campus going *cheep, cheep*. Even the faculty that were disposed towards Cliffe are staying quiet."

"How long do you think that will last?" he asked.

"Not long enough, I'll bet," I said. "The rest of the semester should stay quiet, though."

"I hope so," Nigel said fervently. "We have a lot to get done."

Ellen laid her hand on Nigel's arm. "No. Beryl and Mr. Cathcart have a lot to do. Your job is to get well."

"What's next?" Connie asked.

I shrugged. "I haven't had a chance to talk to Dad, and I'm sure he will want to discuss plans with Nigel, here." I nodded towards Nigel. "I think the Symposim was successful enough that Mid-North could hold it on an annual basis. The first year is probably the worst financially, and we made money. I heard a lot of positive comments, too."

"I really must apologize for throwing a wrench in the works the way I did," Nigel said. "It was stupid and selfish on my part, and I'm sorry."

"It wasn't your fault," Ellen said. "It was a bad situation all around."

"Have we heard from the insurance company, yet?" he asked.

I shook my head. "I don't know." I looked at Ellen. "Did they call?"

"They did, but your dad was over at the church for one of the sessions. I don't think they've gotten back together again."

"And the real estate deal with Lyle Wagar is up in the air, too," Nigel commented.

"Dad has gotten very quiet about that, all of a sudden," I said. "I don't know what's going on."

Nigel looked thoughtful. "He has not talked to me about it recently."

"With Giovanni involved, he probably doesn't want us to hear anything the U.S. Attorney might want to hear."

"That sounds scary," Connie said.

"Oh, it's not really. Dad runs a very straight and narrow operation. But as a rule of thumb, you don't give the Feds any information they don't strictly need to know. And Dad is on good terms with the DOJ."

"I just don't understand any of that," Ellen said. "I thought some of the academic stuff was complicated, but I don't understand what Mr. Cathcart is talking about half the time."

"Real estate and finance has its own language," Nigel said. "I usually have to ask a lot of questions."

I clapped my hands on my knees and stood up. "I suppose we should be on our way, so Ellen can tuck you in."

He folded his hands in supplication. "Don't leave me alone with her, please, Beryl."

Connie and I laughed, but Ellen had a really unpleasant look on her face. There were definite limits to her sense of humor. We left the hospital, and I drove Connie across town to her house. Based upon the previous conversation with Hank Seabrook, the living room was ours after the evening dates. I didn't take liberties, but the chance to steal a few kisses was rewarding.

We usually spent some time reading a Psalm and praying together. We would sometimes dissect the Psalm and pry the marrow of the passage out for further rumination. Connie was a perceptive student of the Word, and could ask some probing questions. I quickly learned I could not skate past her on some of my answers.

"What time are you leaving tomorrow?" she asked.

"Probably whenever I wake up. I'm not planning to sleep late, but there's no need to get up before dawn."

"When will you be back?"

"Probably Monday and Tuesday. I really need to give some attention to my ministry in Appleton. I'll need to head back down on Wednesday and stay through the weekend. Since I'm not in school, there's not a good justification for my being away quite so much. The people there have been remarkably tolerant so far."

"I think I need to be more regular at the dealership," she said. "I don't want to give Mr. Brinker an excuse to find a replacement for me. I need the job too badly."

I briefly hovered on the brink of proposing a quick marriage, so that she wouldn't have to work. I thought we would perhaps be married eventually, but this is something I really didn't want to get ahead of the Lord on.

"Do you dislike your job?"

"No. I love my job. Mr. Brinker has had me taking over more and more of the book keeping. It is really interesting. I like the challenge of getting all the paperwork done properly. Sully does a good job on his sales orders, but he messes up every once in a while."

"I haven't had a chance to really talk to Sully in a while. I was glad he was able to get to some of the sessions at the Symposium."

"He really enjoyed the ones he got to," she said. "He is really growing strongly in the faith."

I was interested in Sully's progress, of course, but the conversation kept drifting off the course I wanted. I guess that was because we both had eclectic interests, and we could spend hours wandering from one topic to another. I had to force it back. I let the silence grow for a bit.

"If we were... to get married, I would not expect you to continue working."

She twisted around on the sofa, so that she was directly facing me. I felt like she was looking right into my soul.

"I have thought about that as well. We know each other well enough now, that I think we should explore the topic."

I felt a wave of affection for this dark-eyed, dark-haired girl. If I didn't start paddling, I was going to drown in her eyes.

"Beryl?"

I shook myself. "Uh. Sorry. I sometimes could lose myself in your eyes."

I watched her eyes shift back and forth slightly as she watched me. I took the opportunity to slip another kiss in.

"Mmmm. That was nice," she said.

"I thought so, too. I guess what I was trying to say was that I would not be opposed to you working outside the home, but you certainly would not need to."

"Daddy told me that with his new job, my contribution to the household was not as critical. He just has me paying room and board now."

That was interesting. I could see things begin to gather momentum. I had been praying about our relationship, and it seemed the Lord was working things out.

She continued. "Something that has become very interesting to me of late..."

I nodded to encourage her to keep talking.

"I think it would be really neat to help out in your family's business. I know I would have a lot to learn, but it sounds fascinating."

That was not what I was expecting her to say. I said so.

"If I have offended, please forgive me," she said quickly. She looked concerned.

"No, no. It's an idea I had never considered. Have you ever thought of going to college?"

"We could never afford it."

"You have intrigued me, Connie."

"You don't like the idea," she said flatly.

"Actually, I'm flabbergasted you suggested it. It makes a lot of sense on several levels. I like the idea, and I think Dad would be extremely honored."

"Please don't say anything to Mr. Cathcart about it. I don't want him to think I am being forward."

"I won't say anything until you ask me to. But, I think he would really like the idea. My sisters aren't interested in the business – well, it's probably too soon to see what Ruth would think. I think it's fascinating, but that's not where my calling is."

"Where would we live?"

"Appleton, I would assume. But we would be commuting to the house up here a lot."

"Your house in Appleton is just darling," she said.

"If we were married, you would probably want to make changes to it. It's kind of a bachelor pad right now."

"Of course, Beryl," she said. "Bachelors are by their very nature uncivilized."

"Well, it gives us something to think about," I said. "And pray about."

"Do you think this was just idle conversation?"

"No, Connie. We've reached the point where we need to start talking about things like this."

She took my hand, and her smile conveyed an inner joy. "I'm so glad."

"We just need to pray the Lord will guide us through this. Right now my ministry occupies a close second place to the Lord. If we get married, you would occupy that position. Ministry would be tertiary. I believe God has called me to a lifetime of service in His vineyards. I would want you as dedicated to that as me."

"I think I understand."

"I think you do, too. But we need to explore it. Together."

I noticed the electric clock on the living room wall indicated ten o'clock.

"I do have a long drive in the morning."

She quickly jumped to her feet. "Oh, I'm sorry I keep losing track of time."

"If I didn't enjoy your company, I would be here that long."

"Well, in that case, let's sit down again." Her impish grin was delightful as well.

CHAPTER FORTY-TWO

"So, are you going to marry her?"

"Probably."

Lane Johnson sat across from me at the diner on Grand Avenue in Galesburg. Harold Dinsmore, one of our elderly church members had recently moved to a nursing home on Losey Street, and we had visited him on Monday morning. Normally, Avis Brody would have made the trip with me, but he was over in Galva visiting a family that had dropped in last Sunday.

"You are a lot more relaxed about this girl, Preacher," he said.

"You noticed?"

"Well, yes. You were stressed all the time when you were seeing that blond girl."

"If you remember, Brother Johnson, there were a lot of things going on besides Ellen this past fall."

"But the one everybody talks about was the girl that showed up on the same Sunday as the Methodists, and looked down her nose at everybody, except Dr. McKisson."

"No she didn't."

He gave me his smile along with a raised eyebrow. "So you think she didn't look down on everybody at the church?"

"As a matter of fact, I happen to know she *did*." I really did not want to admit that, since it opened all kinds of questions that I did not want to deal with. "But if it showed when she was at the church, I would have noticed."

He just grinned at me with that raised eyebrow. Sometimes I felt like taking a swing at him.

"Okay, I'll admit that our dating relationship was an E-ticket ride. But you also have to admit that this period of time included my being run off the road by a madman in a tow truck, and another couple of madmen waving guns around."

"So when you were being chased by the tow truck, you weren't thinking about Ellen then."

I don't know how he did it, but Lane Johnson always managed to back me into a corner. I didn't know how to answer, and he just sat there waiting. It was time for a stratagem. I picked up my toasted cheese sandwich for another bite. I wasn't fooling him, and we both knew it, but I was frantically thinking of a path to drive out of this one.

"I'm just saying there was a lot going on. But, you're right. I am more relaxed with Connie. We are just very comfortable around each other."

"That's pretty obvious to everyone," he said. "When are you going to pop the question?"

Okay, he had gone from picking on me to meddling. "What are you, my mother?"

He laughed then. "Sorry, Preacher. I just wanted to see how far I could push you."

"You already know how far you can push me, and it's pretty far. Honestly, Brother, I don't think I'm very close to popping the question. We actually just discussed it for the first time the other night."

He took a bite of his hamburger and chewed on it as he thought.

"You know, the people at the church are impressed with Connie."

"*I'm* impressed with Connie," I replied. "I'm happy they share my opinion. But I don't expect we'll get engaged at least before Thursday or Friday."

"That will give us time to prepare a wedding. Next Sunday would work." He didn't miss a beat. I should have known by now victories against Lane's wit would be rare.

"Right. You can be the ring bearer."

He immediately responded. "And we could get Minda Cullen to be the flower girl."

Pepsi really burns when you blow it out of your nose. Since my favorite deacon had won game, set, and match, he just leaned back, folded his arms, and watched as I mopped myself up. And since he had swept the field, he decided it was a good time to change the subject. That was probably just as well, since I was tempted to just pour the rest of my soda over his head.

"You know, Preacher, Avis is turning out to be a great visitation pastor."

"Really?" I was still trying to clear my sinuses, and I'm sure I did not present a pretty picture.

"I've been with him on several occasions, and he has a gift at finding the right things to say to people."

"I admire that," I said. "There are times, like when visiting a bereaved family, that I just don't know what to say."

"You do better than you think, Preacher," he said. "But Avis is just very good."

"I'm glad to hear it. I really like him. How's his preaching?"

"Coming along. I don't think he will ever match your skill as a Bible teacher, but he does alright."

"I'm glad he has had the chance to get his seasoning here. The church has been unfailingly patient with me, and I can see the same thing happening with him."

He nodded.

"Certain unnamed deacons excepted, of course," I added.

"Of course. I pray he will get the experience he needs for when he eventually takes a senior pastorate somewhere."

"Is that what he's going to do?" I asked.

Lane nodded. "He told me he would like to learn as much as he can from you, and then take a pastorate."

"He is uncommonly wise for his age."

Lane just looked at me.

"Hey! I'm almost thirty."

He nodded. I guess he decided not to press the issue. "Edgar told me you and he had talked to Dr. McKisson."

"Right," I said. "Uncle Angus would make a place for him. He said as much. I'd like to try to get him moved out to Elmira in time for the fall semester. I think it would be a great experience for him."

"We could help move him out there about the same time I take Artie out there."

Lane's son Arthur was just about done with his sophomore year at McKisson University, and would be a Junior in the fall.

"I need to check the calendar to see when classes start at Mid-North this fall. If I can, I would like to go out there too."

Lane had finished the hamburger and wiped his mouth with the napkin. I hurriedly shoved the rest of the sandwich in my mouth. I hated to keep him waiting.

"Preacher, I think we ought to run up to Oneida and see Denny James this afternoon, if you have time."

"Since you think we should do it, I can make time. What's going on?"

Dennis James was one of the former Methodists who was now a member at Appleton Baptist Church. I had become acquainted with him the previous August when I rescued him from a tractor accident on the Fremont Road.

"There are two or three of our Methodist friends who would like to go ahead and join the church. They've finished the membership class and see no reason to wait."

Since that was the normal procedure, I wondered what was going on.

"And?"

"Denny thinks they don't understand the Gospel, yet."

"Oh. In that case, I think we should go see Denny." I pushed the plate back and stood up.

We went through another one of our little contests, and Lane grabbed the check this time. I waited by the door while he stopped at the cashier, then we got into the Monaco. I headed up Grand Avenue, and then headed north on U.S. 34. This was an old road, and the frost-heaved concrete made the Dodge bound like a speedboat over the ridges in the pavement.

"I wish you would let us pay for your gas, Preacher," Lane said.

"We've had this argument before, Brother Johnson."

"I just don't feel like we're doing our share. You don't ask for much, and we don't give much."

"Let's see," I replied. "We give generous support to a half-dozen missionaries. We support an assistant pastor full-time. For a small church, I'd say we do well."

"I know you don't need the money, Preacher, but I don't want the church people to get in the habit of expecting a free ride."

"We made them cough up for the new furnace last winter," I said. "That wasn't chicken feed."

"No, it wasn't. But, you know what I'm talking about. You already pay your light bill and the phone."

"And you know why."

"Yeah, well, Harold Dinsmore is in the nursing home, now, and is not in a position to complain. Or, even know about it, for that matter."

He did have a point. Harold Dinsmore was the most vocal of the church members who complained about my extensive long distance telephone charges, and that I left every light in the house burning. The truth was, I did run up a lot of long distance charges. And I did keep a lot of lights on – I was prone to stub toes in the dark, against errant furniture.

"Look, I know it bothers people who see the phone and light bill. And be honest, it bothers you too."

He didn't say anything, so I knew I had scored. And I hated to take money from them. I didn't need it. My allowance from Dad enabled me to afford working in a small country church full time. But, he also had a point. The congregation needed to learn its responsibilities in supporting the pastor. In a way, I was spoiling them. I could understand why parents spoiled their children. It was kind of fun.

We drove along in silence for a while before I spoke again. "Perhaps what we could do, Deacon Johnson, is start putting more money into the bank. If we keep growing we are going to need a new building, and I really don't like to see a church go in debt."

"It would be kind of hard to leave that building, though," he said. "There are a lot of memories there."

"True, but aren't you the one who keeps saying we can't get attached to things?"

I looked straight ahead as I was driving and kept a straight face. He decided to be gracious.

"Indeed. I guess I can't argue with you there, Preacher."

"It's just an idea. Maybe you could float it to the other men and see what they think."

"That's a good idea," he said. "The offerings have been good lately, and the bank account is building up."

"We could also use the money to finance a church plant... in Oneida, for example."

It got quiet again, and I looked over at him. He was clearly considering the idea.

"Well, Preacher, as usual you have given me a lot to think about."

"I think if we stay on our knees and keep our eyes on the Word, the Lord will show us what to do when we have to make decisions."

"He surely will," Lane said.

CHAPTER FORTY-THREE

I wouldn't say that everybody at Mid-North lived happily ever after. But things did quiet down after the Symposium. I settled into a routine of commuting to Rockford for a couple of days each week. With Nigel incapacitated again, Dad had his hands full in running the school and trying to manage the fund-raising operations.

I was able to shift a lot of the routine administrative items for him, and Ellen had definitely stepped up her game. She deftly managed the office, and made sure the right papers and right decisions were routed to the right people. She rarely made mistakes and never made excuses. She had matured a lot over the past several months. I briefly considered her growth as the result of my leadership; then told myself I was a fool. Nigel suffered through three surgeries in rapid succession. He was once again ensconced at my parents' house. Ellen recognized she couldn't be Nigel's nursemaid for twenty-four hours per day, although she was over there every spare minute.

I filtered the routine faculty matters for Dad. One of my tasks was to act as the Personnel Director. Dad made all the final decisions, but department heads had begun bringing me difficult people problems. I was always willing to sit down with the parties involved and drive things through to a satisfactory conclusion. The work was similar to pastoral counseling, and I felt like I was pretty good at it. Nigel told me the employees just humored me.

A neatly typed business envelope landed on my desk one day. It was addressed to Nigel, and Ellen had opened it. She had made the decision that whatever it was belonged to me. I slipped the folded letter out and quickly read over it. I got out of my chair and walked over to the doorway into Dad's office and tapped on it.

He looked up as he listened to the telephone, and waved me in. I walked in and sat down across the desk from him. He periodically said, "Okay," as he listened. Finally he said, "Okay. Keep me posted," and hung up.

"I didn't want to say anything quite yet, Beryl, but I think our real estate deal might be coming together."

"For Roland Fordyce's property?"

"For the whole shooting match."

"Including the campus?"

"I think so," he said. "The U.S. Attorney told me they aren't interested in any the property here. It's clean as far as they're concerned."

"That's great news. This means we're going to get a new campus?"

He nodded. "There is still a lot of work and prayer required before this happens. I need to go see Nigel and let him know. Can you come along?"

"Sure."

"And what was it you wanted to see me about?"

I handed the letter to him. He quickly read through it and looked at me with raised eyebrows. "So Alan Carper resigned?"

"At the end of the semester, according to his letter."

"I guess that solves one problem," he said. "Creates another."

"His replacement," I said.

"And Cliffe's replacement."

"We've received about twelve letters of application for Cliffe's job," I said. "Some of them look pretty good. There may be one or two of them in there that we could talk to about Carper's position."

"Do you feel comfortable about interviewing them?" he asked.

"I could do that."

"Let's do this then: go ahead and talk to the candidates over the phone. We can bring the two finalists out, and I'll interview them and make an offer."

"Okay. When are you going to see Nigel?"

"Right now okay with you?"

I looked at my watch. It was four o'clock. "How about if I meet you over there. I'm picking up Connie at 5:30 for dinner."

"I'm glad you got your priorities straight," he said dryly.

"Of course."

Nigel was in the living room chair with a stack of books again at his side. I was still shocked each time I saw him. The weight he had started to pick up before he broke his leg again had melted off. I suspected the gaunt look was the result of the near constant pain he endured. I thought he had had a tough experience before, but he really wasn't bouncing back well this time.

Dad laid the worksheets carefully across his lap and explained the details of the transaction.

"Lyle Wagar will buy Fordyce's property from Giovanni D'Amato. Once he has that locked up, then he signs a letter of intent with the school. Once we close, we will have six months to vacate the property."

"Can we get a new campus built in six months?" I asked.

"Probably not," Dad said. "I would plan to arrange bridge financing to cover the purchase of the land for a new campus and the initial construction." Which meant that Dad would be personally signing the note.

"Which means we will finally be able to get out of this dump," Nigel said, his voice husky.

"Nigel, Dad's house is not a dump."

Nigel looked up at Dad. "Do you suppose he was trying to be funny or just stupid, Mr. C?"

"No telling."

Nigel may have been weak as a kitten, but he hadn't lost his wicked sense of humor. But of course, I had started it this time, so I didn't feel I could complain.

"And you recommend we should do this?" Nigel asked.

"I do. I just got the check from the insurance company for the gym. We would have to tear it down and rebuild it anyway. This way, we save the money for demolition since Lyle is responsible for tearing down the rest of the campus."

"That's good then. What's the status on the new campus?"

Dad folded his hands together and stretched, cracking his knuckles. I winced, and Nigel grinned. I always hated it when Dad did that.

"I've narrowed the search down to four pieces of property," Dad said. If you're up to it, we really need to go see the tracts."

"Let's go," Nigel said.

"Not so fast, Tonto," Dad said. "I thought maybe I could take you on an outing tomorrow."

"Fine with me. Let's talk about them."

I had to bow out because of my pending date with Connie. I wanted to see the new property as well, but the next day was Wednesday, and I needed to head back to Appleton. I was excited about the prospect of a new campus. I couldn't wait to see the surprise this generated among the students. I assumed the employees would be excited about it too, but they would end up with the task of moving the furnishings and equipment to the new location. That was going to be a lot of work.

"I need to talk to Beryl for a minute before he leaves," Nigel said.

Dad raised his eyebrows, but said nothing as he walked out of the room.

"I need you to do me a favor, Buddy," He said.

"Sure, Nigel. Whatcha need?"

"I need you to pick up something for me downtown... without Ellen knowing."

I looked at him curiously. "Sure. When do you need it? I'm leaving for Appleton in the morning."

He looked disappointed. "That's fine. When will you be up here again?"

"I'm coming up again next Monday."

"That would be fine, then. Here's the address." He pulled a slip of paper from a book and handed it to me.

It was the address for Nelson Jewelers. "Nigel."

He waved his hand. "No, no. It's just a little something I ordered for Ellen. She's been working so hard lately."

"She has, at that. Listen, I can stop by in the morning, and then drop it by on my way out of town."

He brightened up. "If it's not too much trouble."

"Hey, I'm glad to help out the cripple."

"Uh huh. Sure you are."

I had to leave then to pick up Connie. The conversation bothered me, though. My first thought was that he had ordered a diamond for her, but Nigel was annoyed at Ellen more often than not. I supposed I should just take it at face value that he wanted to reward her for her hard work. On the other hand, Nigel did not often decide to just buy gifts for people. His mind didn't work that way. So I put it out of my mind.

Connie and I had grown yet closer over the intervening weeks. I had begun to give a lot of consideration to our relationship, along with the wheres and whens. She clearly had too, and the topic began to come up more often in our conversations.

"Assuming we were to get married," I began, "is there a time of the year you would prefer for a wedding? Like summer, fall, winter, or spring?"

"Oh spring is very nice," she said. "But next spring is a long ways off."

She was getting pretty good at telegraphing her thoughts. We were clearly on the same wavelength about getting married. "How long an engagement do you think is best?

"Umm. I don't know. Mama would be upset if it was too short. She told me she was really looking forward to planning my wedding."

"What do you think about that?"

"Oh, I'm fine with it. Mama has better taste than me. And I really would be glad for the help."

"Sooo, like maybe December?"

"That could be really inconvenient if the weather was bad," she said. "And you really can't wear a coat over a wedding dress."

That told me a lot more. Spring would be too long a ways away. She didn't want a December wedding. I would be back in school in the fall. I realized I probably should start making some decisions pretty soon. I had some idea of what my prayer life would look like over the next couple of weeks. If we were going to get married, it would have to be an August wedding, which meant I would need to formally pop the question soon.

"I guess we'll have to think and pray about it," I said. I knew that sounded lame, but I could think of nothing else to say about the topic that didn't push me into a preemptive commitment.

"That's fine. I don't want to push you or anything."

I wasn't sure what that meant, but I decided it meant I was off the hook for that evening.

The next morning I dropped the small gift bag off with Nigel. He was appropriately thankful.

"I really appreciate this Beryl. I needed to get this, but I'm in no condition to get out on my own yet."

"Not for a while, I think," I said.

"Yeah. Ha, ha. Just stuck in this old chair."

Something smelled funny, in the metaphorical sense. Nigel usually didn't talk this way.

"What's in the sack, Nigel?"

"Just a little surprise for Ellen," he said. "I told you that."

"Right. Then how come you're acting so screwy?"

"Come on, Beryl, you're the one who acts screwy."

"Exactly," I said. "You want to show me what you bought?"

"No."

"Nigel, are you getting ready to surprise the daylights out of everybody?"

He gave me a sly look. "I don't know why you're giving me the third degree. It's just a little gift. Let's not spoil the surprise."

Nigel always accused me of being a little slow, and I guess he was right. I was just crossing the Illinois River and on my last leg of the trip before I finally unraveled his evasions and figured out what was going on. The little rascal was getting ready to propose to Ellen. That was the only thing that made sense to me. He had done a good job of keeping me in the dark; I had still labored under the assumption he didn't really like her.

If I was right, he was not only going to seriously surprise my parents, as well as the Holgates, but the whole campus would be shocked as well. I also concluded that his little shenanigan was going to derail the plans

Connie and I were making. At that point I was more than a little disgusted with Nigel. By the time I walked into the house, I had come to the conclusion I wasn't going to let him mess up my plans. Besides, he would think it was funny.

I walked directly through the house, and into my office. I got down on my knees and prayed for fifteen minutes. I felt pretty comfortable at the moment, and I hoped the Lord was with me in my decision. I got up and made two phone calls. I called Avis Brody and asked him to cover the Wednesday night services for me. I called Connie at the dealership and insisted we go to dinner that evening.

I made a stop in the bathroom and got back into the car. After a quick fill up at the station in Appleton, I was on the road to Rockford. I did a lot of praying during that trip.

CHAPTER FORTY-FOUR

"This is awfully mysterious, Beryl," Connie said.

We were in the dining room of the country club. We were both eating a filet and baked potato. Connie was definitely a meat and potatoes kind of girl. I had made a couple of stops in Rockford and arrived at my apartment late in the afternoon. Connie had driven over there, and then rode over to the club with me.

"As I was driving home today, I did a lot of thinking. I reached some conclusions, and thought that there was not time like the present. So I came back to Rockford."

"That's what I mean. Turning around and coming right back is very impulsive."

She looked concerned. As I gazed into her dark eyes, I began to see my actions as impulsive as well. My resolve started melting away, and now I wasn't sure what to do.

"I guess I need your help in working out a problem, but I'm not sure it would be fair to you to talk about it."

"You are making me concerned," she said.

"I'm sorry. I think maybe I've been stupid."

She laid her fork down. "Well, maybe you should just tell me, instead of wandering all around the countryside."

I tapped my fork on the table as I thought. What *had* I been thinking that afternoon?

"I guess it started this morning," I said. "Nigel asked me to pick up a package for him at Nelson's Jewelers. He told me he wanted to give Ellen something as a thank-you for all her hard work recently."

"That is a nice thing for him to do," Connie said.

"Follow my reasoning here. Nigel is not a gift giver. His mind doesn't work that way. If Ellen was doing a good job – and she is by the way – he would tell her so. Buying gifts is not the first thing in his mind, and he wouldn't know what to buy anyway."

"So he was acting out of character?" she asked.

"Yes. And as I drove south on US 51 I asked myself what Nigel could possibly be purchasing from Nelson's Jewelers?" I looked meaningfully at Connie.

Connie stared at me for a moment, then her eyes widened and she jumped. She put her hand over her mouth. I nodded to acknowledge she had come to the same conclusion I had.

"Ellen talks a lot about her plans," she said. "She constantly schemes about one thing or another. She told me she and Nigel were planning to get married. I just assumed it was her talking again."

"On the other hand," I said, "Nigel really could be just giving her a gift."

"Yes he could," she said. "But you really don't think so, do you?"

"Nigel was acting funny about it. He wouldn't show me the gift. When he gets cagey like that, I get worried."

Connie grew thoughtful. "And so you were trying to think of a way to stop it."

"No. Well, I did give that some thought. But no, I don't think I could stop it, although I can't picture those two getting married. And I had another problem."

She tilted her head slightly as she waited for me to explain. I found that bewitching.

"Okay, consider all of the hullabaloo that will be the result of their engagement announcement. What will Ellen's parents say? What will her church say? What about the school? What will my parents think?"

"I'm not sure the reaction will quite as bad as you think," she said. "But there's more, isn't there?"

"Yes. There's you and me. I was working the math, and it seems if we are to get married this year, it will have to be in early August."

She looked down at her plate, and cut another piece of the steak. She seemed to be adopting my habit of using a distraction to give herself time to think. She speared the meat with her fork and popped it into her mouth. I suppose it doesn't make sense to say she chewed *thoughtfully*, but that's what it seemed like to me. I scooped a bit out of the potato while I waited. Finally she spoke again.

"I agree that would have to be the case," she said. She didn't know where I was going with this.

"That being the case, we would need to be engaged soon. You need time to prepare for a wedding. I need time to make the other arrangements."

"I don't think Ellen and Nigel's arrangements would interfere with ours," she said.

"As I was driving home this morning it seemed that things would get complicated. What would happen if Nigel and Ellen announced their engagement, and two days later we did also?"

She pondered some more, then shook her head. Her brunette hair swirled about her face. I sternly told myself to keep my mind on the subject at hand.

"I really don't see that as a problem, Beryl. I think a lot of people would be thrilled if Ellen were engaged. I can't speak for other people, but I would be thrilled to be engaged to you."

Okay, careful there, Beryl, I told myself. *You're on the edge of a precipice.*

"Now that I'm sitting here, I realize you're right," I said.

She chuckled deep in her throat. "And just what act lacking in common sense were you planning, Sir?"

It was my turn to stir the food around on my plate. Now that I was this far along, I really didn't want to admit to her I had been a fool.

"You're going to have to tell me now, you know," she said.

I bit my lower lip. I was embarrassed now and didn't want to tell her. She reached out and laid her hand on mine.

"Do you trust me, Beryl?"

"Absolutely."

"And I trust you absolutely. Trust includes being able to tell each other about things we really would rather not."

I took a deep breath. "As I drove home this morning, it occurred to me that the best way to get out in front of this thing would be if I drove up and proposed to you tonight." It all came out in a rush.

Her mouth dropped open.

"I thought if we got engaged first, then it would neutralize any side effects from Nigel and Ellen."

"You were coming up to propose?" she asked softly.

I snorted. "Wasn't that a silly thing for me to do? I even stopped at Nelson's Jewelry and bought a ring, if you can believe that."

"You bought a ring?" Her voice was slightly husky, and her eyes were bright.

"Yep." I reached in my pocket and pulled out the small box.

She took a couple of quick breaths. "Might I see it?" she asked quietly.

Suddenly the world receded. The sum total of the universe was the table with the small oil lamp in the center. Connie and I were in that universe, and the rest of the dining room became insignificant. I handed her the box, and watched her open it.

It was like the sun was inside that little box. When she opened it the shadows disappeared, and her face lit up in the glow of that diamond tipped dawn. It was a transformation I could not ignore. I cleared my throat, and she looked up quickly.

"Umm. I know this is probably a little unorthodox, but, Connie I love you, and I would like to marry you."

"Yes," she said simply.

All my life I had dreams of proposing to the right girl. It involved my kneeling before her and asking her hand, then sweeping her into my arms. I couldn't do any of that here. All I could do was look at her with my idiotic grin. I hoped she did not suddenly reconsider.

"Yes," she repeated.

I looked around the dining room. The other patrons continued their meals and conversations completely unaware of how the world had just changed. They were oblivious. I looked at Connie's joyous face. She was unaware I had completely taken leave of my senses.

"Umm. What do we do now?"

She looked at me closely, and began with her low chuckle that expanded into a loud *ha, ha, ha*. She reached across the table again and laid her hand on mine.

"Beryl, I love you too. And you're very funny."

I was glad she loved me too, but I didn't think I was being funny at the moment.

"Would it be alright for me to try on the ring?"

"Of course. It's yours, now. I guessed at the size, but the jeweler said he could resize it."

She eased the ring out of the box, and slipped it on her finger.

"It fits. And that is a *gorgeous* diamond."

I suddenly felt myself on the edge of weeping. I guess it was the excitement of the moment. I didn't know why I was such an emotional basket case. And Connie was dry-eyed and practical. This woman was absolutely worth the wait.

"We should go see my parents," she said. "Have you talked to Daddy?"

I slapped my forehead. "No, and he's going to kill me."

"No, he's not," she chuckled again. "He likes you."

"He is going to kill me and brick me up behind the basement wall with all your other former boy-friends."

"No he won't. He buried them all in the garden. He didn't want to waste the fertilizer."

She got me laughing, then. "I suppose it's inevitable. Let's go." I caught the waiter's eye and mimed writing the check. He nodded and walked over, pulling the portfolio out of a side pocket.

"Will there be anything else, Mr. Cathcart?"

I signed the check and handed it back. "No. Thank you. The service was very good tonight."

"Thank you, Sir, and Madam. I trust you will have a pleasant evening."

"He said as I go to my death," I muttered as we walked out of the dining room.

Connie just laughed and grasped my arm. I don't think she realized how nervous I was becoming. Getting engaged was one thing, but the thought of talking to Hank Seabright terrified me. I had no idea how he was going to react.

As we drove across the streets of Rockford, the conversation trailed off. I glanced over to see her studying the ring on her finger with a soft smile.

"I guess we are going to have to pick a date," I said.

I thought I sounded lame, but I was still badly off-balance this evening. Things had not gone quite as I had planned or expected. I had no complaints, though. And all too soon we turned into the driveway of the Seabright house.

"How do we want to do this?" she asked.

I scratched my cheek as I thought frantically. "Okay, how about if you ask your parents to come into the living room, and we can tell them? Maybe your dad will postpone the murder as long as your mom is in the room."

"Don't be silly. How do you know Mama would not help?"

I gave a deep, theatrical sigh. "I suppose we should go in and face the music."

"They'll make it quick."

"By the way," I spoke as the thought crossed my mind, "can you come down to Appleton this weekend?"

"I think so. I can stay with the Brody's again, right? When do you need to leave?"

"Either Friday night or Saturday morning. We can come back up either Sunday night or Monday morning."

"I will need to talk to Mr. Brinker. Under the circumstances I don't think he can complain about my not working on Saturday morning."

Holding hands we walked up the stairs to the porch. She used her key to open the door, and we slipped into the living room.

"Mama, Daddy, can you come into the living room?" she called.

Contessa Seabright bustled into the room. "Yes, Precioso, what is it?" Her slight Italian accent was musical.

Hank followed her into the room, and the slight smile on his face reminded me that he was no fool. He knew what was going on.

I took a deep breath and cleared my throat. "Mr. and Mrs. Seabright, I would like to ask your permission to marry your daughter."

Her mother's face went blank for a moment; then she shrieked and threw her arms about Connie. Hank gave me a big smile and stuck out his hand. Okay the butcher knife would come out later.

"Congratulations, Son. If I have to say so, you have our blessings. We are delighted about this."

Connie's mother stepped back with her hands on Connie's arms. Then she turned and threw her arms about me. Then she kissed me on both cheeks. I quickly learned that Connie's stoic personality came from her father. Contessa was... emotive.

We chatted for a half hour or so, then left to drive to my parents' house. I was curious to see their response, although Connie plainly looked forward to it.

CHAPTER FORTY-FIVE

On the way to my parents' house, we drove down the street where the rebuild of my house was progressing. I was slightly disappointed it was too dark to see much.

"Will we be living here, Beryl?" Connie asked, as we slowly rolled around the curve of the cul-de-sac.

"Sweetheart, I love you so much I am going to give you two houses to live in."

"So we will be traveling back and forth, then?"

"For several years at least. I need to finish a master's degree. Uncle Angus has suggested I also do a doctorate."

"That's interesting," she said. "What's he like?"

"Uncle Angus? If you don't know him, he comes across as a scary old man. You know, he never had kids of his own. He looks at each student as one of his own kids. After you spend some time at McKisson, you begin to realize how much he loves his students."

"I sort of got the idea from Ellen that he was a control freak."

I snorted. "I am tempted to say that it takes one to know one, but Uncle Angus is really not that way."

My right hand rested on the shift lever, and she laid her hand over mine.

"That was mean, Beryl."

I thought about that for a few moments. "Yes, I guess it is. But it is something I could share with you. Plus, it's true. Did she never try to manipulate you?"

"Yes," she said simply.

"Just, yes?"

"She tries to talk me into a lot of things. If I want to do it, I do. If not, I don't."

"And she lets you get away with that?" I asked.

"If she gets oppressive, I just don't go to see her for a while. That usually works."

That was interesting to me. But we had just pulled up in front of Mom and Dad's house, so I couldn't pursue the subject. Connie didn't display the kind of fright I had when we went to talk to her parents. She really was anticipating this.

We walked through the front door and into the living room. Nigel was holding court in the chair in the corner. His leg was completely encased in a cast and rested on the ottoman. Dad sat across from him on the sofa. They both looked up as we walked in.

"Hey Beryl, hey Connie," he said.

I nodded to him and said nothing to Dad – I just pointed at him, and then pointed toward the kitchen, where I could see Mom finishing the dishes.

Nigel looked puzzled as we walked past. I not sure if he figured out what was going on or if he happened to see the ring on Connie's left hand. But he suddenly shouted, "You rat-fink!"

Dad looked at me in surprise, but I just nodded towards the kitchen.

"I'll get you for that, Beryl!" Nigel shouted again. "It'll be an ugly painful death."

"What's set him off?" Dad asked.

"Stuff," I replied. I glanced over at Connie and her eyes were twinkling.

Mom looked at us curiously as we walked across the kitchen. "Dad, Mom, we wanted to tell you that we got engaged tonight."

Both broke into broad grins.

"Oh, that is so wonderful," Mom said as she embraced Connie. Dad shook my hand and then embraced Connie.

"Don't think you're going to get away with this, Cathcart," Nigel yelled from the living room.

Dad nodded towards the other room. "What's all that racket about?"

"I think I stole his thunder."

Dad looked confused for a moment, and then his eyebrows raised. "Ellen?"

I nodded. "I think so, anyway."

"Oh my. Did you do this on purpose?"

"Daryl!" Mom said.

"You know what I mean," he said as he looked at me.

Connie grinned at me. I think she really enjoyed seeing me on the spot.

"It's a long story."

"Well we'd better see to the raging troll," Mom laughed.

We all trooped back into the living room where Nigel was glaring... at me in particular.

"Nigel, just thought you'd like to know that Connie and I are going to be married," I said. "Aren't you excited."

"You did this on purpose, didn't you, you louse?"

"Whatever are you talking about Nigel?" I decided the best defense was a good offense, trite as that may sound. I was going to keep the shoe on my foot as long as possible, because he would be unmerciful otherwise.

"You know what I'm talking about," he grumped. "I hate you and I refuse to talk to you again for the rest of your life or tomorrow morning, whichever comes first." Then he pointed at Connie. "You, I forgive, of course."

"Oh, thank-you Nigel. I worry about things like that, you know." Connie was pretty quick on the draw tonight.

He glared at me some more, then cocked his head. "You were planning this anyway, weren't you?"

I looked around at the people in the room – people I cared most about in this world. Then Ruth came bouncing down the stairs.

"What's going on."

"Come'ere, Cakee," I said.

Ruth walked over to us. "What?"

I held up Connie's left hand so Ruth could see it. She immediately squealed and threw her arms around Connie. Then she hugged me. "When is the wedding?"

Mom and Dad looked expectedly at us. Connie looked at me, so I guessed I was still on. "Sometime in August, we're thinking. There's a lot of · planning to do."

Mom nodded. "I will need to call Contessa. I'm glad we live in the same town. It'll give us chance to get to know your parents better, Connie. Why don't you come back into the kitchen so we can talk?"

So Mom and Connie disappeared to the kitchen, with Ruth glued to them. Dad and I and Nigel looked at each other. Nigel continued giving me a look that could curdle milk.

"As Ricky Ricardo says," Nigel said, "you got some 'splainin' to do."

I walked over and slumped into the couch. Dad sat down, and crossed his arms. He was waiting for me, too.

"Honestly, Nigel, it was spontaneous."

"And the ring just materialized?" Nigel said. "I didn't fall off the turnip truck."

I just stared at his leg.

"Shut up!" he said. "Rat-fink!" he added for good measure.

"Beryl," Dad said.

"Okay, okay. We had been talking about getting married, and it seemed to me that if it was going to happen this year, it would have to be in August. I didn't want to wait another year, and she didn't either. So, working backwards it seemed to me that we needed to be engaged really soon. I mean, like within the next week or so."

"Yeah, that makes sense," Nigel said. "But the ring?"

"As I was driving home today, I was thinking about it. I decided there was no sense waiting. I called Connie from Appleton and suggested dinner. Then I jumped in the car and drove back to Rockford. I stopped at the jewelers when I got in town and picked out a ring."

"And that's it?" Nigel asked.

"Well at dinner tonight I began to think I had been impulsive, so I asked Connie what she thought I should do."

Nigel rolled his eyes and leaned back in his chair with a groan. "Vintage Beryl. You told her about the ring?"

"Yes, and she asked to see it. When I saw the look on her face when she opened the box, I proposed on the spot."

Nigel looked at Dad. "I think you should cut him out of your will. He's not smart enough to be your son."

Dad laughed. He did not laugh often, because he was embarrassed by his high pitched giggle. But he laughed then. It looked like I had dodged the bullet, but I felt a weight on my chest about what I had done to my best friend.

Things relaxed then, and we talked and cut up for a while. I could tell Nigel was happy for me, and delighted as the prospect of our wedding. I felt even worse about what I had done. I wondered how I was going to be able to extricate myself from this mess. In the kitchen I could hear the girls chattering. They sounded like a bunch of magpies.

A little later the four iced teas I had guzzled at the club had their way with me, and I excused myself. When I came out of the bathroom into the upstairs hall, Dad was waiting for me.

"There was more to this wasn't there?" he asked me quietly.

I grimaced and nodded. "He's getting ready to propose to Ellen. I was afraid of the fallout. That's what pushed me into acting. I thought I ought to get our engagement out before he did. When I sat down to eat with Connie tonight, I realized I was being an idiot."

"But, you went ahead anyway."

"It really was spontaneous, Dad."

"You know better than that. You did a horrible thing to your friend. Does Connie know?"

I nodded. "And she still wants to marry you?"

I didn't say anything.

"You can't tell him, you know," he continued in his soft voice. "He would be very hurt. It would destroy your friendship."

"What should I do?"

"I don't know. I am also worried about Nigel and Ellen. I think you're right in assuming that the reaction to their engagement won't be universal adulation."

"He's talked to you about this?"

"Of course. In most ways, he really is my adopted son. He wanted advice."

"And he's not going to listen to you," I said.

"He listened to me, but decided this was something he wanted to do."

"When is it going to happen?"

"Soon." He gave me a sad smile. "I can't tell you how happy I am for you and Connie. And I'm also very disappointed in you, Beryl."

"Dad, I'm sorry."

He laid his arm around my shoulder. "I forgive you, of course, and I love you. But I'm not the one you sinned against."

"What should I do?" I started to feel desperate.

"I don't know, Son. But, you can't ruin Nigel's engagement – however tragic it might be."

"I know that."

"Then come on, let's go entertain your friend. You know he really doesn't have any other family."

"Then I guess we need to be the best family he could have."

"You got that one right," Dad said.

#

Later after we left my parents' house, I pulled over to the curb, and slipped the car into neutral. Connie looked over at me.

"What have you done now?" she asked in her musical voice.

"Connie, I just feel so badly about what I did to Nigel. It was a horrible thing to do. You really ought to think twice about marrying me."

"You want to back out?"

"No, no. I'm just saying that now you have seen what I'm really like, I wouldn't be surprised if you wanted to step away from this."

She leaned across the seat and took my hands. "Darling, I am just as guilty as you. And I feel badly about it. I should have stopped you tonight. We could have waited another week. But it's done."

"I really am a miserable sinner."

"One of the things I love about you, Beryl, is that you don't excuse your sin. We are all sinners, and I wish I was as ashamed of my sins are you are of yours."

"Dad tore a strip off of me," I said.

"I sort of thought he might. I have noticed he misses nothing."

"Very little. He told me I couldn't tell Nigel."

"Of course you can't. We are just going to have to deal with this."

"Could we pray?" I asked.

"Of course we can. I love having you beside me when we talk to the Lord."

The brief prayer time we had together was sweet.

CHAPTER FORTY-SIX

Married life produces increasing joy as the couple grows closer in their love for one another. Yet these first days of our engagement were among the happiest of my life, thus far. There was, of course, the burden we shared about our treatment of Nigel, and neither of us had the slightest idea of how to resolve it. I could remember giving a flip answer during pastoral counseling – *that's just the consequences of sin*. It had an entirely different impact when I applied it to myself. Connie and I had not discussed it further since our prayer session of the other night, but I planned to be more circumspect in my language during future ministry engagements. Right. Based upon experience, I knew I would be fighting my tongue for the rest of my life.

"Do you think your church will be surprised at our announcement?" Connie asked.

We were cruising across Illinois 17 on our trip to Appleton, and I was reveling in the sense of completeness I had when I was with Connie. She didn't exactly say the same thing, but she stayed close.

"Lane won't be surprised," I said. "He knows me too well. The church will be pleased. I think a lot of them have been praying for a wife for me almost since I arrived there."

Out of the corner of my eye, I could see her smiling and nodding. "What?"

"Do you remember Mrs. Fensterer at my church?"

"Is that the spry little old lady who looks to be about one-hundred-twenty-five?"

"That's the one. She came up to me a couple of weeks ago – it was after you and I started showing up together at things – and told me that she had been present at church the day my parents dedicated me. And she had been praying for me since that the Lord would bring the right man into my life."

"Is that so? What did you tell her?"

"I told her, and remember this was a couple weeks ago, that I was becoming convinced that you were the one for me. She said fine, and she would start praying for our children."

"I love little old ladies," I said. "They're just great."

"I never really knew my grandparents. Mrs. Fensterer has sort of filled that role."

"We ought to think of some way we could honor her at the wedding, or the reception, or something," I said.

"Beryl, what a wonderful idea. You really are sweet," and she leaned over and kissed me on the cheek. I could sit all day and soak up her praise, but then again, I am a selfish lout.

I turned on the dome light so I could look at my watch. "It's seven o'clock. I'm getting hungry. How about you?"

"I'm about ready to pass out," she said.

"Why didn't you say something?"

"I was having such a good time talking to you, I didn't think about it until you mentioned it."

"Well, lady, I suppose we had better find some dinner for you."

We were just entering the outskirts of Lacon, and I had slowed down out of respect for the omnipresent small-town cops, and saw the sign for a restaurant.

STORM SWEPT

"The Chuckwagon. What do you think, Sweetheart?"

"Fine with me."

"There is a smorgasboard called the Chuckwagon down in Farmington. I wonder if this is owned by the same people," I said as I pulled into the gravel lot.

She said nothing as we pulled in. It was Friday night, and the place looked busy. I thought that a good sign. This place was not a smorgasboard, but rather seemed to specialize in steaks and roasts. That was fine with both of us. I was amazed at Connie's appetite. As slim as she was, she really could put it away. I was developing a nascent pot belly and had begun to pay attention to my eating. Dad had stayed thin, but his brother had developed a significant gut. It looked like he had swallowed a beach ball. I knew I didn't want to look like him.

Connie watched as I cut my steak in half, and then divided the baked potato.

"May I ask what you are doing?" she asked.

I patted my stomach. "I have noticed a tendency to gain some weight, and I thought I'd better control it now, before it gets out of hand."

"I wonder if I will ever have that problem," she said. "I pretty much can eat whatever I want."

"That's a blessing."

"Well, yes. But when I get hungry, it happens quickly. I asked the doctor about it during my last physical, and he said that I may have to pay attention to my blood sugar when I get older."

"I'm not sure what that means," I said.

"Daddy has the same problem, so I guess that's where I got it. The doctor told me not to overeat, and keep some snacks around for between meals. And to go easy on the sugar."

The Chuckwagon was a convivial place, warm and cheery. After our meal we got back on the road, and made it on through to Appleton. I dropped Connie off at the Brody's. Christine was especially delighted about our engagement, and I had to sternly warn her to not pass the word around. I wanted to surprise the congregation on Sunday morning.

# # #

Because of my absence for most of the week, Saturday was busy. Avis and I spent the day making the rounds of the hospitals and nursing homes to let our elderly people know they still had a pastor. I gave the extra key for the Dart to Connie, and she planned to spend the day shopping in Peoria with Christine.

Avis and I stopped at the McDonald's in Galesburg for lunch. The hamburger joint was gradually transforming itself into a *bona fide* restaurant. A seating area had been grafted on to the front of the walk-up windows, and we were able to eat in comparative comfort. We sat across from each other and reviewed the week at Appleton Baptist, as we munched on our cheeseburgers and fries.

"I really appreciate all the opportunities you've given me, Preacher," Avis said. "Most pastors don't let their lowly assistants in the pulpit that much."

"If I were home all of the time, I'm not sure I would either," I said. "On the other hand, you are developing a fine speaking style, and I really feel obligated to continue your training."

"I did have a question, however," he continued.

I waited for what came next. During the course of his Bible study, he often pondered those questions that men had wrestled with for centuries. He had a key to my house, and I encouraged him to graze in my library when he felt the need. Invariably he would push a topic until he hit the wall, and then come to me. I had come to enjoy chewing the theological rag with him and appreciated the way he would work the topic into one of his sermons. He might not understand everything he was studying, but he was very good at making application.

I looked at my watch. "We don't have to be in any hurry to get over to Victoria this afternoon. What's on your mind?"

"I stumbled across a book in your library where the author criticized the Puritans because their theology made God the author of sin."

"Ha! I hate to tell you this, Avis, but we won't solve that problem this afternoon."

He nodded. "I turned the topic around in my head for a bit, and I didn't see an easy solution. But, it did occur to me that it might be unfair to accuse the Puritans of such. Surely they have thought about this problem."

"And they have," I said. "They have probably put more effort into that problem than just about anybody else. Well, the medieval scholastics probably put a lot of work in it, but they were off-base to begin with."

"So they figured it out, then?"

"I don't believe so. Oh, they have some carefully drawn thoughts about it. The Puritans and the reformed folk tend to operate under the assumption that God gave us a brain, so we ought to be able to figure these things out."

"Isn't that true?"

I chuckled. "To a point, Avis. We can spend our lives mining these precious jewels of knowledge from the Bible and fitting pieces together. And I think God blesses that. It's how we grow. If I were to criticize them, and I would do so carefully because they were extraordinarily Godly people, it would be due to their tendency to keep paving their roads out to where there were no signposts. They may be right, or they may be wrong, but there is no way to prove it either way from the Bible."

"I think I understand what you are saying," he said. "I really can't find anything in the Bible that addresses this."

"Exactly. The truth is, no matter what your theological persuasion, you have this problem of how sin came into the world without God somehow causing it. It's called the mystery of iniquity. It's one of those things we simply won't know until we get to heaven. The Lord will explain it to us, and we will all slap our foreheads and wonder how we could have been so stupid."

"And that's it?" he asked.

"Yep. Oh, our reformed brethren will accuse us of sloppy thinking. But when you really start trying to extrapolate things, you're in danger of going off the deep end. That's how cults get started."

"I don't think I know any reformed people."

I scratched my head, and then wondered if I had gotten French fry grease in my hair. "There are not many in Fundamentalism. As you probably know, Uncle Angus has no use for them."

"He says it kills evangelism."

"And it can."

"Because if believers are predestined to be saved, there's no need to go soul winning."

"That's the theory, anyway."

He looked at me curiously. "It sounds like you don't agree."

I finished my lunch and balled up the paper sack. "I think that you can get wrapped up in almost any doctrine and ride the hobby to the point it kills your evangelism."

"Including Calvinism?" he asked.

"Including Calvinism."

"I gotta think about that, Preacher."

"It's important to keep balance in your ministry. It requires you to pay attention all the time."

We drove out to Victoria to see a family that had recently been visiting the church. They were members of the Methodist Church in Victoria, and had apparently been talking to the expatriate Methodists from the Oneida church, who were now attending in Appleton.

We had intended to just stop by and say hello, but a chance question about the previous Sunday's message changed it into a two hour meeting. This family had never really considered the Gospel before, and I walked them through the Scripture. This was more than just a five minute *Roman's Road* presentation. I started in Genesis and explained to them who God was. I took them through the fall of man, and then several Old Testament prophecies about redemption. With that foundation I was able to present Christ.

They didn't get saved that afternoon, but I was comfortable that we had thoroughly planted and watered the seed. Avis took a piece of note paper, tore into markers and placed them in a Bible. They promised to review the passages before coming to church the next day. With that, we were now running late, so we headed back to Appleton.

"Why didn't you press them to accept the Lord?" Brody asked.

"I can't explain, exactly," I said. "You must remember that it is God, or the Holy Spirit more exactly, who brings them to the decision point. My goal today was to present the Gospel and make sure they understood it – in as far as the natural man can understand. I've learned not to push these things."

"But what if one of them dies tonight?" he asked.

I wasn't sure I wanted to answer that question. "I guess the best way to respond is to note that the question never comes up in the book of the Acts. There are numerous examples of soul winning there, and they don't talk about it."

"I never thought about that."

"In fact, in the worst of situations, when Paul is on the ship that is foundering, notice he doesn't exhort them to get saved before they drown. In fact, the whole point seems to be that we should sow the seed and wait for God to give the increase. That seems to be His job after all."

# # #

It had been a fine, warm spring day. I dropped Avis off at his house, and returned home to find that Connie had arrived before me. She and Mrs.

Marsden were preparing the evening's dinner. Harvey, Mrs. Marsden's husband would join us, as would Lane and Liz Johnson. Mrs. Marsden was excited about our engagement, and I was looking forward to surprising the Johnsons.

Connie seemed to glow. As she worked on the meal with Mrs. Marsden, they discussed plans for the house. She wanted to make slip covers for the upholstered furniture. When I told her I would be happy to buy new furniture for her, she insisted that would be a waste of money. I couldn't convince her otherwise, but I did not try very hard. I was proud she was so careful about money.

"So, Connie, what do you see in our preacher, here?" Lane asked, gently teasing her.

"I see a wonderful man," she replied simply.

"Aren't you concerned about your taste in men?" he asked, pressing a bit harder.

I guess she had been around me enough not to be intimidated by the teasing. "Well, Sir, I guess you obviously do not know him as well as I."

I laughed. When she started using the word *sir*, she was getting ready to get her digs in. It was fun to watch.

"She's obviously much more perceptive than you," I said.

"Oh, good one, Preacher," Liz said. She looked over at Connie. "You don't want Lane to get away with saying things like that. He'll run right over you."

Connie blushed slightly, but said nothing further.

"You can't let any of the men do that," Mrs. Marsden said. "They don't know as much as they think they do."

Harvey Marsden had probably not said two words all evening. He simply smiled at his wife and took another bite of the apple pie. If the conversation was going well, he felt no need to join in. He just rode along and enjoyed the scenery.

416

Lane, Harvey, and I adjourned to the living room as the women cleaned up the meal. During dinner, the warm spring day came to its typical conclusion with a mid-western thunderstorm, and this one was spectacular. Our easy conversation was interspersed with the crash of thunder, but no one seemed terribly concerned. I could tell Lane kept his ear on the storm, as most of the locals did. The freight-train roar of an incoming tornado was not as common as in Kansas or Oklahoma, but it was something to be wary of.

I looked up to see Connie had stepped in the room and had her hand on the doorknob to the bathroom. She was looking around the room.

"What do you need?" I asked. I had to speak louder over the drumming of the rain on the roof.

"I was looking for my purse." Then she snapped her fingers and walked back out of the room.

I looked back at Lane, who continued a story about his dad and brother. Lane was a good raconteur, and I always enjoyed his stories. He had a gift, I thought. He was just starting into another sentence when the room blazed with the actinic glare of lightning. The immediate blast of thunder shook the house. And Liz screamed.

Lane looked over at me with a small smile. "That was close."

I was about to reply when Liz screamed again, this time a scream of terror. The three of us jumped out of our chairs, and moved quickly into the kitchen. Liz was standing at the back door her hand over her mouth, wracked with sobs.

I pushed past her to the door, to see Mrs. Marsden carrying Connie across the yard to the house through the streaming rain. I blasted out the door and leaped across the porch and the steps to the ground.

"Just get the door opened, Preacher," Mrs. Marsden said through clenched teeth.

The old lady stepped effortlessly up on to the porch and into the kitchen. She carefully laid Connie on the floor. Connie wasn't breathing. I didn't know what to do.

CHAPTER FORTY-SEVEN

I just could not believe it. How could God have brought Connie and me all this way and then tear her away from me.

"No! Oh, no," I choked. "Connie!"

I felt Lane's hands on my arms, and he pulled me back. I didn't realize he was so strong.

"Just let Liz work, Preacher. She knows what she's doing."

Liz was on her knees next to Connie and was beginning CPR

After a minute or so, she spoke. "I'm not getting any response,"

I was crying now. I couldn't stop. Mrs. Marsden stepped over and gently pulled Liz away from Connie. What was she doing?

"No," I said. "We can't lose her."

"Peace, Preacher," Mrs. Marsden said. She spoke softly, but I had never heard such authority. I shut up.

She knelt down next to Connie and put her arms around her. After a moment Connie jumped, and I heard her draw a ragged breath.

"You're going to have to get her to the hospital," Mrs. Marsden said, as she carefully stood up. "Harvey and I will stay here and pray."

"Bring your car around, Beryl," Lane said.

I ran out into the pelting rain and started the car. I swung it around across the yard and stopped at the base of the steps. I ran around to the other side and opened the door. Lane and Liz walked quickly out of the house, Lane carrying Connie. She was limp, with her arms hanging below her. And I was still crying.

I held the front seat back, and Liz climbed into the back. Lane put one foot inside the car, and eased Connie into the back seat, and Liz arranged her head on her lap. I ran back around to the driver's side and climbed in. Lane climbed into the passenger seat and closed the door.

I shifted the car into gear, and felt Lane's hand on my arm. "Just a minute, Preacher."

"What?"

He bowed his head. "As always, Lord, we commit our lives, and the life of this your daughter Connie into Your arms." I sobbed again, but he continued. "Give us a safe journey tonight, and please preserve her life. In Jesus' Name."

I let the clutch out and fed the car a bit of gas. The tires started slipping, and I felt the car sink into the yard.

"Well!" I shoved in the clutch and crashed the shifter into reverse. The car rocked back slightly, and I shifted back into first gear. The car began moving, and I quickly slammed it into second. That way I was less apt to get wheel-spin and bury the car. At some level I was still thinking.

There was a slight embankment up to the driveway, and I knew I'd never get the car up it in these conditions, so I just drove out across my front yard to the street. There would be a mess to fix later, but that was obviously not my concern at the moment. I drove across two blocks and pulled out on to the Appleton blacktop. Once across the railroad tracks, I eased into the throttle and let the car stretch out.

"I don't think we want to tarry, gentlemen," Liz said from the back seat.

"How... how is she?" I asked.

"Well, she's breathing on her own, which is a good sign. I thought we had lost her there."

The storm had driven most of the traffic off the roads, and we had US 150 to ourselves. In my rearview mirror I could see constant lightning playing across the sky. The rain had passed, but there was still a lot of standing water on the highway, so ninety was as fast as I dared run. We came to the stop sign at route 97. There were no other headlights in sight, so I shot through the intersection at about fifty and across to the on-ramp for Interstate 74. The road was new and in fine condition, so I dropped the hammer.

I looked in the mirror at Liz. "Any change?"

"No."

I glanced over, and Lane's head was bowed and his lips were moving. That's what we needed. The speedometer needle swept around to where it hovered over the 120 mark. The car had more left in it, but the speed was frightening. We came to a level stretch of the road and got into some standing water. I felt the steering go dead as the tires hydroplaned. I eased off the gas to let the car coast down and didn't make any quick moves.

I felt the tires take hold again and released my breath. I looked over at Lane, whose lips were pursed in a silent whistle. We were still running right at 100, and I decided that was plenty fast. I began thinking about which exit to take that would get us to the hospital.

"Main Street or Seminary?" I asked.

Lane wrinkled his brow. "Not much to choose. Try Main."

And at that point we blew past a state trooper, and we were still running 100. When I saw the flashing lights come on, I pulled over and eased the car to a stop. I got out of the car and met the patrolman as he walked quickly towards me, his hand on his gun.

"My fiancée got struck by lightning. We're taking her to the hospital."

He walked up and shined his flashlight into the backseat.

"Okay, how fast can you drive, Son?"

"I can run as fast as you."

"Okay, just stay behind me. Cottage in Galesburg?"

"Yes, Sir."

"Let's go."

That was one problem solved. The state policemen moved right out, and I got behind him. In less than a minute, we were back up to 100, and he held that speed until the Main Street exit for Galesburg. Police radios are wonderful things. City police had blocked the major intersections as we threaded our way across town, and I followed the trooper right into the emergency entrance of the hospital.

There were several hospital personnel waiting at the door with a gurney, and they started towards the car as soon as I pulled in. They eased Connie out of the backseat and on to the gurney. Liz followed them into the building. I laid my arm across the roof of the car and leaned my face against it. I felt Lane's hand on my shoulder.

"I'll take care of the car. You go on in."

I trotted behind the group that went into the hospital, and got stopped at the waiting room. I slumped into one of the chairs and put my face into my hands. Somebody sat down next to me and I looked up. It was the State Policeman.

"Can you tell me what happened, Son?"

"I really don't know. We were in the living room talking, and Connie was in the kitchen with Liz and Mrs. Marsden. There was a huge crash of thunder and everybody started screaming. When I got to the kitchen, Mrs. Marsden was carrying Connie in from outside. I don't know what she was doing out there."

"I'll need to see some identification," he said.

"I understand." He needed to write me a ticket. I wondered if I should

422

admit to how fast I had been going.

"No, no," he immediately responded, as if he were reading my mind, "I'm not going to ticket you. But since we had the city police out clearing the streets for us, I've got a big report to write."

"I really appreciate your help, Officer."

"That's part of our job. How fast were you going anyway?"

"I was doing 100 when I went past you. I had it up to 120 for a bit, but hit some water and almost lost it."

"You are very lucky."

"There are a number of people praying for us tonight."

"I see." He stood up. "We may need to contact you for more information."

I stood up then. Amazingly, I still had my note cards, and Bic pen in my pocket. I scribbled some phone numbers on one of them.

"This is my house in Appleton. I commute to Rockford, and I can be reached through this number."

"Thank you, Sir. And I hope the young lady pulls through."

"Thank you, once again, Officer."

Lane stepped up to us as the trooper was leaving. "Everything all right?"

"He told me he has to write a report since we called out all the police in Knox County."

"And?" he nodded towards the doors to the Emergency Room.

"They stopped me here. I don't know."

"Then we can pray."

"Wait a minute. We need to call Connie's parents." I was still blubbering and didn't realize it.

"Sit down, Preacher. Let me make the calls for you."

I dropped back into the chair. This time I leaned back with my head against the wall, and closed my eyes. I still could not believe it. Intellectually, I knew the Lord was trying to teach me something, but the impact had staggered me, and I couldn't think clearly.

A little while later, Lane handed me a cardboard cup of coffee. "Here you go, Preacher."

"Thanks."

"I called your parents. They are going to pick up Connie's parents and drive down tonight. They are very frightened."

"I am very frightened. I wish we would hear something."

We settled into the chairs and studied the dust motes on the furniture. A television sat in one corner, and Lawrence Welk softly serenaded us. I had never cared much for him before. Now, I hoped his bubble machine would go out of control and sweep him away. I was impossible someone could be that cheerful. And what was I going to do?

Fifteen minutes later, Avis and Christine Brody swept into the room. We stood up, and Christine threw her arms around me.

"Oh Beryl, we are so sorry. Is Connie..."

"Thanks for coming, guys," I said. "We're still waiting to hear something. She was breathing when we brought her in."

"When Mrs. Marsden called, we could not believe it. She said Connie had run out to get her purse out of the car and got struck by the lightning."

I nodded. "Okay, that makes sense. She was in the living room just before that looking for her purse. I didn't know what happened."

Christine looked at Lane. "Is Liz with her?"

He nodded and simply said, "Yes."

"Before we do anything else, we can pray," Avis said.

We stood in a circle and held hands as he prayed. It was a simple prayer, and I really didn't remember anything he said. But I felt like God wrapped his arms about me. For the first time that evening, I felt the comfort of the Holy Spirit. I broke down and wept, again. I stepped away from my friends, and sat down in the chair, and let the tears flow. I wept in sorrow – for Connie and what might happen. I wept in relief, because I knew we were in God's hands, and He absolutely would allow nothing outside of His will. But I wept, not in despair, because I knew God would work things out to His good pleasure.

An hour later I more or less had myself back together. I had also consumed another two cups of coffee, as we sat in the waiting room and stared at each other. Normally if you put Lane, Christine, and me in a room together, we would soon have lit the place up. Tonight, nobody felt like talking. Avis was the one who kept things moving. He was in the pastoral role and was effective. He didn't try to chatter in my ear, but he did try to make me comfortable. He fetched me coffee, and he read several Psalms to us. I remember thinking about how well suited he was to the task.

Then the door opened, and Liz walked into the room. We all levitated to our feet and gathered around her. I held my breath.

"She's awake and asking for you, Beryl."

At that point all I could do was cry, and say, "Thank God," over and over.

Liz grabbed my arm and shook me lightly. "If we're going to let you into see her, you have to pull yourself back together."

"Okay, okay. I'm fine. Let's go."

"No so fast. They are moving her to a room. They want to keep her for a few days for observation. There are no apparent injuries."

A little later Liz, walked me through the night swept corridors of the Galesburg Cottage Hospital and into a room, where Connie lay in a bed. I thought she looked angelic. I stepped over to the bed and grasped her hand.

"Hey," I said quietly.

"Hey yourself," she replied.

"How are you feeling?"

"Very tired."

"Then I will let you sleep."

"Can you tell me what I'm doing here, Beryl?" she asked.

"What do you remember?"

"We were all sitting around the dinner table – you, me, the Johnsons, and the Marsdens. Then I woke up in a room with different people."

"You don't remember running out into the storm?"

She looked at me in confusion. "Was there a storm?"

"A lot of people are praying for you, right now."

"Oh, I hate to be so much trouble. Can we go home?"

I smiled. "Connie, I love you. They want to keep you here for a couple of days to make sure everything is all right."

"Well, if you feel I must. Can you sit here by me?"

I looked over at Liz, and she nodded.

"Yes. I am here."

She fell asleep with her hand in mine, and we were at peace.

CHAPTER FORTY-EIGHT

In the end, Connie stayed in the hospital for a week. The doctors detected some heartbeat irregularities and wanted to watch her longer. Her memories of the evening were still fragmented. Mine were vivid. I spent every spare moment at the hospital with her. We talked, prayed, read the Bible together, and talked some more.

Hank and Contessa were terrified for their daughter, perhaps not so much as I. But they were gracious, and treated me as one of the family. As we sat in Connie's hospital room together, I grew to know them better and very much liked what I saw. On Tuesday, Dad flew out to Chicago and from there to Rockford. Mom kept the car and stayed in Galesburg.

Wednesday was a day of surprises. I was trying to pull together a message for the Wednesday night services in Appleton. Avis had heroically taken the Sunday services in spite of being at the hospital with us all night Saturday. I needed to give him a break. He had stopped by the hospital several times, and I could see the signs of exhaustion gnawing around the edges.

Connie was sitting in the other chair in the room – they had allowed her out of bed, and she was working on needlepoint. She explained to me that she really didn't like needlepoint as a decoration around the house, but it helped her concentrate and was relaxing.

Hank and Contessa had left a little while previously to find lunch, and I expected them back in a couple of hours. I was taking advantage of the time to concentrate on my study. There was a tap on the door, and Mac and

Martie Holgate stepped in. I was on my feet and over to them in an instant.

"What a surprise," I said.

"We needed to get out of town for a bit," Martie said, "and wanted to come down to see how Connie was doing."

Connie looked at them radiantly. "Oh, thank you so much for coming to visit."

She had told me that the Holgates, Ellen's mother and father, had been like a close uncle and aunt to her.

Martie walked over to Connie. "We have been praying for you, Sweetie. It must have been a frightening experience."

Connie smiled. "For everybody else, I think. I honestly don't remember a thing about the evening until I woke up here."

"We are just glad to see you on the mend, young lady," Mac said. "We ran into your parents outside as we were coming in. They are waiting to have lunch with us."

"Oh, could you bring me a hamburger, please?" Connie said suddenly. "The hospital food isn't much to write home about."

Mac laughed. "Do you suppose the staff would throw me out if I did that?"

Connie had been craving a hamburger all week. I didn't know if that was a side effect of the accident, but the doctors had insisted on keeping her on a strict diet so they could monitor her vitals.

"It would be worth it," Connie laughed.

I thought the Holgates looked tired and strained. After their visit, I followed them into the hall.

"How are you doing?" I asked them.

They looked at each other, and then faced me. "Not to mention Connie's accident, it has been a stressful week," Martie said.

"How so?"

Mac bit his lower lip, and didn't seem able to speak. Martie picked up the thread again. "We had a bit of a surprise on Saturday. Ellen and Nigel eloped."

"They what?" I shouted. I saw heads turning in my direction, and I quickly toned it down. "I don't think I heard you right."

Mac chuckled softly, although he was clearly unhappy. "You heard us right. Ellen called us about nine o'clock and gave us the news. I tried calling Daryl and couldn't get him. I guess they were on their way down here at that point."

I shook my head. "What were they thinking?" I wondered if my actions had precipitated something. This didn't make sense.

"This came out of the clear blue for us," Martie said. "We didn't know Ellen and Nigel were even serious."

"What is it Beryl?" Mac asked. Something must have registered on my face.

I shook my head. "This whole thing has been funny. At different times I would think something was going on, but then Nigel asked me to pick a package for him from a jeweler. That got me thinking. Connie told me that Ellen had been talking about marrying Nigel. She didn't take it seriously because Ellen talks a lot, no offense."

Mac snorted. "None taken. She talked to us about it, but we discounted it too. Hind sight is so comforting."

"I wonder if I precipitated this when Connie and I got engaged."

Mac shoved his hands into his pockets. "I wondered if I didn't directly cause it. Ellen and I had one of our famous fights Saturday morning. She stormed out, and we didn't see her again before she called us Saturday night."

"I'm sure we could all find ways to blame ourselves," Martie said. "I tried to settle her down Saturday morning after her little tiff with Dad. Ellen said maybe she should just move out and marry Nigel. At that point I was a little put out with her and said, *Fine, dear. Whatever you think.*"

Mac looked at her in surprise. "I didn't know you told her that."

"Well, dear, I was afraid that I was the one that caused this mess."

Mac held his palms up. "They're adults. They made their own decision. We're not accomplishing anything by blaming ourselves."

Except I *was* blaming myself. Maybe it wasn't *all* my fault, but I was convinced I had stampeded Nigel and Ellen into making what could have been a very bad decision. I wondered how Dad reacted. This had to have impacted Nigel's position with the school.

"Is this public knowledge?" I asked.

"It soon will be," Martie said.

"I'd better tell Connie. She will be upset if I try to keep it from her."

"Do you think that wise?" Martie asked. "She has been through a lot."

"She more on-balance than the rest of us, I think. She doesn't remember anything about Saturday night."

"That must have been an awful experience."

"You have no idea. In a year of terrifying experiences, this one topped everything."

"Was Ellen a terrifying experience?" Mac asked.

Martie immediately slapped him on the arm. "Mac, stop that! Don't put Beryl on the spot."

"No, it wasn't terrifying," I said. "The ending was unpleasant, but the Lord taught me some things. I hope Ellen learned from it as well."

"I don't think she did," Martie said, "And I was praying she would."

"I don't know what to say," I said. "I'm sorry these things happened."

"Oh, it's not your fault, Beryl," Martie said. "We were both hoping you would be the one to marry Ellen, but we understand why that was not meant to be. And we love Nigel and he will be welcome in our family. But I wish it hadn't happened this way," and she choked up.

We talked for a bit longer; then they both hugged me before they left. I felt lower than something I had stepped in and had to scrape from my shoe. I was convinced my selfishness had ruined at least four lives now, and I wondered when it would stop. I walked back into Connie's room and slipped into the chair. My evening's message was now forgotten as I stared at the wall.

"What's the matter?"

I looked up at Connie and shook my head.

"Has something happened?"

"Yes. I talked to Mac and Martie in the hall after the left the room."

"I thought I heard you shout."

I didn't want to lay this on Connie, but there was no way I could not. "It seems that shortly before our adventure Saturday night Nigel and Ellen eloped."

She gasped and put her hand over her mouth. She rocked back in the chair, her eyes open wide.

"Beryl, we caused this, didn't we?"

I shook my head. "Who knows? Mac and Martie are both convinced they triggered it. Mac had a knock down drag out fight with Ellen on Saturday, and Martie had made a flip response when Ellen said something about marrying Nigel. And who really knows at this point?"

"The Holgates must be crushed," she said. "We must pray for them."

I stepped over, knelt by her chair, and took her hand. My already high opinion of Connie climbed further when she prayed. She knew how to talk to God. I somehow managed to muddle through. I looked up at her when we finished.

"We're going to have to talk to them, to apologize to them."

"Oh, I know, Beryl. The guilt just keeps getting worse."

"There's no other way out."

I moved back over to my chair, and we talked for a while. I was able to get back to my message. In the middle of the afternoon my mother walked in.

"I just saw the Holgates," she said. The look on her face told me she had received the news.

"They told me, and I told Connie," I said.

"What were they thinking?" Mom asked. "Nigel told your father he was going to move into the old provost's residence, since we hadn't hired anybody. It's a ranch house, and we thought it was a good idea – it would be easier for him when he eventually moves home. We had no idea what he was planning."

"Wasn't he at your place Saturday night?" I asked.

"No, he wasn't. Ellen told us she was taking him to the club. We thought it was a good idea for him to get out of the house. When Lane called, we tried to get them at the club, and they weren't there. Then we had to leave. I just feel like this is all my fault. I could have stopped it or something. I knew something was going on, but I never dreamed."

"Apparently a lot of us are blaming ourselves," I said.

"You too?" she asked.

"Us too," I replied.

She looked quickly over at Connie, who nodded.

"Oh my. Connie, this isn't something you should fret over. Nigel and Ellen made their own decisions."

"That's what everybody keeps saying," she replied.

"When Mac and Martie told me, I went to a pay phone and called your father. This was the first he had heard about it."

"I'll bet he was surprised," I said.

She gave me a nervous smile. "You might say that."

"Since Dad found out about it from you, that means Nigel and Ellen haven't come up for air."

"Beryl!" both Mom and Connie said.

I shook my head. "Sorry. That wasn't what I meant."

"I never know with you," Mom said.

"I'm trying to do better. Connie beats me when I don't behave."

"And I promise you I will have a word with him later," Connie said. She gave me a meaningful look.

Mom laughed. "My prayers go with you, Connie. You may be able to accomplish something I have never succeeded in, and that's keeping Beryl's mouth under control."

"I'll give it my best shot."

I decided to get back into the conversation. "And her best is very, very good."

"I came in to tell you," Mom said, "that I'll probably head back to Rockford tomorrow. It appears I have some other wild children to corral."

"What's Ruth done, now?" I asked.

"Ruth is not the problem," Mom said sternly.

"Okay."

"Connie's parents want to wait until she gets out of here, and then ride back to Rockford with you."

"That would be fine," I said.

Once we had sorted out the logistics, I had asked Avis to bring the Dart for Hank and Contessa to use while they were in Galesburg. When we headed up, I assumed we would have to drive past my house to leave the other car.

"I'm ready to go now," Connie said. "Sitting around this place gets old."

When I considered what might have happened, I had no problems with it. I still wasn't sure what Mrs. Marsden had done to get Connie's motor started again, and I needed to ask her. I wasn't sure she would tell me, though. There were times I caught glimpses of things in the old lady that puzzled and frightened me. I was just thankful that things had turned out okay.

When I thought of what might have happened, I almost broke down again. It wasn't just an angel standing in the snowy road protecting us. This time we had all felt God's direct hand upon us. It was both terrifying and reassuring at the same time.

CHAPTER FORTY-NINE

"Your dad is not speaking to me," Nigel said.

"I'm not surprised," I said.

We were sitting in Nigel's office on the campus of Mid-North College on a Tuesday morning in April. The previous day I had ferried Connie and her parents back to Rockford. She seemed none the worse after her accidental electrification and a week's enforced rest in the hospital. The only side-effect I had observed was during the thunderstorm that brewed up on Friday afternoon. She had cried, and gripped my hand so tightly she left marks.

The trip to Rockford was pleasant. Connie and her mom rode in the back seat, and Hank rode up front with me. As I got to know them I recognized them for the sweet gracious people that they were. Also, they were entirely different from Mac and Martie. Connie was all set to go back to work on Tuesday, whereupon Hank put his foot down. Connie was unhappily confined to the house for the rest of the week, except for some short excursions with her fiancé – something I had to negotiate with him.

Now, sitting in Nigel's office, I was dealing with the other nightmare that had enveloped everyone over the past week. He and Ellen had appeared the previous Friday to assume housekeeping in the former provost's residence. And he was absolutely right about Dad's refusal to speak to him. Dad was furious.

"I made sure everything was completely legal," Nigel continued. "I even got Reverend Friessen to perform the ceremony."

"Julius Friessen did it? How did you ever talk him into that?"

"Well, it wasn't pretty."

"How long did you argue with him about it?"

"About fifteen minutes. I threatened to go to a Justice of the Peace to tie the knot, and he gave in."

"Listen, Nigel," I said, "I'm not interested in starting a fight, but what precipitated this?"

"Well, we had been talking about it, and that package you picked up for me was the ring – which I assume you figured out."

And I felt a pang when he mentioned that.

"But I guess it was the arguments Ellen had with her parents that week. We talked about it, and we picked up the license on Friday. We were going to tell her parents and invite them to a small ceremony. But she called me Saturday morning and said we needed to do it. So we did."

"Pardon me, but getting married because your girl had a fight with her parents strikes me as not a very good reason."

"I figured you would say that. That's one of the reasons we didn't tell anybody," he said. "They would have tried to talk us out of it."

"Nigel, listen to yourself."

"I know, I know. I just got tired of imposing on your parents. We had decided to get married anyway, and the timing otherwise was perfect."

I sighed. "I suppose I shouldn't be the one to criticize. I'm just as bad."

Nigel cocked his head and studied me. "I suppose you are going to do a guilt trip on yourself, so that I'll feel bad. That's the way you usually operate."

"I did something stupid, Nigel, and I feel very bad about it."

"Uh huh, uh huh," he said. "Why is any different than any other week in the life of Beryl Cathcart? You do dumb things all the time, and feel bad about it. Sometimes you're such a schlepper."

"No, seriously, Nigel..."

"I don't want to hear it."

I stared at him, trying to figure out a way to get through the impasse. I needed to apologize to him, and he was being difficult. Finally he rolled his eyes and threw his hands into the air.

"All right. If I don't let you go on with this, you'll be giving me that whipped puppy look all day."

"I don't look like a whipped puppy!"

He didn't say anything, just raised an eyebrow. Sometimes I wanted to slap him.

"Are you going to tell me what's bothering you, or not?" he asked.

"Good grief, Nigel, I'm trying to apologize to you."

"Oh, so you *do* want to do the guilt trip on me."

"Sheesh!" I got up and headed for the door. Sometimes Nigel was impossible. I was beginning to think he and Ellen were made for each other.

"Siddown, Beryl," Nigel yelled. He had his exasperated voice on now. "What's on your mind?"

I sat down again. "Listen. I picked up that package for you at Nelson's, and I figured out it was what it was."

"Yeah, I sort of thought you did."

"Well, anyway, Connie and I were getting close to an engagement. I was afraid that if you and Ellen announced, it would mess up our deal. So, when I got home, I turned around and came back. We got engaged that Wednesday night."

"I know what you did," he said. He then shrugged. "I thought it was funny."

"You don't understand, Nigel. I was thinking of myself. I purposely pulled the trigger on this thing just to get ahead of you. I thought maybe that was what caused you and Ellen to elope."

"We didn't elope. We merely had an impromptu wedding. And your engagement to Connie had nothing to do with that. I was happy for you."

I looked at him carefully. "Can I still apologize."

"You're going to have to wrestle me for it, and I think I can take you."

I quickly stepped behind his desk, and forced his head to the desktop, and pulled his arm behind his back. "Give?"

He struggled for a bit, trying to extricate himself – difficult because he was dragging around that cast. Finally he looked up at me. "Had enough?"

I staggered across his office and collapsed in his sofa in helpless laughter from the break in tension. Nigel laughed too, and had tears coursing down his cheeks. I thought my lungs were going to collapse. I finally managed to suck in a load of air, and I'm sure it sounded like my pneumonia was back. I looked up, and Dad had stepped into the office looking completely flabbergasted. I stopped laughing, and Nigel struggled to get control of himself.

"Nigel, while I am deeply unhappy about what you did, the way I have been treating you this morning is completely inexcusable. I wish to apologize."

"You're going to have to wrestle him for it," I said, as Nigel and I both collapsed again. Now Dad just looked bewildered.

"Sometimes I just don't understand you two," he said, shaking his head. He turned and pulled the door shut as he left.

"There has got to be a Lone Ranger joke that covers this," Nigel said, laughing.

"Don't get me started. Connie backed me into a corner about my mouth, and I'm really trying to lose the off-color humor."

He leaned back in his chair and smiled at me. "Aren't we a pair, Beryl? I mean, I understand what you are saying. Ellen has been working on me about my more objectionable habits."

"If she did that, there wouldn't be anything left of you."

"I told her that, but as you know, Ellen has a whim of steel. That's why I love her so."

"You never told me you loved her," I said.

"That's kind of personal, isn't it? You never told me you loved Connie."

"I guess that's a point for your side," I said.

"So I can warn Connie that she's getting ready to marry a loser?"

"Ha! You would think both Connie and Ellen had better taste in men."

"No argument," he said. "I know a lot of people are upset with us, but we still think we did the right thing."

"I still think it was an insane thing to do, but I'll drop it. As Julius probably said, *for better, for worse.* You're married. That is now God's will for your lives. Don't screw it up, Nigel."

"I don't plan to. My parents were married four times, twice with each other. I don't want my kids growing up in that kind of a household."

I had never heard that before. Nigel never said much about his background, and I could understand.

"Is Julius going to keep mentoring you guys?" I asked.

"That was his one iron-clad arrangement that he refused to negotiate on. And I'm glad to have his help."

Listen, Nigel, if that fails, I can give you lots of advice on marriage."

I had to quickly duck, since he picked up the book on his desk and threw it at me. We laughed some more and began settling back into our comfortable friendship.

"You know, Beryl, for both of us this is the beginning of the rest of our lives."

"I hadn't thought about that, but you're right of course."

"Of course I am. I'm always right. But, what I was saying is that Ellen and I have started a life together. You and Connie soon will as well. I want it to be dedicated to the Lord."

"I agree." I decided to ignore his flippant remark. "Connie and I have been praying to that end."

"As have Ellen and I."

We sat in companionable silence for a few minutes before Nigel stirred again.

"Well, I suppose I need to apologize to your dad. He's worse than you are when he gets his feelings hurt."

"Not my dad."

"Right. Why don't you hie yourself back to his office, and ask him to come see me."

I stood up. "Thanks, Nigel."

"What for?"

"How about... the rest of my life?"

"What are friends for? Now, get out of here before I find something else to throw at you."

THE END

ABOUT THE AUTHOR

Marvin Reem lives in Greenville, South Carolina with his wife. A college professor and an Information Technology professional, Reem writes Adult Christian Fiction, and Christian Science-Fiction. Visit his web site at www.MarvinReem.com. He can be reached at mpreem@gmail.com

37648025R00256

Made in the USA
Charleston, SC
13 January 2015